UPON A
WINTER'S
NIGHT

KAREN HARPER

UPON A
WINTER'S
NIGHT

ISBN-13: 978-1-62490-975-7

UPON A WINTER'S NIGHT

To the great readers who have enjoyed and written to me about my previous seven Amish romantic suspense novels. And as ever, to my #1 fan, Don.

1

The Home Valley, Ohio
November 24, 2012

Melly was lost in the storm, and Lydia was determined to find her. But it was hard going since huge flakes of snow fell thick and fast on top of the six inches already on the ground.

Josh had corralled the rest of his manger scene animals, but Melly, an eight-foot-tall female camel, loved to wander. Josh had told Lydia to stay put in the barn and Melly would find her way back, but while he was feeding his sheep, Lydia had gone out, anyway. Though she was annoyed with the big beast right now, Melly's waywardness made Lydia love the camel even more. She sympathized with the animal's stubborn nature.

"Melly! Melly!" she called. The bitter wind bit deep into her throat and seemed to puff back out in each cloud of breath she exhaled. Swirling flakes made her feel she was inside a shaken snow globe—one like her mother had owned years ago, now hidden under Lydia's bed. "Melly, you bad girl, where are you?"

Lydia was grateful for her deep bonnet brim and warm cape, but her long skirt and apron were a problem as she lifted booted feet to plod toward the tall woven wire fence that kept the animals in Josh's large enclosure. Josh Yoder considered her just another of his helpers. He thought she should take care of the docile sheep and cows he rented out to communities and churches for Christmas tableauxs. But it was the camels and donkeys she cared about. And secretly, she cared about Josh, too, and her joy in working near him was worth more than he could ever pay her.

She nearly slipped but managed to right herself. This was no time for daydreaming, but Josh Yoder often intruded on her thoughts, even when he wasn't near. Despite going into the wind, Lydia quickened her steps. Josh would be angry if he had to come looking for her. Though he tried to stay calm and trusting in all trials, he did have a bit of a temper.

She tried not to picture him angry. Broad cheeks, square chin—he was still clean shaven. The men in their Amish church had the choice of beginning a beard either when they joined the church or when they wed, which he'd never done. Josh was a member in good standing, but as yet had no wife or *maidal* he courted—maybe because he'd lived in the world for several years. So handsome with his green-blue eyes and gold-as-wheat hair, he was tall for an Amish man. *Ya,* she looked up to him in more ways than one. If only she could say that about her come-calling friend, Gid Reich, whom her *daad* kept inviting to dinner, even though she saw him each day at work. She didn't want to let her *daad* and *mamm* down, but she'd tried to tell them Gid wasn't for her. Still, on paper, as they say, he seemed the perfect match.

Lydia stopped for a moment to get her bearings. Surely, she wasn't walking in circles. Her parents would scold her for going out in a storm, because they were very protective. She understood that. They had lost their only other child in a tragic accident. Just beyond the fence was Creek Pond, where her five-year-old brother, Sammy, had drowned years ago. Her mother, who blamed herself for the boy's death, didn't want her daughter anywhere near the pond, summer or winter.

Lydia traced her way along the fence. If worse came to worst, it would guide her back to the big Yoder barn where Josh housed and tended his menagerie. But—oh, no—the back gate was open several feet! It had a latch, so could that crazy camel have escaped through the gap and be wandering back toward the pond? Would Melly's weight crack right through the ice? Sammy's screams clawed at Lydia's memory again, but it was just the shrill shriek of the wind. A tear froze on her cheek, but she kept going.

She reached out and dragged the narrow gate closed and latched it. She'd have to head straight back to tell Josh now. Who could have left the gate ajar, let alone opened it? Surely, not the wind. All Josh's other workers, some hired, some volunteers like her, knew to keep the animals in this big field and they'd gone home hours ago—Saturday night, time for courting.

Josh had kidded once about how Melly "liked to swing for the fences." The camel loved to scratch her sides on the woven wire. Lydia could picture the big baby, along with her cohorts, Gaspar and Balty, poking their furry-lipped muzzles through the fence in good weather while they watched buggies and vehicles go by on the road. Talk about stopping traffic! The sight of camels in the heart of Ohio Amish country had caused more than one fender bender.

As Lydia trudged back toward the barn, praying she'd find her favorite camel, she stumbled over something low, sprawled under the white shroud of snow. She let out a little scream. Thank the Lord, it was too small to be Melly. She backed away. When the person—it was a person—didn't move, she bent over it—her—then fell to her knees.

The woman lay facedown. Lydia started to speak to her in Amish *Deutsche,* then saw by her short, curly hair—blond hair iced with snow—that she was *Englische.*

"Wake up. Hello? Are you all right? My name is Lydia Brand. I want to help you, *ya,* I do."

No answer, no movement. Unconscious? Dead? Had she opened the gate and come in? But from where? A narrow dirt lane, woodlot, fields and hills lay behind.

Lydia dusted off the woman's face as best she could and put her own nearly on the ground to get a better look at her. She didn't recognize the woman, wasn't even sure how old she was—sixties? Older? Ripping off a mitten, Lydia touched the white, icy face with two fingers, then fumbled for a neck pulse. Couldn't tell. She had to get help soon—now. She'd never be able to carry her. And if she dragged her through the snow, she might hurt her more.

The woman was not even wearing a scarf, hat or gloves, so was she off her bean? Clutched in her hand was a small, square piece of paper, like those sticky notes. Maybe it had her name on it or a message for someone. Lydia took it and held it close to her face. Words written in blue ink smeared the sodden paper. Not able to read it through the scrim of flakes, Lydia thrust it into the mitten she'd pulled back on, so the paper lay damp against her palm.

Panic pulsed through her as she took off her warm woolen cape and draped it over the woman, as if tucking her into bed. Josh would have to go for help in his buggy to the Stark family down the road, since they were *Englische* and had cars and phones. They could call the volunteer emergency squad and Sheriff Freeman.

Despite sweating in her frenzy, Lydia felt the gnawing cold even more without her cape. Could that woman have frozen to death? Fearing the flakes were turning to ice pellets, Lydia skimmed her hand along the wire fence, and calling out, "Melly! Melly!" stumbled through the deepening snow toward the barn.

Josh Yoder breathed a sigh of relief when the last camel, Melly, ambled into the barn, blinking ice crystals from her two-inch lashes and shaking the snow off her shaggy fur. He put her in her stall on camel row, then realized Lydia had not followed the big beast into the barn.

He ran back to the single tall door the camels used and pulled it back open. The wind howled at him, and snow fell like wool at shearing time. He had partly inherited this big, old milking barn from his father and had bought his brothers out. But it was no longer the Yoder Dairy. He'd kept four of the cows and acquired other animals to breed, but mostly he hired them out for living Christmas tableaux or holiday pageants in December. Spring through autumn, he ran a petting zoo, and a wagon pulled by his big Belgian horses took tourists on a ride so they could see and feed, and, of course, pet, the tamer animals in the back fields. But in wintertime he kept them inside.

Still no sign of Lydia. Surely, she'd have come in with Melly if she'd brought her back here. The barn was a shelter from the storm, a lofty, wide place with one long wing that held the old milking stanchions and rows of cattle stalls he planned to replace soon. The main building boasted two spacious haymows above the barn floor, one for fodder and straw and one to store other food supplies. He and his workers tried hard to keep the place clean. It actually managed to smell sweetly of straw, hay and warm bodies most of the winter. He only wished he'd known this sudden storm was coming.

Squinting against the spin of stinging snow—ice pellets now—and cupping his hands around his mouth, he bellowed out the door, "Lydia! Get in here! Don't you walk home in this! I'll take you in the sleigh or your parents will have my head. Lydia, get back here!"

Ach, that woman was willful, always had been. But she was sure-footed and bright, too. At age twenty, she was a *maidal* who had blossomed into a beauty from the pesky, skinny tomboy she used to be. She was a distraction sometimes, bending over to feed the animals, humming, shooting those quick smiles at him. In the four years he'd been away from the Home Valley, she'd become a desirable woman, though one who would be a lot of trouble for the man she married. She was being courted by Gideon Reich, who worked for her father, so there was probably a wedding in the offing. Gideon was a widower, so maybe he knew a thing or two about women, but good luck to him taming Lydia Brand.

Really worried now—could she have fallen or twisted an ankle out there?—Josh grabbed his heavy coat and flap-eared hat. Should he just run outside, yelling for her? Harness Blaze onto the sleigh and try to catch her before she went into the thick woodlot that lay between his place and the Brand house?

Then he saw her emerge from the curtain of snow, half stumbling, half running. He rushed out and put an arm around her shaking shoulders. "What happened? Where's your cape?"

Her cheeks were pink with cold, her lips blue, her teeth chattering. At least she still wore mittens and boots. He picked her up and carried her toward the barn. Despite her trembling, she held tight to him.

"C-c-cape c-covered a woman, lying in the s-snow. By the back g-gate," she stuttered through chapped lips. "It was open, but I closed it."

He sat her at his worktable and put his coat around her. He poured hot chocolate from his thermos into a plastic cup and held it to her lips until she took a swallow and brought her mittened hands up to hold it. A woman out in the snow? And it upset him about the gate because he didn't need more *rumspringa* kids sneaking in to ride or scare the animals. The animals could get hurt and the kids, too, but what had happened to the woman?

"Not sure whether to take the sleigh for her or go

to the Starks to get help," Josh muttered as he ran to harness his mare in the nearest corner of the barn.

"I'll g-go with you either way," she called after him.

"No, you stay here. Is she hurt? Alive?"

"Not sure. F-frozen, I think."

"You didn't recognize her?"

"No. Not Amish."

"No one else lost out there?"

"Don't know. I'll help you harness B-Blaze, then—"

"Drink that. Stay put."

It would be quickest to take the sleigh. He'd refused to rent it out recently for a Santa pageant. When he'd returned after four years of working at the Columbus Zoo and joined the church, he'd promised Bishop Esh that the animals would be rented out strictly for religious events. He could go find someone to help. But no, he'd go check on the woman first.

He heard knocking and a shout at the far end of the barn, closest to the road. If only it was someone with a car or a cell phone! He paid his *Englische* friend Hank to do his bookings on his cell, but Josh wished he had his own now.

He sprinted the width of the barn, past the donkeys braying at the intrusion, and swung the door open. Lydia's father, Sol Brand, stood there. Snow etched his brimmed hat, narrow shoulders and graying beard. He was a head shorter than Josh. If any Amish man could be considered a loner in their friendly, tight church community, even though he worked with many people every day, it was Solomon Brand.

"Liddy here?" he asked, frowning, as he stepped inside. "Hope you didn't let her walk home in this." Beyond him Josh saw two horses hitched to a big buggy.

"She's here, Mr. Brand. She was out in the snow, but she stumbled on an injured or dead woman on her way back, and we need to get help. Since you're hitched up, could you go down the road to the Starks' and have them phone for help? I'll go out for the woman and, if she's alive, bring her back to the barn."

"Don't like to bother the Starks myself, but for this... How 'bout you take my buggy and go? Is it someone Amish?"

"A modern."

Sol frowned again at Josh as if that were his fault. "Liddy, you all right?" the older man bellowed so loud the donkeys began braying again.

"Ya, daad!" she called, walking toward them. "Glad you came so you can help!"

Sol shook his head when he saw Lydia wrapped in Josh's coat. Josh knew the Brands didn't like their daughter spending hours working with his animals, especially on weekends like this. But she'd stood firm on helping here. Her father often came after her since they didn't want her out in her buggy after dark. No doubt her come-calling friend, Gideon Reich, didn't want her here, either, "dirtying her hands," as Josh had heard, but Lydia had a mind of her own. And, while her mother scolded her a lot, her father seemed to love her dearly.

"All right, I'll go," Sol told Josh. "Liddy, don't you go back out in the storm! I'll be right back—let Connor Stark do the calling for help."

He lifted a quick hand to his daughter, turned and went back out. Josh had intentionally not mentioned where the woman lay, back by the gate to Creek Pond. Sol and Susan Brand's five-year-old son, Samuel, had drowned there when Lydia was about ten and Josh was twenty. He understood that was one of the reasons the Brands sheltered their remaining child. They had Lydia working during the week as the receptionist in their family-owned Amish furniture store on the edge of town, and, otherwise, tried to keep her close to home.

Josh hurried to Lydia and steered her back toward the worktable where she'd been sitting. "I can't believe *Daad* went to the Starks. He thinks they're prideful, even though they've bought a lot of our furniture."

"He's going, and I'm going to try to find the woman near the gate, bring her here. You wait here for the sheriff or the squad. If I'm not back and they need to drive vehicles out there, they should take the dirt road outside the fence, if they can find it in this snow. I've got Blaze half-hitched. Sit down here by the front door and rest."

But she followed him over to the sleigh, where he finished hitching the black mare. "You'll need this coat," she insisted, and took it off. "I'll get a blanket from your buggy to wrap the woman in."

She held his coat for him while he turned his back to put it on.

"Stay warm," he told her when he spun back to face her. He gave her a quick hug that he didn't know was coming, and she obviously didn't, either. She went stiff in surprise for a moment, then hugged him back so fast and hard that it surprised him, too.

He tossed Blaze's reins into the sleigh, jumped up into it and, when Lydia opened the camel gate for him, giddyapped the horse out into the storm.

2

Lydia didn't hear a siren, but about twenty minutes later, Sheriff Jack Freeman opened the far barn door and came in with his wife, Ray-Lynn, who ran the biggest restaurant in town. He wasn't in his usual black uniform, but he held some sort of little flat phone in his hand. As Lydia hurried to meet them, she realized they were dressed real fancy. Ray-Lynn had a fur collar on her bright blue coat and shiny, knee-high boots.

"Lydia, where's Josh?" the sheriff asked.

Sheriff Freeman managed to know most of the Amish names, which was appreciated. Of course, he'd met a lot of her people in the restaurant he and his wife co-owned uptown. Right now, there was no time for small talk. He was obviously in full take-charge sheriff mode.

"He went out to see if the woman's alive," Lydia told him, gesturing toward the back of the barn. "He's going to bring her into the warmth if she is."

"If she's not, I hope he leaves her there and the scene untouched, though this snow will mess things up. I hear you found her. I'll need a complete statement later. I think we got us a possible ID on the woman. Connor Stark's aunt wandered off today, been missing a couple hours since they found her gone, and that's pretty close to here. They been searching their land through all those Christmas trees. Ray-Lynn and I been to a dinner in Cleveland with friends—had the day off. Just on our way back through this surprise storm."

Though the Amish didn't much trust government officials or law enforcement, Sheriff Jack Freeman had passed muster with the Eden County Amish a long time ago. And everyone liked his new wife, who was not new to the Home Valley or the little town of Homestead. Ray-Lynn hired lots of Amish girls in her Dutch Farm Table Restaurant and had helped more than one of her workers through tough times. The Freemans were quite a pair: the sheriff trim and erect with his clipped comments; Ray-Lynn, a shapely, flaming redhead with a slow, Southern drawl.

"I didn't know there was an older woman living at the Starks' house, besides Bess Stark when she comes home," Lydia said to Ray-Lynn since the sheriff was back on his phone.

"There's a lot we don't know about the private lives of the rich and famous like matriarch Bess Stark. Ohio Senator Stark, that is. Got to watch those politicians! Who would've guessed the lady missing is Bess's older sister, Victoria Keller, not married, more or less a recluse, I take it. She's lived with them for a couple of years and—" here Ray-Lynn paused and whispered "—has severe early onset Alzheimer's, so I hear. You know—out of her head. Says weird things. Since Bess is a state senator ready to run for governor, the family decided it was best to keep her at home—or so the story goes."

"Oh, I see. That's what my people would do, keep the ill, older generation at home, but I didn't think the Starks..."

The door to the barn shoved open to admit Connor Stark, son of Senator Stark and, evidently, nephew of the poor woman out in the field. Hatless even in the storm, he wore tight black jeans, black tooled boots and an unzipped leather jacket. In his mid-thirties, he was now the mayor of Homestead, strikingly handsome with chiseled features and slicked-back, dark hair already threaded with silver at the temples. But a cold wind blew in behind him and he didn't close the door.

Lydia had known him from years ago when Senator Stark used to be so kind to her, but she didn't go over there anymore because her mother had found out and had insisted that the Starks weren't churched and were a bad influence. Besides, she'd claimed, you have to either serve God or mammon, which meant money. Lydia had to look that word up in the dictionary at her reception desk at the furniture store. She thought her mother might be the pot calling the kettle black, because their own family was real well off, at least among the Amish.

"I was in my office, but my wife called me when Sol Brand showed up," Connor said, addressing the sheriff and ignoring Lydia, who went to close the door. "I was trying to coordinate a broader search for early tomorrow morning. Damn hired help tending to Aunt Victoria let her get loose. She alive? Where is she?"

The sheriff punched off on his phone call. "Josh

went out to bring her back here if she's alive, Mayor. Lydia found her."

"She say anything to you?" Connor demanded, turning toward her as she came back from closing the door. "She's had dementia for years, so nothing she says makes much sense. She's in a fantasy world."

Before Lydia could reply, the sheriff interrupted, "I'll ask the questions here. I know you're used to being in charge, Connor, but not right now."

Lydia figured Connor, who was only recently elected, looked as if he was actually going to cuss out the sheriff. But, at the other end of the barn, the camel door swung open and, through the blizzard of flakes, they could see the silhouette of Josh's horse and sleigh.

They all hurried toward him.

"I left her out there, 'cause she's dead for sure," Josh told them, out of breath as he led Blaze in, dragging the sleigh across the floorboards. "Frozen to death or something else, can't tell. I'll take anyone out there who wants to go. I left her like she fell, except for Lydia's cape over her, in case there was any foul play."

"Good thinking," the sheriff said.

Connor faced Josh. "Foul play? That's ridiculous! She's out of her head! She just wandered off and picked a deadly time to do it."

Sheriff Freeman ignored the outburst, but Lydia and Ray-Lynn exchanged uneasy glances.

"I'm the only one going with you, Josh," the sheriff said, then got back on his phone. Lydia realized he was talking to the county coroner.

Connor's shoulders slumped, and he walked away, punching numbers into his cell phone, evidently to call his wife or his mother. Lydia thought for sure he had

huffed out a sigh of relief—or was it exasperation?—
when he'd heard his aunt was dead, but then she knew
from her own family that people handled shock and
grinding grief in different ways.

Oh, *ya,* she thought as her father arrived at the far
door with her mother hurrying ahead of him toward
Lydia. She sure knew all about that.

Lydia wanted to stay in the barn until Josh and the
sheriff came back from the field. She felt she should in
case the sheriff had questions for her. But her parents
insisted she go home with them and the sheriff could
interview her later. Ray-Lynn said the men would be
out there a long time, waiting for the coroner, and she
was supposed to go home, too.

With a buggy robe wrapped around her like a shawl
and another one over her knees, Lydia sat wedged between *Mamm* and *Daad* on the short journey home.
It was so cold it hurt to talk, but *Mamm* was doing it,
anyway.

"See what I mean about the Starks? *Ach,* who knew
they had an ailing aunt stashed over there? Secrets all
around, oh, *ya.* I wouldn't be surprised they took her in
just so when she passed they could get her money, too."

"That's enough," *Daad* said.

"Well, she's a Keller, evidently an old maid Keller,
and it was her and Bess Keller Stark's family that had
the seed money for all they do. Obviously, they can
buy anything they want, including people's silence,
because they must have had someone taking care of
her. Connor just grows and sells those pine trees so
he's not completely bored playing big man in town
and now mayor."

"Let's not judge others," *Daad* said.

"I try. I tried for years, but I'm only human. And, Lydia, see what a stew you got yourself into working over there with those animals!"

"It was a blessing I found her body, *Mamm*. And we've discussed my working with the animals before. Christmas is coming, and Josh needs help preparing them for manger and crèche scenes. It's a good service to let people know about the real meaning of Christmas, and anytime people mingle with animals, it reminds them of God's creation."

"Don't you preach at me, too."

And that was that until they were home. The two women hurried into the house while *Daad* stayed behind in the barn to unhitch and rub down the horse. Lydia went upstairs to take a hot bath, but, as usual, the frosty air between her parents didn't thaw even later when *Daad* stomped into the mudroom at the back of their big house and *Mamm* stood stiff-backed at the stove, making them cocoa and putting out friendship bread and thumping down jars of apple butter and peach preserves on the table.

Lydia thought *Daad* had been out in the barn pretty long on such a cold night, but it seemed he always spent hours out there as well as at the Home Valley Amish Furniture store he'd inherited from his father and had built up even more. Then, too, Solomon Brand often spent time in the side parlor of their house with the secret he kept from all the world except his wife and his daughter: Sol Brand loved to hand quilt.

True, that traditional craft belonged in the realm of Amish women, like keeping the garden, and making clothing and watching the *kinder*. But he was so skilled at it with his tiny, even stitches, intricate patterns and unique colors, especially for a man who oversaw carpenters, joiners, sanders and stainers at the store workshop. Neither Susan, though she belonged to a quilting circle, nor Lydia, who draped some of his quilts near the oak and maple bedsteads and headboards they displayed at the store, ever admitted who was the maker of his stunning quilts.

Besides luring customers into the store, his "Amish-made" quilts covered beds and lay like buried treasure in the chests and closets of their home. Amish women never signed their handwork, anyway. Many were cooperative efforts, and no one wanted to be prideful by boasting or asking who made the ones for sale. But how often Lydia had wanted to tell someone, "My *daad* made that, and isn't it grand?"

Once, she recalled, Sammy had blurted out to several church leaders that his father "quilts," but he was such a youngster that Bishop Esh had thought he'd said "*Daadi* builds." One of the elders had said, "Oh, *ya,* but really he oversees what other men build at the furniture store." And, of course, Sammy, flesh of her parents' flesh, while Lydia sometimes felt bone of their bone of contention, never got scolded for telling the family secret. Oh, no, Sammy never made a mistake. Except the day he disobeyed and sneaked out of the house to go swimming in the pond when he was told to take a nap because he'd had a summer cold—and he drowned.

Lydia had heard his desperate shrieks. *Mamm,* hanging clothes, had, too, but they were both too late by the time they ran clear out there. Lydia had thanked the Lord more than once that she wasn't supposed to

watch him that August day but had been told to weed
the side garden. She could not imagine his death having been her fault. But it was so sad that her mother
had never stopped blaming herself.

How different Connor Stark had reacted today
when a member of his family wandered out and died.
Though he'd said they had hired help watching his
aunt, would he blame his wife over the years for not
seeing Victoria Keller sneak out the way *Daad* must
surely blame *Mamm?* Or so Lydia had figured all these
years since they were always on edge.

After her little brother was lost, it had come as
a shock to Lydia when her father told her, with her
mother hovering, that she had been adopted when
her parents, *Daad*'s distant cousins, were killed in a
buggy-car accident. She had only been an infant—
and, thank the Lord, *Daad* said, she was not in the
buggy with them.

She'd cried and cried at first, but *Daad* had assured
her that the accident meant she was chosen to be their
child, not just given from on high. And *Mamm* had
blurted out once that they had believed Sammy was a
special gift from God because they'd taken Lydia in.
Just like Sarah and Elizabeth in the Bible, all those
barren years—and then a son!

But to be adopted in Amish country with its big
families was something that marked Lydia, at least to
herself. Even though people seldom mentioned it, she
felt she carried that scar deep inside. She had tried
to talk about it with Bishop Esh. He had said that the
Lord and her parents loved her very much, and that she
should "learn to be content" and ask no more questions

about her "real" parents—that Solomon and Susan Brand were her real parents.

Josh knew he wouldn't sleep even though things were calm now. Finally, silent night. The storm had diminished to spitting snow; the sheriff and the coroner's van had gone; Mayor Stark had finally departed, too, once he'd viewed his aunt Victoria's body to identify her. Turned out the woman was only sixty, though in death she looked much older.

Carrying a lantern, Josh left the barn and slogged through the new foot of snow to his house to be sure the faucets were all dripping to keep the pipes from freezing. He wanted to build up the stove and hunker down by it, but he was too restless, running on adrenaline, as they said in the world he had sampled for four years.

He had liked living in Columbus, working with ruminants at the zoo, getting to know the famous and admired Jack Hannah, the former zoo director, who had built the place up to one of the best in the country. Josh had learned some important things about vet medicine, the history and habitats of different breeds, and animal conservation in the wild. But his people, his calling—the dream of having his own animals to share with others—had brought him back to the Home Valley.

The big house he'd grown up in felt achingly quiet and lonely tonight. Its bones creaked in the cold. How would it be to have a family to fill the place, a wife waiting for him, kids calling down the stairs, his own little band of workers for his furry, hairy crew?

He locked the farmhouse again and trudged back to

the barn. Despite the cold, he'd sleep on his cot there tonight, comforted by the gurgles of the camels and the snorts and snuffles of the other animals. An occasional *baa* or *moo* never bothered him. Hopefully, the donkeys were asleep, his security alarm system for now, though come spring he was going to buy a couple of peacocks to take over the job. No good to have tourists arriving with youngsters for a petting zoo and hayride only to be greeted by barking watchdogs.

It bothered him that Lydia had found the back gate ajar, though Victoria Keller must have been the one who opened it. Lately, Amish kids in their running-around years had sneaked in that way, so maybe he needed to put a padlock on it. It was hard to get used to that kind of thinking, but major crimes had found their way into Eden County. When he was growing up, a lot of folks didn't even lock their houses.

He had generator-powered blowers and heaters in the barn—which blew out cool air in the summer—and he shoved his cot over so he'd be in the draft of warm air. He put the single lantern on the board floor far away from any loose hay or straw. He saw Lydia's cape on his cot where he'd spread it to dry—*ya,* the blowers had done that now, and he'd be sure she got it back tomorrow. He hoped her parents would still let her help him after all this. The cape even smelled of her, though he knew she didn't use perfume. It was a fresh scent that reminded him of nature, of the outdoors and freedom. Lydia was a natural with the animals, as well as a natural beauty.

Groggy with exhaustion, he lay down and tugged up the two blankets and her cape over him, the cape she'd given up to help warm that poor woman. He hugged it to him, thinking of how he'd hugged Lydia tonight. She meant more to him than just a helper, just the girl—woman—next door that he'd thought of as a kid most of his life...

But it was pretty obvious she was to be betrothed to Gideon Reich. Josh didn't know the man well, but he had piercing eyes and a big, black beard when most Amish men had hair and beard that were blond, brown or gray. Ray-Lynn at the restaurant had told him that Lydia and Reich were tight, said they sometimes came in together for lunch. Lydia never mentioned the man, but with the Plain People, courting was often private until the big announcement of the betrothal, followed several months or even weeks later by the wedding. Reich's house was way on the other side of town, so Josh knew he'd lose her help—lose her—when she wed.

Sometime in the dead of night, Joshua Yoder dropped off to sleep and dreamed of an oasis in the desert with a warm wind and camels and black-bearded Bedouins and a veiled woman. No, that was a prayer *kapp*. She had big, blue-green eyes and then her *kapp* blew off and her long, honey-hued hair came free. He went out into the sandstorm and picked her up in his arms before anyone else could get to her. When he lay down again, she gave him a big hug and then he kissed her and held her to him and pulled her into his bed.

It was the dead of night, but, in a robe and warm flannel nightgown, Lydia sat at the kitchen table, sipping cocoa, remembering how Josh had poured her some of his cocoa, even raised it to her lips. How warm his coat had been around her, and then that hug he started but she finished well enough.

"Lydia," *Mamm*'s voice cut into her thought. "You're daydreaming again, and that's a waste of time. Wishing and wanting doesn't help."

Lydia knew better than to defend herself, so she just reached for a piece of bread. *Mamm* started to make up her grocery list as if nothing unusual had happened tonight. *Daad* sat at the other end of the table, eating, quiet. Lydia was aching to talk about finding the woman, and a thought hit her foursquare: that note the dead woman had in her hand was still in her mitten.

She stood and hurried into the mudroom where she'd left it. Not much of the message could be read, she recalled, but what had the remaining words said? She'd have to tell the sheriff, give the note back to Connor or the deceased woman's sister, Bess, when she returned for the funeral—if there was a funeral, given how secretive they had kept Victoria Keller's presence. Word about a strange recluse living in the mayor's mansion would have traveled fast as greased lightning in this small, tight community.

Lydia checked the first mitten pinned to their indoor line. Nothing. Had she lost it? But there it was in the other mitt, still damp.

Lydia held the paper up to the kerosene lantern hanging in the window and squinted at the writing, mostly blue streaks.

"What's that?" *Daad* asked, popping his head around the corner.

"Just something I forgot," she said.

"Don't mind your *mamm*'s fussing," he said, keeping his voice low. "Dreams are fine if you are willing to work for them."

"Danki, Daad," she told him. She almost showed him the note, but as he went back out she was glad she hadn't. When she tipped it toward the lantern, she could read a few of the words, written in what looked to be a fancy cursive in a hand that had trembled: *To the girl Brand baby... Your mother is—*

She couldn't read that next word for sure. *Your mother is alert? Your mother is alike?* No, it said, *alive.* Alive! *Your mother is alive. And I...* And I, what? Lydia wanted to scream.

From the kitchen, *Daad* called to her, "Don't worry about talking to the sheriff tomorrow or on Monday, Liddy. I can be with you when he interviews you, if you want."

"Danki, Daad, but I'll be fine. There isn't much to say."

Alone in the dim mudroom, Lydia stood stunned. *Alive? Your mother is alive? And I...*

She'd just told *Daad* there wasn't much to say. But after tonight—finding Victoria Keller, Josh's hug, now this—she wouldn't be fine, maybe ever again.

She had to be "the Brand baby," didn't she? Everybody knew who Sammy's mother was, and she was the only girl. Dare she share this with the sheriff, the Starks or even her own parents? And could she trust a demented woman that her mother was still alive?

3

Lydia was grateful for a quiet Sabbath morning. It was the off Sunday for Amish church since the congregation met every other week in a home or barn. *Daad* always said a special prayer after the large breakfast *Mamm* and Lydia made before they went their own ways for quiet time. But Lydia hadn't slept last night. Her mind had not quit churning and she couldn't sit still.

In her bedroom, she stared again and again at the note she'd taken from Victoria Keller's hand. Had it been meant for her, or at least was it about her? Then why was the woman evidently heading for Josh's big acreage? Or, since she had what Connor called dementia, had she mixed up who lived where in the storm, stumbled on past the back of the Brand land and the woodlot and gone in Josh's back gate by mistake? Surely she wouldn't know Lydia worked for Josh. If the woman was one bit sane, she would not have gone out in that storm, or had it surprised and trapped her, too? And why now? Why had she waited twenty years after the Brand baby had been born—if it referred to Lydia—to deliver the note?

Yet Lydia felt that finding the woman and the note must have been a sign from heaven, a sign that she should not only learn if the note was true but also find out more about her real parents. She'd had questions pent up inside her for years. She didn't want to hurt her adoptive parents or make them think she didn't love and respect them, yet she had to get to the bottom of this, maybe without telling anyone. But she knew she'd be better off getting help. She had to start somewhere.

A car door slammed outside. She went to her second-story bedroom window and glanced down. It was Sheriff Freeman, in his uniform and with his cruiser this time. She slid the note she'd dried out between two tissues back into an envelope and put it under her bed next to the snow globe. When she was twelve, her father had given that to her and said not to tell *Mamm,* that it had belonged to her birth mother and had been left by someone at the store. No, he'd insisted, he knew no more about it.

Lydia smoothed her hair under her prayer *kapp* and went downstairs as she heard the sheriff knock on the front door. His words floated to her before she got all the way down the staircase.

"Afternoon, Sol, Mrs. Brand. Oh, good, Lydia. I knew there wasn't Amish church today but wanted to give you some catch-up time after last night, and Ray-Lynn and I were at church. Lydia, Ray-Lynn's on a committee for our Community Church doing a living manger scene, so we're hoping to use some of the animals you help tend."

"Oh, that will be good. Josh will be happy to take

the animals to a church that's nearby. He and his driver, Hank, usually have to go much farther."

Daad gestured them into the living room and, to Lydia's chagrin, sat in a big rocking chair near the one the sheriff took. Lydia perched on the sofa facing the sheriff while *Mamm* hovered at the door to the hall.

"Always admire the furniture from your store," the sheriff said, taking out a small notebook and flipping it open. "Hope to buy Ray-Lynn a corner cupboard there real soon. Now, since Lydia's the one I need to talk to—won't take long—I hope you won't mind giving me a few minutes alone with her. Turns out the victim, Victoria Keller, suffered a blow to the back of her head. That could be significant—or not—since she wasn't real steady on her feet. The coroner will rule on that. Meanwhile, I'm trying to put the pieces together."

Daad said, "I'd like to sit in. Won't say a word, and Susan can fix us some coffee for after you're done."

He shot his wife a look; Lydia sensed *Mamm* would refuse, but she went out.

"I understand your protective instinct," Sheriff Freeman said to *Daad,* "but your daughter's able to answer on her own as an adult."

"That she is. I will be in the kitchen with my wife, then," he said, slapping his hands on his knees. "I know Liddy will help you, though she doesn't know much besides finding the woman and leaving her cape. And she shouldn't have been out looking for a camel in that storm. Josh Yoder should take better care of his animals over there."

Though she had several things to say about that, Lydia kept her mouth shut until her father left the room.

"That's terrible about the blow to her head," she

said, leaning farther forward, hands clenched on her knees. "But in her condition and that storm, it doesn't mean someone really hit her, does it? I think she might have had trouble opening the gate, because I had trouble closing it, dragging it through the snow the wind had piled up there. But unless she fell into it, I doubt it could hit her hard. It wouldn't swing open or shut in that snow."

"Okay, that's a start. She may have hit her head on the gate. Now tell me what you saw from the beginning."

Lydia talked about looking for Melly, how the camel liked to cling to the fences. "Her real name is Melchior," she told him, feeling more nervous every second. "The other two Bactrian camels we—I mean, Josh—has are Gaspar and Balty, short for Balthasar. You know, the traditional names of the three wise men. The three dromedaries he owns are Angel, Star and Song. He needs at least six to cover the manger scenes and pageant orders, like you mentioned Ray-Lynn's in charge of."

"And Bactrian means...?" he asked, pen poised, looking up at her.

"Oh, sorry. Bactrians have two humps, and dromedaries have one. It's really not true that camels are nasty, though if mistreated they can spit and balk, but Josh's are not that way. Camels are like dogs in that respect—some good, some bad, all depending on how they're treated, and Josh is good to his."

"So you believe a camel, this Melly, even if she was startled or panicked in the storm, wouldn't slam into or kick someone who should not be on the grounds?"

"Melly? Oh, no. She might be curious, but— No."

Lydia's heartbeat kicked up. "You don't think that Melly knocked her down?"

"Don't know what to think yet. What about if the woman was already down and Melly stumbled over her? Josh says Melly just came loping into the barn by herself and that's when he realized you might be the one missing."

Her mind racing, Lydia stared the sheriff down. Surely someone like Connor wouldn't insist Melly be put down or give Josh trouble over this. It was his aunt who was trespassing, poor soul, not the camel.

"No, Sheriff," she said. "I don't think Melly would kick her, and if she stumbled over someone already on the ground, it was an accident."

"Okay, so is there anything else you can tell me about what you recall, anything at all?"

Lydia thought she could hear someone in the hall. *Mamm* with the coffee? *Daad* waiting until they were done? Now, right now, she should tell the sheriff about the note she found, but it was so confusing, only a partial message, and so—personal. Hadn't the Lord meant for her to find it and use it? Maybe the sheriff could help her learn what it meant, but wouldn't that make it all public again that she was adopted, upset her parents... She started to sweat, her stomach cramped.

"Lydia? You all right? Is there something else?" the sheriff asked, leaning closer.

"Oh, sure. I— Of course, you know this, but I put my cape over her, tucked it in, so I hope I didn't disturb anything."

"Right—the cape. I took a good look at it, no blood. I told Josh he could give it back to you. So, that's it?"

She nodded, perhaps a bit too hard, as if she were

a little kid defending a fib. This man was used to putting clues together, figuring out when someone was lying or guilty. Did he know something was wrong, that she'd held information back, maybe something very important?

"Okay, then," he said, and rose, flipping his little spiral notebook closed and putting it in his shirt pocket. "The Starks are planning a small, private funeral later this week. Connor said you'd be invited for all you did to try to help his aunt."

"I'm sorry she was mentally ill and so young— I mean, even at sixty, that's young to—to lose your mind. And she had no family but the Starks here?"

"Never married, no children. And now she's not even alive..."

Your mother is alive. And I... The haunting words of the note echoed in Lydia's head and heart.

Mamm suddenly appeared in the doorway with a tray of mugs and a plate of sliced friendship bread, and Lydia hurried to help her.

Josh had to admit he was nervous, taking Lydia's cape back to her house. Over the years, he'd visited there various times, but everything felt different today. And it was a Sunday, when unwed Amish men, termed *come-calling friends,* visited women they hoped to court and eventually marry. If it had been a church day, he'd have been sure she got the cape back before this.

No doubt, in a family as well off as hers, she'd have more than one cape. He'd actually had to get out his iron and ironing board to smooth it out after he'd evidently bunched it around and under himself last night. That kind of labor was frowned upon on the Sabbath, but he could hardly give the cape back in a wrinkled mess, even though it had been tucked around the dead woman in the snow.

Victoria Keller died alone, yet she'd received that loving act of kindness on her cold deathbed. He shifted uneasily on his buggy seat. Would that be his fate when he died—the kindness of a stranger—if he never wed?

He'd left two of his best workers, teenage brothers Micah and Andy Beiler, with the animals, but he still couldn't stay long at Lydia's. They were kids he trusted, though, unlike the wild *rumspringa* ones who drank and smoked and ran around out of control.

Often Lydia came over on a Sunday afternoon to help him feed or curry the animals, but after all that had happened he wasn't banking on that today. As he turned into the driveway he saw the sheriff was just pulling out. Though Blaze was immune to cars coming at her, he got the buggy over as far as he could on the snow-covered, narrow gravel lane.

Jack Freeman rolled his window down and leaned out. His words puffed clouds into the brisk air. "Everything okay today, Josh?"

"Back to normal, I hope."

"Coroner's early report says Ms. Keller was struck on the back of the head with something. If she was down on the ground, could that camel have accidentally kicked her?"

"Doubt it. Even in thick snow, camels see great—double eyelids and really long lashes. They're built that way because of sandstorms. It's highly unlikely, Sheriff."

"Got that. Lydia says the camel has a nice disposition and clued me in on their names and humps. 'Preciate it. You did a great job yesterday, helping me get to the body. See you later, Josh."

Hope not, Josh almost said. It was kind of like dealing with a doctor. You might like the person, but you didn't want to see much of him.

At the front door of the Brand house—tire tracks showed him that's where the sheriff had parked, too—he got down from his buggy and draped the cape carefully over his arm. A Shaker-style hardwood oak bench and matching table were on the deep front porch, even in this weather, as if to advertise the heirloom quality of the family furniture. Josh owned only one piece of inherited Brand furniture, his dining room table. It was beautifully built, but Amish craftsmen always had high standards.

Lydia opened the door before he could knock.

"Oh, how kind of you to bring that back. Please come in."

He stepped inside, onto a dark wood, gleaming-clean floor. She closed the door behind him.

"I saw the sheriff just leaving," he told her. "He said he talked to you about Melly. You fill him in on everything?"

She nodded, but he would have sworn she looked as if she was going to cry. Had the sheriff been that hard on her?

"I was going to come over for a little bit, anyway," she said. "Help the boys with the camel and donkey grooming—do Melly myself."

"I wasn't sure they would want you to after last night," he said, keeping his voice low and glancing around. She would know who "they" were, not the Beiler boys but her parents.

"So nothing's changed, but everything's changed," she told him with a huge sigh, not that he was sure what she meant. She added, "*Daad*'s working in his lair, and *Mamm*'s lying down upstairs. I'll leave them a note and just hitch a ride back with you. I have to get something from upstairs. Just a minute."

"I'll make sure you get home— Or, I know, your father might come for you."

"I'd like to get out, like to talk to you." She darted away, up the stairs, hardly making a sound.

He went a few steps down the hall and looked in the big parlor. Again, he admired the amazing furniture. Yet despite it being Lydia's home, there was something stiff about the entire place, like it was part of the showroom at their store with the construction area hidden behind the formal facade.

Lydia came back down the stairs. He swirled the cape around her shoulders, thinking of how they'd hugged when she'd held his coat for him last night. That reminded him he'd been trying to remember a dream he'd had last night, something he wanted to recall but couldn't…something just out of reach…like Lydia.

She closed and locked the door quietly, and he helped her up into the buggy before he saw, in the large, clear plastic bag she held, an old snow globe and an envelope. As he turned Blaze to head out, he also saw, in a second-story window, Lydia's mother. He didn't mention it to her since she seemed so on edge. Mrs. Brand was, he thought, just watching them, but behind the shiny window glass, she looked as if she, too, like the poor dead woman last night, was coated with ice.

4

"You don't mean the cause of that woman's death might have been kick-by-camel?" Ray-Lynn asked her husband over their midafternoon Sunday dinner. "And in the heart of Amish country?"

She'd had to hold dinner for him, but she was used to that. She'd known about the life of a sheriff—even a small-town, rural county sheriff—going in. But Jack was worth it.

"Delicious ham and sweet potato casserole, honey," he said as he took second helpings. "No, I'm not arresting the camel. I only mentioned that since you seem so set on getting one for the church's living manger scene. Josh Yoder's camels sound tame enough, but I don't want you getting near them since you're going over there to talk to him about the manger scene. And forget anything but having one camel standing off to the side of the manger. No wise men riding them, or we're the ones could be in for a fall. If something happens to a cast member or observer, the church doesn't need a lawsuit."

"I hear you, Sheriff," she said, smiling at him. "But

with a gig just a few miles from his property, I'll bet
Josh himself will come with the camel and maybe
Lydia Brand to help out, too. They'll keep a good eye
on things."

She spread marmalade on a made-from-scratch
yeast roll. She loved cooking and baking for just the
two of them, even though she oversaw so much food
during the week at the restaurant. Honoring Amish
tradition and beliefs, she kept the Dutch Farm Table
closed on Sundays. If she had not, she would have lost
her staff of Amish servers and cooks and been politely
boycotted. No Sunday Sales, read many handprinted
signs in Eden County. And her Amish friendships
meant a lot to her. From the youngest server to her
oldest cook, she felt honored to be entrusted with their
joys and sorrows.

"I've been thinking, Jack…"

"Uh-oh."

"Don't tease. This whole thing with Victoria Keller
living like a specter in the Stark mansion reminds me
of Miss Havisham, the character who was stood up at
the altar and turned into a recluse. She went a little
crazy, too."

"I missed that one in *Gone with the Wind*."

"It's not from *Gone with the Wind* and you know it.
It's from Charles Dickens's book *Great Expectations*.
Didn't you ever have to read that in high school?"

"Nope. Nor your *GWTW.*"

Everyone who knew Ray-Lynn was aware she was
a rabid fan of *Gone with the Wind* and anything to do
with it. Their house was a treasure trove of pictures,
plates and figurines of scenes from the movie. They'd

even worn Civil War costumes for their wedding and reception.

"I'm listening," he said. "You've got good instincts about people, Ray-Lynn, but I don't want you poking around in the Victoria Keller investigation, so just tell me what you want to say."

"Well, first of all, Charles Dickens was a genius at naming his characters to give his readers a hint about them and their secrets. Miss *Have-a-sham,* see? A *sham* is a trick or hypocrisy. She wasn't what she seemed to be."

"What did she seem to be?"

"A spinster recluse, sad and broken over having been jilted by her bridegroom at the altar. But in reality she wanted others to suffer, too. She wanted revenge. And she was wealthy enough to get it. She picked especially on one innocent person, but I won't go into that."

"Honey, we don't know whether Victoria Keller had any motive for going out in the storm to help or hurt someone, get revenge—whatever, and we may never know. She had severe Alzheimer's. I think we can trust Connor and Bess Stark, when Bess gets here from Columbus today, to tell us if there was anything suspicious we should know. And, no offense, but you better stick with Scarlett O'Hara. Now promise me you'll steer clear of this Keller-Stark real-life minidrama and just worry about ordering some of the Yoder animals for the manger scene."

She sensed he was about ready to close this case as soon as he talked to Senator Stark, but Victoria Keller fascinated Ray-Lynn. Hoping he didn't notice she hadn't sworn on a stack of Bibles to stay out of his investigation, she asked, "Are you ready for some mincemeat pie?"

"*That,* I'm ready for. Let me help you clear these dishes, and I'll tell you how big a piece I can handle after all that good cooking—one way to a man's heart, anyway."

"And this," she said as they both stood, "is another," and she stretched on her tiptoes to give him a long, slanted, openmouthed kiss.

Strange, Lydia thought, but the only person she could trust to help straighten out her worries over Victoria Keller's note was Josh. He would understand the background circumstances, her rush and panic that night to help the woman. He wouldn't go all emotional or feel she was challenging him in any way as her parents might. He'd probably tell her she had to show the note to the sheriff right away, but at least she could get his advice first.

The minute they got into his open corner "office" in the barn, while the Beiler boys were feeding the sheep across the building, she said to him, "I'd like your opinion about something—something strange."

He turned to her, nodded wide-eyed, then gestured her toward the bales of straw in the corner. Knees almost touching, they perched on two adjacent ones. Bless him, he seemed instantly intent. His warmth radiated, bathing her in friendship, and she saw in his eyes—something more? In her lap she clutched the envelope with the note and the plastic snow globe with its little scene of a child standing and an angel hovering overhead. An undecorated Christmas tree was off to the side. The liquid inside had gone a bit murky, but if she shook it hard, it still snowed.

"Last night," she began, choosing her words carefully, "when I found Miss Keller, she had a damp, blurry note in her hand. I tried to read it then but couldn't, so I stuffed it in my mitten and didn't think to look at it again until I got home last night. Very little of it is readable."

"And what did it say—the part you could read?"

She reached into the envelope and extended it to him.

"You still have it? The sheriff let you keep it?" he asked as he held it up to the kerosene lantern light and squinted to make out the words.

He glanced at her. She tried hard to blink back tears.

"Did Sheriff Freeman give you a hard time about not handing this over right away? But why—"

"I didn't," she said, her voice shaking. "I didn't give it to him—didn't tell him. I know I should have—have to, but I think it's about me, the Brand baby. And if so, it says my mother—my birth mother—is still alive and that Victoria must have known something about her, like maybe where to find her. I don't— It can't mean, can it—that she is—was my mother?"

"Victoria Keller? I don't think she's ever lived around here before lately."

"I know I'm clutching at straws, but I've been so desperate to know more about my birth parents. I haven't acted on it because it would hurt my parents so. *Daad* would take it personally and *Mamm* would— I don't know. She puts on a good front, but she's very fragile."

He nodded. Did he realize that? Most people who

observed or knew Susan Brand thought she had a prickly personality and figured it was because of Sammy's loss. Some thought she blamed herself for that—even blamed God.

He said, his voice low, "I had a friend when I was in Columbus who researched her roots, as she called them, online. You know, a computer, but that would be tough in this case if you can't get information directly from your parents. You'd need to hire a researcher privately."

"Somehow, I have to get answers on my own."

"Like how? First of all, are you sure Victoria wrote this? If she's as out-of-it as Connor says, couldn't she have picked it up, found it somewhere in their house, then out in the snow, it got all wet and smeared."

"I don't know! I don't know where to start. I only know I have to do something. I thought my parents might overhear if I gave it to the sheriff. Then the note would become public property, bring up things I've learned not to ask or talk about. Even Bishop Esh told me 'to learn in whatever state I am to be content.'"

"That's in the Bible. But I do have one idea. This friend of mine, Sandra Myerson, who was researching her family tree, is also a writer who was doing a doctoral paper on Christmas customs of immigrant people in the Midwest. She's a real go-getter."

"She's a doctor?"

"Not a medical doctor. She's working on a university degree that will give her the title of doctor so she can teach sociology at the college level."

"Oh. So I could write to her with what I know? Maybe trade information about an Amish Christmas for her looking up some things for me? Should I tell her about Old Amish Christmas and how upset our people are about what's happened to the worldly one? About how Bishop Esh said he'd almost like to kill that other Christmas?"

"I spent a lot of time trying to convince Sandra that the German immigrant Amish do not have fancy Victorian Christmas trees and lots of wrapped gifts. I explained we have a plain and simple family day without secret Christmas customs. But to most outsiders, I guess Old Amish Christmas is a secret. I'm sure she'd like to meet you, and you can back up what I said. Yet our Christmases are always, well, just plain beautiful."

"Yes. Yes, they are. So was she working at the zoo, too?"

"I met her at a social event there my second year in the city, ironically a Christmas tree holiday extravaganza called Wildlights. We became friends, did some things together. She tried to talk me into going to vet school at Ohio State University by working my way through, but it wasn't in my plans. I can have Hank phone her for you, ask her to come out to visit. You could meet with her here instead of your house."

"Was this Sandra like a social friend? I mean, you dated her?"

"Something like that, but our lives were on two very different career paths. No way a humble, plain life is for her."

Lydia's heart was beating hard. Her face felt flushed. Had Josh been in love with Sandra Myerson? Had he been heartbroken to leave her when he came back here? He had never mentioned her. Of course, she could have visited here. Still, it sounded as if he hadn't seen her for a while.

"Lydia," he said, his voice gentle, as he reached out to give her the note back, "she didn't like animals, except her three cats."

"Oh."

"What's with the snow globe?" he asked. She could tell he was itching to change the subject. And had he read her mind about his relationship with Sandra?

"*Daad* gave it to me a long time ago. He said it was my mother's. My real mother's. Someone had dropped it off in the furniture store, but he didn't know who and said not to ask more about it. I just—I thought I should hide the note with it."

"Will you tell the sheriff about the note?"

"Will you tell on me?"

"No. It's your decision, though now you've made me an accomplice."

She almost smiled at that, but she bit her lower lip. "He—the sheriff said I was to be invited to the private funeral for Victoria. I may ask someone there about it."

"Connor?"

"Maybe his mother."

"At least they were trying to do the right thing, taking her in, keeping her there."

"Then, would she have run away? I need to know more about dementia, I guess. Yes, if you could have Hank contact your friend for help with tracing my family tree—quietly—I would appreciate that. There must have been newspaper articles about the fatal buggy accident. There always are."

"But it would be almost twenty years ago. There was no local paper then. Maybe we could ask Sandra to check the *Wooster Daily Record.* Do you know the date of the accident or your parents' names?"

She shook her head and could not stem the tears. "Not even that," she whispered. "They were distant cousins of Solomon Brand, but I don't even know if their last name was Brand. They were Amish, though."

Josh covered her hands, clasped over the snow globe, with one of his. So warm, so steady, so reassuring. Except that her stomach flip-flopped and her pulse pounded when he so much as touched her.

Feeling more upset that she didn't even know her real parents' names, when she knew the ones for every animal in this barn, Lydia worked hard at grooming the camels. It bothered her, too, that Sandra Myerson, the woman she'd agreed to have Josh bring out to Amish country, was probably a woman he'd really cared about. What was that worldly saying? Oh, *ya,* maybe she was an old fire of his—no, an old flame.

Lydia kept up a string of talk to the camels, not only to calm them but to calm herself. She rubbed their ears, cleaned their eyes and brushed their heads. She was glad they weren't shedding this time of year and she didn't have to work through dirt, mats and mud balls. She had to smile when Gaspar tried to gently shove Balty out of the way to be next in line.

When she heard a woman's voice, she peered around Balty's chest. Coming down the center aisle with Josh was Senator Bess Stark, taking long strides and dressed in black slacks, white blouse and unbuttoned bright green coat. And here Lydia looked like this, red-eyed and dirty with her hair flopping loose because Melly had playfully pulled her prayer *kapp* off and her long braid had broken free.

But she smoothed her skirt and apron and stepped

out into the aisle to greet them. Mrs. Stark's gaze went over her thoroughly, but she didn't let on one bit how bad she looked. Josh was staring, kind of hot-eyed at her hair. Just because he'd never seen her with her hair loose? That was reserved only for husbands among the Amish. Nervously, she tossed her long hair back behind her shoulders and was really surprised when the senator stepped forward to give her a light hug.

Elizabeth Stark, called Bess, was in her early fifties and a striking woman, though Lydia had never figured out why she'd suddenly appeared with all silver-white, sleek hair when she'd looked real nice with just a dusting of silver in her sandy-colored tresses. Her eyes were as green as grass, and her teeth were white and perfect. She'd been a widow a long time, since Connor was about twelve. Rumors always flew around that she was dating someone important in Columbus or Washington, D.C. Everyone in this area was proud of Senator Stark, even the Amish, who had no truck with politics, but more than once she'd helped them out and always supported their charity events.

Whether Bess Stark was a politician or not, Lydia had always liked her. Though she wasn't around much anymore except at holidays or when she was campaigning for reelection, years ago she'd give Lydia cookies and lemonade when Lydia used to play in the rows and rows of pine trees the Starks grew. That is, until Connor told her to stay on her own property. She'd never told anyone—and *Mamm* forbade Lydia to go over there, anyway.

As Bess pulled back and held Lydia at arm's length for a moment with her hands on her shoulders, Lydia saw there were worry lines on the senator's forehead.

Of course, she'd been grieving for her sister's sad death.

"My little next-door neighbor from long ago! You have certainly grown up from that tomboy in a skirt and bonnet, Lydia. Hasn't she, Joshua?"

He cleared his throat. "For sure," he said, sounding breathier than usual.

"We are so sorry about your sister," Lydia said, as Bess stepped away and pulled her shoulder purse up, which had slipped down her arm. It was real fancy, bright yellow leather, big, too, almost like a small, soft suitcase.

"I can't thank both of you enough for what you did to try to help her last night. Sadly, she's been slipping from us for a long time, wasn't herself, didn't know what she was saying or doing."

Lydia's hopes that the note could mean anything fell. Those who knew Victoria Keller best had said the poor woman was completely out of touch with reality.

She glanced at Josh, who nodded. He seemed to have read her mind again and knew that she was undecided whether to show the note to Bess Stark or not. Lydia's heart beat faster. Did she dare to show her the note? But then she'd take it, wouldn't she?

"I'm late and have to run," Bess said, as if deciding for her. "I haven't even been home yet, just saw Joshua out in front as I drove by. So much to do to plan the funeral, but I would like you two to attend. The sheriff and Ray-Lynn will be invited also, so it will just be the four of you from the community with our family and friends. I hope your parents will let you take a break from the furniture store, Lydia. Wednesday afternoon at one, our house. We're interring her in the Wooster cemetery on our family plot near my husband, but we won't expect you to go to the cemetery—can't be away from the animals too long. True?"

"*Ya*. You're right about that," Josh put in.

"Lydia?"

"I would be honored to be there. I'm sure *Daad* will let me go."

"I hope so," she said, frowning, seemingly lost in thought about the funeral again. "If Victoria had been in her right mind, she would have thanked you both. Joshua, I've written a check—" she fumbled in that big purse and dug it out "—to help toward all you do with your animals at Christmastime. For feed, gas for transporting them—whatever. Just a little something. And don't you mention it to anyone else."

His eyes widened when he glanced down at the check she handed him. "But—four thousand dollars. I can't take that for a human kindness, Senator Stark. It's enough to rebuild one entire wing of the old dairy!"

"I hear Lydia loves the animals, too, so half of it is her contribution. Yes, get some good Amish builders in here. All of us need to promote jobs right now. You go ahead—remodel and rebuild. Everybody needs to do that from time to time, especially in great loss and tragedy. Don't you dare tear that up," she insisted, walking away from him. "I think you're doing a great service to the community I represent with your petting zoo and the holiday events. And I will see both of you on Wednesday at one. Now I have to go see the sheriff and then the coroner about releasing her body despite all this nonsense about an investigation into her death, but I think they will agree with me."

"Oh, *ya*," Josh said to Lydia as they stood in the door to watch her drive away, "I think they will."

5

Because Christmas was barely a month away, the Home Valley Amish Furniture store was abuzz with business. Although the Amish gave only single, simple gifts to commemorate the Lord's birth, the *Englische* world, despite a supposed recession, seemed to be buying every piece of solid hardwood furniture in sight.

It was the Monday morning after the tragedy of the weekend, and Lydia still felt shaken. At least being so busy meant she had little time to agonize over her decisions. She would meet and hope to work with Sandra Myerson, Josh's more-than-good friend. And she was dedicated to learning all she could about her deceased parents—if her mother really was dead.

Greeting customers kept her occupied. She let Naomi, one of their seasonal staff, answer the phone while she darted here and there with inquiries or to pair up shoppers with particular salesmen. Although the store hired *Englische* delivery vans, some folks came in to pick up their orders. She could see out the row of side windows that not only workers' buggies but worldly pickup trucks filled the parking lot.

To answer customer questions for salespeople on the floor, Lydia practically ran from her front desk to the side showrooms, which displayed the various styles the craftsmen, who worked out back or in their homes, produced: Shaker-style, Mission-style and traditional furniture of all kinds. Now and then, she darted to the offices between the spacious showrooms and the large, rear workshop to ask someone a question.

"Can we do a custom stain on maple chairs? I told the buyer that our kiln-dried northern hardwoods have their own beauty." Or, this question for Gid right now: "The buyer for that huge walnut dining room outfit—ah, number 1088—wants to know if he can make the first payment after New Year's instead of right before." He nodded and gestured her in, but she stood her ground.

She tried not to go into the bookkeeping office because that was Gideon Reich's realm, but when she needed to, she went, standing in his doorway with the door open, telling him, "Sorry, can't come in now," she added. It's too busy out here." Lately, she tried not to be alone with him even here at the store.

"Lunch, then? I can send someone out for food for us, for your father, too, if you want. I brought my usual bachelor's packed lunch. I envy the men out back. Most have wives to pack their lunch boxes," he said with a wink before he sobered. "And I'm sorry I was away visiting this weekend when everything happened. I wanted to talk to you about that."

With an exaggerated shrug, she told him, "It's pretty much over," even as she realized that was a big, fat lie. Why was she telling so many lately?

"But it's another reason not to hang around Yoder

and those animals," he insisted, standing and coming around his big cherry desk toward her. "That sudden storm that could have trapped you, then a possible murder..."

"Are people saying that? I think the poor lady hit her head pulling open the back gate. I'll bet she had to tug hard, to drag it through the snow where it was maybe frozen fast, then it came loose and hit her when she was bending low." She cleared her throat. "I know the coroner hasn't ruled yet, though."

Gideon Reich was a powerfully built man, although he was not fat or tall. Lydia looked at him eye to eye. Gid was in his late thirties, a childless widower who had never remarried. His father had worked for her grandfather, who had started a small furniture work-shop on this property. In the twenty years Gid had been employed here, he had worked his way up to head bookkeeper and general manager, at least if her father was not on-site. Gid's home was large, second only to the Stark mansion and chock-full of beautiful Brand furniture.

Despite the usual privacy of Amish courtships, it was no secret to anyone here, in town or in their church, that Gid had his eye on Lydia. To her mind, the real question was why, as she not only tried to discour-age him but had made it clear he should try to court someone else. With all the trouble she gave him, she wondered if he persevered only to court her parents because she came attached to the store and its profits.

"And," Gid went on, his voice rising, "you were chasing a camel in the storm when you should have been inside—inside your own house, not the Yoder barn! Lydia, I know this isn't the time, and I'm busy, too, but stray animals are all you're chasing over at Yoder's place, aren't they?" He came even closer. "As your come-calling friend, who admires and appreciates you and wants only what is best for you, I've warned you again and again that your working in an animal barn isn't suitable. You know that your father also agrees that—"

"As ever, thank you for your concern, but you have heard again and again how I feel about helping out at Yoder's. And your mentioning my father reminds me I need to pop in to see him, too. As for lunch, that's very kind of you, but I have an errand to run."

She darted out, closing the door on him, quietly but firmly, almost in his face. How she wished she could close the door on any future with him. She feared he was going to press her for a promise. And when she said no, it was going to complicate everything at home and here at work. True, she was ready to leave her parents, but not to become Gid Reich's bride.

As she headed toward her father's office, she saw he was sitting not behind his massive desk, but in a big hickory rocker with one of his new quilts draped over his knees—a wedding ring design, no less. As lovely as it was with its leaping blue-and-yellow hues, she hoped he hadn't made it for her. Sol Brand had an open-door policy here not only for her but for anyone who had a question or concern, from the lowliest sweep-up boy out back to his key advisor and master bookkeeper, Gid.

Although no one was in his office now, she knew he was busy, even overworked. He seemed tired, older than his age, even distressed. She'd forgotten there were drafts in here this time of year, and he looked a bit chilled.

"Liddy!" he said, glancing up from some sort of document he was reading. "I've recently had an inquiry I think you can answer."

"Oh, sure. Anything to help."

"A certain buyer has asked me to find out if you would prefer a blanket chest, pie safe or jelly cupboard for a gift in the near future," he said with a lift of his eyebrows and a tight smile. "Sounds more like a betrothal gift, eh?"

Lydia's insides cartwheeled. "*Daad,* I can't commit to such a gift or something like a betrothal right now."

"You've said that before. When, then? And why not, my girl?"

"I'm not ready in my head and heart. And if it's Gid—"

"*Ya,* of course, it's Gid. Do you think I would want just anyone for my only daughter? Your mother and I would miss you, but it's time you consider that fine man. And, in a way, since all of this will be your inheritance someday—" he swept his arm to indicate the wood-paneled office lined with metal file cases "—you will need someone who knows the business, values it and not something far different."

"*Daad,* I know my friends are getting married off right and left, but I need some time. And, if you and *Mamm* really want me to be happy, you will give me more time and help me convince Gid that it's not a done deal. I have an errand in town to run at lunchtime—just wanted to let you know," she added, backing away. "Got to get back to my desk..."

She'd forgotten why she'd come in here. What

would she do if her father turned against her the way she sometimes felt her mother had? Worse, as she hurried back out into the showroom, she saw Gid had emerged from his office and was watching her from the display of blanket chests any good Amish girl would want to use for a hope chest.

Ray-Lynn spotted Lydia Brand right away when she came into the restaurant. She seemed to be in a hurry, alone and skimming the lunch crowd for someone. Ray-Lynn handed the coffeepot to Amy, one of her Amish servers, and asked her to keep refilling cups.

"Lydia, looking for someone?" Ray-Lynn asked, thinking, since she'd come in without her father or Gid Reich, she might be meeting Josh Yoder. She'd picked up vibes between the two of them this weekend. And she really liked Lydia. Despite the fact her family was the Amish answer to the local *Lifestyles of the Rich and Famous,* Lydia was always down-to-earth and concerned for others, evidently even Josh Yoder's camels.

"Actually, I was hoping to talk to you," Lydia said. She was out of breath and flushed. "Something kind of personal—you know, private. I know it's your busy time right now, but I need to ask you a quick question, if you'd agree to help."

Ray-Lynn put a hand on Lydia's caped shoulder and steered her down the narrow hall toward the restrooms and her office. "Let me get someone to cover for a few minutes, and I'll see you in my office. Just go in. The door's marked. And if this is your lunch hour, I'll order both of us a sandwich and soft drink, okay?"

"Thanks, Ray-Lynn."

At the counter, she put Martha on the front desk and ordered two roast beef sandwiches with slaw and two colas to be sent back to her office. When Ray-Lynn joined Lydia, she'd taken her cape off—the same cape she'd put over the dead woman?—but was still standing. Or had she been pacing?

"Sit and talk to me," she told her, taking one of the two chairs in front of the desk and patting the arm of the other.

"It's a favor," Lydia said, perching on the edge of the chair. "I know you hear a lot of things in the restaurant, know a lot of people."

"That, I do."

"Would you happen to know who had the jobs at the Stark house—overseers or nurses, I don't know— to take care of Victoria Keller?"

Ray-Lynn leaned closer to Lydia over the arm of her chair. "Until Saturday, I didn't even catch a whiff that they had Senator Stark's demented sister living there."

"Oh, right. So you wouldn't have any idea about—"

"I didn't say that. The sheriff intends to interview both of the caregivers to learn more about Victoria's state of mind, and he mentioned who they are—both Amish. You probably know them, though they're older than you. Connor wasn't too pleased about the interviews, but he had to cooperate and give their names. The woman who was on duty when Victoria sneaked out came under scrutiny, of course, for dereliction of duty."

"Are their names law enforcement business, and I can't find out?"

"Before I answer that, why do you want to know? I mean, the coroner just declared Victoria Keller's death

accidental this morning. He ruled that evidence in-
dicates she caused her own demise by yanking that
swinging gate open in the eight or so inches of snow
and hitting her head—which I believe was a theory
you gave the sheriff. So, it's all over, Lydia. Did you
just want to know more about Victoria from those who
tended her? At the funeral Wednesday, I'd be glad to
help you ask Senator Stark, or even Connor's wife,
about her for you."

Lydia looked as if she were about to cry. Her lower
lip trembled and she gripped her knees. Ray-Lynn
covered the girl's cold hands with her own.

"I know you've helped several friends of mine,"
the girl whispered. "But the fact that you're married
to the sheriff and shouldn't keep anything back from
him, even if he can't sometimes tell you everything..."

"My dear girl, you have a lot to learn about marriage. I will always be faithful and true to Jack Freeman, but that doesn't mean I have to tell him absolutely
everything I happen to hear, everything I know. Do
you have some kind of information about Victoria?"

"Do you know if there's any such thing as privileged
information with the sheriff?" the young woman countered. "I mean, if I show or tell him something that
could hurt my family—not about her death exactly—
would he have to make it public?"

"I do know there are things the police hold back to
use in interrogations or in court, so they can be sure
they have the right person arrested, charged and con-
victed."

Martha knocked and came in with the tray of
food and drinks and set it on Ray-Lynn's desk. They

thanked her but neither of them made a move toward it or said anything else until she went out.

"It's just," Lydia said, her voice a shaky whisper as she dabbed at tears with her fingers, "I don't want to hurt my parents."

"How would it hurt your parents? Listen, Lydia, do you want to just tell me, or do you want me to call the sheriff and have him come over to hear it, too? In a way, you can trade what you know for the caretakers' names. Unless he's gone out in the last half hour, he's just across the street. And if you ask him not to tell your parents, even if you're under their roof, I'm sure he would agree. You're considered an adult among your people, so surely you can make your own decisions."

"Make my own decisions," she repeated, nodding. "*Ya,* I intend to. And I hate doing things in secret, but sometimes it's best."

Ray-Lynn went for the phone on her desk. She used the speed dial to get Jack, then pushed the food tray toward Lydia.

"If he's not there now, I'll have to head back soon," the girl said, stabbing her straw into her soft drink.

"Ray-Lynn, you okay?" came the familiar voice she loved.

"Just fine. Jack, Lydia Brand and I need your help. Can you drop by my office at the restaurant?"

"Right now? Something about the Keller case?"

"She'll have to tell you, but she has to go back to the furniture store soon."

"Sure, honey. For you and one of your little Amish friends, be right there."

* * *

Lydia wasn't as nervous as she thought she'd be, especially since Ray-Lynn stayed when Sheriff Freeman arrived. He sat in the chair Ray-Lynn had vacated, while she sat behind her desk. Putting his hat next to their half-eaten tray of food, he leaned his elbows on his knees but looked up toward Lydia.

"Okay, talk," he said with a nod and small, encouraging smile she appreciated.

In a nearly breathless rush, Lydia explained what she knew—and suspected—about the note. "I'm sorry I don't have it here," she said. "It's hidden under my bed at home."

"You shouldn't have withheld evidence," the sheriff said, sitting up straight. "But I see why you forgot about it that night in the barn and why you didn't want to tell me with your parents hovering. I'll need that note."

"Not to show it to them or the Starks?"

"The case has been closed with an accidental death ruling, but it does throw light on what the deceased might have thought she was doing or where she was going. But she has no connection to you, right?" he said, frowning, with a shake of his head.

"No. Not that I know about now. She can't possibly be my real mother—I mean birth mother."

"I'll keep it in my evidence file and only mention it to Connor if something else comes up. I think they're eager to get her buried proper and go on with their lives."

"*Danki,* Sheriff. I—"

"But that's only because I talked to one of her caregivers from the Starks' home and got the deceased's medical records from the place she was being treated in Cincinnati, a top-of-the-line Alzheimer's care facility. She was mentally bad off, Lydia, just like Connor said. Victoria Keller was delusional, claiming wild things, and tried to wander off there. That note probably means zilch, so don't get your hopes up— or down."

Ray-Lynn had been real quiet, which seemed pretty unusual, but she piped up, "So there's no harm in letting Lydia talk to the local caregivers?"

"I hear you, honey," he told his wife without looking at her.

"Ya," Lydia put in quickly. "Just a private talk. I'll tell no one what they say—except you or Ray-Lynn, if you want, Sheriff. My mother is still fragile over my brother's drowning years ago. I didn't want to upset her or my father, because they're touchy about my looking into my birth parents."

"I can see that when they always told you your parents were dead. *'Your mother is still alive, and I...'"* he quoted what Lydia had told him about the note. "Tell you what now. You get me the note to examine and put on file. As spacey as Victoria Keller was, I repeat, it probably means nothing. Meanwhile, you have my permission to talk to the two women who were watching Victoria, though one of the caretakers just moved out of the area. 'Cause with Victoria's medical history, far as I'm concerned, this case is closed. But you let me know what you find out. Connor Stark's not one to be crossed, and I had to come down hard on him not to press charges of negligence against the two women. As it is, he refused to give them their last month's paychecks."

Ray-Lynn gave a loud snort. "Our rich/cheap, kind/cruel new mayor," she muttered.

"Now, Ray-Lynn," the sheriff scolded, but his voice was gentle. "So here—" he reached for a pen and paper on the corner of the desk "—are the two women's names and the one's address I can recall offhand because the other one lives up near Cleveland. They're both members of other Amish churches—not yours. But you keep things low-key with them, okay?"

"Low-key, *ya,*" Lydia promised, gripping her hands in her lap so hard her fingers went numb.

But how could something so momentous in her life be "low" anything? As for a key, since she wasn't exactly sure what he meant, this just might be the key to answering questions about her past—and her future.

6

Even though Lydia stayed later than usual at the furniture store that same day, she lit out in her buggy just before *Daad* and Gid closed up the place. She hurried home and unhitched her horse, Flower. Relieved *Mamm* was still taking her nap, Lydia grabbed the precious note from under her bed, snatched a container to protect it and walked down to the road to wait for Ray-Lynn to pick her up.

Their cover story was that Lydia was going with her to Josh's to help her place an order for manger animals for the Homestead Community Church Christmas tableau. Actually, Lydia was to give her the note so it could be delivered to the sheriff. She also planned to feed the camels while Ray-Lynn and Josh sealed the deal. Like most Amish, Josh never worked with contracts but believed in a handshake and trust, even though he did take careful notes about what animals would be delivered where and when by him and his *Englische* driver, Hank.

"Here it is," Lydia told Ray-Lynn as she climbed

into her van. "I sealed the note in a Tupperware sandwich box to keep it safe."

"Good. Just slide it under your seat, and I'll be sure my man gets it. Speaking of which, you and Josh are pretty good friends, right?"

"Well, we've known each other for years," Lydia said, fumbling for words, realizing she was talking in almost as slow a drawl as Ray-Lynn used. Why didn't she just spit it out? She cared about him more than he did her. At least the drive to Josh's was about one minute long, so she didn't have time to explain—and explain what, she wasn't even sure.

"Oh, look!" Ray-Lynn cried, pointing. "Wonder who that is. A long-lost friend of Josh's, for sure."

Lydia's gaze followed her friend's finger. Not by the barn but over on his front porch, Josh was hugging a woman with long auburn hair. And she was sure hugging him back. She wore a short denim skirt, boots and red jacket and, despite the cold wind, looked pretty warm—hot, like worldly folks said. Lydia couldn't see her face but the rest of her looked pretty good.

Then she realized who it was. Sandra Myerson was here.

"I think that's an old friend of his from Columbus," she told Ray-Lynn, trying not to gawk. And here she'd blown up the importance of her and Josh's hug in the barn last Saturday night. It hadn't been like that long, hard hug with Sandra at all. It had meant so much to her but to him...

"Quite a flashy car, too," Ray-Lynn said as she pulled up by the barn and stopped in one of the two parking spots next to the hitching post for buggies.

Lydia darted another glance at Josh. The hug was over, and she'd hardly noticed the low, small red car parked in his driveway. Oh, now he was taking Sandra—if that's who it was—into his house.

"Well, if he's preoccupied, I can't wait around," Ray-Lynn said, hitting her fist on the steering wheel. "Listen, Lydia, hugs and kissy face are common in the world, so don't let all that get to you."

"Get to me? I'm glad she's here as she knows how to trace family trees, and that's what I hope to do."

"Oh, you know her. Ding-dang, you've got to forgive me for jumping to conclusions. Jack says it's my weakness, but I know it's only one of them. By the way, Josh did wave to acknowledge he saw us, or maybe he recognized my van. Can I drop you back at home or are you staying?"

"I came to take care of the camels," she told Ray-Lynn with a forced smile. "I'll just go in the barn and maybe meet her later, as I've only heard about her so far."

"Will you tell Josh for me that the Community Church would like to rent a manger scene? One camel, one donkey and a couple of sheep for Wednesday, December 12, in the evening, like six to nine? We intend to really kick off the Christmas season for the area."

"Sure, I'll tell him. That early and the middle of the week, it will probably be fine. I'll bring you a list of the prices next time I see you. Ray-Lynn, *danki* and thanks, both!"

As Lydia started to get out of the car, Ray-Lynn grabbed her arm. "If you need to talk to someone who cares, you come see me."

"I will," she promised. As she got out of the van, she glimpsed the pale green plastic sandwich box with the note in it sticking out from under the seat. She hated to give the note up but she was getting much in return. The sheriff, maybe thanks to Ray-Lynn, wasn't angry with her. He had given her the names of Anna Gingerich, who lived about twenty miles away, and Sarah Miller, who lived up near Cleveland. So there was a place to start, a trail to follow, people to question. Now, if only Sandra Myerson could help her out without trying to get Josh back—because, of course, she must have been in love with him.

With a wave at Ray-Lynn, Lydia hurried into and through the barn, greeting animals by name, petting her favorites among the donkeys who pushed against their bars to get their ears scratched and a dried apple to eat from the bin. "Melly, Balty, all of you are expected to be on your best behavior today," she told the six camels as they swung their curved, shaggy necks over the railings to greet her with fluttery, fat-lipped air kisses.

"Hugs and kissy face!" she told her avid furry listeners. "What do we care about all that in the big, bad world, right?"

Since she had left the donkeys with only one apple apiece, they brayed in protest, and the sheep murmured their *baa-baas*.

Lydia wrote Ray-Lynn's requests on a piece of paper on Josh's barn desk—long oak boards on barrels—then turned toward the camels just as the back door opened and Josh stood there. Hatless, his hair blew free in the wind. Vital and strong, with the crisp blue, winter sky behind him highlighting the color of his eyes, he seemed to fill and warm the large door frame.

"Lydia, glad you're here. As you may have seen, Sandra's here from Columbus, wants to stay a day or two—that is, at the Plain and Fancy B and B in town. She'd rather not come out to the animal barn, but can you come in the house? She's pretty excited to meet you and exchange some genealogical help for info on Amish Christmas, if you're still willing."

Oh, *ya,* Lydia thought, she was still willing, despite the fact Josh's face looked much more flushed than the winter wind usually made it.

Up close, Sandra Myerson was very pretty with auburn, arched eyebrows and full lips that smiled easily to display snow-white teeth. Her expressions came quickly and were full of emotion and life. She shook Lydia's hand, then pressed it between both of hers. Her brown eyes were alert and sharp and warmed when she looked at Josh. Lydia tried not to take that all in and instead managed glances at Josh's living room.

She hadn't been in his house since he'd bought his brothers out. She figured the place must tell a lot about him. A spacious, two-story white farmhouse with high ceilings, it was well-lighted from the tall windows. Maybe a bit sparse on furniture but what he had was well arranged. On the table next to the comfy-looking dark blue sofa was a stack of zoo and animal magazines, and the calendar on the wall had a picture of zebra in the snow for the month of November.

"Josh had his friend Hank fill me in on the phone about you, Lydia, but I'd love to hear your take on everything," Sandra said. "I'd be happy to help you try to trace your biological roots and take in trade anything you can tell me about an Amish Christmas here in Eden County. Not that Josh and I didn't have some go-arounds about that, but women see things a lot differently from men."

Sandra gave Josh a playful punch in his midriff, which Lydia figured was a lot more intimate than a punch to his arm. Oh, well. She had to work with and get along with this woman. And if these two still meant something to each other, Lydia had to accept that, at least for now.

"I don't even have names to start tracing," she admitted as Josh sat in his chair and the two women took the sofa, facing each other. "But there has to be a newspaper record of my parents' deaths, because car-buggy accidents are always written up. I do know the week they died because I was ten days old. It was the second week of February 1992."

"You mean you weren't even told your parents' names?"

"It was— I just sensed it was difficult to ask. As if I would be disloyal if I did. Actually, I did ask once and *Mamm* said that she and *Daad* were my real parents now, so I got that message loud and clear. I didn't want to upset her more and wanted *Daad* to know I loved and trusted him—which I do," she added hastily.

Sandra raised an eyebrow at Josh. "Well, more of a mystery, then, though I've seen other situations where key information had been lost or even lied about. I can check the database archive from the *Cleveland Plain*

Dealer online if it goes back that far, but is there a more local paper?"

Josh put in, "Homestead has a weekly paper but it's only about nine years old. We'd need to go into Wooster in the next county to check on articles from the *Daily Record*."

We'd need to go? Lydia thought. Was Josh going to help Sandra? But this was his busiest time for the Christmas animals. Or did he automatically think of himself and Sandra as a team?

"Is there any way you could go to Wooster with me now?" Sandra asked Lydia. "I saw a mileage sign a ways back that I think said thirtysomething. I can call ahead to check on the paper's closing time."

Lydia's head was spinning. Go in that little red car right now when her parents would think she was working over here?

"I came to work with Josh's animals so—"

"I can take care of them," he said. "I know how much this means to you and how much you've meant to the animals and me."

Lydia's gaze met and locked with his for a moment, but it seemed a long time. Sandra cleared her throat. "Let's do it," Lydia heard herself say. "I can't thank both of you enough for your help."

"Besides, we need to get to know each other better, since we're going to work together," Sandra said, bobbing up from the sofa. "Who knows? Maybe their archives are online."

"Don't bet on it," Josh said.

She got a flat, little thing out of her purse, flipped it open and started stroking the small screen. "I'll just check the closing time of the *Wooster Daily Record* offices or else get their number and call them. And thirty-some miles means you can talk about your genealogy project en route and about an Amish Christmas coming back."

"You'll be surprised how complicated my problem is compared to how simple our Christmas is—both of them," Lydia told her as she and Josh stood, too. She wished she'd dressed better than her barn clothes but that wouldn't stop her from going to Wooster. She was too eager to get started on finding out who she really was—and who this Sandra really was, especially what she meant to Josh.

By the time they pulled up in front of the *Daily Record* newspaper office in Wooster, the county seat for the next county, Lydia had talked a lot but learned a lot. One thing, though she hated to admit it, was that she liked Sandra Myerson. She seemed honest and straightforward, as Josh had said, a go-getter who knew what she wanted from life, and Lydia couldn't help but admire that. Sadly, the woman did not like animals except cats, but surely there were worse flaws in human beings. At least, Lydia thought, that probably meant Sandra and Josh were not meant for each other, except for the fact Sandra had carried on about what a great, genuine guy he was.

Dusk was descending as they hurried into the *Daily Record* office and told the curly haired woman at the reception counter what they hoped to find. She didn't blink an eye that the two of them looked so different, but Wayne County had plenty of Amish, too.

"Okay," the receptionist said when she'd heard their inquiry, "a double death, car hits buggy. That or a court case means a clip should have been kept, though only events from the last ten years are stored in our computer system. From the time period you want, our clips are not in a database but should be in an envelope filed in the morgue."

"The morgue?" Lydia said.

"Just our slang. We don't have a librarian anymore, but some of our veteran editors know how to find stuff in the morgue—it's kind of like a library. Let me see if someone can help you, but several have gone home already."

They waited about five minutes until a plump, sixty-something woman named Monica Jordan came out to help them. They wrote out their information for her and sat down to wait again.

"I've done research in the States and Europe," Sandra told her in a quiet voice. "It's sometimes just like this—fill out forms and wait, but then—*voilà!*—some hidden gem falls right in your lap.

"So what's this about two Amish Christmases?" she asked. "Josh only told me about one, December 25, a family day, keep-it-simple, sometimes home-made gifts, a traditional meal. It sounds like the rest of us except for the lack of razzle-dazzle and ooh-la-la, no over-the-top decorations and Santa stuff we moderns enjoy."

"For sure no Santa stuff."

"But how about decorated trees? I passed a Christmas tree farm near Josh's."

"That's the Stark tree farm on the outskirts of

Homestead, but the Amish don't buy those. The moderns do, though, and the farm ships truckloads of trees to local cities to be sold on rented lots. That's Ohio Senator Bess Stark's family business, though she's almost never here, and her son oversees it."

"Boy, that's a good one. Snarky Stark's family sells Christmas trees."

Lydia didn't know what *snarky* meant but she didn't want to ask. Sandra used all kinds of strange words like *voilà*.

"So, go on about Christmas," Sandra prompted.

"The truth is that many Amish want to ignore the December 25 celebration, since the world has commercialized it so much. We struggle to ignore outside temptation and keep the day focused on our faith. But as for the second so-called Amish Christmas, we just call it Old Christmas because it went with the historical religious calendar from centuries ago. We close our stores on that day, too. It's January 6, called Epiphany, the traditional day of the arrival of the wise men from the East—probably the first non-Jews to see the baby Jesus, and that shows anyone can approach Him."

"So you celebrate January 6, too, while the rest of America does not? I don't think that's very well-known. Great, I can use that in my dissertation on immigrant holidays. The modern-day Amish are against commercialized Christmas, so they cling to another day when the wise men brought their gifts to the manger."

"But it's a simple day, too, sometimes spent with extended family. You know, that's one of the things I might have missed, being adopted. I have a few cousins on my father's side, but they don't live within buggy distance, so I see them mostly at weddings and funerals. Mother's family is from Pennsylvania, so the same there. But maybe if I learn who my biological parents were, there will be new cousins, even some in buggy range."

Sandra leaned closer and put her hand on Lydia's arm. "Don't dream too big. They might not even find the old article of the accident. Then, if you still don't want to involve your adoptive parents, we'd have to start asking around on the sly."

But her voice trailed off as Monica Jordan came back out to the front desk with a manila folder in her hand. "Ladies," she said, "I think I've found what you're looking for."

They rose. Lydia's heartbeat kicked up. They approached the counter where Ms. Jordan spread open the folder, filled with old newspaper articles that looked more black-and-yellow than black-and-white. And on top lay one with a photo of a crumpled buggy in a ditch and a dead horse.

Lydia sucked in a sob. Any hurt or killed animal got to her, even when the local men went hunting. But this—her parents' death scene...

"Could we look at this over there?" Sandra asked the woman. "We'll be very careful with it."

Evidently noting Lydia's distress, Monica said, "It's almost closing time, but I can photocopy it for you."

Lydia carried the warm copy of the article outside into the thickening dark. She cradled it to her cape; it seemed to burn her hand. When they got back in Sandra's car, the overhead light popped on. Lydia was suddenly afraid to look at the picture again, though it didn't show dead bodies. Sandra turned on the ignition and the heater, but it blew out cold air at first.

"Can you read it out loud or should I?" Sandra asked.

"I can. I want to—have wanted to for a long time," Lydia whispered. Then, despite feeling chilled from within, she read aloud, "'Young Amish Couple Die in Buggy Accident. Driver Cited.'"

Lydia frowned. "Driver cited?" she muttered as Sandra leaned closer to look at the photo. The article was trembling in Lydia's hand.

"That means the driver of the car. Go on, and I'll make notes," she said, fumbling in her big purse for a pad and pen.

Her voice shaking, Lydia went on.

"A young Amish couple from the Charm, Ohio area, David Brand, age 24, and Lena Hostetler Brand, age 23…"

Her voice caught. *David and Lena, David and Lena…* Their names were David and Lena… And her mother's people were Hostetlers. She knew of some in this area, though not in the Homestead Amish church.

She cleared her throat, blinked back tears and continued.

"…were pronounced dead at the scene after a vehicle carrying four tourists from Parma, Ohio, struck their buggy at approximately 9:00 p.m. on Wednesday.

Clinton MacKenney, the Holmes County sheriff at the scene, theorized that skid marks indicate the vehicle, a station wagon, careened over the hill behind the buggy at a speed of at least fifty miles per hour, could not stop in time and hit the buggy from the rear. Marvin Lowe, 65, was cited for driving over the speed limit with reckless abandon. Further charges of double manslaughter may be forthcoming.

Lowe made no statement but said he will soon have a lawyer. His vehicle sustained minor damage…

"Minor damage," Lydia whispered, blinking back tears. "It isn't fair. So perhaps there was a trial."

"But this gives us all we need to know to start searching."

"And there's no way my mother could still be alive," Lydia admitted with a sigh. She'd told Sandra about the note. "Talk about getting my hopes up…"

Sandra shook her head. "So sad. A tragedy that could have been avoided. Do you want me to read the rest of it?"

"Okay but I'm fine. Well, not really, but I want to find out no matter what."

Sandra took up where she'd left off.

"Since it was nearly four hours after dark, the Brand buggy had two lanterns on the back, both surprisingly found still lighted in the ditch when medics and the sheriff arrived. The horse was also killed. The couple had wed barely a year

ago and leave one infant daughter who is staying with relatives. David Brand was a tree cutter
with a company in Amity."

"A tree cutter," Lydia repeated. "I wish it said if
they left behind other family—siblings, cousins."

"I can search for their obits later, and those might
tell."

"Maybe. The Amish come from far and wide for
funerals. More likely their obituaries appeared in *The
Budget,* the national Amish newspaper. But I'm sure no
one keeps clippings from that in folders or databases."

"I forget I'm dealing with an enclave culture here."

Another word Lydia didn't know but she got the
idea.

"I just wonder," Sandra said as she turned off the
light on the car's ceiling and backed out, "if the relatives you were staying with the night of the accident
or thereafter are your adoptive parents or if there were
others who took care of you at first. What's the relationship between your adoptive father and your biological father?"

"I'm not sure. A cousin, not first cousin. *Ach,* our
people value family, even extended family, and many
know their roots way back to the few Amish families who migrated from Europe to escape persecution
there. And here, I know next to nothing," she added,
blinking back tears again.

"But you know a lot more than a few minutes ago,
and it gives me information to start digging. It's obvious your real mother died in this accident," she said,

"but Victoria's note gives us such an interesting twist we might still want to check it out."

"Yes, I still do," Lydia told her, stroking the old photo of the scene of the double murder—that's what it was, murder! Nothing to do about that this late, of course, except try to forgive. But unlike what her *daad* and *mamm* wanted, after today, she could never forget. Like she'd heard Josh say once when he was talking about his time in the world, *A little knowledge is a dangerous thing*.

7

"Lydia, it's so raw outside, and I'm afraid I'm getting a cold," *Mamm* told her late Tuesday afternoon, the day after Lydia and Sandra had been to Wooster. She did, Lydia thought, sound nasal and had been blowing her nose, though sometimes she thought *Mamm* had private crying bouts and sounded like that, anyway.

"I know you're heading for the animal barn," *Mamm* said, "but could you take these four loaves of bread outside to Mattie Esh for the Stark funeral?"

Although Lydia had overheard that some local Amish women referred to her mother as "Sad Susan," *Mamm* was also known in the community for her generous gifts of what most outsiders called Amish friendship bread. She gave loaves of it away for Christmas gifts and anytime the church had a special event. Even the local *Englische* knew to look for it in her plain brown wrappers at Amish benefits and yard sales.

But *Mamm* kept the starter yeast mix and recipe to herself. Lydia had once asked why, when the sharing of those things was part of the idea of friendship. Her mother had simply said that the bread alone was her gift to her people. But Lydia came to believe the cinnamon-crunchy sweet bread was *Mamm*'s way of trying to make up for a tart tongue and sour outlook on life. And *Mamm*'s sending anything to the Starks surprised Lydia, though *Mamm* often contributed bread to local funerals.

Pointing out the window, *Mamm* went on, "Mattie and Anna Kauffman are buggying up the lane right now, see? Since I'm on the church list to donate bread for local events, I could hardly say no when the Starks, living next door all these years, have a family funeral—which I wish you were not attending, you and Josh."

"*Mamm,* we're honored to represent the Amish community. Sure, I'll take the bread out to them, then just head over to Josh's. I'm going to walk through the woods because Flower got chilled waiting for me in the store barn all day."

"Flower! You and your animals. Here, the bread's in this sack."

"And smells wonderful, as usual!" Lydia lifted the sack and gave her a quick kiss on the cheek. She had tried very hard since yesterday to be affectionate toward both her parents. After all, they'd taken her in after the tragic death of her birth parents. They had treated her as their own when she'd lost David and Lena Brand...David and Lena... She loved to recite their names to herself. Lydia wondered what else Sandra might have found, cross-checking other sources, as she'd put it.

In the mudroom, she quickly donned her bonnet and warmest cape—the one she'd placed over poor Victoria Keller—stuffed her feet into boots and tied a woolen scarf around her neck. She yanked her gloves on, picked up the sack of fragrant bread and hurried outside. Lacy snowflakes sifted down, but they didn't seem to be piling up fast. The two women, Mattie Esh, the bishop's wife, and one of her good friends, were in a large family buggy.

"Hello, Mrs. Esh and Mrs. Kauffman," Lydia greeted them. As she lifted the sack to Mrs. Kauffman, she saw the backseats were full of baskets and bags. "Oh, my, what a lot of food!" she blurted.

Mrs. Esh told her, "The church really wanted a special outreach to the Starks to show our love and concern for them."

"And not because Connor is mayor now," Anna Kauffman added with a sharp sniff. "Nor because Bess Stark has worldly political power. But we want to extend the right hand of fellowship to those who seem trapped in the world's ways. Speaking of hands, we could use an extra couple of strong ones to unload, sure we could. Lydia, can you ride along with us next door to help drop these things off? It won't take long, and we'll bring you back home."

Though she was eager to head over to Josh's, she told them, "*Ya,* of course, I'd be glad to help." She climbed up in the buggy and held the sack of still-warm bread in her lap so she could fit on the second seat.

Mrs. Esh turned the buggy around, and they headed back down the lane. "How are Hannah's twins, Mrs. Esh?" Lydia asked. Her daughter Hannah had gone to the world for a while to pursue a singing career, but had returned home, wed Amish and sang now only at their weddings.

"Big for their ages, and lungs strong like Hannah's. They will be two strapping boys, Lord willing. You know, she sings to them all the time. Hannah's little adopted four-year-old girl, Marlena, is a big help."

Oh, ya, *that's right,* Lydia thought. Hannah had more or less adopted Marlena when she married the widowed Seth Lantz, but Seth was the girl's real father, so she'd never actually been orphaned. And Lydia just bet Hannah and Seth told their little girl all about her real mother and didn't try to ignore or hide the truth.

"And how is your daughter Sarah doing?" Lydia asked Mrs. Kauffman. A noted Ohio artist, Sarah had been shunned for painting the faces of people she knew and for wedding an outsider. But Lydia knew the Kauffmans still saw her and her husband and their little daughter from time to time. What would happen when *Mamm* and *Daad* finally learned that their own daughter had defied them?

"Sarah's doing good but should still stop painting faces for her work," Mrs. Kauffman said, and Lydia realized that was that.

Soon they were buggying past the rows of Christmas trees the Starks sold this time of year. The big banner was up over the lane that led a short way to the barn where they bundled their yearly crop of firs and pines, the short-needled ones barely dusted with snow, others bowing their branches under its weight. Those who lived near the tree farm knew it was almost a year-round task to care for the trees. The seedlings were planted mid-April, and shearing and shaping went on through the hot months of June and mid-July. In the late autumn, skilled workers with rotary pruners trimmed the trees which went on sale late November and December. The familiar banner read, Stark Choose-and-Cut Christmas Tree Farm. Open Now to Christmas. Hay Rides, Cider, Cocoa Free.

More rows of trees, some tall, some growing for future years, sped past Lydia's gaze. The Starks had twenty-five acres of trees, just the right size farm, she'd heard, for a family to run with only seasonal help. She had not been at the Stark house for years, not since *Mamm* had laid down the law about her visits there. The fragrant, crisp scents of blue spruce, Fraser fir, Scotch and white pine vied with the smell of the bread in her lap. The rows of trees wrapped around the slant of the hill on which the Stark mansion perched. When it was lighted at night, Lydia used to think the house was like its own star atop a giant tree.

The horse team pulled the big buggy easily up the lane, since it wasn't slippery. Years ago, the Starks had put some sort of heating pipes under the pavement, so the snow and ice melted off. It sure saved a lot of shoveling. Who knew what wonders were to be found in their house itself after all these years.

At the side door, they unloaded their goods, met not by a family member but by a woman in a canvas apron. "Hi, I'm Jenny from the caterer's," she told them. "What wonderful gifts. Perhaps we can have an entire Amish table at the funeral, and the family will be so grateful. Senator Stark's in town with her daughter-in-law, but Mr. Stark is out in the trees somewhere. They will all be delighted. How kind of you."

The three of them and Jenny carried the baskets and boxes of food inside to a pantry area with Jenny's continued thanks. From the vantage point of the side porch, Lydia could see that Connor was not down by the barn, with the other seasonal workers, but in a row of about five-foot trees on a slant of the hill overlooking her house. She would, of course, have a chance at the funeral tomorrow to tell him she was sorry for his loss, but he'd be busy with other people. He'd been so upset that night they found his aunt in the snow.

"If you don't mind," she told Mrs. Esh, "I'll just walk back to my house. Cutting down the hill will be much shorter."

"Of course, my dear, and we thank you for the help, we surely do. We will be in prayer tomorrow that you and Josh Yoder will represent our people well at the funeral."

"Danki," she told them. "I appreciate all the prayer support I can get."

"Lydia's late," Sandra told Josh when he came back to the house to see how she was doing. She was sitting at his dining room table still typing away on her laptop about, he guessed, Old Amish Christmas. "She's not in the barn, is she? I'd rather go over a battle plan with her in here."

"A battle plan?" Josh said as he poured himself a mug of the now-tepid cider he'd left for Sandy and Lydia. He threw his coat over his chair and sat across the table from her. "You still have a lot to learn about our ways."

"Our meaning the Amish, or you and Lydia? I can see you care for her, and she— Let's just say the same." As if they were making a toast, she leaned across the table to clink her cider mug to his.

"Lydia's just the tomboy next door who grew up," he countered.

"And so doesn't know her own power over men yet? But you do, right, and you're very surprised. Besides, you sound defensive, my friend. By the way, you know what she asked me?"

"I'm afraid to hear it. She really cuts to the heart sometimes."

"Touché. She said since I didn't like animals, why was I at the zoo in Columbus where you and I met?"

"*Ya,* I did mention that. So you told her you got the ticket free and as a starving grad student couldn't turn down wine and a buffet?"

"I told her I was hunting for a rare beast to study and I found one. No, don't look at me that way. I told her grad students seldom get invitations like that, and I was always up for a new adventure, at least at a place where the animals were all in cages. She also asked me why I didn't like animals— Was I afraid of them because of something that happened to me when I was young? You never asked me that. Lydia's bright and perceptive. You'd think she was a soc or psych major, for heaven's sake!" she said, leaning back in her chair and closing her laptop.

"She's a rare one, exotic in her own way," Josh said. "Good with animals and good with people. Most girls—young women—who weren't being told about their real parents by their adoptive ones wouldn't be so careful not to hurt them, at least I think so." He leaned forward in his chair. "But did something happen in your past that kept you from liking animals, at least some animals?"

Sandra jumped up from the table and started to pace, dining room to living room and back with jerky steps.

"I wish I had a cigarette or a drink," she muttered, wrapping her arms around herself as if she were cold.

"I'm proud of you that you gave up smoking, and cider's the strongest thing I have in the house."

"I wasn't being serious! But—but yes, I once closed a closet door on my brother's puppy when I was about six. I—I smashed his head, and he yelped and cried and I felt horrible when he died. I ran and hid in the basement, but had to face up to what I'd done. I swear, my brother hated me for months after that—years— and nothing my parents said about it being an accident made things better for me."

She sniffed hard and strode away again. "The thing is," she said, her voice shaky and almost choked, "I think I meant to do it— I mean, looking back at it now, analyzing, playing my own shrink. Grandpa had given that dog to him, not me, and everyone was fussing over it. I was the first born, used to be the family princess, and then here came my brother and everyone doted on him…

"Oh, damn—sorry," she blurted out, but he wasn't sure if the 'sorry' was for swearing or for telling him her painful story. "You just heard true confessions about what an idiot I was—still am."

He stood and snagged her arm when she passed again, hugged her awkwardly with one arm around her shoulders. "We all have things in our past that haunt us. Look at Lydia, even me."

"You? Such as what?"

"I agonized over jumping the fence, you know, leaving home to pursue my dream of working at a zoo for several years. I hurt my mother. I'm regretful to this day that her grieving, even though I hadn't yet joined the church and so wasn't shunned, probably made her cancer worse and hastened her death. And that I was too late getting a ride back here and didn't get to say a final goodbye. But you're not going to hurt animals ever again, or be hurt by them, and my mother needed to accept my dreams, even if they weren't to work the fields and milk cows with *Daad* and my brothers."

She pulled away and blew her nose. "That— You helped me. Lydia did, too, like you say, cutting to the heart of things. You know what? I have a bumper sticker I should put on the back of the car that says, I Brake for Squirrels. I do, really. Now, camels and donkeys, I don't know, but maybe later, sometime while I'm here, I'll go out to the barn with you or Lydia. Now, what in the world is keeping her?"

"You been up to the house?" Connor called to Lydia as she approached him down a row of white pines that were not quite as tall as he was. Next year's trees, she guessed. "My mother's in town with my wife."

"I heard. I was just helping some of our women deliver food for the funeral and thought I'd walk home. This is like a well-ordered forest," she said, with a sweep of her gloved hand at the acres of trees. She noticed he had hastily put aside what looked like a spray paint gun. *Ya,* she could see he'd been spraying some of these trees with a green paint that smelled. On closer look, some did seem a bit brown on the tips—wilted.

"Not that well-ordered. It's a struggle. I was just touching up some of these with insecticide where a beetle's been at them. See. They have a few dead needles, but I just knock those off."

Though she was no expert, Lydia knew this wasn't

the time of year to be spraying for insects. And that was paint for sure, so was he doing something wrong by covering up the wilted branches? She decided she'd better not ask or let on she suspected him of lying and maybe more. For a moment, she just watched him handle two pitchforks, one in each hand as he quickly knocked dead needles off the tree. But it seemed to her the needles falling to the snow were more than a few.

"Besides," he said, "the darn deer have been nipping the tops off seedlings on the other side of the hill, and here I am worrying about pests I can't even see. But," he said, stepping closer, "I'll find a way to get rid of them."

"Hopefully, these trees will be all right by next year."

"They're for this year—apartment size."

When he frowned at her, she said in a rush, "I wanted to tell you I'm sorry about your aunt—that she died that way. I know you'll be too busy at the funeral and meal to tell you then, but please accept our sympathy, from both Josh and me."

Her voice broke. She shouldn't have spoken for Josh. It almost sounded as if they were a couple. As usual, she felt awkward around Connor Stark, especially since he had a pitchfork in each hand. But he stabbed them through the snow and into the ground where they shuddered a moment, then stilled. Although Connor had been around as long as she remembered, she hadn't been alone with him for years.

"You heard the coroner's ruling?" he asked, examining another tree limb that looked diseased, even to her untrained eye.

"*Ya.* Ray-Lynn Freeman told me."

"Whatever you hear about Victoria Keller, Lydia, we tried our best with her, but she was, to put it nicely, beyond help."

He moved around her to examine a tree slightly up the hill as if he didn't want her to be looking down on him. When there was no snow on the ground, he often rode a golf cart around, but he'd obviously walked here today, carrying that equipment. And if his work was all on the up-and-up, why didn't he send one of his seasonal workers to take care of it?

"So," he said, shaking snow from a tree bough and staring at it, "would you like a job working at the tree barn for the next couple of weeks? I know you work for your father, but Gid Reich mentioned how good you are with customers there. It would be only for a couple of hours an evening, if you want. You wouldn't have to run the cash register. Just oversee doughnuts and cocoa, chat people up."

"Gid suggested it? That figures. He doesn't like me working with the Yoder animals."

"He's pretty sweet on you, I'd say, and probably doesn't want you to get hurt—by the animals or the situation."

Lydia was going to ask him what situation he was referring to, as if she didn't know, but Connor went on, "Gid's one of my new investors in the tree farm. I've taken several locals on and plan to buy more land to the north, hire on some extra help since I'm now also 'Mr. Mayor' and my mother's gone a lot."

"I thank you for the job offer, and your family has always been kind to me, but—"

"My mother, especially. Some like to help stray animals, but she is always into causes for people—in her capacity as state senator, I mean. So, you'd better be heading home."

Connor's words reminded Lydia about the time he'd ordered her off their property years ago. Of course, it must have been hard on him to lose a father he'd adored to an illness with the big name of multiple myeloma. He was being kind now, at least, wasn't he? Yet she sensed an edge to him. Others had mentioned it, too—their smiling new mayor with the invisible chip on his shoulder when he seemed to have so much going for him.

"See you tomorrow, Connor. I appreciate the job offer, but no thanks."

"Yeah, sure. I'll see you."

Lydia did not look back as she hurried down the hill, taking small strides so she wouldn't slip. She'd pop in to tell her mother she was heading straight for Josh's and she was late.

Still, it was the strangest thing. Maybe it was because she thought she'd caught Connor doing something bad, but every step she took down the hill, she was certain she felt his eyes boring into her back.

8

The next day, the morning of the Stark funeral, Lydia made breakfast for the family as she often did. She had not slept well last night, with disjointed dreams haunting her. More than once in the still-dark morning she caught herself staring out the window at her reflection. The glass was like a giant mirror, and she was wondering how much she resembled David and Lena Brand...David and Lena Brand...

Mamm seldom joined them until later, though this morning *Daad* had not appeared, either. As usual, Lydia and *Daad* would buggy separately to the store as soon as dawn lit the sky. Halfway through her oatmeal, she was surprised to hear him emerge from the side parlor, his private abode, instead of coming down the stairs. His firm closing of the door behind him echoed like a single knock as Lydia popped up to ladle out his oatmeal.

"You haven't been working all night on a quilt, have you?" she asked, half-teasing.

"Maybe something I want to finish before Christmas, eh? I heard you stirring."

"Ya," she said with a little laugh. "Stirring the oatmeal for three and hoping it doesn't clump up before *Mamm* gets down here. I told her I don't make lumpy oatmeal, only if it sits for a while until she gets out of bed to eat it."

She thought *Daad* might say something about the need to understand her mother, but he didn't comment. He sat and bowed his head in a brief, silent prayer while she poured him orange juice and coffee. When he opened his eyes, they looked tired and bloodshot.

Lydia was barely back to her own oatmeal when *Daad* said, "Gid came calling for you last night after you lit out. Said he wanted to continue a conversation you two started yesterday. He wasn't too pleased when *Mamm* told him you'd gone over to the Yoder barn. And he was really upset when he saw you and an *Englische* woman in a little red car, roaring out of Yoder's and heading away from town. Just a warning he'll probably bring it up when he sees you at work this morning."

Her spoon dinged against her bowl. "Now he's taken to spying on me—and reporting back to you as if I were ten instead of twenty!"

"Liddy, he happened to see an unusual thing. The woman he loves—"

"I don't think he lo—"

"Don't interrupt," he scolded, thumping his index finger on the table in her direction. "I repeat, the woman he loves and wants to marry was riding with an *Englische* stranger in a car, heading who knows where. That might upset any good Amish come-calling friend."

"She's a friend of Josh's from his days in Columbus,

visiting here, and I was showing her how to get into Wooster. She had business there. She's writing about customs of Amish Christmas."

"And thought to ask you about that instead of Josh?"

"As well as Josh."

"Liddy," he said, reaching over to cover her hand with his, "do you love Josh Yoder?"

She was shocked he'd asked. Ray-Lynn had, too, more or less. Was it so evident? Couldn't people just accept she wanted to help him with the animals? And was that the real reason she kept going back?

"I—I care for him," she stammered. "Also for the animals, of course. I think it's good what he's doing for people who celebrate Christmas, and with the petting zoo for the local kids and worldly visitors."

"But when it comes to you, what is he doing? How does he feel about you? More than just gratitude that you are such a good friend and free help to him? You're not a lanky kid anymore."

"*Ya,* like you said, we're friends," she faltered, desperately blinking back tears.

"He won't ever want to run a big furniture store, now will he?"

"Should that be what matters most?"

He sighed and pulled his hand back. "Liddy, I want the best for you, and I think that's Gid Reich. And, *ach,* I know people can be wrong about the ones they love, make bad choices and suffer long for those."

Lydia almost asked if he meant his sad marriage with *Mamm,* but she held her tongue on that. "Does *Mamm* know?" she asked. "I mean about my going with Josh's friend in her car?"

"*Ya,* but I told her I'd talk to you about it and how

you're hurting Gid. And I told her you had to find your own way to a husband, though you know how we both stand on it. I repeat, we only want the best for you."

Lydia almost blurted out to him that would mean sharing all they knew about her real parents…and that it didn't mean she loved or honored them less. She almost told him what she'd learned, thanks to Sandra Myerson.

But instead she finished her nearly cold oatmeal, which sat like a lump in her stomach. She hurried to wash their dishes and darted out to the barn to harness Flower before *Daad* came back downstairs to harness his buggy horse. It was bad enough she was dreading a confrontation with Gid this morning and probably with *Mamm* later.

As she buggied past the dark Stark house on its hill, she thought about Victoria's sad, cold death and realized something in her had died, too: her childhood. Her dependence on her adoptive parents was finally gone, though she would always love them. She wanted to learn more about her real parents and she wanted to pursue the man she really loved and wanted. And, for sure, that was not Gid Reich.

To Lydia's amazement, Gid was kind and proper that morning. He wished her well at the Stark funeral. "I'm going to be partners with Connor in a limited way," he informed her as he cornered her in the store's small employee coffee-and-snacks room. "I'm buying into his tree business to help him—and me—expand."

She was tempted to warn him that she'd caught Connor spraying sick trees he intended to sell anyway, but she didn't want to chance upsetting Gid's apparent good mood. Nor did she want to have him questioning or confronting Connor. It was possible she'd misunderstood why he was spraying those pines. Maybe the pesticide was in the paint and would work quickly to heal a sick tree.

Taking a snickerdoodle from the plateful someone had brought in, she told him, "He mentioned your new partnership with him when he offered me a seasonal job. But I'm stretched pretty thin, so I told him thanks but no. He said you suggested it to him."

Gid began to walk with her when she left, wending her way back toward the front desk amid the aisles of dining room tables and hutches. Holding her cookie and cup of cocoa, she still expected a lecture about working at Josh's barn.

"Just thought you might like a short-term job at Stark's for a while," he said. "You told me once—I think it was when we went together to the county fair last July—that you used to love going over there but didn't anymore, that it upset your mother. I thought that would be my way of weighing in to help you with her. If your *mamm* thought it was my idea, she wouldn't complain."

In the aisle with the tall, ticking grandfather clocks, Lydia stopped walking, that is, stopped hurrying to escape this man. What he'd said—his insight and kindness—touched her. This wasn't the Gid she'd known for months, since she'd tried to slow him down and hold him off. Today he had been thoughtful of her, calm with no scolding or mention of the red car or Josh.

She glanced at one of the clocks. Ten-thirty. She was meeting Josh in two hours at the barn, and he would buggy them to the Starks'. Surely, Gid had known that, too, yet no dire warning, no mention of it. Had *Daad* warned Gid he needed to mend his ways to win her hand? And what would Gid think if she told him that Sol Brand, owner of this large store and workshop, was not her real father. No, her real father was not a shop owner but a laborer who had merely cut the trees that became the furniture for all this Brand bounty.

She was surprised again when Gid glanced quickly around, then bent to peck a kiss on her cheek. With a raised hand in farewell, a wink and a smile, he backed away and left her standing there.

Would wonders never cease? A new tactic to woo her? So far, this day was full of surprises, and she hoped there wouldn't be any more of them, especially at the funeral.

Perhaps because they'd arrived together in the only Amish buggy parked among the cars, Lydia could tell that guests she didn't know—most of the people here—assumed she and Josh were a couple. Strangely, she felt they were and loved the feeling. How Josh felt she couldn't tell.

"We certainly appreciate your coming," Bess Stark told them as she greeted them inside the large living room in a sort of reception line with Connor and his wife, Heather, just beyond her. "Especially since it's starting to snow again, and I'll bet those steel buggy wheels can be slippery on the roads." She shook Josh's hand and gave Lydia's shoulders a light hug. "If Victoria—we always called her Vicky—were here, if she were herself, which she hadn't been for several years, she would thank you, too. Josh, are plans afoot to expand or redo that barn?"

"As soon as the weather gets decent, *ya,* for sure." He leaned closer and lowered his voice. "As you know, Senator Stark, in big cities, they like to name stadiums and hospital wings after their donors. But I promise you, I will not call the new animal wing the Elizabeth Stark barn."

Though Bess looked tired and it seemed to Lydia new creases lined her forehead and her upper lip, her face lit in a smile. "Actually, I wouldn't mind a bit," she said. "But let's keep it our secret. Best that not get out."

"Best what not get out?" Connor asked, leaning toward them. "Ah, the Amish contingent. We're pleased you could come, of course. The sheriff and Ray-Lynn are over by the casket paying their final respects. Closed casket, the close of a sad life. I try to remember Aunt Vicky as she was, but these last years have been so difficult—for her, of course, as well as for us to see her slip away like that."

"Did she still read or write?" Lydia asked. "I mean, anything normal like that?"

She felt Josh's arm touching hers stiffen. He knew that she was digging for information about the note. The fact he took her elbow as if to steer her on made her realize he didn't think it was a good idea—not here, not now. She could almost hear his thoughts.

"She scribbled crazy things, pictures, like senseless doodles," Bess said. "She used to want to be an artist, but gave it up for a career in journalism. She was a bright woman. Her Alzheimer's doctors used to try to decipher her scribblings and pictures, but that, too, went nowhere."

Others had come in the door; they had to move on. Connor introduced them to his wife, Heather, a pretty, slender woman with long blond hair streaked with auburn. Heather Stark seemed nervous. Her eyes darted past them as they spoke briefly. She thanked them for what they had done the night Aunt Vicky died, then told them, "Please take a chair over by the casket. People have sent such lovely flowers. I'm going to have to duck out and see how our twins are behaving. Seven-year-old boys at something like this need a bit of watching, so they don't show up in a Darth Vader mask or tell people what they want for Christmas. I'm pleased you're staying for the buffet."

She darted off. "Twin boys just like Hannah has," Lydia told Josh as they moved on. She could tell some of the *Englische* folks were watching them. She'd been so few places lately where they were in the minority that she'd forgotten the feeling.

"Tragedies and blessings fall on the Plain People and the fancy ones," Josh said as they headed for the Freemans, who had sat down in the back row of wooden chairs facing the flowers and the casket, where the funeral service would evidently be held.

Lydia was awed by the huge array of summer flowers this time of year and by the rest of the living room she'd been stealing glimpses of. The family had apparently cleared furniture from this end of the room. Through a veil of falling flakes, the array of windows on the east and west sides displayed the white Home Valley below. It made her feel they were in a snow globe.

On a third wall was a ceiling-high stone fireplace and mantel with an oil painting over it of Bess, Connor, Heather and the twins. How her artist friend Sarah would love to see that, she thought, with their unique facial expressions: Bess, prideful; Connor, possessive; Heather, loving; and the twins, one a bit smug, the other looking as if he'd rather be elsewhere.

Although the floor underfoot was polished oak, foreign-looking area rugs with ornate designs were scattered throughout. As they approached the Freemans, Lydia glimpsed the dining room off to the side. Two long tables were not yet laden with food, but linen tablecloths, plates and utensils and more flowers were in place. Beyond that, in yet another living room or den, she could see small, round tables set with candle and pine cone centerpieces.

And on the polished coffin, beside a draping of red roses, was a photo of a much younger Victoria—Vicky, they had called her—sitting at a writing desk with pen in her hand, looking off into the distance. Though her own people would have judged that as prideful, Lydia was glad to see the picture. After she had found that note, it was almost a sign from heaven that the deceased woman had pen in hand.

"Glad to see you all," Ray-Lynn interrupted her thoughts. Some others were taking seats in the eight narrow rows. After Josh and the sheriff shook hands, Lydia sat next to Ray-Lynn with Josh on her other side.

"Quite a place, right?" Ray-Lynn asked Lydia out of the side of her mouth. "And what a view. Can you spot your house from here?"

"Not from this room, but I'll bet from the north windows. I just wonder if Victoria didn't look out and see our place and try to walk to it that night with the note."

"We'll probably never know," Ray-Lynn said. Then, leaning over Lydia, she said to Josh, "There was a friend of yours came in the restaurant for breakfast and lunch today. Sandra something. She asked me and others a lot of questions about Amish customs, created a bit of a stir. No one wanted to tell her much at first— you know, small-town rules and Amish humility— until she said she was a friend of yours. And of Lydia's, too. She doesn't quite get the Amish privacy and don't-push thing, because at first she tried to use a little voice recorder and had a camera."

Shaking his head and frowning, Josh told them who Sandra was, explaining she was writing a disserta-tion—maybe even a book later—about immigrant Christmas customs. He said he'd talk to Sandra about not coming on so strong like that.

Lydia said nothing, but she was upset. She had ex-pected Sandra to keep a bit private here, not interview anyone and everyone. She stared hard at the photo of Victoria Keller with the pen in her hand, but her face blurred to Sandra's.

After the funeral, the casket was carried out to the hearse and the guests went through the buffet line be-fore they joined the procession to the cemetery or left for their homes. As they took plates, Josh whispered to Lydia, "Sorry to hear Sandra came on like gang-busters. I thought she'd know better, but I'm sure she didn't tell any of your story."

"My story?" she said, taking a spoonful of pasta salad. "I'm not even sure what my story is."

People were heading down both sides of the table, and the man across from them was saying to another in a quiet voice, "Seems she's laying the groundwork to run for governor and, if she gets that, the sky's the limit."

"Namely 1600 Pennsylvania Avenue," the other muttered with a tight grin. "Yeah, I think we're ready for a woman president."

Lydia almost spilled the spoonful she was taking of some kind of fancy potato salad. They had to mean Bess. Governor? President? Of the whole country?

"Oh, by the way, Josh," Connor said, walking by with one of his sons in tow, "that female writer friend of yours is going to interview me tomorrow morning before she heads back to Columbus. Says she wants to know how it feels to be selling one of the major symbols of Christmas in an area where the Amish want nothing to do with decorated trees. I figure it will be good publicity for us."

"Publicity, publicity—not today," Bess Stark said, coming up and tapping Connor on the shoulder while holding her other grandson by the hand. "Today, just family, friends and down-home memories. And I really don't think the boys need to go to the cemetery, Connor. Not only is it snowy and cold, but all this is enough."

It was enough all right, Lydia thought. This huge house was more than enough. Maybe trusting Sandra Myerson was too much. So she'd make the next moves on her own. This weekend she'd find a way to visit Victoria's caregiver Anna Gingerich. But first, she was going into the nearby town of Amity to see if she could talk to someone at a tree cutting business there who might have known her father.

* * *

Lydia and Josh sat in his buggy atop Starks' hill, watching the hearse lead the line of cars away. Soon the funeral caravan was lost in the swirl of snow. Lydia recalled Bess's concern for their buggy wheels slipping in bad weather, but the steep lane down the hill was no problem with the snow melted off the pavement. She saw a few customers at the Christmas tree barn as they passed. Her people would have closed for the day, but life—and Stark Christmas business—went merrily on.

They buggied past Lydia's house. *Daad* would not be home yet. *Mamm* must be baking bread because the kitchen light was on. She made extra loaves of friendship bread at holiday time and froze them in the generator-run freezer in the basement.

Despite Lydia's sadness over losing the chance to talk to Victoria Keller, and being upset with Sandra overstepping in town, it was wonderful to be with Josh, to feel all sealed in with him by the fiberglass buggy and the Plexiglas screen they added for a windshield in such weather. And they shared a warm lap blanket as if they were cuddled up in bed together.

When they turned in the lane to his house—she'd left her horse and buggy not in the big barn but in his small stables—he was the first to mention Sandra again.

"Sorry Sandra's making waves when I know you thought she'd be more, well, quiet. Unfortunately, that's not her way, but I didn't think she'd do public interviews in a strange place. I guess I should have warned you about that, but, as I said, I'm sure she'll keep your secret."

"Especially if you remind her. I can tell she cares about you, so you two know each other pretty well."

He didn't follow up on that little fishing expedition but jumped down to open the stable door—so she thought. Instead, he hurried around and helped her down, almost as if they were a courting couple. "She said the same about you, Lydia—that is, that you care about me," he told her as he slid open the stable door.

"Of course I do. Even more than I care for Melly and Balty."

Now, she thought, why had she blurted that out? Because she didn't want him to know how much she was attracted to him? "Actually, a bit more than that," she added with a little laugh, hoping he hadn't taken offense.

He hadn't. It was great to be with someone who had a sense of humor, since that was in pretty short supply at her house. As he unhitched Blaze and hitched Flower to Lydia's buggy, he grinned at her more than once.

"We have fun together," he said, with a wink. "Since it's so beautiful out, want to make a couple of snow angels before you head home—for old times' sake, though I like the new times better. The menagerie can wait a few minutes. I trust the boys to take care of them. Of course, you'll walk into your house with your backside all wet as if we've been rolling in the snow."

"Which we will have been. I'll just take my cape off."

She untied and swirled it onto her buggy seat. On the day of a funeral, a day when their mutual friend Sandra had let them down, she knew she shouldn't be so excited. Josh had taught her and some friends how to make snow angels years ago. She'd had a schoolgirl crush on him then, but now...

"Race you outside!" he shouted, as if he recalled that day, too.

He threw off his hat and winter coat on the way out. His small backyard, fenced off from the large animal field, looked pristine with the big flakes falling fast.

He took her hand. Laughing, they flopped down together, about two feet apart, and moved their arms and legs to make the wings and skirts.

"Angels from the realms of glory..." he started to sing, slightly off-key, but she didn't care. The lacy flakes wet her face and stuck her lashes together when she blinked. Again, she felt she was in a snow globe and someone was shaking it, shaking the very earth when she lay so close in body and heart to this man.

He helped her up and, careful of their creations, which could soon be covered with snow anyway, they walked back toward the barn, his arm around her shoulders, hers around his waist. He turned her to him, she thought at first to give her a boost up into her buggy, but his mouth descended on hers.

And it was swirling snow again, but this time in her head and heart and oh, so warm, so hot. She tipped her head so they wouldn't bump noses, and opened her mouth to his invading tongue.

It was a whole new world. Gid had never kissed her like this, and she didn't want him to. She hadn't realized it could be this way, pressed to Josh, her soft places fitting perfectly to his muscular, angular ones. She had to concentrate on breathing, on not just grabbing him to her.

Too soon, he set her back. "I can't apologize for that," he said, sounding not quite as breathless as she felt. "If you're promised to another, don't kiss me back like that."

"I—wanted to."

"Better get going before someone comes after you."

"Gid saw me leaving here with Sandra in her car."

"You mean he's been watching or following you?"

"Just bad timing, I think. But he was very polite today, like he was sorry."

"Polite. And I guess I wasn't right now."

"I didn't mean that. You were—just right."

But it surprised her that, despite the kiss and her telling him about Gid, and despite how much she secretly, deeply cared for Joshua Yoder, she didn't tell him her plans to look more into her real family. He might tell Sandra, and she might tell someone she shouldn't. No, Lydia was going to buggy into Amity on her own to find someone who might have known her father or her family. After all, she told herself, Josh had helped her a lot and she didn't want him to think he should leave the animals this time of year to go with her. She'd tell him, maybe Sandra, too, if she learned anything useful.

He boosted her up into the buggy and handed her Flower's reins. She told him, "I won't be here after work tomorrow but Friday evening and Saturday for sure, though I might be late. I have to run some errands. And thank you for everything—and I do mean everything."

He patted Flower's flank, but she could almost feel he'd patted hers. She smiled down at him, and he grinned like the *rumspringa* boy she remembered the day he'd first taught her to make snow angels. When she giddyapped Flower outside, the snow had suddenly stopped. At least their angels would still be holding hands, not buried in more snow. Feeling like an angel from the realms of glory, she could almost have flown.

9

The next day Lydia asked *Daad* if she could combine her morning break and lunchtime to leave early to run an errand in Amity.

"As long as you're not just stepping out to avoid Gid," he said. "It's natural he would want to know how an *Englische* funeral goes—especially one the Starks arranged."

"He hasn't asked about it yet, but I've hardly seen him today. I was surprised *Mamm* wanted to know all about it—and you really didn't."

He frowned. "I have more things to worry about than the Starks."

"*Daad,* you're looking tired. I know it's the busiest time of year, but you just seem, well, like you are pushing yourself too hard."

"As do you. Work here, work at Josh Yoder's barn. Avoiding Gid. By the way, your mother asked him over to evening meal Sunday."

"As long as she asked him, he's not my guest, so I won't expect to be left alone with him afterward. It will be a family thing, the Brands entertaining their general manager, bookkeeper and common friend."

"Listen to me, Liddy," he said, then just threw up his hands. "*Ya,* go to Amity if you must, but you could probably buy the same here in Homestead, eh?"

That made her realize she'd have to come back with something unique from Amity. Maybe some quilting material from the dry goods shop there. She or *Mamm* usually bought material for *Daad* here in town on his strictest orders of what he wanted.

After glancing repeatedly at the big oak-case clock over the front door, Lydia left her helper, Naomi, at the greeter's desk and slipped out the front door promptly at three o'clock. To avoid having to walk past the offices or through the workshop, she went outside to the building in back where they kept the horses. At least the weather was calm and sunny, though not warm enough to melt any snow.

After a forty-minute fast trot, she tied up in Amity and bought *Daad* a bolt of bright blue cloth and *Mamm* a pillow that was embroidered with the saying, Mothers Are Forever. Now why, she wondered, had it not read, A Mother Is Forever. No, for Lydia, at least, this was the right gift. And she was wise to come in here because her chat with the saleswomen told her what she needed to know. There was only one tree cutting farm around, and it had been in business a long time.

Rabers Cutters and Trimmers, the sign read on the Amish house just outside of town where the women sent her. Lydia could tell the place was Amish because there were no electric or phone lines going into the house, no lightning rods on the buildings and no TV antennae or disks pointing skyward. And the big giveaway, even in this weather that froze material stiff:

the familiar black-and-pastel dresses, broadfall trousers and shirts hung on the clothesline.

She pulled Flower into the driveway where she saw a smaller go-round-in-back sign, so she went a little farther and parked the buggy on the far side of the barn next to a field full of dried corn stubble. The wind had mostly swept its snow cover bare. What must be the Raber family's unhitched wagons and two buggies took most of the best parking space back here.

Her knock on the back door was immediately answered by a woman about *Mamm*'s age, wearing glasses, though she still squinted. "Welcome," the plump woman said with a nod and a small smile. "Business for the men?"

"Oh, no, sorry. My name is Lydia Brand from Homestead." Suddenly, just to say the next words aloud made her almost stammer. "I believe my father, David Brand, used to work with the Rabers cutting trees. A long time ago. Twenty years. He died in a car-buggy accident. I—I was just hoping someone would still remember him, because I don't. My adoptive parents took me in when I was almost a newborn."

"Ah," she said, seeming partly surprised, partly sympathetic. "Step in, step in. Cold out there. I'm Miriam Raber. The men got picked up by their taxi van to get all their tools sharpened, better job than they can do themselves. But I bet *Grossdaadi* can help you, my husband's father. He had the business then. You just sit, and I'll tell him you're here. A good day for a visit, so I'll pour some tea."

Lydia's hopes had fallen when Miriam had said the men were away, but now she trembled with anticipation. So easily accomplished? *Thank you, Lord.*

And the Rabers were just far enough away they didn't belong to the Homestead church, where word might spread that Lydia was asking questions.

Miriam left for a few minutes, then bustled back in and poured three cups of tea. "He was asleep in his rocking chair, *ya,* he was, but he'll be glad to talk to you. David Brand, he remembers him. Here, some fresh cookies, too," she said as she added a small plate to her tray.

Reminding herself to keep calm, Lydia followed Miriam through the tidy house. As they approached the front parlor, the woman stopped and whispered, "Forgot to tell you *Grossdaadi* is nearly blind—macular degeneration—but his mind is sharp."

Lydia's pulse picked up as she was ushered to a straight-backed chair across a small table from the old man in his rocker. He had a shock of white hair and a long white beard and was so thin that he made Miriam look fat. He had a blanket over his legs and a quilt folded over the back of his chair, which he leaned his head against. Miriam fussed over their tea, made sure her father-in-law knew right where it was on the table, then said, "*Grossdaadi,* this is Lydia Brand from over Homestead way. If you can tell her something about her birth father, she will be glad."

"Oh, *ya,* Mr. Raber," Lydia said. "So grateful. I was a baby when my father, David Brand, and his wife, Lena, died in a car-buggy accident, so anything you can remember will be a gift to me."

Miriam hovered a moment at the door, then left them alone. The old man cleared his throat. His blue eyes looked glazed, but they moved in her direction as if he could see her. When he spoke, she hung on every word.

"Eager to learn a trade, he was, David. Had to teach him most things, but he learned fast. Bright and agile. They lived out a ways, still in Eden County, though."

Lydia blinked back tears. "Did you—ever meet my mother?"

"Couple of times. Once I think, when we had a picnic for our workers right here. Short as he was tall. Quick movements. But ah, your father. Just like me, David Brand loved to climb, more than my own boys, not a bit afraid of heights. Up he'd go with his shoe spikes on, up with his ropes." He gestured toward the ceiling, smiling and looking up as if he could see him climbing yet. "Learned the knot-tying fast, too, so the limbs can be lowered and not just fall. Sad to lose him for me—and tragedy for you."

He took his teacup for the first time and put the tip of a crooked finger in it, evidently to test its temperature. Lydia had a hundred questions, but she kept quiet. He'd volunteered so much on his own that she didn't want to interrupt. The old man—she realized she didn't even know his first name—took a sip of his tea and continued. "They wanted children bad, he told me. But they sure kept you a secret. Never heard him say you were on the way. Linda—I mean, Lydia— here's the thing. If there's something bad, you want to hear it, too?"

He tilted forward in his rocking chair with his cup of tea cradled between both hands. She leaned closer, too. Her stomach clenched when he hesitated to go on.

"Was there a trial for the man who hit them?" she

asked. "Did it get public when our people would just have them gone and buried and forgiven the man?"

"Yes, a trial and the man went to prison. But I don't mean that. It's just that I think you were born before your time. I saw Lena Brand maybe a month before the accident and—I'm just an old man now—but she wasn't showing any baby, and I've seen a lot of that in my years."

"I was born premature? You said before my time."

"Just they had no child—and then they did."

She knew now he was mixing things up. He must have heard that she was given away, adopted by a Brand family. He'd confused that with David and Lena Brand not having a child—then suddenly having her. He'd said her mother was petite. Sometimes small, young women held in their pregnancies until real late, and with the way Amish garments were loose anyway, and maybe his eyes were going bad even then, he might not have noticed her mother was expecting. But rather than explain all that to him, since he obviously prided himself in what he did recall, she thanked him.

When Miriam returned, Lydia thanked her also and said goodbye to Mr. Raber. But before she could follow Miriam out, he asked, "So who was that other lady came yesterday, asked a lot of the same questions? Spoke *Englische,* not *Deutsche.* Said she was a friend of the Brand family that has the furniture store over in Homestead."

Sandra! She had tracked this man down even before Lydia had. She stumbled to give an answer, said she didn't know her friend had come here, taken his time, too…

But Lydia did know she had to corral Sandra Myerson and not just leave it up to Josh.

"Well, I didn't know you'd be so upset by my doing
some extra research on my project," Sandra told Josh
as they stood next to her car on the lane between the
animal barn and his house. "Sorry I flashed my camera
at people in the restaurant. I should have known word
would spread around here. I could have taken photos
with my phone, and they'd never know."

"They'd know! Most of my people have had those
little phones pointed at them. And using both my *and*
Lydia's names as a calling card isn't good!" He tried
to control his temper and his voice. "Come on, Sandra, think! It links Lydia and me publicly."

"So what? You two are linked. I can see it, I—"

"You've got to tread lightly here. Our customs don't
include tabloid talk about who is dating who. Even
betrothals are secret until invitations to the wedding
are sent out, and everyone thinks Lydia is more or less
pledged to another man."

"See! So there is talk about who goes with whom.
It's human nature, Amish, English, Spanish, Turk-
ish…"

"Would you just listen?"

He forced himself to stop yelling, something he
struggled not to do when he got angry. This day had
started out with someone stealing one of the expensive camel seats the wise men rode on in the Christmas pageants, the saddle with dark green fringe. He'd
left it outside the back door to clean and use this afternoon. It was smart to reacquaint the camels with the
saddle before they were ridden every year, but stupid

to think nothing would go wrong out back anymore. He had to put a padlock on that back gate where some *rumspringa* kids and Victoria Keller had wandered in.

"I'm sorry I raised my voice," he said, realizing he still sounded steamed.

"You tend to do that, oh Josh of the humble folk. Look, I said I'm sorry and I'll be more careful doing interviews with your Plain People around here. I was going to ask you if I could stay here at your place when I come back, but I won't even mention that. The B and B is great, even reasonable, but it adds up. Gas for that car," she said with a nod at it, "is enough to crimp my budget."

"You're right, you can't stay here. And I'll cover the gas next time you come. Maybe you'll find the time and courage to come out in the barn and see my animals."

"Only if you have house cats out there."

"Actually, I do, barn cats, at least. A tabby cat just delivered six kittens up in the loft."

"Oh, I adore kittens! Now, that's my style of pet, and that's my let's-change-the-subject-and-stay-friends farewell for now. I'll let you know through your friend Hank when I'm coming back. Tell Lydia I'm sorry if I upset any Amish applecarts, and I may have more to tell her about her biologicals when I get back."

She gave him a peck on the cheek, got in her car, honked and drove out. He felt strangely relieved to be rid of her, yet it annoyed him even more when she turned toward town instead of taking the road out to the highway. Then he remembered what Connor had said at the funeral: she planned to interview him, too. Josh could just see her trying to pit the Amish against the Starks about Christmas trees. Worse, if Bess Stark was still home and Sandra ran into her, would she try to interview Bess, too? Lydia said Sandra had referred to the senator as Snarky Stark for some reason.

Muttering under his breath, he hurried into the house and headed upstairs to the bathroom. One of the things he'd liked about the homes of moderns he'd known in Columbus was that most of them had bathrooms on the first floor as well as upstairs, but in an old farmhouse, you went with tradition. On the small landing that marked the turn in the two flights of stairs, he glanced out the window at the two snow angels he and Lydia had made yesterday. He liked seeing them there, but—

"What in the—?"

He pressed his forehead to the cold windowpane and scraped away the frost in the upper right corner. Not only had someone put carrot horns on the angels but they'd drawn a pitchfork in the snow where the angels held hands as if to make them into demons. Worse, two real pitchforks were stuck in the ground—right where the angels' hearts would be.

Upset again by Sandra—and by Mr. Raber's ominous words that she was *born before her time*—Lydia strode toward her buggy. She gasped. Flower had been freed from the traces and was missing!

She spun around to scan the area, especially the barren cornfield where the mare could have wandered. Had Flower been stolen? No one had come into the house who might have unhitched the horse and put her in the barn, but she'd have to look there. She'd also have to get Miriam Raber's help. She ran back along the fence and saw a place where it was broken. Could Flower have gone through the opening? But still, who would have loosed her? And where was she?

Lydia tore behind the barn and found her mare tied by her halter and a rope to an old water trough. But her relief soon turned to shock. The nervous, stamping horse bore on her back one of Josh's camel saddles, the one with the dark green fringe.

That evening, after feeding the animals, Lydia and Josh huddled in the hayloft, though right now it was half-full of loose straw. They had fed the mother cat and were petting the newborn kittens when they weren't nursing. Josh had hung a lantern on a hook in the rafters, which cast wan golden light. Despite the fact the other workers had left, he'd started whispering, and she'd gone along with him.

"It could be anyone trying to scare us, since Sandra broadcast she was friends of both of us," she told him. When she'd returned his stolen camel seat, he'd showed her the defaced snow angels. She didn't like the look of the horns or the pitchfork they were holding. He'd said he found them like that, nothing else, though. She in turn had admitted she'd been to Amity and that Sandra had been there before her.

"Best scenario," he said, "Sandra was just trying to find out more information on your parents to help you out."

"Worst scenario?" she prompted.

"She's trying to ruin our friendship. But why? She knows there's no future for the two of us—her and me."

"Maybe she thinks she's onto something she can

turn into a scandal to get publicity for her writing. You know, sell it to make money."

"Or maybe she's trying to learn something about Bess Stark by casting a wide net. Gain influence, find bigger topics to write about, though politics is hardly Sandra's field of study. But she did refer to Bess as Snarky Stark."

"Which means what?" Lydia demanded, feeling instantly protective of Bess.

"Snarky? Like sarcastic, smart-alecky."

"But Bess is not that way."

"Not to you. Not around here. But she is a public person, a politician, who has to take a stand and defend it. Lydia, I read the Columbus paper for four years. She's what they call a mover and shaker, and she has a staff that would go to the wall for her—protect her at any cost."

"Well, we're not involved in that part of her life. We know what a good person she really is."

Under the watchful gaze of mother cat, they went back to petting the tiny balls of fur that had newly opened their eyes. Josh said, "You should have told me you were going to interview someone who knew your father."

"With Sandra grilling anyone and everyone at the restaurant, I thought I'd just do it myself, without getting you involved again."

"But someone still played us for fools, tried to scare or warn us, but of what? I think, next time you plan a detective expedition, I should go, too."

"It's your busiest time of year, Josh."

"But with all the volunteer hours you've put in with

me, I can afford to go with you. Okay, I can see you have something else in mind. What's up next?"

"I want to talk to the woman who tended Victoria Keller, not the one in Cleveland but the one who lives closer."

"Connor probably scared both of them," he said, "but I hope she'll talk to you."

"Could he be behind any of this?" Lydia asked. "Maybe he knows his aunt did have something sane to say and he's afraid we'll find out what that is."

"*Ya,* but you said Gid Reich saw you leave with Sandra. So maybe he's seen other things, following you. Like us making snow angels, like you leaving work early and heading for Amity. Maybe he sees me as some sort of rival and he's out to warn or scare us. Besides, as you know, hefting around that camel saddle is not easy, and he looks stronger than Connor."

Lydia heaved a huge sigh. She'd had to drag it on the ground after she took it off Flower and then had to winch it into the back of the buggy with the rope Flower was tied with. Josh had been shocked when she'd returned it. Now she said only, "Gid has changed his coat of many colors lately—turned kind, more polite."

"*Ya,* so you said. And you said that former caretaker lives about twenty miles away. That's a long buggy ride. How about we save time and horses and have Hank drive us? The three of us can stop for lunch somewhere. Besides, I need to check out the town square in Hillside where we'll take some of the animals next weekend, and that's up by where she lives, right?"

"After what's happened today, we can hardly say we're mixing business with pleasure."

"Oh, I don't know," he said, reaching out his hand to slowly trace the slant of her cheek and jaw, then her chin and throat with his knuckles. He stopped just above her collarbone, but it was as if he stroked her clear down to her toes. "I owe you big-time for getting that camel seat back for me," he went on. "And I'd like to pay up, but not with a roll in this old straw—you'd have it in your hair and clothes when you went back home to the lion's den, if you'll excuse me for putting it that way. But being near you does give me pleasure."

Of all the things that had frightened Lydia today, this scared her the most. That is, that she would risk her reputation and her future and her parents' goodwill to want to roll in the straw with this man right now. She wanted to throw herself in his arms and tell him how much she loved and needed him. But that might scare him, too, as much as angels being made to look like devils with a pitchfork drawn in the snow. So she just turned her head real fast and planted a kiss on his cheek, then jumped up and made for the ladder. It was a long ways down, and she liked it up here. After all, David Brand had liked heights.

"I'll take you up on the ride with Hank on Saturday if you can arrange it," she said, poised at the top of the ladder. "Meanwhile, I think our enemy is Sandra. She can drive that car fast from place to place and she was already at the Rabers' house. Maybe we'll find she's been to see Anna Gingerich, too."

"I just hope," he said, following her to the ladder, "she doesn't get in cahoots with Connor."

Lydia didn't know what *cahoots* meant, but she got

the message. Connor had always seemed like he had a big bone to pick with her. Yet Lydia trusted Bess Stark when Sandra evidently didn't.

As for the pitchfork that was drawn in the snow angels' joined hands, devils were often pictured with them, but around here, pitchforks were just useful tools anyone could use. Josh often pitched hay to his animals with one. She'd seen workers at the Christmas tree farm use pitchforks to shake the snow off trees after a storm. Connor had used two of them at once when she saw him knocking dead needles off the trees he was spraying. Why, even *Daad,* who didn't farm a lick, had two of them in their barn.

10

On Saturday morning, the first day of December, Lydia sat between Josh and his driver, Hank Habeggar, as Hank drove them northwest into the next county, following the sheriff's directions, to the home of Anna Gingerich. Always flexible and cheerful, Hank took all Josh's phone calls and made deliveries of animals and their supplies. Hank was Mennonite, a group often confused with the Amish but much more liberal. Cars, phones, electricity, college for their kids, some TV—it was a much bigger world for the Mennonites, but they shared many of the same core beliefs as the Amish.

Lydia liked Hank, though she didn't know him very well. With his red hair and beard, freckles and easy grin, he seemed younger than he was—probably in his late thirties. He had a wife and four kids and made a living doing odd jobs for various people in the area. He didn't seem to be aware of continually whistling off-key, but apparently it only bothered her and the donkeys. It occasionally set them to braying, and that made the perfect chorus.

"Do you want me to go in with you?" Josh asked

her as they turned onto Willoway Road, the street they had listed for Mrs. Gingerich.

"I think it would be easier on her if you didn't. You know, woman to woman."

"What reason are you going to give for talking to her?"

"I'd like to tell her the truth, but I don't want things getting to anyone else. I will ask her if Sandra's been to see her, though. But for openers—I'm not sure."

Hank's whistling stopped. "I'd say it's that run-down house there." He pointed. "Yep, 1650. See the mailbox?"

"I was expecting a farmhouse," Lydia admitted, looking at the small home with siding and a chimney that needed work. "But then, if she was well-off, why would she be getting a ride clear into Homestead every day to tend an ill woman?"

"No wonder she's still here," Josh said as they pulled in the cinder driveway. It crunched under the unshoveled snow, which also weighed down the un-trimmed hedges. "Not enough money to leave for a while, maybe no money to get clear in from Cleveland like the other caretaker. What was her name, the one the sheriff said lived farther away?"

"Sarah Miller. The sheriff has her address, too, but let's just see how this goes."

"We'll wait in the car. You need us, just come to the back door."

"She may not even be here."

"Someone's here," Hank observed. "I see a little trail of smoke out the chimney."

Lydia had to watch her steps on the back walk and concrete stoop, which were both glazed with ice under snow. She knocked on the door. Waited. Knocked again. There was no screen or storm door. She looked back at the men in the truck and shrugged. But she breathed in the scent of woodsmoke, and no other house was nearby. As she turned back to knock again, the dark blue door curtain quivered. Two eyes in a pale face under a prayer *kapp* looked out.

Lydia raised her voice. "Hello! Are you Anna Gingerich? I'm Lydia Brand from Homestead. Please, can I ask you a couple of questions?"

The lock turned; the door opened about an inch. "From Homestead? Are you sent by Connor Stark?"

"No. I came on my own. I think Victoria Keller may have been trying to find me the night she died. I would be grateful if you could tell me what she was like—even when she was so ill."

"Those men not coming in?"

"No—friends. They'll wait for me."

"You could ask your town sheriff. I talked to him."

"I'm asking for myself. Please, I—"

The door swept open with a strong smell of woodsmoke from within. Didn't this woman know how to vent her stove or fireplace?

"Cold in and out," Mrs. Gingerich said. "Best keep your cape and bonnet on."

"That's fine. I'm sure you're busy." Lydia stepped in. "I won't stay long, but I would be grateful for anything you can tell me about Victoria Keller that might give me an idea why she wanted to contact me."

"Who says she did?"

"I—she had a note with her, and it seemed to be addressed to me. I'm the one who found her, got her help, but it was too late."

"Too late for her for years," Mrs. Gingerich said, closing the door and gesturing for Lydia to sit at a square Formica table in the small kitchen. The gaunt woman, who was probably in her sixties, sat across from her but didn't pull her chair up. She seemed stiff and wary. She wore a coat over her clothes. The smoke inside the house made Lydia's eyes sting and water. It looked as if the woman had been crying, but it might just be the bad ventilation.

Suddenly, Mrs. Gingerich said, "She liked to draw, not good but kind of like cartoons in the newspaper. You know, telling a story."

That fit what Bess had mentioned at the funeral. "The same story?" Lydia prompted. "Different ones? Did they make any sense?"

"To her, I s'pose. At least it kept her quiet and occupied for a little while, but she looked real angry, almost fierce, when she drew them." Mrs. Gingerich slanted a glance toward the kitchen's only window. She obviously didn't want to meet Lydia's intense gaze. "Victoria was always upset and restless, but Mrs. Stark—Victoria's sister, not the younger one—said never to tie her down. You swear you're not here for Mr. Stark?"

The woman seemed not only nervous but genuinely afraid of Connor. Lydia hardened her heart toward him even more, but, of course, he had been upset with the caregivers that Victoria got out of the house. And it had caused her death.

"No, I am not here for him but for myself. Did she tend to repeat her drawings?"

"Oh, yes. Sorry I don't have any of them left. I used them for fire fuel here. But her stories, *ya,* I guess. Her reaching for a baby with wings, like a baby angel, and it flying away. In the last square each time, it flew high out of the picture."

Lydia sat stunned. Perhaps Victoria had had a child out of wedlock and decided to give it away—or was forced to. Or it died and she pictured it flying toward heaven. But what could that have to do with her? Victoria had never lived near Homestead until recently. But if the demented woman was obsessing over a child she lost, could she have gazed out her window, seen Lydia coming and going and decided she was her child?

"Did the baby with wings look like a cherub? Are you sure the woman in the drawings was Victoria?"

"A cherub, maybe," Mrs. Gingerich said, finally meeting Lydia's eyes. "She drew her own self really good. I could tell right who that was. But after drawing the same thing each time, she got even angrier and scribbled it out real hard. So I didn't feel bad bringing the papers home to burn, and I sure didn't want Mr. Stark to know we let her have pens and paper."

"Why would that have upset him? Was he afraid she'd hurt herself with something sharp?"

"'Cause he would want her tied down in bed— Oh, I know he would, but he didn't dare because of his mother. And here he blames me and Sarah when she managed to get out!"

"He hasn't threatened you, has he?"

"He scairt Sarah for sure, and she was glad she lived a far piece away. Me, I'm a widow, want to stay here, got nowhere else to go. If it weren't for my church, especially now, I'd scarce get by."

"Did you ever overhear things about Victoria's past—from her or from the family?"

"I was told she was a maiden lady, liked to write and draw. No children, of course, like me. And you thought Victoria had a note for you? Doubt it. The Starks were right about one thing. Nothing she did made sense, all gibberish."

"But did she always speak the same gibberish, like the drawings were the same?"

"Why, mostly she said things like, 'Got to tell the truth. Got to let them know. I have to tell the truth. It's not right. Taken away, not fair...' On and on like that."

"She said 'taken away'?"

"Oh, *ya*. She was always fussing they'd taken her away from her home or the clinic and brought her to their house. That's what Sarah and I figured. Her career, her independence—her family took all that away, she must have meant, when, of course, it was her failing mind. But she needed to be cared for. She was always seeing other things that wasn't there. She could look right through you, like you was a ghost, when more like, she was."

Anna Gingerich shuddered. Lydia did, too. Not from the cold in here but from the thought of a talented, bright woman trapped in her own mind, haunted by something she could no longer grasp. And that baby? The note read, *To the girl Brand baby... Your mother is alive.* Victoria Keller must have overheard the name Brand. After all, they were the Starks' neighbors, and Lydia's house could have been visible from Victoria's rooms.

"Mrs. Gingerich, did Victoria spend much time

looking out the windows of the top floor? That is where she was kept, right?"

"Oh, *ya*. I got to admit the downward view of the valley was real pretty, but she liked to look at the sky. Looked up, always looking up. Had a nice big room with north and west windows. I think she was look-ing for something in the sky and sometimes she cried when the sun went down."

"You have been so kind and helpful. Has anyone else besides the sheriff been to question you about this?"

"No one. I shouldn't even talk to you, so please, don't you tell anyone in Homestead."

Well, Lydia thought, at least Sandra had not beat her here. "Mrs. Gingerich, would you mind if my friends came in just to see why it's so smoky in here? Maybe there's a stuck flue in the chimney or—"

"Oh, no! Used to it. No men in this house since my Silas passed, 'cept the bishop, that's all right."

Lydia wondered if the woman was still afraid that Connor had sent the men, but at least she'd been kind to her. The Amish were that way, and how she'd like to help this woman somehow, especially since she'd heard Connor had refused to pay the caretakers for their last month's work. She realized also that this was the first Amish home she'd ever visited where she hadn't been offered something to eat or drink. Perhaps Anna Gin-gerich had nothing to offer.

As the woman showed her out, Lydia managed to drop a twenty-dollar bill from her pocketbook onto the faded, gray linoleum floor.

"So how did it go?" Josh asked as Hank drove them out of the Gingerich driveway and turned toward the

little town of Hillside. He'd been real nervous while
Lydia was inside. He was feeling overly protective of
her lately.

"I'm actually not sure she told me anything useful.
Victoria did draw the same thing repeatedly, though,
and there was a baby involved. I'm wondering if she
didn't just long for children she never had, and she got
stuck on that. Mrs. Gingerich is very poor and afraid
of Connor."

Josh asked no more, partly because they hadn't told
Hank about the note or Lydia's being adopted and her
search to find out about her birth parents.

When Josh patted her arm, Hank put in, "Lots of
folks in town should be afraid of Connor. Instead,
they vote for him, think he's the best thing since sliced
bread. Too much power and, with him, maybe not
well used. It's like he wants to be his mother but on a
smaller scale."

"Smaller scale for sure," Josh said. "But he doesn't
have Bess Stark's warmth or personality."

"That's the truth," Lydia agreed. Josh noted she'd
finally stopped gripping her hands together so fiercely
in her lap. For the first time since she'd shared her
quest with him, he hoped Lydia would just let it go.
She knew who her real parents were now, and they
were gone. Victoria, if she'd ever known anything,
was gone, too, and he thought that was a wild-goose
chase. He'd have Hank phone Sandra today and tell
her to stop stirring up trouble. He realized that he
wanted not only to protect Lydia, but to win her heart
and hand. Now, if only he could find some way to get
Gid Reich out of her life.

* * *

Sunday evening, Lydia tried to concentrate on the talk over supper. Sometimes it turned into a three-way conversation among Gid and her parents while she just nodded and smiled until someone prompted her with a question or comment. Her mind kept straying to Anna Gingerich's descriptions of Victoria, then skipped to Mr. Raber's insisting she was *born before her time.*

She also kept recalling how, after they had talked to the committee for the Hillside town square manger scene yesterday, she had waited in the truck while Hank called Sandra on his cell phone for Josh. The message was not to come back to the Home Valley until they called her again, but Lydia had seen Josh take the phone from Hank and speak to her himself. He looked pretty upset, pacing, gesturing. Hank had moved away as if to give Josh privacy. When Lydia had asked Josh later what he'd said to Sandra, he'd just told her not to worry about it and put her off.

"Can't put off Christmas," her mother was saying. "I've been turning out my bread, Gid, buggying here and there to give it to people in need. Though you aren't in need of much, I want you to take a fresh loaf home with you."

"It's a real talent you have for baking," Gid said with a nod and a smile. He had cleaned his pumpkin pie plate so well, it looked as if he'd licked it. "I'm sure some of your kitchen talents have rubbed off on Lydia."

"When she takes the time, *ya,* indeed," *Mamm* agreed.

"Each one of us has God-given talents," Gid said with a smile at Lydia. She'd been silently scolding herself for not taking a loaf of that bread to Anna Gingerich, but then she would have had to explain to *Mamm.* "It is just a question of how we use them," Gid went on. "And we are blessed to have the furniture doing so well in these difficult times, Sol."

Difficult times, for sure, Lydia thought, but she said, "There are lots of Amish furniture stores in Ohio, but *Daad*'s dedication to detail and quality makes all the difference. Here, *Mamm,* let me help you clear," she said the moment her mother made a move to rise.

"No, you sit with Gid, and *Daad* will help me."

"Then I'll just fetch that loaf of bread for Gid," Lydia said.

"Actually," Gid admitted, looking a bit guilty, "I did promise Connor Stark I would stop there on my way home to give him a check for my share in the new partnership—extending his property for more plantings. At least in about five or so years, his trees are ready to cut whereas the hardwoods we use take decades to grow."

Lydia was surprised Gid was leaving early tonight. He used to make excuses to hang around. When Connor Stark commanded, people jumped. Or was this just part of Gid's new tactic of acting uninterested, just as she always had? If he thought that would make a difference about how she felt toward him, he was wrong—and yet it had gotten her attention.

Since he seemed willing to leave, Lydia agreed to go out to hand him the loaf of friendship bread and say good-night. He was already in his buggy, so there was no question about a good-night kiss for once. Maybe he had taken her advice and had begun to court someone else, even though he'd have to, of course, still be kind to his employer's daughter.

"My thanks and see you tomorrow at the store," he called to her. The only kiss was the one he blew to his horse as the buggy moved away into the dark.

Or, she thought, could Gid actually be behind the stolen camel seat and the defacing of the snow angels? Was he really keeping close tabs on her and Josh and pretending disinterest so they would not suspect?

Wrapping her cloak around her in the cold night, she glanced over toward Josh's place, wishing he'd been the one her mother—her adoptive mother—had invited tonight. Though the woodlot trees between here and there looked like twisted skeletons with their clothes stripped away, she'd love to walk through them to visit Josh right now. Thinking of how Victoria had always looked skyward, Lydia raised her eyes to the pinpoint array of stars in the moonless night. Maybe the poor woman's love of the sky, of heaven, was why she'd drawn flying angels, and Anna Gingerich had just thought it was a baby. Maybe—

Lydia gasped when a strange man appeared from nowhere in the dark. She hadn't heard or seen him approach. How long had he been there?

Her first instinct was to run for the house, but he blocked her way. She opened her mouth to scream. Even as she made a sound, he said, "Shut up. I'm gonna say this quick and fast, and you better listen."

She could not make out his face, but his bulk and apparent lack of neck between his big, bald head and broad shoulders made her realize she didn't know him. His breath made clouds in the cold darkness.

"You've mistaken me for someone else, so—" she began before he interrupted her.

"Lay off sending that reporter around, sniffing about what's long past—the buggy accident. My dad paid six years of his life in prison for aggravated vehicular homicide. The judge said it was reckless driving, but it was that dark buggy's fault. His business was ruined when he got out. He's eighty-five now and needs to be left alone."

"You're—you're Marvin Lowe's son?" She was shaking all over. She wanted to run, but her feet felt rooted to the ground.

"Damn right. He paid his dues. Slow buggy, after dark."

"A buggy lit by two lanterns! But what reporter?" she asked, though she was afraid she knew that it was a writer and not a reporter, a friend of Josh's who had somehow turned into a monster. Had Sandra told Josh on the phone she'd talked to the man who had hit her parents' buggy and that's what Josh was yelling about? Surely, it was not someone from the Wooster newspaper who had decided to do a follow-up story when the old car-buggy accident was called to their attention.

"You know who I mean," the man said, his voice gruff and low. "Ms. Myerson. She used your name. Now call her off and steer clear, or you'll be sorry! Don't think I won't be watching."

She was grateful the man turned and ran away, heading into the woodlot toward Josh's. Could he have been the one who was warning both her and Josh by stealing things and ruining something as harmless as snow angels? And was he harmless? Maybe she should tell the sheriff, and—

"Liddy? You still out there? It's cold, girl," *Daad*'s voice rang out in the darkness. "Your *mamm* thinks you're still with Gid but I know better 'cause I saw him leave."

She tried to call, "*Ya,* coming, *Daad,*" but her voice stuck in her throat. On shaky legs, she ran toward the house, kissed her father on the cheek as she hurried inside and told him nothing of what had shaken her so.

11

Monday after work, Lydia buggied directly to the Yoder barn. Deeply shaken by being accosted in the dark outside her home last night by Marvin Lowe's angry son, and learning that Sandra had been to see Mr. Lowe as well as Mr. Raber, she needed to tell Josh everything.

"I can't believe she'd dare all that," Josh said when she'd explained. His voice level rose so fast that the sheep he was feeding shied away. He climbed out of their pen and took Lydia's upper arms in his strong hands. "And then the man threatens you! Hank's here, and I'm going to borrow his cell phone to call Sandra and stop her. You're going to have to tell the sheriff, too."

"Won't he want me to press some kind of charges? You know our people can't do that. Besides, once again, my parents could find out all I've been doing behind their backs, and they'd be devastated."

"First things first. I swear I had no idea Sandra would cross the line like this," he said, heading toward Hank so fast she had to run to keep up.

"Lowe's son called her a reporter. It's like she's turned into one who is after some sort of story way beyond the customs of Christmas."

In Josh's makeshift barn office, Hank had been making phone calls to clients, checking dates and times for delivering animals.

"Can we borrow your cell?" Josh asked him.

"Wow, must be something pressing. Sure, go ahead. I'll just give you some space and go use the 'men's room' at the house." He gave Josh a light punch on his shoulder as he handed over his phone.

"Her number will be on here somewhere," Josh told Lydia, and started touching the little window on the phone.

No buttons to push anymore? Lydia wondered. Of course, Josh had lived in the world for four years and probably had a phone there, maybe even a small, flat window phone like that one. But what bothered her, on top of everything, was that he must be able to recognize Sandra's number from Hank's list.

Exactly what *had* their relationship been? Just friends? Could Sandra still care for Josh enough that she meant to put Lydia in some sort of danger? But she'd been so kind and supportive the day they drove to Wooster and found the article about her parents' death.

Lydia watched Josh pace back and forth between his office and the camel pen. Melly and Gaspar looked faintly interested until they realized they were being ignored. Lydia wondered if she should stand here where she could hear, or if he wanted privacy. She retreated into the corner and perched on a bale of hay.

At first she couldn't hear what he was saying, but he must have gotten hold of Sandra. Had he held her, kissed her, made love to her in better times? Were they still more than friends?

Typical of Josh, she could tell he was having trouble controlling his temper. "But the guy could have really hurt her. You're going too far with this. She knows who her parents are—were—so you don't need to do in-depth investiga…Yeah, yeah, I know, but you need to lay off. I strongly suggest you not come back here since you seem so tempted to interview everyone in sight…Yeah, she's here."

He held the phone behind his back and came over to Lydia, whispering, "She wants to hear from you that you want her to lay off. You mind talking on the phone?"

"It looks like a tiny TV," she protested, but he put it in her hand, and she talked into it just like she'd seen him do.

"Sandra, I thank you for your help in the beginning, but *ya,* please, this has to end."

"I wanted to give you a more detailed portrait of your parents, so to speak," Sandra said in a rush. "Listen, I didn't realize that Leo Lowe, Marvin's son, was such a hothead. You should get a restraining order on him, scare him a bit."

"But that's the thing. You just don't understand Amish ways. We don't do things like that, legal things, court things, police business. I have no intention of 'scaring him a bit' even though that's what he did to me. Our way is more like turn the other cheek, go the extra mile."

"Sorry, really. And about Mr. Raber, too. I just thought if I did the asking around, you wouldn't have to so that you don't upset your adoptive parents. I'll be more circumspect next time, make it up to both of you, maybe later this week. Actually, I've learned something else you should know but I'd rather tell you in person."

"Just a second," Lydia said, then put the phone behind her back and whispered the way Josh had. "She wants to come back—maybe later this week."

Shaking his head and rolling his eyes, Josh took the phone. "Listen, Sandra, I think we'd better give all this a rest, let things calm down. Lydia agrees...Okay, but can't you just tell her or me over the phone?...Right, right. I think it's great if you're ready to see my animals, but—"

Despite wanting Sandra to stay away, Lydia wondered if the something else she'd turned up was valuable, or just something Lydia already knew. But asking Josh about that flew right out of her head when she saw who had come in and maybe overheard—how much?

Lydia's mother had suddenly appeared in the barn with a loaf of bread in her hands when she'd never set foot here on her own before. Josh turned off the phone, obviously surprised to see her, too.

"Oh, you—Lydia, too," *Mamm* said, "using a cell phone? You know the bishop has ruled against that. I brought you this loaf of friendship bread, Joshua, but I hope your friendship with my daughter is not leading her astray with a phone or anything else."

Ray-Lynn was surprised to see Lydia Brand appear for the early bird breakfast at the restaurant on Tuesday morning. It was usually just wall-to-wall men in here this early.

"If I take a back booth," Lydia told her in a quiet voice, "would you have a second to chat?"

Actually, she didn't, because she was a server short, but the look on Lydia's face told her something was really wrong. "Sure. Let me put your order in, and I'll be right back with coffee. Black?"

"Yes. Thanks, Ray-Lynn. Just scrambled eggs, sausage and toast."

Well, Ray-Lynn thought, she'd never been able to turn down helping one of these genuine, young Amish women this area seemed to breed. Last time Lydia had been in here it had turned into police business. Ray-Lynn knew better than to dabble in that. But she was still fascinated by poor Victoria's death and how the Starks had chosen to bring her secretly to live with them instead of leaving her in a top-of-the-line Alzheimer's clinic. It was hardly a money issue, so why isolate the woman and put that burden on themselves? The Amish might keep such family members at home, but the well-to-do, so-called moderns? Not often.

She put in Lydia's order, then poured both of them coffee at the booth. "How can I help?" Ray-Lynn asked, sliding into the opposite seat.

"I guess you know I need help," the young woman said, staring down into her coffee as if she could read answers there. She gripped the mug with both hands. "At first, I was just going to ask if you knew anyone from the Hostetler family who came in here. I've found out I'm somewhat related to them."

"I know a few. You want me to ask them to contact you?"

"No! I'd rather have it the other way around. I could go to see them."

"And what else? That's not really what's upsetting you, is it?"

"I have a problem."

"Let's hear it. No beating around the bush. Something else about Victoria Keller and that note?"

"It's complicated, and I know you're busy. I don't mean to make you a middleman—woman—to the sheriff all the time, but I just want him to know that I was approached by the son of the man who hit my birth parents' buggy and killed them years ago. His father went to jail for double manslaughter back then, and he thinks I'm bringing it up again, which in a way I am, but I don't intend to bother them. You know I can't have anything to do with asking for charges or a restraining order but—"

"Did this man hurt you?"

"Just with words. Threats."

Ray-Lynn leaned even closer across the table. "Such as?"

"He said, 'Don't think I won't be watching.' And I'd be sorry if I didn't call off my friend."

"Josh?"

"No, Sandra Myerson went to question his father. He got some crazy idea she was a reporter. His son is afraid someone will open up the case, I guess."

"As you know, Sandra Myerson caused a real stir in here last week. Somebody ought to put the skids on her."

"The man's name is Leo Lowe, from Parma. Just so the sheriff knows."

"I hope you and Josh can shut Ms. Myerson up before she does more damage. I don't want to see her in the Dutch Table again with her little camera and recorder."

"Honestly, Ray-Lynn, she was trying to help me, but she went—went over the edge with it."

"I'll tell the sheriff, and he'll understand why you can't get more involved. Amish ways and— Are you still keeping your parents in the dark about looking for your birth family?"

She nodded solemnly. "I suppose I should tell them—maybe after Christmas. *Daad*'s busy at the store, *Mamm*'s delivering bread..."

"Wish I could get her to bake that for the restaurant. She makes the best in the area. And you and Josh are getting ready to liven up our manger scene."

Lydia forced a little smile. "You're a heaven-sent friend," she said, reaching out to grip Ray-Lynn's hand. The girl's fingers were cold and trembling.

When Lydia's breakfast came, Ray-Lynn excused herself to get up, then thought of something else. "By the way, I heard tell that Connor more or less threw Josh's so-called friend Sandra out when she came to interview him. Anyhow, it didn't go well. Plus, she got a speeding ticket from the sheriff while she was leaving town, and she told him Connor Stark was a pompous, well, to put it in Yoder rent-an-animal talk, a pompous donkey."

"Sandra's not what—who—she seemed to be at first."

"Hell on wheels in more ways than one, and don't tell Bishop Esh I said that." Ray-Lynn squeezed Lydia's shoulder and went back to work, but she was already planning how she'd tell Jack without getting him all riled up that she was nosing in on his official business. After all, the girl had come to her.

Lydia knew the Bible said "Do not fret because it only causes harm," but she couldn't help herself. After Leo Lowe frightened her, she was tempted to put a rearview mirror on her buggy to be sure she wasn't being followed by him or Gid. But she'd need the bishop's permission for that. And then he'd want to know why, and one admission would lead to another. Years ago when she'd asked him for advice about trying to find her real parents, he had counseled against it. If he found out to what lengths she was going now, it could even lead to a public confession before the church. But it did make her feel guilty she was keeping so much from *Mamm* and *Daad.*

The continued but welcome frenzy at the furniture store hardly took her mind off her worries. Gid was still polite and kind, but that bothered her. Why had he changed? Was he hoping it would intrigue her and she would ask him? Was he waiting for a sign she really did care for him?

Daad, as busy as ever, seemed even more frail and gaunt. In the New Year, hopefully he would get more rest.

When the bishop's son-in-law Seth Lantz came into the store with his little girl to pick up a new chair for his wife, Hannah, Lydia wondered if it wasn't a sign from above that she was to consult the bishop again. Ray-Lynn had mentioned Bishop Esh, and, after all, Lydia had not been an adult when she'd talked to him before about her adoptive parents. Maybe she'd taken what he'd said wrong. Since he'd suffered so much with losing his daughter Hannah to the world for a while and had now gotten her back, maybe he could better understand her plight and give her his blessing to search for relatives and more information about her birth parents.

So on the way home, Lydia pulled her buggy into the Esh farmhouse to see if Bishop Esh had a free moment to speak with her. While Mrs. Esh fussed over them with tea and cookies, Lydia cleared her throat and began, "I would be grateful for your advice, Bishop Esh."

"You mind if Mrs. Esh stays?" he said. "Maybe a woman's point of view as well as mine and the Lord's, eh?"

In the stark winter light reflecting off the snow through the window, Lydia noted how Bishop Esh had aged. He almost reminded her of old Mr. Raber in Amity. His wife, Mattie, fetched the German Bible for him, and he put it next to his teacup, resting one gnarled hand on it. How many people had the elderly bishop advised over the years? Bishops were chosen by lot, not by an election, and their burdens of preaching and counseling must be unbearable at times.

"Years ago," Lydia began, her voice not sounding like her own, "I came to you with questions about my birth parents. You told me then to let it be, and I assure you I do love and respect my *daad* and *mamm,* but I still yearn to know about the—my first parents."

"You know we are called to think of others first, Lydia," he said. "'Think not only of your interests, but also for the interests of others.' And in this case, the living others are Sol and Susan Brand. *Ach,* what pain we could cause those who are good to us, who love us. Even if the goal seems right, the end cannot justify the means at times."

Her hopes fell. Anger rose in her, but she beat it down. Wasn't the bishop wise enough to realize how important this was to her? "So whether I tell them my need or keep a secret, it will hurt them. Is that what you mean?" she asked a bit louder than she intended. Maybe Josh's bad habit of showing a quick temper was rubbing off on her.

Mrs. Esh looked as if she'd like to say something. She was fidgeting worse than Lydia, but she held her tongue.

"Lydia, believe me, trust me," Bishop Esh said. "Best you be content and not begin to search the past or tell others of your wandering thoughts. I can only counsel you to remember one of the Ten Commandments to honor your father and your mother."

"But that's what I would be doing, for my birth father and mother, while still respecting and honoring *Daad* and *Mamm*. You preached not long ago on another piece of Bible wisdom, 'Know the truth and it shall set you free.'"

Mattie Esh had tears in her eyes as she showed Lydia out to her buggy. Having lost her own daughter for several years, perhaps she was sympathizing with Lydia's mother. Or did she know something— something that Lydia could get her to tell?

"Mrs. Esh, I know it must have grieved you when Hannah did not take your advice and went her own way—did what she had to do. But here she came back and things are even better now because she chose to return. If you can help me in any way, I—"

"I wish I could, but can't," she said. She tried to

smile but it came out as a grimace that made the lines on her face cobweb even deeper. "It's best— Just can't." She turned and hurried into the house, glancing back just once.

Lydia heaved a huge sigh that turned cloudy in the frosty air. As the early evening darkness descended, she knew it would have been a waste of time to ask permission for a rearview mirror. But, though she was bucking what the bishop had said, she vowed she was going to continue to look not only forward, but back.

12

At dinner that evening, *Mamm* had not said one word about catching Lydia and Josh on a cell phone in the Yoder barn. She wasn't sure why *Mamm* had not mentioned it. Maybe she had wanted to see if Lydia would bring it up or apologize on her own. Maybe she had not wanted *Daad* to know—or not wanted him to know she had taken friendship bread to Josh. But Lydia recognized her familiar knock on her bedroom door later and steadied herself for questions.

"Come in, *Mamm*," Lydia called. She was walking back and forth from bed to dresser, brushing her long hair. *Mamm* came in and sat on the edge of the bed, so Lydia did, too, though they were both facing forward.

"So you and Josh were using a cell phone?" *Mamm* said, her voice unusually quiet and calm, though the little vein at the side of her neck pulsed as it always did when she was upset. "I thought his friend did his business calls."

"That was Hank's phone Josh just borrowed. You may be glad to know we were trying to convince Sandra Myerson, the woman Gid told you I went to

Wooster with, not to come back. She upset Ray-Lynn and both *Englische* and Amish at the restaurant by asking too many questions."

"And with a little camera, so I heard. She's not coming back?"

"Maybe just to see Josh's animals. He said she's been afraid of them and wants to get over that. Besides, she's crazy about cats—"

"Crazy in general!"

"—and there are new kittens in the loft. I'm not sure, but maybe she wants to—well, adopt one."

"That is enough of someone prideful and pushy like her, at least around my daughter. So you won't see her again? I had a bad dream you got in her red car again and left us for good."

Lydia shook her head. She would never leave the Home Valley but she sensed *Mamm*'s hidden fears in that dream. She'd had some, too, lately, ones where she was climbing a tall tree, searching through its thick leaves, looking for her birth parents, fearful she'd fall. Beneath her, someone was cutting limbs off the tree with a loud, shrill buzz saw coming closer and closer.

Again she wondered how much her mother had heard of their conversation. It was so hard to believe she'd brought a peace offering of bread to Josh, though it was the Christmas season. Surely, that had not just been an excuse to see what they were doing in the barn.

She turned more toward her mother on the bed, bending one leg on the quilt bedspread. "Don't let bad dreams upset you, *Mamm*. You haven't had the one about hearing Sammy calling from out by the pond again?"

"No, and don't speak of that. I don't want them to start again. But I can't bear to lose you, too, Lydia, in a red car or any way— Well, only if you'd agree to marry Gid, I guess."

"He's backed off a bit, and that's fine with me."

"Just don't you misuse our trust in you to get all mixed up with worldly folk, or even ones who lived in the world for a while. It changes them, rubs off on others. They are what our people call yanked over."

Lydia fought to keep from arguing to defend Josh and herself. "Let me only say it was kind of you to take Josh the bread, and he was most grateful."

"So he said, but I did it because I liked his parents. They were good neighbors."

"And he is not?"

She shrugged and sighed. "In the summer, too many cars for the petting zoo, and when it's warm the camels smell."

"Way over here? I've never noticed that. And it's just the camels?"

"No, but if you tend them so close, you must notice, too."

"I haven't smelled them here, ever. With help, Josh keeps his animals well fed and cared for."

Mamm rose quickly and went to the door. "That's enough talk for now," she said. "If Sandra Myerson comes back, at least you won't be near her again. Let *him* entertain *her* by himself." On that she closed the door.

Lydia shuddered at that thought. *Mamm* always knew how to twist a nice enough thought to a sharp point. Tossing her hairbrush on the bed, she knelt beside it, not to pray but to pull out her birth mother's snow globe from the darkness. She held it up before the single kerosene lantern on her bedside table. As she shook it gently, its insides swirled and spun. The old snowflakes seemed to turn to silver glitter around the angel and the child inside, and she recalled making angels in the snow with Josh.

Josh thought he heard something besides the wind outside the barn. He wished darkness didn't come so early in the winter months. He patted Noah, his strongest donkey, the one who always carried the "pregnant" Virgin Mary in pageants, but the animal seemed nervous, too, maybe since two of his asinine—Hank's joke—buddies were still outside. Turning the lantern down so he wouldn't be seen as he stepped out, Josh grabbed his coat and muffler-eared hat, slid the big back camel door open and looked out.

Braying. Something was bothering the two donkeys he had yet to corral. He slid the door closed behind him and edged around the corner of the barn in the direction of the noise. He whistled for them. That usually brought Jonah and Enos, at least when they were hungry.

He heard a human shout, then more braying. Someone from the road trying to ride the animals? Harm them? Take them?

"Hey, stop!" he shouted into the darkness lit only by starlight. He ran toward the fence along the road, still unsure of what he'd find. The two donkeys rushed at him, past him. He gasped as he stumbled over a body on the ground and nearly sprawled into the snow face-first. Somehow he kept his balance and grabbed the fence. He pictured again poor Victoria on the ground, frozen, dead. But this bundle of flesh and bone yelped and rolled away.

"I just saw the donkeys and wanted to have some fun!" a muffled voice called in Amish *Deutsche.*

"Amos? Amos Baughman, you been trying to ride a donkey again?" Josh shouted and pulled him up by the scruff of his coat. He gave him a little shake, then let him go. The boy was only twelve and had helped with the animals off and on in the summer. "I told you that you could get kicked!"

"But—but someone else was here and scairt them bad. I was doing good on Enos, but a person was there by the barn and got them riled and Enos bucked just when I was gonna get off. But you said once he was as good as a horse ride."

Josh backed the boy up against the fence. "What do you mean someone else was there? How do you know? What did you see?"

"Honest, Mr. Yoder, a dark form over there close to the barn. Didn't see him right away."

"It was a man?"

"Don't know for sure in the dark, with a bulky coat, hat and all. He—or she—moved away quicklike. I thought it was you at first and was gonna hightail it out, but then Enos got spooked as bad as me and—"

"You just get on home. Your *mamm*'s going to be worried about you and blame me. You want to help me with the animals next summer on salary you better mend your ways. Now you get going. But watch the slippery spots. I can't leave the animals to take you home right now."

The boy only lived a ten-minute run up the lane on the north side of the road, the opposite direction from

Lydia's. Through the wire-fenced gate, Josh watched the boy go until he disappeared into the darkness. Josh closed it quietly and carefully. He had put a combination lock on the back gate Victoria had come through, and now he'd have to lock this one. Muttering, he latched it the best he could.

He went back inside, got the lantern, turned up the wick and brought it out to look for tracks. *Ya,* someone had been standing tight against the barn, maybe trying to stay out of the wind. Then he or she had shuffled along to the barn door closest to the house, but stopped there. And then—the boy was right—the person had evidently been disturbed by Amos trying to mount the donkey, and he or she had taken off around the front of the barn. Josh followed the footsteps as far as the woodlot that led toward the Brands' property.

Shaking his head, Josh trudged back into the barn and put the bar down on the big door. Could the man who'd bothered Lydia Sunday night be hanging around here? She said he'd hightailed it toward the woodlot. Surely Sandra hadn't come back already. Being secretive wasn't her style, but she'd really surprised him lately. He had trouble believing it could be one of the *rumspringa* boys. Maybe he should lock the house up tight and sleep in the barn tonight. Last time he'd done that, at least he'd had a great dream about making love to a woman he now knew was Lydia.

He sighed and went to feed the two donkeys that had been outside. Too bad they couldn't describe the intruder on his property, but they hardly had the eyesight of those cats up in the loft. When he stopped by to see Ray-Lynn Freeman tomorrow about the arrangements for their church's manger scene, he'd give her a note for the sheriff telling him someone had been trespassing, and he had no clue who.

After she'd popped into *Daad*'s office at the furniture store the next morning and got permission to fill a rush Christmas order, Lydia lingered a moment, then asked, "I just wondered if *Mamm* told you about Josh and me using a cell phone. You didn't bring it up at breakfast, but…I just wondered," she repeated.

He looked up again from behind his big desk. "*Ya,* she did. And later told me you were both speaking with Josh's friend from Columbus, Sandra Myerson. I met her, you know."

He ignored Lydia's small gasp and went on, "She asked for an interview about how a big Amish-owned-and-staffed business operates. Since she said she was a friend of yours, I told her she could drop by. She came after most here, including you, had left."

Lydia leaned against the door to steady herself. That woman had dared to meet her father—her adoptive father—to interview him? And just about his Amish business? Sandra had probably slid in a couple of questions about his family and about her. What if he guessed that Lydia had been asking around about her birth parents?

"You look surprised, Liddy," *Daad* said. "Sit down. And close the door because I discussed some interesting things with her."

On shaky legs, Lydia closed the door and sat perched on the edge of a chair across from his desk. She had to remind herself to breathe. Had Sandra risked asking him if his daughter was adopted? But he'd not alluded to that, not seemed different lately, except maybe more tired and distracted.

"When was she here?" Lydia asked.

"Not sure what day it was." He gave her a little smile. "One of the days she was running amok in town, I suppose."

So he knew all about that. Realizing there was an awkward silence, Lydia said, "Josh is sorry about loosing her on everyone. As *Mamm* said, she can be pushy and she doesn't understand our ways."

"Despite it all, I liked her."

"You did?"

"She has a fine mind and she really loved my quilts. Of course, I didn't tell her I had made them, but I almost did. She bought two off the floor here and said she wished she could afford more. She went on and on about the designs and workmanship, which, of course, she thought was work-womanship."

Lydia breathed an audible sigh. They had talked about quilts. "They are wonderful and should be admired as well as used."

"I don't mean to be prideful, but she made some clever observations I had not thought about, not in all the hours I spend making them."

"Oh. Like what?"

"She recognized that the quilts, even ones unsigned by our people, are expressions of a personality, not just fabric but stories. And she must have had some hard times in her life because she asked if quilts ever— what was her word?—*memorialized* a love one who died. She talked about the Christmas season, too, how it brought back sad memories as well as happy ones."

Lydia twisted the paper in her hand so hard it

reminded her of how *Grossdaad* used to wring a chicken's neck before *Grossmamm* plucked and fried it. So Sandra had been fishing for information, maybe hoping *Daad* would bring up his son's death and say something about his daughter. Lydia had suspected for years that some of *Daad*'s quilts with squares of fabric that looked like dark, rocky water were made while he was missing Sammy—a silent memorial to the drowned boy. And Sandra was right that memories of Christmases past could be painful. Sammy had always been so excited on Christmas day.

"She's right, you know," *Daad* continued, interrupting her agonizing. He leaned forward in his chair with his hands folded before him on his desk. "At Christmas, the past is present again. Those we've loved who have gone on before, people who have not walked the earth for years, are in our minds and hearts again. A holiday time warp, Sandra called it. But the best thing she said was that when you see a quilt, if you look closely, you see a soul. See a quilt, see a soul, was how she put it."

Lydia nodded, noting her father was lost in his own thoughts, his eyes distant, not on her now. It was true that Sandra could be almost two people, helpful and kind or contrary and pushy. She guessed that if Sandra made a quilt, and if "See a quilt, see a soul" was true, the design would be a big, open mouth. But would it be a mouth puckered up to kiss a man she'd once dated and might still want?

Josh stopped at the Dutch Farm Table Restaurant when he knew the lunch crowd would be thinned out and the early dinner rush would not have yet begun.

With his copy of the list of animals and the time of delivery for the Homestead Community Church just outside of town, he sat at the end of the counter and waited for Ray-Lynn. To his surprise, she came back and took the tall, rotating chair next to his.

"Thanks for stopping by. I've got the down payment for you." She slid a check toward him on the counter. "A check's okay, isn't it?"

"Fine, thanks. I just wanted to go over a few things with you. The camel will not be ridden, but Mary, with Joseph walking beside her, will make an entrance on the donkey, right?"

"Yes. I hope it's not a rainy or cold night since we're obviously doing this alfresco."

"The basic three-sided manger you've asked for will block some of the wind and put a roof over the heads of the central figures, though bad weather would sure cut down on viewers driving by in buggies or cars."

"And freeze the four girls who are going to be angels and stand on top of a back platform we're building for them."

"It was probably a cold night when Jesus was born, too—real to life. By the way, this camel is well behaved but put out the word people should not come too close or startle her. I'll be there, but just a word to the wise."

"My husband thought of that already—no problems, no lawsuits. By the way, will Lydia be coming, too, or your helper, ah…Henry?"

"Hank. He'll be dropping me off with the animals but will be leaving early for his son's birthday. Whoever plays the shepherds will have to keep an eye on the three sheep. They love to do their own thing."

"Don't we all?"

"Ray-Lynn, I've written a short note to the sheriff about someone hanging around outside my barn last night—spooked my donkeys and spooked me." He extended it to her. He'd decided not to mention little Amos because he didn't want the sheriff questioning him and getting the kid in trouble with his parents. He wouldn't have brought the intruder up at all with worldly law enforcement, except that Victoria had died on his land and Lydia had been harassed nearby.

"Could it be the same guy who scared Lydia, the son of that man whose car hit her birth parents?" Ray-Lynn asked.

"She told me you knew about her quest to learn more about them and that she'd told you about Leo Lowe showing up and threatening her."

"She said you and that Myerson woman were helping her, though I guess she's been a bit out of control and needs to be stopped."

"*Ya,* don't we wish. If she comes back for a quick visit, I'll put an end to her 'Amish research' if I can."

"But you used to be close, right? I mean the two of you—Sandra and you, so—"

He frowned at her, and she stopped in midthought.

"A good friend from the city," he said, "but one who doesn't fit in here or with my new life, my real life." He stood up to leave. "See you with a menagerie in tow, Ray-Lynn. Will the sheriff be there?"

"He'd better be because he's on the committee with Mrs. Sheriff, but you know how sudden problems can take first place sometimes. I married the man and the job, and that's the way it should be."

"I hope to have a marriage like that," he said, then realized he was about to confide to the woman in town who probably talked to more people than anyone else. He trusted her on business matters, but on ones of the heart? "Thanks," he added, picking up his bill and hat as he headed out. "For everything."

After work, Lydia couldn't believe Josh wasn't in the barn feeding the animals and waiting for her. She couldn't find him anywhere. She knew the Beiler boys couldn't be working tonight as they'd both managed to come down with bad chest colds. The handwritten note on the desk in the barn said so.

Nor was Josh over at his house. She'd already checked, rung the doorbell and knocked on the back door. The house was dark, the sky was darkening, and she was getting nervous.

Taking one of his flashlights, she even looked in the stables and his large, back storage shed—garden tools, a hand push lawnmower, rolled-up wire fencing, a volleyball or badminton net stretched across the wall, but no sign of Josh. Worse, his unhitched horse and buggy were here. Her heart began to pound. She'd checked that all the animals seemed to be in the barn, so he wasn't out searching for one.

She saw something protruding from behind the shed and, her heart thudding, she went back to look. He didn't own any big farm machinery.

Sandra's red car! It glowed scarlet in the flashlight beam. So she *was* back, maybe had been for a while, and Josh didn't want anyone to know, so he'd had her park here. Maybe they were in the house together, not answering the doorbell and ignoring her knocking.

She flashed the beam of light in the car. Of course, no one was in the front or backseats. She touched the sleek red hood. Oh, still faintly warm, so she must not have been here long. But where was she—and Josh? Hurrying out from behind the shed, Lydia looked up at the second-floor bedroom windows. Dark. No one was up there. Or were they?

Her stomach clenched. Had Sandra been coming back secretly, and Josh tried to keep others, especially her, from knowing? But to leave his animals when it was feeding time...

Lydia stomped back through the snow to the barn and went in. She'd feed his animals for him, but if he and Sandra were meeting in secret, that was that. She bent to her work, tears in her eyes, making two Mellys, two bags of grass hay feed.

She'd trusted Josh, cared for him, but something could still be wrong here. Lydia fed the sheep, who *baaed* in thanks before sticking their snouts in the feed, and then she tended to the cantankerous donkeys. She remembered Josh had been taking a pan of milk up to the cats in the loft and wondered if they'd been fed.

Feeling drained, still fighting back tears, she rounded the camel pens toward the distant corner of the straw-strewn barn floor beneath the haymow loft. The ladder was there, not straight up, but tipped at a strange angle.

When Lydia saw what lay beneath, she shrieked so loud the animals shied and snorted, kicking their pens. In a leather coat, slacks and boots, her gloves on, Sandra lay sprawled on the floor of the barn, her limbs positioned all wrong, her head twisted at a terrible angle. A puddle of blood had formed under her open mouth. She didn't move, and her unblinking eyes stared straight at Lydia.

13

Lydia stared in horror. Sandra looked dead. Lydia leaned over to peer closer but couldn't bear to touch her. She must have gone up the ladder to see the kittens and she fell. That's exactly what it looked like.

Lydia felt she shouldn't leave her, yet she wanted to flee. At first her feet would not even move. Where was Josh?

She turned and tore out of the barn to her buggy. She had to get the sheriff, maybe the emergency squad—the coroner. The Starks owned the closest phone so she headed in that direction.

"Giddyap! *Schnell! Schnell!*" she cried to Flower, and the buggy lunged forward. She turned out onto the road and drove past her house. *Daad*'s buggy was just going into the barn so he was home early for once. No light in the kitchen. *Mamm* had been delivering loaves of friendship bread lately but she was usually home by now.

As dusk deepened, the Stark acreage with its rows of pines and spruces flew past. She turned Flower into their driveway, but an SUV heading toward her with a big Christmas tree tied to its roof made her pull up and get the buggy off the lane. Under strings of lights at the sales and hospitality shed, shoppers were paying for their trees or waiting while they were put in net bags. A few stood around with hot drinks, talking.

Of course, someone would have a phone out here, and she wouldn't need to go all the way up the hill to the house. Lydia turned Flower a sharp right toward the lighted area.

To her surprise and relief, the first person she saw was Bess, sitting in the golf cart Connor sometimes used to ride around on their land. She must have been talking to the workers and customers. When Lydia reined in, jumped down and rushed toward her, she saw there were two loaves of *Mamm*'s distinctively wrapped bread on the seat beside Bess.

She had started to drive away but stopped when she saw Lydia and got out. "Lydia, are you all right? Your mother just left if you're looking for her."

Ordinarily, the fact *Mamm* had so much as set foot anywhere near Stark land would have been a shock, but Lydia was beyond that. She tried to whisper so everyone wouldn't hear.

"I need help—a phone." Her voice sounded shrill and much too loud.

Bess put an arm around her shoulders. "What is it?"

"Please call the sheriff and tell him there's been an accident at the Yoder barn."

"Josh is hurt?"

"His friend Sandra Myerson. I think she's dead— fell from the ladder or the haymow loft."

"Oh, no! Where's Josh?"

"Don't know."

Bess reached back onto the floor of the cart and grabbed a small phone. A young Amish worker Lydia knew, Silas Kline, a man her age, smiled and waved at her, but she felt frozen in place, her face a mask of ice. Bess pulled Lydia away from the lights and people. Her feelings were so jumbled she hardly heard what Bess was saying into the phone at first.

"Yes. Yes, the same Yoder barn. Yes, Bess Stark making the call for Lydia Brand." Bess punched off her phone. "Lydia, let one of our helpers care for your horse and buggy and come with me." Bess took her hand as if she were a child. "I'll go back with you, wait with you. We'll find Josh."

Bess led Lydia to the golf cart and sat her inside it. Lydia watched as Bess spoke with Silas, pointing to her buggy. He nodded and gave Lydia another quick glance. Bess got in the cart beside her. It made a humming sound as they zipped up the hill. In the triple-car garage there were only two cars. She saw Connor's was out. Bess took a key off a hook and put Lydia in the front seat of her car, even snapped her seat belt closed for her.

"You talked to the sheriff?" Lydia asked as Bess got in the other side and started the engine. Her thoughts were running together, all around.

"No, his 9-1-1 operator. She's sending him and the E.R. squad. After all, Ms. Myerson may not be dead."

Bess turned her bright lights on and drove fast down the hill, honking to get a couple of people out of the way near where they were selling the trees. She turned left on the road and sped up even more.

"I—I couldn't bear to touch her," Lydia admitted.

"Speaking of which, she sure touched a lot of sore

spots around here. I heard about her *Candid Camera* trick at the Dutch Farm Table, and Connor had to ask her to leave when she got pushy at our house." She heaved a sign, then added in a rush, "I'm glad I didn't talk to her."

That's right, Lydia recalled, though her thoughts seemed soaked in molasses. And after Connor got rid of Sandra, she'd been arrested for speeding, so at least the sheriff already knew her. Thank heavens, Sandra hadn't bothered Bess like she had so many others.

Bess slammed the car to a stop outside Josh's barn, and they rushed in. The animals seemed restless, as if they knew what had happened. Still no Josh, but a flashlight sat upright near Sandra's body. He must have been here just now, but why did he need a flashlight when lanterns still lit the barn?

Lydia began to shake. Had Sandra lain here when Lydia first arrived and began to look for Josh and then fed the animals? If she'd found her sooner, would she have still been alive?

"Wait, I hear a buggy!" Lydia cried and ran back to the front barn door they'd just come in. It was Josh, urging Blaze to a gallop out of his driveway.

"Josh!" she shouted, cupping her hands around her mouth. "Josh, I got help! Bess is here, too!"

He reined in at the bottom of his driveway, then turned the buggy sharply toward her. Surely, he had not been running away. He must have been going for help.

He didn't even tie Blaze to the hitching post but tossed the reins and leaped out of the buggy. "She's dead—inside, Sandra," he cried. "Fell from the loft or ladder!"

"I know. I saw her. Where were you?"

"For a while, hiding in the woodlot, waiting to see if the intruder came back toward the barn."

"Hiding? What intruder? I—"

Bess came out to them through the barn door. Her sharp voice interrupted Lydia's questions. "Best you two come inside and wait for the sheriff. He'll want to talk to both of you, and you shouldn't compare notes. It looks like an accident, but you never know."

Josh blurted, "Sandra told me she would come back just to see the barn animals—especially the kittens in the loft. She should have waited for me."

"Come inside," Bess insisted. They walked slowly toward her. "Listen, you two, there will probably be questions, an investigation, and I will help either or both of you if you need it. I know your people don't trust or use lawyers, but just keep what I said in mind. It took a couple of days to close the case when my sister died, but this will take at least as long. Come on now, let's sit down to wait. I just hope this doesn't turn into a media circus. Oh, I think I hear a siren."

Ya, she was right. A distant shrill sound pierced the crisp night air, but Lydia saw no blinking lights down the road yet. She felt so blessed to have Bess here. She leaned slightly against her as the older woman put her arm around her shoulders again and they went inside with Josh out of the cold night air.

But was Bess suggesting this could be murder? A lot of people didn't like Sandra, but surely with that ladder tipped…the kittens in the loft… Of course, it could have been set up, but surely not by Josh.

At least, Lydia thought as they went into the barn and the animals looked up and stared, Josh's explanation meant he didn't even know Sandra had parked behind his shed. And they hadn't been together in the house or the loft—had they?

As if the nightmare of Victoria Keller's death was haunting him again, Josh saw the sheriff rush into his barn, which had once been a haven for him and his animals. The volunteer emergency squad arrived and pronounced Sandra dead, then the sheriff phoned the coroner while Josh, Lydia and Bess waited in his office area. His bringing Sandra here in the first place was a terrible decision, but it wasn't his fault she'd turned out to be poison. Everything had happened so fast—out of his control.

Once the coroner arrived, it seemed an eternity before Sheriff Freeman left the far corner of the barn where the body lay and approached them. "Josh, I'd like to talk to you first since Ms. Myerson was your friend and her death was on your property. From a card we found in her purse, we got next of kin and made that call. Her purse was in the loft, so she did climb up there. It's all roped off now, but, of course, I'll leave the animal pens and stalls accessible for you."

"Next of kin is her mother in Akron?" Josh asked.

"That's right. I called the local police there, and they'll go to her door. No good to get a call after dark in the holiday season—but then there's no good time for this."

"Can't you question Lydia first so she can go home? What are they doing with the can of spray paint over there, anyway?"

"No, Lydia needs to stay for a while. They're outlining the body, so we can study how she fell later, match it with any internal injuries."

"My flashlight has a ring around it, too."

"Standard procedure since it's in the vicinity of the body."

Josh's stomach clenched. His prints would be on the flashlight, but so what? He had to stay steady. He'd seen too many forensic and criminal TV shows when he'd lived in the world.

"A BCI tech's on the way from Columbus, too," the sheriff said. "He'll take a lot of photos. BCI, Lydia and Josh, is Bureau of Criminal Investigation. We rural sheriffs call in help when it's needed."

"Criminal investigation?" Josh demanded before realizing he was speaking much too loud. "You don't think she just fell off the ladder?"

"How 'bout I ask the questions, starting with—" he turned toward Bess and Lydia "—Bess. Would you mind waiting with Lydia at the other side of the barn by the front door? I'll be over to talk to her soon as I can, then she can go home. If you need to leave before Lydia does, I'll be sure she gets there safe and sound."

"Of course, Sheriff," Bess said, getting to her feet. Josh was glad she was taking care of Lydia. "By the way, I know the attorney general who oversees the BCI, if you need anything special. I think they do a good job, but they're not as low-key as they used to be. No more flying under the media radar since he likes the publicity of protecting the public. I intend to call him anyway and tell him this is in no way connected to my sister's death and I want him to keep a lid on the two-women-die-on-same-property angle. Come on, then," Bess said to Lydia, and Josh watched them walk away.

He blinked back tears as Lydia patted Melly and Gaspar on her way past them. It was the first time it had occurred to him that Lydia had obviously fed the animals. But as distraught as he was, it wasn't the first time it had hit him what a great wife she would be.

As soon as they were alone, Josh told the sheriff, "I had that ladder nailed down, and I can't figure how it came loose. If someone loosened it, it wasn't me."

"Listen, Josh," Sheriff Freeman said as he sat down next to him, "I gotta warn you that the BCI guys aside, the Columbus media, probably Cleveland folks, too, are gonna swarm in here with questions and cameras. No matter how much clout Bess Stark has, they'll jump on the two women dying on the same property, all that. I don't know what your past with the deceased was, but the press will ferret it out. You think Sandra caused a stir with her camera, you haven't seen anything yet. And here I thought," he added with a sigh, "after the other upheavals round here, we were gonna have a nice, peaceful holiday season. It won't help that Senator Bess Stark was in on it, either—another news angle they'll exploit."

Josh put his elbows on his knees and his head in his hands. At least the sheriff already knew about his intruder and that Leo Lowe had threatened Lydia. Sheriff Freeman wouldn't think he was making it up, since there was another witness. Josh had not wanted to get young Amos Baughman in trouble with his parents for trying to ride the donkey, but he was going to have to give the sheriff the boy's name.

Josh wasn't an idiot. He'd lived in the world and

heard media stories of murders. If there was any chance of foul play, they always looked at the husband or boyfriend of a dead woman first—former boyfriends, too. At least the sheriff had not read him his rights—and as an Amish man, he would not call in a lawyer, anyway. Man, he wished this would not have happened! For Sandra, of course, for himself... for Lydia. And Sheriff Jack Freeman was looking at him with narrowed eyes and a poised pen on paper as if he were waiting for a confession right now.

Lydia felt she was standing outside herself, like this was happening to someone else. After the sheriff talked with Josh for about a half hour, he sat down with her on a bale of straw near the front door of the barn. Josh had hooked a kerosene lantern to a big beam over their heads. He had nodded at her. She could tell he tried to smile to buck her up, but his face seemed gaunt and stiff, not his own. They were both in disbelief, like this was some horrible nightmare.

It scared her silly that it could become common knowledge that Sandra had come to the Home Valley to help her find her birth parents. Worse, if the sheriff thought for one moment that either Josh or Lydia would lure her into the barn, then push her off the loft or ladder, he was dead wrong. *Ach,* why had she thought of it that way?

"Sorry you had to be the one to find both bodies," Sheriff Freeman said as he sat on the bale of straw catty-corner from her. "Pretty bad coincidence."

"The Lord must have wanted it that way for some reason we can't understand. His ways are higher than ours."

"That's for sure. Speaking of high, were you ever up in that loft?"

"*Ya,* once to see the new kittens, the same reason Sandra was probably up there. Josh said she loves cats and wanted to see them."

"Did she? Josh told you that, huh? When were you up in the loft, and were you alone?"

"No. Josh was showing the kittens to me. Let's see, today's Wednesday. It was—I think it was last Thursday."

"That would be November 29," he said, writing even that down. "Did the ladder seem steady to you when you climbed it? Did it shake or tip?"

"It seemed steady."

Her voice was quavering. She was afraid she was going to get sick to her stomach. She told him in a rush, "That Leo Lowe I told Ray-Lynn about was angry with Sandra as well as with me."

"I remember that, and that he was lurking in this area. I'll find him and talk to him. Calm down now. I'll be having a chat with several folks in town who had run-ins with Ms. Myerson in case this is not an accidental death. Coroner will rule on the cause ASAP."

"Will you be talking to Mayor Connor Stark?"

He glanced up and looked her straight in the eye. "Who told you he had a run-in with her?"

"Bess mentioned it tonight."

"Anyone tell you before tonight?"

"Actually, it was Ray-Lynn."

"That right? Then I must have been the source for that, and I'll have to have a chat with her about what to say and not to say." He leveled another stern look at her, then looked back at his notes.

That was a good thing because Lydia could feel herself beginning a blush. What if he thought she was withholding information? The last thing she wanted to do was get Ray-Lynn in trouble or Connor, either, but should she tell the sheriff about how Connor had threatened the two caretakers who had worked for the Starks? Still, she didn't want to upset Bess, who had been so kind to help tonight.

But now that she was thinking clearly again, Lydia realized getting Ray-Lynn and Connor in trouble was the least of her worries. The worst would be if her parents learned why Sandra came to visit in the first place. But she might have to admit that publicly so it didn't look like Sandra just came to see Josh, maybe to start up their relationship again, which could have panicked or angered him.

Her mind raced. The sheriff might interview Hank, who could mention how upset Josh was with Sandra lately, how he'd yelled at her over Hank's phone when they visited Hillside. After all, Josh and Sandra had some sort of emotional past, and he still had a bad habit of losing his temper. But surely, *surely,* Josh couldn't have a thing to do with Sandra's death.

14

"You're late," Ray-Lynn greeted her husband at the back door of their mudroom. "I thought you said you'd be coming home early, and I was worried."

He hugged her hard—no kiss—then pulled away to hang up his utility belt. It didn't take much to realize he was really upset.

"Something big came up, and I didn't have time to call you," he said. "Sandra Myerson's dead. She evidently fell off a twelve-foot-high loft or a ladder at the Yoder barn and broke her neck. Least that's the early guess—and my hope that's all that happened."

"That's terrible! You—you don't mean it could be a suspicious death?"

"Dang it, Ray-Lynn, you're starting to think like me. If it turns out that way, you'll probably be the first to know—and not because I told you. That gab 'n' gossip you got going in the restaurant's better than using Google online."

"You sound angry with me." She put her hands on her hips, then just crossed them over her breasts. But after he untied his shoes and kicked them off, she rubbed his back lightly. His muscles felt like carved wood.

"Not exactly, just angry in general," he muttered, his back still to her. "It's really gonna hit the fan tomorrow—outside law enforcement, media, and at this time of year. Better get some more food into the Dutch Farm Table 'cause the swarms of meddlers will be there with cameras a hundred times bigger than Sandra Myerson's and questions that make her annoying Q and A in the restaurant seem like nothing."

"You keep coming back to that. Jack, the so-called restaurant gab 'n' gossip is not only a big part of our livelihood but our outreach to the community. More than once, gab 'n' gossip I've related to you has helped you solve a crime and helped me help others."

She followed him into the kitchen. She'd tried to keep his dinner warm, then had put it in the fridge. Taking it out now, she placed it in the microwave and punched in the time. Of course, he was upset, but she was, too. He knew when he married her that her relationships at the restaurant—the hospitality at the restaurant itself—meant everything to her. And she was helping him, not hurting him, by what she learned there. Couldn't his job be part of their partnership as much as hers was?

"Aw, I know the benefits and blessings of the restaurant, honey," he said as if he'd read her mind. He almost collapsed into his chair at the table, stretching his back with his arms over his head. Despite the cold weather outside, he'd been sweating under his armpits. Nervous? Was he upset he had to, no doubt, grill Josh?

Lowering his arms and shaking his head, he said, "I'm just ticked off you hear some stuff before I do, that's all. Between the privacy the Amish cling to and this young woman's death, which is now gonna be breaking news—and break up this community in this supposed season of joy…"

"I know. It makes me sick, for Lydia, too. It makes Victoria Keller's loss seem small next to a young woman's death. Josh wasn't with her when she fell, was he?"

"He says no, that he was outside. Lydia found her, and that's bad news in more ways than one."

"That poor girl! She'd put such trust in Sandra, who turned out to be a Jekyll and Hyde."

He braced his elbows on the table and his head in his hands, not even moving when the microwave dinged and she put the hot plate of meat loaf, hash browns and creamed corn in front of him. Then, to her surprise and relief, he hooked one arm around her waist to hold her where she was, next to his chair.

In a softer voice, he said, "Sandra's take-no-prisoners approach to interviewing around here gives me a too-long list of persons of interest if there's any hint it's a murder and not an accident. I hope the Lord is especially tuned into prayers near Christmastime. I swear, I'm gonna outpray the Amish on this one."

"Because, if it was foul play, you'll have to look at Josh."

"And Lydia," he said, starting to pick at his food.

"What? No, you can't—"

"Shh, sweetheart. Here I go scolding you for knowing too much, and I'm still unloading on you. I gotta get me a new deputy in here so you and I can have more time—time where we're not talking about crimes. Sorry I blew up about the restaurant, but it just bugs me you know more than I do sometimes, and I know you've held things back."

"Only if I've promised someone." Without even being asked, she got him a beer and upcapped it. She put it down in front of him. "Glass for that, handsome?"

"No, I'm fine, and I'll be fine. Thanks, honey."

She sat catty-corner from him, leaning forward. "The thing is, Jack, if some of my sources thought I ran right to you, I'd never hear a thing."

"I just don't want info flowing in the other direction—stuff I tell you."

"I don't. I wouldn't! I kept my cool when you said the restaurant was a gab 'n' gossip place, but— I don't know why I thought I could be a small-town sheriff's wife!"

He raised his voice, too. "Lydia admitted to me you told her that Connor threw Sandra out of their little chat and then I got her for speeding."

"Lydia and I are becoming friends and, I guess, that just came out. Okay, I don't tell you everything, but you don't tell me everything, either. We have to work together to—"

"To make this marriage work," he cut in, grabbing her wrist before she could jump up from the table. "I want us to have lots of time together, but one more problem. You'll have to take me off the Living Christmas Pageant committee at church. Folks will understand. Besides, you'll do things just fine with it, and I'll still try to provide security from six to nine."

"I understand," she assured him, but she wished things wouldn't have to be so tense—and at Christmas. "Eat your food while it's hot." She squeezed his shoulder and stood up. Blinking back tears, she got herself a drink of water at the sink. The window above it was

like a big black mirror, except for the motion light over
the garage that popped on. Probably a deer had come
into the edge of town, looking for scarce winter food,
but she saw no deer. A human form scuttled from the
shadows into the darkness.

A neighbor out this late? The Collisters' house next
door looked dark. Could it have been her imagination?
No way did she want to send Jack out there to look
around. He might even think she'd made it up just to
change the subject or play up the way she always told
him she felt he protected her. Besides, someone could
have been out for a walk and was just hurrying home.
Some crazy joggers around here didn't care if there
was snow or ice underfoot.

"Ray-Lynn?" he said, rising and coming up behind
her to put his hands on her waist. "Let's not get all up-
tight, okay? Sorry I brought my work home with me
tonight, but it's been a real hard day. And if Josh Yoder
had anything to do with that woman's death, it's gonna
break a lot of hearts."

Lying in bed that night, Lydia wet her pillow with
tears. *Daad* had driven his buggy over to wait for her
outside the barn until the sheriff was finished interviewing her. He'd caught a chill, since he couldn't
come in. The front barn door as well as the loft and
the floor where Sandra fell had been closed off with
bright yellow police tape. Then *Daad* had insisted on
taking her over to the Starks' tree lot to get her buggy
back from the workers there. And when he'd gone
up to bed, after ordering her to stay away from Josh
and the barn after this latest catastrophe, *Mamm* had

started in on her as Lydia had sat at the kitchen table while *Mamm* had kneaded bread dough.

"It's a sign to you from God that you've defied us to work over there with that man and his animals." *Mamm*'s words still rang in her ears. "You want to work with animals, marry an Amish dairy farmer. You don't want to let Gid be your come-calling friend, you want to let the store your grandfather and father have worked to build up—with Gid's help—slip from control of our family while you milk cows or get up at the crack of dawn to shove hens aside to take their eggs, then—"

"Mamm," she'd cried, "this isn't about me. A woman is dead."

"Probably Josh's woman, at least while he left our people," *Mamm* went on, thumping her fist into the pile of dough, not even looking at Lydia. *"Ach,* and who knows why she kept coming back, and you getting more and more sweet on that man! He should go live in the world with his old friends, have electric in his house, drive a car…and get his own cell phone."

Lydia couldn't help but think that she'd rather go through another talk with the sheriff instead of one with *Mamm.* When he'd asked her to go step-by-step through what she'd done when she arrived on Josh's land today, she'd told him about Sandra's car parked behind Josh's shed. But she hadn't told him at first that she was afraid they might be upstairs together. She had mentioned that the hood of the car—the engine, as the sheriff had put it—was still warm. To Lydia that meant Sandra and Josh could not have had much time together, even if he knew she had arrived, but Jack

Freeman had not wanted to hear her theories—only what had actually happened.

It made her wonder about his own theories. Hopefully, he believed that Josh had told the truth about not seeing Sandra until he found her dead. She prayed Josh and Sandra hadn't argued in person like they had on the phone, maybe while they were up in the loft, looking at the kittens. If Sandra was afraid of being around the big animals, would she have gone into the barn without Josh?

"Are you listening to me?" *Mamm* had demanded. "I said, you're always going to the Starks for something or other."

"I saw the bread you left there for them. At this season of Christmas, you reached out to them, and that made me happy to see—"

"Not that I wanted to go there."

"And you brought a loaf to Josh when I was over there. Can't we just all get along and—"

"Lydia, we are Amish, not *Englische*, not those who cuddle up to the rich and powerful. Maybe I took that bread over to the Starks—and there was Bess, so I gave it to her—because the Word says if you 'feed your enemy, thou shalt heap coals of fire on his head. Be not overcome of evil, but overcome evil with good.'"

"But the Starks aren't our enemies—only different. I know their ways are not our ways, but they have been kind and—"

"Enough said. You needed a phone fast, so you ran there. Enough said for one night or one lifetime," she'd muttered, and turned back to making her friendship bread—yes, even late into the night—without another word.

Now Lydia kept trying to fall asleep but she'd cried so hard she couldn't breathe out of her nose. She reached for a tissue on her bedside table. She still couldn't bear to tell her parents why Sandra had come to town the first time, why Lydia had gone with her to Wooster. And what had Sandra meant when she told both her and Josh that she had something else important to tell Lydia and it would best be told in person? It must have been more information on her birth parents. And shouldn't she have told the sheriff that so he didn't think Sandra came back here to settle an argument with Josh?

She wiped tears away and blew her nose. Then on a whim, from under her bed she pulled out the pillow in its plastic sack, the one she'd bought the day she went to Amity to interview Mr. Raber, who had known her real father.

Her real father... She should not think of it that way. Who could have been a more real, loving father to his Liddy than Sol Brand had been? And now, because he had waited for her in the cold and insisted she get her buggy back from Silas Kline over at the Starks', he had evidently caught a cold. She could hear him coughing from down the hall, so *Mamm* would blame her for that, too.

In the dark, Lydia let her fingers run over the stitching on the pillow she'd bought for *Mamm,* then decided to hold it for Christmas. Mothers Are Forever, it said, and to Lydia, in secret, it would always mean both of her mothers. She knelt again by the bed and pulled out the snow globe *Daad* had said belonged to her birth mother—but he'd vowed he would say no more on that. When he felt better, when things calmed down around here and the coroner declared Sandra's death an accident, dare she ask him more about the globe? He'd said someone had dropped it off at the store, but who?

As she shook it—though she could not see it in the dark—its smooth plastic slipped from her hand. She heard it hit the wood floor and felt the gush of its glittery liquid on her bare feet.

"Oh, no! Oh, no! Please, Lord, no!" she whispered as she knelt and felt for it.

Its gooey insides were in a small puddle on the floor. Feeling along, she found first the plastic dome, then its base with the hovering angel, Christmas tree and the little girl. She got back in bed, sat cross-legged and cradled the pieces on her lap. She'd fix them somehow, put water inside, glue the dome back on, even if the lost glitter never made it snow again. But could she fix the mess she'd made of things, still obsessed with learning more about her biological parents, still wanting to meet her birth mother's Hostetler kin?

And Josh—loving Josh, wanting Josh, believing in Josh, when so much as being near him might be even harder now.

Midmorning the next day, Josh saw Hank approach the back door of the barn in his truck. Right now that was the only way into the barn, but at least, because of the animals, the sheriff had not barred that door. Hank must have figured out either from the neon-colored police tape across the front of the barn or by having to honk his way through the crowd of TV trucks out front that this was the best way in.

"The sheriff came by and told the reporters they'd have to stay off the property, but they're like a swarm

of wasps out there," Hank said. "They're staying on
the road but shouting questions at me like I was the
president—or at least Congresswoman Stark." He
grasped Josh by his shoulders hard—a kind of hug,
he figured.

"You know what happened?" Josh asked.

"It's not in the papers or on the TV yet, but it will
be," Hank told him. "Yeah, I know. Sheriff came to
the house to interview me at the crack of dawn and
filled me in. I told him that you told Sandra to keep
away in no uncertain terms, so she shouldn't even have
been back here."

Josh just nodded. He hadn't slept and he felt dizzy
and weak-kneed. If Hank thought revealing that was
doing him a favor, he didn't realize it could work
against him, too.

Hank said, "One more thing you ought to know,
because the sheriff does. I was saving this to tell you
today." He took out his cell phone. "He made a recording of this, but at least he didn't confiscate my cell,
'cause we've got events to work on and set up today.
You—you are still wanting to work, aren't you?"

"Sure. Why wouldn't I be, except it's been a long,
sad night. I'm grieving not only for Sandra, but for
her mother and for the friends we had in common in
Columbus."

"Yeah, well, I'll bet they'll talk if those wasps out
there can find them. So—so how tight were you and
Sandra?"

"She dazzled me at first. That's the word for it. She
was so different—assertive. And I'm sure I was some
kind of novelty for her, too. How about that's all I say

in case the sheriff comes back for a second chat with you? But why would he want to take your cell phone?"

"Oh, yeah, got off the track there for a sec. Because Sandra left a voice message on it for you, came in yesterday afternoon, I guess. She said— Well, here, I still got it, though, like I said, the sheriff made a copy of it."

Hank touched the screen to get voice mail and held it up for him. Josh shivered to hear her voice again.

"Hi, Hank. Sandra Myerson here. Message for Josh Yoder. I've learned something interesting about Lydia's mother, but I'll save it to tell either you or her. I wasn't going to tell her at first because it's pretty upsetting. But I'm coming back to show you I can face those camels, cows and whatever else you have stashed in that barn. Maybe you'll let me have a kitten for old times' sake, or are they too young to leave their mother? Can't wait to see them. Josh, don't be mad at me. Sorry we had that fight. We can make up and be close again, even if we're apart. See you soon."

Josh stood transfixed. Something about Lydia's mother. Her birth mother, evidently. But he was analyzing what the sheriff would have learned from this message. It was good she'd said she planned to go up in the loft, but bad news that she'd said he was mad at her. And be close again? The only woman he wanted to be close to was the one this scandal might have made him lose forever.

15

By midafternoon the day after Sandra's death, the parking lot and front yard of the Brand Amish furniture store looked as if it was having a yard sale. Reporters' cars and television trucks sprouting antennae took most of the parking spaces, forcing buggies and customers' cars onto the snow-covered lawn. Some of their customers milled around outside, looking at the biggest vehicles. Live at Five, Cleveland News, one truck had written large on its side. Another read, Six on Your Side, Columbus.

Even the brisk, icy wind did not deter them. In came a small group of men and one woman, straight toward Lydia's reception desk. One, no, two cameras! Naomi was running an errand back in the store, so she couldn't leave. The phone was ringing again, but Lydia didn't answer it because callers wanted interviews, not furniture. Without even picking up the receiver this time, she put the caller on hold. Was Josh facing the pestering press, too, or had they all come over here?

"Mike Jenson, *WCOL News,* Columbus," the tallest man said. "You are Lydia Brand? We learned in town this is where you work, that your family owns this store. You are—were—a friend of Sandra Myerson and Josh Yoder? How well did you know the deceased? What's your relationship to Mr. Yoder?"

"Yes, I'm Lydia, but I have nothing to say about all that. You should ask the sheriff—"

"I understand Mr. Yoder and the deceased had a past relationship they had broken off. Then why did she come to the Home Valley?"

Gid appeared with the megaphone they used to run the summer games for the staff. His voice boomed so loud through it that even Lydia jumped.

"Please leave the store unless you are shoppers," he announced. "This is a place of business, and we have just placed a sign on the front door allowing only customers here."

A long pole with something on the end of it swung away from Lydia toward Gid. The two men with cameras on their shoulders turned them toward him, too, then at *Daad* when he appeared, trying to usher people out. Oh, no, they were taking their pictures, capturing their images, as Bishop Esh always called it. "You have stolen me!" he had shouted one time at several people snapping pictures of his face. Sometimes the *Englische* just didn't understand that photographs violated God's law about not making graven images.

Some of the invading crowd—maybe only about ten people but it seemed a hundred—backed off a bit, but one man yelled at Gid, "You're interfering with freedom of the press!"

"The press," Lydia repeated when *Daad* hustled her away into his office and closed the door. "Now I know how those people got that name. Press, press, press for information, my relationship to Josh—"

"I hope your mother never sees a newspaper that talks about that."

"—and about how well I knew Sandra, like why she'd come to the Home Valley."

"And why did she?" *Daad* countered, then began a coughing fit. She poured him a glass of water from the pitcher on his desk. He slumped into his rocking chair. He meant why Sandra came back yesterday, not originally, Lydia figured. The aftermath of Sandra's death made her realize she needed to tell her parents about the search for David and Lena Brand before these meddlers turned it up. But she wanted to have her parents together for that, at home, not in this turmoil.

Keeping her voice calm, Lydia said, "She has been afraid of most animals for years and wanted to face up to that, get past it, so I guess that's why she went into the barn alone. I—I think she was also going to take a kitten from the haymow loft for a pet. And she probably wanted to say goodbye to Josh."

"Goodbye or a new hello? Your mother thinks it wasn't goodbye. By the way, you realize today is the day she's decided to bring in the loaves of bread for the entire staff."

"Oh, no! She didn't tell me, and if she gets into that mess outside…"

"I'd better go wait for her, get her in without being attacked by our visitors."

With a huge sigh, even a groan, as if getting to his feet was too much for him, *Daad* went out again. Lydia thought he looked so bad that maybe she should play the sacrificial lamb and face the media mob herself, hopefully get them to disperse. But if she was answering their questions and *Mamm* arrived… No, once *Mamm* saw what was going on here, surely she'd buggy right by.

Gid knocked, opened the office door, came in and closed it. He leaned against it. "Your mother's here. Sheriff Freeman is, too, and has made the raving horde get off the property. Now they're parked up and down the road instead. You'll be fair game once you're outside, so you might want to lie down in the back of my buggy and let me cover you up with a lap blanket, take you home a back way. Someone else can bring your buggy around to you later."

Lying down, covered up in Gid's buggy was not something that excited her, but it did seem practical. And he had been kind and controlled lately.

"I may take you up on that," she told him. "But they may try to question you, too."

He just snorted. "Of course, where it would be idiotic for you to go is to the Yoder barn—ever again. It's like the biblical handwriting on the wall, Lydia. This is all a warning to you." He held up his hands as if holding off the protest he knew was coming. "Don't argue. Let's go out into the workroom while your mother delivers her gifts. Sol, Susan, you and me. Let's present a united front in the face of this worldly chaos."

She agreed with him again and yet she didn't like the way he'd put that. It sounded as if they were all co-owners of the store, even family. Gid was slowly but surely trying to corral her, she thought, just the way she herded stray animals in, not with shouts and quick movements but with a steady hand and calm talk.

Lydia went out with him and headed through the

now-quiet showroom toward the large back workshop. She realized that, for once, Gid wasn't going to wear the plastic oxygen mask he sometimes used in the workroom because he was so sensitive to the smells of shellac and stains. He held the door for her, and she went in to join her parents.

Unlike Gid, she had always loved the smells of the low-ceilinged, large workroom where Amish craftsmen of different ages sanded, stained, buffed and assembled the furniture, those pieces at least that weren't finished throughout the valley in what *Daad* called "the cottage industry part of our shop." Today the distinctive scent of cinnamon from *Mamm*'s bread mingled with the smell of sawdust and wood stains. Gid took out a handkerchief and blew his nose, but of course, he wouldn't want *Mamm* to know even the smell of her bread could bother him, too.

The twenty-four men and six sweep-up boys who were being apprenticed had left their tasks and gathered in the middle of the shop. They surely knew what was coming since *Mamm* was there with her sacks of bread every year. Two weeks' extra wages in a plain envelope with a thank-you card came later.

Gid held up his hands for quiet. "It's not quite Christmas yet, but a good time to kick off the season of giving," he announced in his strong voice, which did not need a megaphone. "Those of you who are veterans here know that means Susan Brand's delicious friendship bread. That's the perfect name for it since we consider all of you friends as well as fellow workers."

Gid was making himself one of the family again, Lydia thought. *Daad* had always made this speech before, but, with his cold, he'd probably asked Gid to do the talking. She'd just die if Gid, *Daad* or *Mamm* actually thought Gid would soon be her betrothed. For sure, she had to tell her parents three things fast, however bad *Daad* looked, however upset *Mamm* got. One, she'd stand her ground that she was still not going to get betrothed to Gid. Two, once the reporters left, she was going back to work with Josh and his animals, at least during this busy season of the year. And three, she would have to tell them that Sandra had actually come to the Home Valley the first time because their own daughter had asked for help tracing her birth parents.

The workers stepped forward in orderly file, each one typically giving way to the others while *Mamm,* not really smiling but more pleasant looking than Lydia had seen her in a while, handed out the loaves. Gid was the one smiling. And *Daad* grabbed at his chest, cried out and collapsed onto the concrete floor.

Josh had wiped off the large wooden assembly pieces that made up one of the two construct-on-site mangers he rented out, when he heard a car pull around in front and kill the engine. To his surprise, the front barn door opened. Someone was ignoring the police tape, and he'd have to warn them off. But Sheriff Freeman himself came in, looking as if he was in a hurry.

"I see the media mavens have decamped to the Brand furniture store," he said. He closed the barn door behind him.

"I was hoping they wouldn't go over there," Josh said, wiping his hands on the rag. "Is everyone there all right?"

"Yeah, far as I know. Heard tell they hid Lydia and

shooed everyone out, but I didn't go in, just cleared the media off their property. Her mother drove in with loaves of bread for the staff. Listen, Josh, I've got some bad news for you, which I haven't told anyone in the community yet. The autopsy on Sandra—"

"I didn't know they'd have to do that!"

"Calm down. Standard procedure with something like this. It indicated that a cylindrical object struck the back of her head. With the fall, that probably killed her, but more tests are to come."

"The blow to her head could be from when she fell and hit a rung of the ladder."

"Maybe. I'm gonna have you saw off a rung and take it with me. That flashlight of yours—it wasn't on the floor or in the haymow loft where she could have hit her head on it?"

Josh's eyes widened. The sheriff must suspect he'd hit her with the flashlight and shoved her out of the loft. He realized he was hesitating too long, but that was his biggest fear, that all this would somehow point to him. And hadn't Victoria Keller possibly died of a blow to the head, whether it was from her swinging the gate closed…or something else?

"No, I had the flashlight out in the woodlot—turned off—while I waited to see if that intruder materialized again."

"I talked to Amos Baughman about his ride-the-donkey fiasco. The kid wouldn't make up an intruder just to get you from blaming him, would he?"

Josh could read between the lines here. Cleverly, carefully, the sheriff was questioning him again, implying that if Amos had concocted an excuse for why he was thrown from the donkey, Josh could have con-

cocted that same intruder to get off being accused of
much worse. His stomach clenched. He tried to keep a
tight rein on his temper to avoid shouting at the sheriff
that he understood how he was tightening the screws.
If the Amish trusted worldly lawyers, which they did
not, he would have retained one quick.

"I don't think he made up the intruder any more
than Lydia made up Leo Lowe accosting her," Josh
said as slowly and as calmly as he could manage since
his heart was pounding hard enough to shake the raf-
ter beams.

"As a matter of fact, a visit to Mr. Lowe is on my
docket today."

"Here, Sheriff, let me saw off a ladder rung for
you, or as many as you'd like," he said. "Hope you
don't mind if I bring down the mother cat and her kittens first, at least until I get another ladder. I've been
feeding her."

"She climb that ladder—the mother cat, I mean?"
the sheriff asked as he followed Josh across the barn.
The animals were keeping quiet, Josh noticed, almost
as if they knew something was wrong or could go
very wrong.

"*Ya,* far as I know. I didn't ask the Beiler boys who
work here if they gave mama cat a boost up there in
the first place."

"I'll have to interview them, too, case they saw anything strange. Too bad your animals can't talk. Isn't
there some Christmas story where the animals in the
manger talk?"

"*Ya,* an old European legend, I think. Sandra mentioned it a couple of years ago when she started writing
about immigrant practices at Christmas. The legend

says the animals speak only on Christmas Eve, and people should not eavesdrop, or they'll hear that the beasts don't think much of their human masters— something like that. Another superstition she mentioned was that oxen will kneel each Christmas Eve in their stables in honor of the Christ child, too. I've got to admit I've seen them kneel, but not just at Christmas."

Josh realized he'd been yammering too much about Sandra's work and to the wrong person. Unbidden tears filled his eyes as he recalled all the talks he and Sandra had enjoyed when they were seeing each other. But had he really ever known her?

"I ought to get a copy of Sandra's work and let Ray-Lynn read it," the sheriff said, leaning closer as if to study each pore on Josh's face. "You think there's anything there that would help me know Sandra better, maybe info about someone she interviewed I don't know—someone she angered?"

"I couldn't say," Josh said, turning away. "You mind if I go up first to bring the cats down? I won't touch anything else up there."

"Sure. Fine. Everything up there's being tested for evidence by the BCI techs in their lab, or will be soon, so your leaving DNA now won't change a thing about what they find."

Again, Josh's insides twisted. How had all this happened? He blamed himself, but no way should he blurt that out.

Since the sheriff only wanted one rung, he changed his mind about going up. He went over by his office to get a saw when he heard the sheriff's phone beep. He spoke hurriedly to someone, nodding, frowning. More trouble with the media? Josh wondered.

"Saw me a rung off quick," the sheriff ordered. "That lower one. Sol Brand collapsed over at the furniture store, and they used the business phone to call for help. Probable heart attack. I'm going to lead the EMR to Wooster Community Hospital. His wife and Lydia are with him."

Though his hands were shaking, Josh cut off the lowest ladder rung as fast as he could and handed it to the sheriff as if he were brandishing a club. "Tell Lydia I'm very sorry, and I'll be praying," Josh said as they both sprinted toward the front door.

"Will do." Sheriff Freeman ducked under the tape outside and tore toward his cruiser.

It was only then that Josh realized that "tell Lydia I'm sorry, and I'll be praying," could have sounded like a confession of sorts, about Sandra's loss and not the rush to save Lydia's father.

"I'll take care of things here," Gid told them as Lydia wedged in next to *Mamm* on a hard bench along the side of the big, square, red EMR vehicle parked behind the furniture store. The driver slammed the door shut on the concerned faces of Gid and several staff, then got in the cab. They pulled quickly away. Lydia knew both local volunteer medics, one driving, one tending the IV drips in her father's arms. *Daad* looked absolutely gray-skinned around the edge of the oxygen mask. In truth, he looked dead, but the heart monitor said he was still alive.

Mamm gripped her hands, her own hands, rather than reaching for Lydia's. "Too much strain," *Mamm* whispered. "All this you got yourself into…"

In other words, Lydia thought as she tried to steady

herself and fight breaking down, *Mamm* believed this was her fault. Suddenly, telling either of her adoptive parents that she was searching for her birth parents seemed the height of stupidity and impossibility.

As they started out through town and sped past their house, the sheriff's car appeared from somewhere ahead of them, lights flashing, siren wailing to lead the way. She glimpsed Josh standing outside his barn. As they rushed past it looked as if the bright yellow police tape strung there had caught him in some strange spider's web.

Just like when Lydia was in Sandra's little red sports car, the houses and fields blurred by. *Daad* had to live. He just had to! Why hadn't they insisted he rest more, lie down, leave more store business to Gid at this busy time?

But that thought terrified her, too: What if *Daad* didn't make it? She would have to work more closely with Gid. The pressure from *Mamm* and the expectation from others would be overwhelming for her and Gid to become partners in more ways than one.

Suddenly, she recalled a saying—a superstition, her mother had called it. Years ago Connor had told Lydia that deaths came in threes and, back then in the community, they had. Now Victoria Keller was dead, Sandra was number two, but *Daad*—that was different, wasn't it?

When they turned onto Route 30 East toward Wooster, the same way she and Sandra had driven there, the EMR turned on its siren, too. Though somewhat muted by the vehicle's interior, the siren's sharp shrieks and *Mamm*'s awful sobbing stabbed deep inside Lydia. She reached out to *Daad*'s booted, bouncing foot and held on tight. If she lost him, she would be so alone, even in her own home.

16

That evening, Lydia and *Mamm* sat slumped in the surgery waiting room at the hospital. Their shoulders touched—at least something did. *Mamm* either kept her eyes closed or stared off into space. She had not drunk the tea Lydia had brought her from the cafeteria. How Lydia wished *Mamm* would say something, but, on the other hand, it might be more accusations.

Lydia guessed it was pretty much after hours for scheduled surgeries, because they were alone, like two strangers who hardly spoke.

Finally, around nine, a surgeon, Dr. Bryan, still dressed in his light green outfit, came out to talk to them. "Mrs. Brand?"

They both stood. "*Ya,* and our daughter, Lydia," *Mamm* said, and those few words brought more tears to Lydia's eyes.

"Solomon came through the procedure quite well. During the angioplasty I explained earlier, we inserted a stent, a wire mesh tube to keep the offending artery open. That will improve the blood flow to his heart and relieve the angina—the pain. With new medications and rest, he should make a full recovery. But time will tell."

"Thank you, Doctor," Lydia put in while *Mamm* just sucked in a sob and sat back down.

"One of you can stay in his room this evening, though he'll be heavily sedated. He'll be in cardiac care on the first floor. Mrs. Brand, have you thought of the name of his blood pressure medication? I know under the strain, neither of you could recall it before. Of course, we can phone his doctor for it tomorrow—"

"If *Maam* stays and I can find a way home, I can bring you the bottle of his pills so you can see the dosage and all," Lydia offered.

"Ya," Mamm said. "In the medicine cabinet in the bathroom. Sorry, I can't remember, but it was a strange name."

"I understand," Dr. Bryan said. "Lydia, can I call for a driver to take you back to Homestead?"

At that very moment, a miracle. Two miracles in one night, because she'd been praying *Daad* could live a normal life again. And now Hank stood in the door with car keys in his hands as if delivered by an angel. If only Josh could be with him!

"Just one moment," she told the doctor. "I see someone from home who has a truck." She hurried over toward Hank.

"Josh isn't here but he sent me," Hank blurted. "How's your dad doing?"

"As well as can be expected. A heart attack."

"Josh said that's what the sheriff thought."

"He was there questioning Josh again?"

"More or less. They did an autopsy on Sandra. It may have been a blow to her head. Hopefully—if I can say it that way—when she fell, not that someone hit her."

Though Lydia's stomach had felt cramped for hours, she felt worse now. "It can't be murder," she whispered, then shook her head to get back to this reality. "Hank, if you're heading home, I need a ride. My mother's going to stay, but I have to get some things for her and *Daad,* including the name of his medicine."

"Sure. That way you can report into Josh instead of me. But I'll be out of town tomorrow, so I can't bring you back here."

"You're a godsend as is. Just a minute."

She promised her mother and the doctor she'd be back with clothing and her father's medication first thing tomorrow.

"How did Josh's worker know to come?" *Mamm* asked as the doctor left them. She glanced over and nodded at Hank, even gave him a little wave.

"The sheriff told Josh, who called Hank, I guess. I'll be back as soon as I can tomorrow. Gid will have to run the store, then I'll try to get in to help him as soon as I can."

"*Ya,* you two work together, that's good." To Lydia's surprise, *Mamm* gave her a brief, stiff hug.

"Take good care of *Daad,*" Lydia said, and hurried away.

"You're not kidding, are you? So it might be murder?" Ray-Lynn asked Jack when he stopped at home for a quick sandwich and told her the current findings. As horrible as the possibility was that Sandra could have been killed, at least Jack was still confiding in her, though she knew all this would be common knowledge tomorrow.

He'd only taken two bites and was already on his way out the door again, sandwich in his hand. "I said the autopsy shows a blow to her head, that's all," he added, talking with his mouth full.

"But that could mean Victoria Keller's death might be murder, too. Maybe bumping into that gate didn't cause her death."

He turned back in the half-open door, despite the cold air swirling in around him. "Don't go doing my thinking for me, honey. The coroner's accident versus murder disclosure is going to hit the big newspapers tomorrow, and I'll be double busy. Thank God I've got the BCI techs helping. I think I can do the necessary interviews myself, but if not, I'll call in one of their agents, too."

She tugged him back in and closed the door. "So, am I supposed to tell you what I overhear at the restaurant tomorrow? My new manager and the servers sometimes report in to me so—"

"Marva is gonna work out as assistant manager? Hope so, to give you more free time. Then if I get a deputy in here, maybe we can live normal lives, but not now, not yet. Got burned with that last deputy, but I'm ready to try again. Thanks for the sandwich and the coffee. It's a bit of a drive to Parma." He reached for the doorknob again.

"Which means you're going to talk to that guy whose father killed Lydia's parents years ago?"

"Yeah. He's kind of a hothead—but then I get the feeling Josh Yoder has a temper, too."

"No way you're going to look at Josh for this attack!

I mean, you aren't, are you? Sandra Myerson ticked off a lot of folks around here in a very short time, and that guy you're going to interview had a motive, so please be careful."

"Now, why in all that's holy do I think I need a new deputy when I got you? Speaking of holy, the manger scene committee meeting go okay tonight?"

Ray-Lynn nodded. "Except I'm hoping you'll be there for the presentation to keep the peace. Last year in Youngstown, some kids intentionally scared the animals and—"

"I know, but with all this going on, I'm not gonna chase camels and donkeys across the fields beyond the church. Ray-Lynn, I gotta go, and you're obstructing justice, honey!"

He kissed her hard. His breath smelled of peanut butter, and he was rushing off again. But she loved him more than ever.

It was pitch-black as Hank's truck rolled through the countryside, heading home. Lydia felt exhausted but somehow alert. Hank had said that Josh was staying strong through all this, focusing on the animals and the sets for the coming manger scenes at Ray-Lynn's church and Hillside's town square.

"I hope I can help him, especially the Community Church, since you can't stay for all three hours of that," she said. "I want things to go right for Ray-Lynn. She's been good to me."

"Yeah, well, I gotta say Josh is worried about you getting pulled into the media stuff surrounding Sandra's death. Maybe it's best you not help him right now—"

"No! I think that would look even more suspicious. I want to stop by the barn on the way home to tell him I'm on his side, Hank. Cheer him up. So have you heard anything else besides Homestead being infested with reporters?"

"Not about that. Saw them up close and personal, though, 'fore the sheriff cleared them out."

"Then they migrated to the furniture store," she said with a huge sigh. "I can't blame them for *Daad*'s heart attack, but they didn't help."

"There is one thing you should know, and Josh gave me permission to tell you, to let you hear it."

"Hear what?" she said, turning toward him despite her seat belt.

He reached for his phone, which rested in one of the circular holes for drinks in his truck, hit a button, and this came out, *"Hi, Hank. Sandra Myerson here. Message for Josh Yoder. I've learned something interesting about Lydia's mother, but I'll save it to tell either you or her. I wasn't going to tell her at first because it's pretty upsetting. But I'm coming back to show you I can face those camels, cows and whatever else you have stashed in that barn. Maybe you'll let me have a kitten for old times' sake, or are they too young to leave their mother? Can't wait to see them. Josh, don't be mad at me. Sorry we had that fight. We can make up and be close again, even if we're apart. See you soon."*

Lydia realized she was holding her breath. Hank clicked it off; the light on the phone went dead as he said, "She sent it the night before she came back to the barn and fell. And yeah, the sheriff heard it."

"But about my mother—which one?" she whispered. "She must mean my real mother, Lena Hostetler Brand. Maybe now I'll never know what she found out. I'll have to go to the Hostetlers in the area, try to learn more about her, but what could it be that was upsetting? And if the sheriff heard that recording, it lets him know Josh and Sandra had a fight."

"Yeah. Thought about that. Josh has, too, I'll bet."

"Now I definitely want to stop there to see him. If you have to go on, he can take me home or I can walk."

"Sure, yeah, we can stop there. Lydia, one more thing Josh doesn't know yet. I saw Gid Reich sort of hanging around your place as I drove by on my way outta town to the hospital."

She sat forward so fast the seat belt pulled her back. Gid had followed her at least once before. She groaned, then realized why Gid might have been there. "Maybe he was overseeing getting all three of our buggies home from the store, maybe feeding the horses."

"Yeah, that could have been it. But he was walking around your house, not the barn, when I saw him. Hey, we're almost to Josh's. Let me make sure he can take you home 'fore I head out."

"Hank, I don't know what he would do without you, and now me, as well."

"I think you mean you're thanking me, but you make it sound like he can't do without you—and that just may be true. Maybe you two should join forces, and one thanks to me will be enough."

She blinked back tears as he turned the truck toward the Yoder barn, then drove around to the back. "It's a thought," she whispered, "but the reality of Josh and my really being together is pretty hard to get to from here, for now."

Hank knocked on the back barn door and a weary, mussed-looking Josh opened it. He hadn't even shaved, so did that mean he was starting his beard? Yet he'd never looked better to her. She almost threw herself into his arms but stood her ground.

"How's your *daad?*" Josh asked when he saw her behind Hank.

"A heart attack. They put a stent in, and he should be okay, but he'll be there for a little while, then need a lot of downtime. *Mamm*'s with him. I came home to get some things for both of them."

"Thank the Lord, he'll be all right."

"Can you take her home if I leave now?" Hank asked. Lydia realized she and Josh had their gazes locked as though no one else was there, so she tore hers away.

"*Ya,* sure, I can get her home," Josh told him. "I owe you big-time."

"Just glad to help. See you tomorrow," he said, then patted Lydia's shoulder and walked away.

"Come in," Josh said, taking her hand to pull her inside. "Everyone here has missed you so much."

They only got as far as his office when his arms went hard around her. They clung together, then the kissing started. He picked her up, sat down on a hay bale with her sprawled across his lap. If the sheriff suspected Josh of hurting Sandra, she didn't. She trusted him, needed him, wanted him.

Her bonnet dropped back, her prayer *kapp* went askew and her braid fell free. She didn't mind the roughness of his beard against her cheeks, but craved his kisses that went on and on, warming her, no, burning her clear down into her belly. His hands raced along her back, cupped her bottom. His free hand seized her ankle, then ran up her stockinged leg to her knee and thigh, ruffling up her coat and dress. They ignored the random brays and camel snorts and *baas* as they breathed in unison, and her lips opened under his to give him access to her mouth, her tongue. She couldn't breathe, she couldn't think—

Breathing hard, Josh finally broke the kiss and smoothed down her hems. "I've got to get you home. You shouldn't be here—at least not this late. I don't know what I'd do without you, through all this. But I do know what I want to do with you, and we can't— like this."

Still feeling dizzy, she held hard to him with her head on his shoulder, pressing her lips into the warmth of his neck, not sure she could even stand up on her own. When she opened her eyes, hoping to stop the spinning of the world, she glimpsed the mother cat and kittens in a feedbox nearly at their feet.

"You—you brought them down from the haymow," she whispered.

"Ya," he said, not looking at them but nuzzling her neck under the tumble of her hair. "The sheriff was here again, gave me permission. That's when the call came in to him about your father collapsing at the store."

He set her aside, stood and lifted her slowly to her feet. "Did Hank let you hear Sandra's last phone call like I told him?"

She nodded and reached back to pin up her heavy braid then shoved it back under her *kapp.* "When I can, I'm going to reach out to the Hostetlers in the area, my birth mother's family. I'll bet Sandra interviewed some of them, and they told her something really disturbing about Lena Hostetler Brand."

"You also realize from that call that the sheriff has proof that Sandra and I had a falling-out."

"Well, she and I did, too, and I'll tell him that."

"You know I wouldn't have hurt her!" he insisted, gripping her shoulders in his hands to make her look up at him.

"I believe her death was an accident, or I wouldn't be here."

"But the sheriff has new evidence that her head might have been hit with a cylinder-shaped object—maybe a ladder rung when she fell."

Lydia drew in a sharp breath. "Like the gate hitting Victoria's head?"

"I just want you to know—to believe—I did not hurt Sandra, however much I was upset by her, whatever past we had."

"Was it a past either of you wanted back?"

"We both knew it would never work. It never came up."

"You didn't answer my question."

"No. The past was the past with us. It was intense for a while, just because we were so different from each other, I think. But it was over."

"Intense. Like what just happened between you and me?"

"Not exactly like that because I never loved her!" He'd raised his voice so fast she startled.

She stared at him. Even lit by a distant lantern, his eyes seemed to glow. The passion that emanated from him—was that a temper on a leash right now or maybe desire? But love? Did he mean he'd never loved Sandra or that he now loved her, Lydia? Whatever the intensity of his relationship with Sandra, at least it was before he and Lydia became close. She mustn't feel betrayed by his past feelings for Sandra, but his caring for another woman still hurt. And that passion and power that blazed from him sometimes—surely it would not have turned to violence.

He sighed and let go of her shoulders. "I'll take you home," he said.

Suddenly eager to change the subject, she told him, "Hank phoned Ray-Lynn for me, and she can get me to Wooster tomorrow morning before work. She has that new manager, Marva, to help with the restaurant, you know."

"Lydia, I want you with me, but not if it hurts your reputation right now. You have a lot to worry about."

"But," she said as he went over to Blaze to get his buggy hitched, "I intend to pay back Ray-Lynn's kindness to me by helping you with her church's pageant, so I'll be here to get everything ready…when I can. With *Daad* at the hospital for a while, I'll have to try to keep an eye on things at the store."

"With Gid Reich there, who will keep a good eye on you."

"But I can handle him."

"Just so he doesn't handle you—keeps his hands off you. Once this mess over Sandra's death is cleared up, I want to court you. Whatever your parents or Gid say or do, I want to be your come-calling friend, if you will let me."

"When the time's right and things are cleared up, *ya,* Joshua Yoder, I will let you for sure."

17

"I'll come inside until you get a lantern lit," Josh insisted when he helped her down from his buggy by her back door. From the seat behind them, he lifted the lighted lantern he'd brought along.

"I think Gid made sure the buggies were back and the horses fed, but I should take a look in the barn first."

"I can do that after you're inside. Or...let's just do it together," he added and, trying to shield his lantern, he went with her through the wind toward the Brand barn. Over its double doors was painted a large quilt square done by a local artist, Sarah Kauffman, who had married an outsider and gone to live in the world. But *Daad,* a secret artist at heart, had hired her to paint a large square both on the side of the furniture store and on their barn before she was shunned. This one was a design called *Sunshine and Shadows,* because *Daad* said life was like that.

As cold as it was right now, Lydia felt the warmth of her love for Josh. Strangely, the light parts of the design above their heads seemed to glow ghostly white tonight, as if lit from within.

"If I can't come calling on you, with your *Daad* needing quiet and all," Josh said, "we may have to sometimes do our courting in my barn. You know, upon a winter's night like this—like a little while ago."

She tingled from tonight's memory. While she held the lantern, he unlatched the barn door and slid it open. They went in together, out of the slap of the wind. She knew he was partly teasing about the courting in the barn, yet she couldn't quite picture Josh calling for her at the store after work or *Mamm* asking him to Sunday dinner. Once the sadness of Sandra's death was behind them…then?

"Things look normal in here," she said, hanging the lantern from the crossbar hook and glancing around. "Gid did bring all three buggies back. The horses look curried and fed," she added as she went over to pet Flower, who nuzzled the palm of her hand.

"Maybe he had help."

"He'll need it at the store, too."

"From you?"

"And others. I got the idea from the surgeon it would be a long haul for *Daad* to get back to normal. He'll need rest, lots of it. I have to take his medicine back with me, and I bet the surgeon will change it again. It took him a long time to adjust to it. The first one his regular doctor put him on gave him a bad cough, and the second made his hands shake, which bothered his quilting. Oh," she gasped, turning to look at him, "I haven't let that slip ever with anyone else!"

Josh came closer and put a foot on the lowest stall rail. "Your father likes to quilt?"

"The family secret, one of them, I guess. He's good at it, does beautiful work."

"I won't tell anyone I know—especially him. I'm hoping he will honor me with his friendship and counsel someday. As for your mother, at least I got a loaf of friendship bread from her. It was delicious, though I had the feeling she came over partly to keep an eye on us."

They left the barn and went out into the wind again. She didn't want to worry Josh by repeating what Hank had said about seeing Gid circling her house when he drove by. Gid was probably just being helpful again, making sure none of the shutters were damaged, that everything looked all right outside.

"Here, let me," Josh said, and took the key from her trembling, gloved hand to unlock the back door of her house. Inside, he lit both kerosene kitchen lanterns so that warm light bathed the room. They stood awkwardly across the corner of the kitchen table from each other.

"I'd like to kiss you good-night," he said, twisting his hat in his hands. "But I don't know if I'd want to leave then, and I hear Melly and Gaspar calling." Despite his little joke, he looked painfully serious. "I'd better get going. You sure you'll be all right? You've never been alone here at night, have you?"

"No, but this is home—for now. I can't thank you enough for delivering me safe and sound."

"With all this media attention about Sandra, it's best that no one sees my buggy here tonight. I'd better get going," he said again.

"I think the media folk have cleared out, though."

"I'm praying they won't be back. And that the blow

to Sandra's head fits the loft ladder rung I cut off for the sheriff."

"You did? If it fits, then she hit her head falling, because no one could lift that ladder to hit her. Oh, but—" she felt her stomach go into free fall "—someone could still have pushed her out of the loft." And, she recalled, Josh's flashlight had been there, but—

"Lydia, I swear to you, if someone hit her, it wasn't me."

"As I said, I believe you, or you wouldn't be here. I wouldn't have come to you tonight—kissed you back."

They almost swayed together, but he picked up his lantern, went to the door and put his hand to the knob.

She called after him, "Josh, an Amish man's word is his bond. You don't have to swear you're telling the truth—about Sandra, about me." *About love,* she almost added.

"And a good Amish woman trusts her man. Now lock this door behind me." He went out and firmly closed the door.

She locked it and watched through the kitchen window as he drove away into the windy darkness. Suddenly, she realized she was hungry and took cheese and milk from the fridge. Things looked a little rearranged in there since she'd fixed breakfast this morning, but *Mamm* had probably been making more bread. She must have been distracted, though. She'd put a jar of honey in the fridge where it would crystallize, so Lydia took it out and put it back in its place in the cupboard. Mamm had obviously used a lot of it, and it wasn't for her bread recipe. The outside of the jar was sticky, so she must have really been in a rush. Things were usually immaculate in *Mamm*'s kitchen.

Lydia got some crackers and ate them with cheese washed down by a glass of milk that tasted much colder than usual. The house seemed so chilly and silent—"Silent Night," but somehow, not "Holy Night." She hoped both of those were included in the carols Ray-Lynn's friends would sing at their outdoor manger scene. She liked most of the worldly Christmas carols.

"It came upon a midnight clear," she sang, but the house seemed to swallow her words. Besides, singing right now didn't cheer her up. It was near midnight but cloudy, not clear outside, as if another storm was hovering. The thought of *Daad* so ill hung heavy on her, especially in the wake of Sandra's death and Victoria Keller's. At least Josh's almost-profession of love, her growing friendship with Ray-Lynn and renewed one with Bess Stark lifted her spirits a bit. But then there was the eternal tension with *Mamm*...

She shook her head as if that could clear it. She had to gather a change of clothes for her parents and above all find *Daad*'s blood pressure medicine. It was in the medicine cabinet, *Mamm* had said. Taking one of the two kitchen lanterns, she went up the stairs. They creaked, which she hadn't noticed before. The house was cold to the bone, and it was windy. The gentle hiss of the lantern was drowned by other sounds.

And it seemed so dark up here when one lantern had often lit her way. Shadows loomed from the open, silent mouths of the doors. Even the thought of a bath and her own bed didn't comfort her.

She went into her parents' bedroom and put the lantern down on the cherry dresser so she could see into their drawers. Yes, a change of undergarments for both, easily spotted, and another shirt for *Daad*.

She took the pile of clothing to pack and, carrying the lantern, went into the bathroom to get the medicine.

She hesitated at the door. The dark green bathroom curtain was pulled shut when *Mamm* liked it open to air out the tub and the tiles. There were no mirrors to reflect the light like in *Englische* bathrooms she'd seen, and her own huge shadow seemed to leap at her.

Though she knew it was a crazy idea, she yanked the curtain open. An empty tub, of course, but water speckled the tiles and—yes, the bottom of the tub. *Daad* took a shower at night, and she and *Mamm* had baths then. No one would have used the tub since last night so the water would not have stayed here like this.

Her pulse started to pound. The house had been closed up. And with the shower curtain closed, the water hadn't dried up, that's all. She was letting everything get to her. The medicine—just get *Daad*'s medicine where *Mamm* said it would be.

She opened the pinewood cabinet. As usual, it was immaculate with perfect placements of over-the-counter remedies for headaches, bug bites, bruises and—sleeping pills, no doubt *Mamm*'s! When had she started taking sleeping pills? But she didn't find *Daad*'s prescription bottle. Had she missed his medicine beside his bed? No, if *Mamm* said it was here, surely it was.

From the cabinet, Lydia took *Daad*'s hand razor. No Amish beards were cut or trimmed, but the men shaved above their mouths to keep a mustache at bay. That was a tradition from the terrible days when European soldiers who sported mustaches hunted down the Amish and dragged them off to torture and death.

Lydia pictured one dreadful drawing in the Amish book called *Martyrs' Mirror* and shuddered again.

She also gathered their toothbrushes and toothpaste, a brush and comb. She'd already taken some money for *Mamm* from her top dresser drawer.

Frustrated, wanting to get to sleep—maybe on the sofa downstairs because she didn't like the idea of being up here alone tonight—she hurried down to the kitchen.

No medicine bottle there. Maybe the surgeon would have to phone *Daad*'s doctor, but what if he had not been taking his pills? Maybe he had lost them or thrown them away. That would need to be reported, too. As stubborn as he was, perhaps he'd brought about his own heart attack. He'd looked especially bad these past few weeks. After those first two medicines gave him bad side effects, what if he'd gone off the latest one on his own?

Once she'd checked the dining room table and the end table by his favorite chair, Lydia decided to look the only other place she could think of—the side parlor, his quilting room. She'd been in there before but not for several years. She'd had the feeling he would still welcome her there, but he didn't want *Mamm* coming in, and he could hardly bar just one of them.

It was locked, but she knew where he kept the key, under the back foot of the table near the sofa. She put down the pile of clothing and tried the door.

Feeling like a naughty child about to be caught at something, Lydia unlocked the door, lifted her lantern and went in. Bolts of cloth were neatly stacked on the shelves of walnut cabinets once used for books. Several evidently completed quilts were piled in the rocking chair near the door.

A large frame stretching a nearly completed quilt—a Christmas gift for her or *Mamm?*—claimed the center of the high-ceilinged room. Two straight-backed chairs faced the quilt as if a specter quilter joined him in his solitary abode. No doubt he just didn't want to move a chair when he changed positions. An unlit, suspended double lantern hung over the quilt frame, but now her lantern cast the only light. Things seemed to shift in shadows as if an unseen hand were quilting, moving the material.

She got hold of herself, whispering a little prayer of thanks that *Daad* would be coming back to finish this beautiful quilt, dominated by Christmas colors, white-and-gold squares on a dark green background. The Amish avoided red, the color of martyrs' blood.

The quilt was upside down from her position, but she could see it did have a Christmas theme with an angel in every fourth square. It also featured repeated sheep and donkeys—even camels! Could it be intended as a gift for her? Was he honoring her work with Josh's animals or was he simply using manger symbols?

As she started to walk around the quilt to see it right side up, she caught sight of a pill bottle on a lower shelf, nearly hidden by scissors and spools of thread. That had to be the blood pressure medicine. It better be because her heart was pounding so hard she probably needed it herself.

She picked up the bottle and turned the label close to the lantern. *Ya!* His Hytrin medicine. *Mamm* just hadn't known he'd moved it here. And beside it, or rather behind it, another bottle of pills. She squinted in the dim light to read Paxil, whatever that was. Oh, around the back of the label it read, "for depression."

Daad was taking medication for depression? Sure, her people used modern medicines and saw worldly doctors when they needed to. The bishops had permitted that for years. But *Mamm* couldn't know this, could she? Besides, it seemed to Lydia that *Mamm* was the one depressed, not *Daad*. He'd only seemed tired to Lydia. Of course, she'd have to tell the surgeon this. Was *Daad* unhappy with his life? With his tense marriage? Could he have been upset that she didn't like Gid, who could run the store for him someday?

Holding both medicine bottles in her left hand, Lydia lifted the lantern higher to examine the quilt from the bottom up. How lovely the angels were. They looked just like the one in the precious snow globe she had broken and must get fixed. On the main border of the quilt draped over the frame, the star of Bethlehem was sewn around the edges in a repeating pattern, and, just above that, an inner border was stitched with the scripted German words *Vergeben Sie Vater*—Father Forgive, the Lord's words from the cross.

Or, since those two words were duplicated over and over with no punctuation between them, did it say, "Forgive Father"? No, it must be the Bible quote, but it puzzled her. That was an Easter, not a Christmas quote. Another mystery like Victoria Keller's half-written note to the girl Brand baby. And if this quilt was meant as a Christmas gift for Lydia, what was the message? At least, if it was to be hers, she could ask *Daad* when and if he gave it to her. It wouldn't be a strange message as if from the grave, as Victoria's had been.

With a final glance at the quilt she knew she must keep a secret, unless *Daad* figured out where she found his meds, she tiptoed out, relocked the door and replaced the key. Though she didn't usually think this way, she wished she could phone Josh just to hear his voice. Or Ray-Lynn. Sometimes she wished her people had phones that were in the house, not way down a dark, cold road in a common booth. Even another voice from a radio or TV would help right now. Not that she was disloyal to her people or usually felt that way. But tonight, at this moment, she felt so alone.

She decided she would sleep downstairs but she'd need to wash up and get her nightgown and a fresh dress for tomorrow from her bedroom. The dress she had on looked as if she'd slept in it, and she longed to take her hair down and brush it.

First, she went into the pantry to get two of *Mamm*'s bread sacks to put her parents' clothing in. She noted that several were pulled off the shelf and lay on the floor. Any sort of disorder was unlike her overly tidy mother, but then she'd probably been in a rush to get all that bread ready to take to the furniture store staff today. Or the sacks had slid out, and she hadn't seen them. Lydia put the bags back in place, then labeled the two she needed *Daad* and *Mamm* and slid their personal items inside. Taking her lantern again, she hurried upstairs. As tense and nervous as she'd been today, exhaustion was starting to take a toll on her.

She stripped off her clothes in the bathroom and washed quickly with soap and warm water. Trembling from the cold, with a towel wrapped around her na-

kedness and the lantern in her hand, she tiptoed—
now, why tiptoe?—to her bedroom and went directly
to her closet. Putting the lantern on her tall dresser,
she slipped on a warm flannel nightgown and robe and
jammed her feet in her woolen slippers.

She should take her clothes for tomorrow downstairs, too— No, she'd come up tomorrow to wash up
better. She'd just take her pillow and a blanket. She
could use one of *Daad*'s quilts from the living room,
too, and pretend she was wrapped in the Christmas
quilt.

But as she turned to her bed, she gasped. She'd
made it this morning, all smooth and straight, but now
the sheets were yanked awry, pillow punched and in-
dented. She moved a step closer. It looked as if someone had slept in it, twisting and turning, writhing!
And strings of sticky honey were dribbled on the pillow, all around!

She gasped, and the walls seemed to echo the
sound. The house creaked as if its very bones were
breaking. She recalled that little fairy tale she'd read
from the library bookmobile years ago, before *Mamm*
found out and took it away from her as being "worldly
nonsense."

"Who has been sleeping in my bed?" said Mama
Bear, Daddy Bear and Baby Bear.

Lydia staggered back against the wall, barely
breathing, trying to sift out sounds. No footsteps, no
one else in the room, but some evil presence had been
here and still lurked. Had *Daad* given Gid a key? He'd
been walking around the house. No, he wanted to gain
favor with the Brands. He'd never do something like
this—sacks on the floor, water in the tub, honey in

the refrigerator and in her bed, and who knows what else she'd missed?

Reminding herself to breathe, she approached her bed and ripped the upper covers back, terrified she'd see something dreadful there, a threatening note at least. Nothing, but the sheets were damp as if the invader had taken a shower, then come straight here to roll in the honey, punch her pillow and violate her bed.

18

Crying and shaking so hard her lantern quivered, Lydia searched room after room in the house. All she wanted to do was run outside, but she was afraid to go in the barn alone or race through the woodlot to Josh. Besides, perhaps the person who had done this wanted her to be outside alone, like that night Leo Lowe accosted her. If she could only hitch Flower to her buggy or run to Josh, spend the night there—but what if this was a setup to force her to do that, catch them together late at night?

Because she couldn't bear to search the attic or basement, she locked both doors and wedged ladder-back chair under their knobs. Yet surely no one was hiding upstairs or down there. She would hear them, sense them, wouldn't she? At least Ray-Lynn would be here early tomorrow. Emotionally and physically exhausted, Lydia decided she'd get dressed again and sit on the sofa downstairs, keep the curtains closed and lots of lanterns lit. And with *Mamm*'s heaviest wooden rolling pin in her hands.

But sometime in the night, amid the shrieks of wind

and creaking house, she dreamed her own voice was shrieking. She was gripping a rung of a ladder or the smooth wooden limb of a tall tree, climbing amid thick leaves and straw, searching for Sandra. Was she still in the loft? Sandra had to tell her what upsetting thing she had found out about her mother—and which mother? But as she climbed the tree, people snatched at her skirts, Leo Lowe, Gid, even Connor, who was trying to spray the tree. *Mamm!* Mamm was below, too, scolding her to come down. Where was Josh? She needed Josh!

Lydia woke to the sound of someone cutting the tree down with a hatchet, *rap, rap, rap*—and then realized someone was knocking on the back door. She forced her eyes open and jerked awake.

"Connor," Ray-Lynn called as she got out of her car in the Brands' driveway, "what are you doing here so early? I thought Jack told you Sol Brand had a heart attack and is in the hospital in Wooster."

As she had driven down the lane, she'd watched Connor walk from the line of spruce trees that edged his property, across the driveway and up to the back porch, where he had knocked on the door. He looked startled to see her. "Oh, yeah, he did. My mother went back to Columbus overnight. I called her to tell her, and she said to check on Lydia."

"So you know her mother's staying in Wooster, too? I'm here to drive Lydia to the hospital, then back," she said as she walked up to join him on the small back porch. Like a young kid caught doing something wrong, he jammed his hands in his jeans pockets.

"Oh, so she'll be here tonight, too? I'll tell Mother."

He seemed frazzled, as if he'd been up all night

just as Jack had. Surely, the duties of mayor weren't weighing Connor down, but maybe selling Christmas trees was demanding, even though he had a large staff.

Still looking nervous, he started down the steps. "Mother told me to see if Lydia needed any help, and she'd be back tonight—my mother, from Columbus, where she had some business."

"Got it. Lydia may be sleeping in. It's been quite a time for her. I'll give her your message."

The back door opened, and Lydia stood there. Dark half-moons shadowed the underside of her eyes, and her clothes were mussed. Her hair looked as if she'd combed it with her fingers beneath her lopsided prayer *kapp.*

"Oh, Ray-Lynn," Lydia said. Then she added, "Connor! Is everything all right?"

"My mother just asked me to stop by to see if there's anything she—we—can do. A ride to Wooster, anything."

Lydia looked as if she was still waking up. Her voice sounded shaky and she kept blinking, either bothered by the light or maybe the sight of Connor at her back door.

Lydia told him, "Please thank her for me, and I'll let her know. *Daad* came through well. He'll need rest for a while, though."

"Sure. Been losing a bit of sleep myself—with my new duties in town. Just let us know if we can help," he repeated, and walked down the drive until he could cut across to his own property. As cold as it was, as early as it was, Ray-Lynn thought, why had he walked over here instead of driving?

"Ray-Lynn, come in," Lydia said. "I'll change really quick. Want something to eat?"

"Now, you know us Southern girls don't stir outside in the morning without our makeup, coffee and grits." Ray-Lynn tried for a light tone as Lydia closed the door. But when she saw the tears clumping Lydia's eyelashes together, she hugged her. "But you're the one with grit, my girl. And I'm right here to help."

Lydia hugged her back, then stepped away, wiping tears from her wet cheeks. "Oh, Ray-Lynn, someone was inside the house while we were all in Wooster. Moved some things around in the refrigerator, took a shower, got in my bed and made a mess of it."

"What? You mean like a break-in? Like someone ate your food and dared to sleep here?"

"Not exactly," she said, shaking her head hard. "I think it was to scare me, hurt me. I searched the whole house except for the basement and attic—that's why the chair is propped there," she said with a nod at the basement door across the kitchen.

"I can call Jack. He can come over and look around. He drove to Parma last night to see Leo Lowe, but he wasn't there, and his wife claimed she didn't know where he was. That's the guy who was hanging out in your backyard before, right?"

"*Ya.* But I don't think there was a break-in, so where would he get a key?"

"I don't know, but Jack's got the Parma police looking for him."

"I'll give you and the sheriff the details later, but I've got to get some things to the hospital," she said, moving away. "If I leave a key under the mat, can the sheriff have a look after we leave?"

"Not a good idea if you've had an intruder. I'll call Jack and let him know, let him put two and two together about Leo Lowe. When I bring you back here, he can take a look around."

Lydia rushed upstairs to change. Ray-Lynn walked around the house, wanting to look out, but Lydia had all the curtains drawn. That figure Ray-Lynn had seen outside her and Jack's house the other night—coincidence? Jack had said once that in police work there were no coincidences, but this was still the heart of Amish country, the Home Valley in Eden County, for heaven's sake. So why did another serpent have to slither into their little piece of paradise?

Lydia asked Ray-Lynn to wait in the hospital lounge while she headed down the hall toward the room number she'd been given for her father. Carrying the two paper sacks with her parents' clothing, she held both plastic containers of *Daad*'s medicines tight in her hand, along with the sleeping pills she wanted to talk to *Mamm* about. What a good sign that his doctor was walking toward her with a laptop computer in his hand!

"Ms. Brand, it looks as if you could use some rest, too," he said, stopping beside her. "Did you find your father's BP meds?"

She handed the bottle right over. "Yes, here. I had to really look for it. All I saw in the medicine cabinet where my mother said to look were first-aid things and her sleeping pills."

He looked up from studying the label on the bottle. "Does she have trouble sleeping, too? Your father said he did."

He seemed so kind and interested that Lydia almost launched into the sad story of the family losing Sammy, but she said only, "She does sometimes." She showed him the bottle of *Mamm*'s pills. "So is that a good sleep medicine?"

"A powerful one. People taking it have been known to have waking-talking blackout periods. They can function as if awake but they do things they later don't recall, kind of like sleepwalking. I knew someone using this med who fixed a large breakfast for people and didn't recall a thing—thought someone else had been in her kitchen. What's really bad is that some people drive after taking it. In a couple of recent criminal cases, the accused have claimed they weren't responsible for an accident because they were under the influence of the drug."

"And you can buy something scary like that in a drugstore or grocery store?"

"No. It's prescription only and comes with all sorts of warnings." Taking the container from her, he observed, "She's peeled off the label that gives the doctor and pharmacy. I'm just giving you a heads-up that if your mother is taking this on a regular basis for insomnia, she might not be a very good nurse for your father, but at least she'll have you to help. Thanks for this." He indicated the Hytrin medication. "I just checked your father out a half hour ago. He's resting well, but we'll be sure he gets onto a good blood pressure med. So, what's in that other bottle you're holding?"

"Oh, I almost forgot. I grabbed this medicine of *Daad*'s, too, in case it makes a difference in what you prescribe. It's Paxil, and I didn't know he had it. It says 'for depression.'"

The doctor's eyebrows shot up. He took it from her and glanced at the label. "It's the same doctor he had for the blood pressure meds. But you had no idea about this?"

"No, and I'm not sure *Mamm* did, either. I found it in his—in his private study with the Hytrin bottle. He's looked tired lately and has a lot of pressure at this time of year in the store, but… Could these have hurt his heart?"

"As with the sleeping pills, there are side effects, so I'm glad you turned these up. Don't get him or your mother more upset talking about it until I check things out. I'll speak to him first in private."

"I understand. I won't bring it up." She almost told him that she had bigger secrets than that. Keeping both of *Daad*'s pill vials but handing *Mamm*'s back, he gave her an encouraging nod and went on his way. Lydia just stood there a moment, her mind racing. *Daad*'s depression was one thing, but she had no idea *Mamm* had been to a doctor for sleeping pills, though she had taken a lot of naps lately. But with those strange side effects, why didn't she choose another kind? And had her doctor explained the risks to her?

She tiptoed into *Daad*'s room, a private one with one bed, though *Mamm* was curled up on a couch along the far wall. Machines with moving lines on their screens were attached to *Daad*'s arms like power cords going into an *Englische* home from telephone poles. She decided not to upset either of them by telling them what she'd found at home. Besides, Ray-Lynn would go in with her when they went back, and then she planned to buggy straight to the furniture store. Ray-Lynn had called the sheriff. The two of them planned to meet Lydia at the house so that she could walk him through it in a similar setting as she'd found the place.

"Liddy," came a quiet voice from the bed.

She hurried over and put her hands over her father's left one atop the sheets. He whispered, "Had a tube down my throat...hurts."

"Don't talk, then," she whispered, nearly matching his raspy voice, hoping not to wake *Mamm.* "You'll be fine, but it will take some time. You'll be home soon, and I'll help."

He mouthed his words this time. "You already do."

"Ray-Lynn has volunteered to drive me back and forth. Even Connor came over this morning to say his mother was worried about us."

His eyes widened in obvious surprise. Tears glazed his eyes but did not spill. "You can trust her—Bess," she thought he said, but he seemed to have fallen asleep again.

She stood there for a while, holding his hand, watching the little lines go up and down each time his heart beat. She nearly jumped through the roof when someone touched her from behind.

It was *Mamm,* motioning her out into the hall. She, too, looked so strung out that Lydia decided right then she wouldn't tell her about the disarray in the house until later. Even if *Daad* had been in great shape, the thought of an intruder would upset her mother.

"You found his medicine?" *Mamm* asked.

"Yes, and I gave the bottle to the doctor. I brought things in sacks for both of you," she added, "on the chair next to his bed."

"Good girl. Lydia, I know I sound like a scold sometimes, but I only want what's best for you. You know that, don't you?"

"*Ya, Mamm,* of course." And, Lydia thought, the fact her mother had not been sleeping well for who knew how long could make anyone on edge. She wondered again if *Mamm* knew about *Daad*'s medicine for depression, but that would have to wait.

"But now you must also do what is best for the family," *Mamm* went on, "and that means helping Gid at the store. I can take care of things here and when we get *Daad* home. No need to whisper to your father, say things that might upset him, and the same for him."

"I—I wouldn't. But 'same for him'? I don't know what you mean."

She shrugged. "In his condition, he might say things he doesn't mean. He had some sedation."

Lydia almost asked her if she knew the side effects of her own sleeping pills, but she decided to save that, too.

"Ray-Lynn is still here?" *Mamm* asked.

"She said she'd wait."

"Don't keep your friend waiting. It was so nice of her, but she has a business to care for just like you do now."

Lydia nodded. At least *Mamm* had more or less apologized for seeming to scold all the time. And she was right that she should check in at the furniture store, for surely *Daad* would want that, too. But what sort of sickbed confessions had she been afraid her own daughter and *Daad* would be whispering about? Maybe she was afraid that, since *Daad* had faced death, he would insist they tell Lydia all about her "real" parents.

* * *

About halfway home, Ray-Lynn said to Lydia, "Not to change the subject when you have a lot to worry about already, but I did end up talking to a Hostetler. You told me you might want to reach out to your birth mother's family."

"Someone came into the restaurant?" Lydia asked, coming instantly alert and sitting up in the passenger seat.

"Actually, it's our custodian at the Community Church, Nathan Hostetler. He's about fortysomething, I guess. He's not of your faith anymore, but he and his family turned Mennonite. He was around during our manger scene planning, and I just thought I'd ask him if he was related to a Lena Hostetler Brand from over near Amity. He is—was—her cousin. One of many, I take it."

"You didn't say more to him about that, did you?"

"Only made sure he'd be at the outdoor manger scene, because I thought you could talk to him there, so you wouldn't have to make a big deal of going to his house, lying to your parents. And I knew you'd be too busy to look him up right away."

"Ray-Lynn, you're the best! I don't know what I'd do without you and Josh."

"Well, ding-dang. But somehow I know you don't put us both just in the good-friends category. Lydia, what are you going to do about Gid Reich when all this smoke clears?"

"I'm going to make sure he understands we can be partners at the store until *Daad* recovers, but not in life."

"It may not be that easy. You just be careful."

"Don't I know it, because Hank saw Gid walking around our house, though he did bring our buggies back and was probably just making certain things were secure. I need to bide my time with him—and everyone. Not jump to conclusions."

"Such as that he was the one in your house? You know Jack and I will help."

"*Ya,* and I'm so blessed by that. I want to find out, with the sheriff's help, who it was. Then I'll have to wait until it can be proved Sandra's death was an accident. Ray-Lynn—it just had to be! And I need to get *Daad* healthy again so I can tell my parents I love them both but I need to know about my real parents. Sandra sent a voice message to Josh on Hank's phone that said she had something else to tell me about my mother. It sounded like something bad—"

"Which mother?"

"My birth mother, of course, Lena Hostetler! That's what Sandra was researching for me, even if she went about it the wrong way."

But after so vehemently answering that question, Lydia agonized silently the rest of the way home. Sandra had sought out *Daad* at the store and somehow won him over, partly because of her admiration of his quilts, of course, partly because she didn't tell him her real intentions.

But could she also have dared to meet with or question *Mamm?* And if so, was there any way she'd won her over, too? No, more likely Susan Brand would have reacted just the opposite, because *Mamm* had bad-mouthed Sandra when she, supposedly, hadn't even met her.

19

Although it was midafternoon with sunlight glaring off the snow and slanting through the windows when Lydia entered the barn to harness Flower, it suddenly seemed a dark place to her. Her parents would not want her to padlock it at night, yet what if the house intruder did something in here? Someone had unhitched and moved Flower when she was in Amity, and that would be easier in a dark barn.

She fed all three horses, putting a feed bag on Flower while she harnessed her. Same as last night, every little creak of wood, even the horses shuffling through straw, alarmed her. She could not and would not live in fear, she vowed, but her pulse still pounded.

As she led Flower outside pulling the buggy, then went back to slide the barn door closed, she thought of it. She was an idiot! Why hadn't she remembered that before? *Daad* kept an extra house key on a hook at the back of the barn. Could someone have found that— used that? Gid and who knew who else had been in here just yesterday to bring the buggies home.

She went back inside, remembering again that

someone strong must have taken Josh's camel seat, followed her to Amity and unhitched Flower from her buggy the day she interviewed Mr. Raber about her birth father. Gid? Leo Lowe, whom the sheriff couldn't find at his home last night? Surely not Connor.

But there was the key. Of course, it could have been used and returned. Oh, no. It was hanging on a big nail next to the hook where *Daad* kept it! Had it been used, moved, or could *Daad,* as distracted and ill as he'd been lately, have moved it himself? But he had keys to the house and store on a chain. And that chain had probably been left somewhere in his office when the emergency squad came to take him to Wooster.

She grabbed the key and stuck it in the top of her stocking. After closing the barn door, she rushed to her buggy, climbed up and giddyapped Flower away. She had to oversee more than the front desk at the store. She also needed to carefully, cleverly, keep an eye on her would-be come-calling friend, Gideon Reich.

"You're up early, Sheriff," Josh greeted Jack Freeman at the back door of his barn. At least he had knocked this time and not just walked in as if the place was under his ownership or control.

"More like I haven't been to bed," he said, scratching the stubble on his chin. "Knew if I did I wouldn't get up. Slept in a chair and Ray-Lynn gave me holy hell for not coming to bed. Sorry to put it that way."

"That's okay," Josh said. "But there's Hell, and there's what's holy, and never the twain shall meet. Lately, though, it's been more like Hell around here."

"Got some more-or-less good news for you."

They stood facing each other between the camel

pen and the loft where Sandra had died. "I could sure use some of that," Josh admitted as his hopes soared.

"Putting it in layman's terms, the coroner's official report will be that Sandra's death was caused by a traumatic blow to her head and a broken neck. Probable cause—her head hitting the lower ladder rung, so that eliminates a blow to her head by a second party."

Josh exhaled. "A tragic accident. I had nothing to do with it, or at least, I wasn't there."

"What's that mean? 'At least' you weren't there?"

"Indirectly, I might have been the reason she climbed up there. I think she wanted to prove to me that she was willing to come in the barn with the big animals. She'd been afraid of any animal much larger than cats since she was a kid. She told me once she'd accidentally fatally injured her brother's puppy and everyone made a big deal of it, not thinking of her feelings. And then, once she was in the barn, she must have wanted to see the cat and kittens I'd mentioned to her—and somehow fell."

"You're a smart guy," the sheriff said, "so help me with a couple of things. You mind if we sit down?"

"That's fine. You can have the one chair I've got out here."

"A hay bale will do," he said, going over to Josh's makeshift office and sinking onto one.

"Coffee? I brought some out. I've got cups."

"Sure, thanks."

Josh poured, hoping what was coming next wasn't some complication to the so-called "good news" he'd just shared. Not wanting to tower over his guest, Josh sat on a hay bale, too, one a few feet away.

"You know what I'm gonna say?" the sheriff asked after he took a long sip of the coffee.

"That two women have died on my property by blows to their heads?"

"That, too. No, I'm thinking, even if Sandra fell and hit her head on the ladder, that would not have been enough to make it come loose from its moorings considering the way you had it nailed down. The ladder must have been wrenched or the nails removed to come away from the loft like that."

"Maybe when she fell, she grabbed the ladder and pulled it loose."

"Then took a header into the bottom rung? Like you say, maybe. With her injuries, she must have fallen headfirst, and it's still hard for me to picture her not clinging to the loft or ladder, then falling feetfirst, unless she was pushed. A broken leg maybe, but not a broken neck."

He drained his coffee cup. Josh was amazed the man could drink coffee that hot straight down.

Staring at Josh again, the sheriff continued, "Her head hitting the lowest rung clears up any worries about your flashlight being involved. That brings up another problem for me, though."

"Sheriff, if you can take fingerprints off the wood of that rung, of course my fingerprints would be on it, but yours would be, too."

"I'm not talking about that. That rung had traces of her blood on it."

"Blood? I didn't see any blood on it. Did you? We both handled it."

"Nope, but that's why I have the BCI forensic guys involved. Under a powerful microscope, the blood—

a match to her blood—showed up on that rung. Now, here's the kicker, Josh," he said, leaning closer, elbows on his knees, his empty cup dangling in his big hands. "You and I didn't see any blood on it—and I got scolded for how carelessly we'd handled that piece of evidence—because the traces were in the grain and cracks of the wood. Someone had tried to wipe wet blood from that rung and drove it into the crevices, and since I don't think it was the victim—yeah, the victim—I think we still got us a case of possible murder. And if Sandra Myerson was murdered by a blow to the head, or being shoved out of the loft headfirst, maybe more than an icy cold gate caused Victoria Keller's death, too."

"But nothing links those women!" Josh protested, realizing he was getting loud again, angry, feeling trapped.

"Other than they were both on your property, got to agree with that. For now, at least."

Trying to keep calm, Josh told him, "But there were no other footsteps in the snow, like someone had been following Victoria."

"True, but the falling snow and strong wind could have obscured some of that. However, we do have Lydia's footprints coming up behind her and then a lot of yours when you went out to help. So anyway, the coroner's ruling is accidental death—again, just like Victoria's. But I gotta admit, I'm not willing to let it go, and if you cared for Sandra, which your mutual friends in Columbus say you did, you won't let it go, either. You'll help me find the truth."

You'll help me find the truth. The sheriff's parting

words rang in his ears. But he was terrified the sheriff's version of the truth could still be focused on him.

Lydia knew she'd have to tread carefully to find the truth about Gid. She already knew he'd been walking around the outside of her house. He had been in her barn. He coveted this business and perhaps wanted her as his ticket to owning it in the future. But could all that have anything to do with Sandra's death? Since she seemed to have talked to so many people, could she have talked to Gid, maybe let on she was investigating whether Lydia's parents really were her parents, so he'd wanted to shut her up? After all, if Lydia was not the true heir, how would Gid solidify his future claim to the store? She knew he wanted to own, not just manage it for Lydia if she married someone else.

One of their young shop apprentices, Amos Getz, was in the horse shed at the store and took care of unhitching Flower for her, so she hurried inside. It took her a while to get through the shop, where she announced *Daad*'s good progress and accepted the well wishes and promises of more prayers from everyone.

To give herself some time to get her courage up before facing Gid, she went directly to her father's office. She was both annoyed and panicked to see Gid sitting behind *Daad*'s desk.

"Oh, Gid. Why aren't you in your own office? Can't you run things from there?"

"Lydia! I didn't know you would make it in today," he cried, popping up and coming around the desk. "I've been back and forth—needed some things he had here."

She stood her ground, one hand on the door, barely

outside it, hoping that barrier and her sticking to the public hall would keep him from hugging her.

"He's doing as well as can be expected," she told him, not budging, so he stopped a few feet from her. "He's talking. I'm still not sure when they'll release him."

"And your mother's staying with him?"

No way was she going to let this man know she might be alone again tonight. "That's not decided," she lied. "Ray-Lynn's coming over tonight." That, at least, was true, Lydia thought as she walked past him and sat in her father's big chair herself. The sheriff was coming to look at the things disturbed in her house, and Ray-Lynn said she'd come, too.

"Oh, good," he said, but he didn't sound sincere. Yet that might just be because most Amish did not have close *Englische* friends, and certainly not the sheriff's wife. "But, aren't you going to the front desk where you can keep an eye on the store? I have everything under control here."

"I'll help Naomi on the desk when I can, but, of course, while my father's away, I'll be keeping an eye on things in his office also."

"When he talked to you at the hospital, he suggested that?"

"He expects me to report in to him—about everything."

She leveled the calmest, coldest look she could at him. He almost flinched. He did seem especially nervous, didn't he?

"We'll have to work together more closely than ever," was all he said. "Now, I've got things to do."

She breathed a huge sigh when he walked out. She

looked down at the file drawer open in the desk. If he'd come in here for something, why did he just walk away without it now?

She leaned closer to look at the file he'd partly pulled out. Accounts payable—nothing unusual there. But she noticed another desk drawer was also ajar and pulled it open. She gasped. A kind of junk drawer, though one neatly arranged. But something stood out. Amidst the tidy compartments of paper clips, stamps, pens and business cards, *Daad*'s chain with his keys—for the store and the house—had been hastily dropped or thrown here, and hardly in its proper place, an empty section of this big, clear plastic organizer. Had Gid been looking for these, or was he putting them back?

Lydia carried the keys when she went out into the store, jingling them to make sure that Gid saw she had them as she passed him chatting with a salesman. She had no intention of letting this chain out of her sight any more than the key from the barn that she had hidden in the top of her stocking.

Lydia had just finished talking to Naomi about any problems she'd had at the front desk. And, even without Gid's consent, she'd promised her a small raise for running the front desk without Lydia until *Daad* returned.

She also had subtly learned that Isaac Gerber, one of the men who had helped Gid drive the Brand buggies back to their barn, and who had eyes for Naomi, had said that before Gid drove the three men back here in his buggy, he had returned to the barn alone and then walked around the house, looking in windows to check that everything was all right.

Lydia was planning to personally thank—and carefully quiz—all three men who had accompanied Gid by driving a Brand buggy that day. But as she worked her way toward the back of the store, she heard the front door open and a familiar voice.

Bess Stark was here.

"I see the sign on the front door about customers only." She was evidently talking to Naomi. "But for a place of business that's discriminatory at best, illegal at worst."

Naomi's voice. "It was just to keep the media people out, then we forgot to take it down."

"Much as we'd all love to keep them away, freedom of speech and all that, my girl. Freedom of religion, too, that's the best part for your people. But I think you'd better take that sign off the door. Oh, Lydia, there you are! I'm so sorry to hear the latest. And if that sign is company policy and you intend to toss me out, I came in to buy a gun-rack cabinet for Connor for Christmas."

The entire place seemed to be brighter with Bess here. Although Lydia saw Gid heading toward them, she indicated Bess should come with her and took her around the other way.

"I came in the back and forgot Gid had put that sign up," Lydia told Bess as Naomi scurried toward the front door. "Thanks for sending Connor over to check on me. Let me show you the cabinets you're interested in."

"But let's talk first things first. How is your father? Connor said a heart attack but improving?"

"Ya," she told her friend as they walked toward the back of the store, winding their way through the larger dining room pieces and kitchen cabinets. "The doctor put in a stent and is changing his medications, I think. *Mamm*'s staying with him. I got the idea he'll be released fairly soon but will need a lot of downtime."

"Ah, downtime. What's that, right? I'll bet you'll be especially busy here now. Any time left to work with Josh's animals—and the male animal?"

Bess's eyes seemed to twinkle. For the first time in days, Lydia smiled. "I'm helping him as best I can, especially when he goes out with a menagerie for a Christmas pageant. We're helping Ray-Lynn Freeman put on her church's living crèche scene next week. It will kind of, as Ray-Lynn says, kick off the Home Valley holiday season, though your trees have set the mood, too."

"Well, maybe not the entire mood, as your people's dedication to your faith means much more than festive decorations. I admire that—need that," Bess added under her breath as they stopped in the back corner where the three styles of gun cabinets were displayed.

Before Lydia could talk about the cabinets, Bess said, "We always have to worry about our loved ones, don't we?" Evidently not expecting an answer, she rushed on, "Poor Connor's been so strung out with juggling the tree farm, mayoral duties and problems with his boys acting up because they're used to his being home more. He's not sleeping, worried about some of the trees dropping needles early."

Oh, *ya,* Lydia thought, rolling her eyes. Bess obviously hadn't walked out to look at those trees herself. Lydia figured he'd been spraying bad trees and was scared he'd get caught, by his mother or customers. Lydia could just see the headline in the papers, Son of Senator Stark Caught Covering up Sick Trees, or something shameful like that. Lydia was almost tempted to tell Bess about seeing Connor doing exactly that, but she didn't want to be a telltale or to get Connor upset with her. He'd been touchy over the years, and she didn't need that again with everything else going on.

"Well, maybe a nice gift like this will cheer him up," Lydia said. "As you can see, two of these walnut pieces have glassed-in fronts which can be locked. We always like to stress safety, especially if there are little ones in the house like your twin grandsons."

"Believe me I appreciate that. Gun safety and gun control are big issues these days."

"So, about how many hunting rifles will Connor want to store? These racks, as you see, have places for eight locked up."

"That will surely do it. I'd shoot Connor myself if I didn't know he kept his considerable arsenal unloaded and under lock and key."

Under lock and key... The words revolved in Lydia's brain as she showed Bess the lower part of the cabinet, the fine workmanship, even the price, at which she didn't blink an eye. Connor could be her family's enemy—say he wanted to drive them off their adjoining property so he could expand his holding for trees more easily. He was now in partnership with Gid, at least on a small financial scale.

It was news to her that Connor had a gun collection. She'd known he'd loved to hunt, was good with a rifle, of course. Years ago she could recall him bang-ing away at tin cans somewhere on the Stark acreage. Lately, he'd complained that deer were eating some of his seedlings, so he'd no doubt shoot them. But was he also good with locks and keys? Maybe she was wrong that Gid had to be the intruder.

"I said I'll take the large one. Lydia, are you listening? Are you certain you're all right?"

"Oh, sorry. Just exhausted. Thinking too much."

"Thinking too much can be bad, and I know it. Would you believe I have pressure not only to run for governor, which I may do, but to consider a later run for a much higher office? Isn't that all I need on top of all my other stress? Now, I'm trusting you not to tell anyone, especially your friend Ray-Lynn, I said that."

"I won't. But I think you'd be great at whatever you do, and I also think the cat's out of the bag on that, too."

"What do you mean?" she asked as they walked back toward the front desk and cash register.

"Just that two of your worldly funeral guests were whispering the same thing, two of the men."

"Aha. Good ears and a retentive mind. I ought to hire you to keep me informed, my girl," she said with a tight smile, and gave Lydia one of those one-armed hugs again. Lydia liked the nickname "my girl," but then she'd heard Bess had called Naomi that, too. She silently scolded herself for selfishly wanting Bess to be her special friend. Bess might sometimes live next door, but surely they were really worlds apart.

20

"All right now, Lydia," Sheriff Freeman said, "you just take me and Ray-Lynn through the house the way you saw things. I've got a flashlight here in case something needs a good look, but you go ahead and lead the way with your single lantern."

He had checked the basement and attic. On the first floor, he'd found no indication someone had broken in. Lydia first showed them the inside of the generator-operated refrigerator, though *Mamm* would have a tizzy if she knew she was letting strangers, especially worldly ones, peer inside. The Freemans both bent down to take a look.

"Things are just not the way my mother would leave them—kind of disturbed," Lydia explained, pointing. "The honey jar, which she never would have put here, was out of its place in the cupboard and right there where the honey smears are. At first, I just figured she was in a rush."

"You asked her about any of this yet?" the sheriff said.

"No. I thought she had enough to cope with since

Daad was so ill. This will really worry him, too. And it will out-and-out panic her."

"But, I'll bet," Ray-Lynn put in, "not as much as when you tell her about your search for information on your birth parents."

"Every time I get close to telling both of them about that, something worse happens," Lydia said. "And now with *Daad*'s heart attack my mother would have a heart attack of a different kind."

"Ray-Lynn and Lydia, let's just stick to the here and now," the sheriff said.

Lydia saw Ray-Lynn roll her eyes, but she didn't say another word as Lydia showed them where she'd put the honey jar.

"No!" he said when she reached for it. "If worse comes to worst, I can get that fingerprinted, but I'd have to print you and your mother to eliminate yours. Just leave it there for now. It's pretty sticky."

"That's because the intruder poured honey in my bed. The intruder went into the bathroom first, so I'll show you that."

She held the lantern high as they followed her upstairs. She just bet they were thinking the Amish were off their beans to live by lantern light. She showed them the shower—*Mamm* would have a tizzy over that, too—although the water splashes were now dried, so she had to describe the wet tub and tiles as well as the closed shower curtain. Then she took them into her bedroom. Ray-Lynn gasped when she saw the bed.

"Well, truth is," Lydia told them, "I ripped the covers down to see if there was a note or something like that, but it was a mess before I touched it. Like some-

one rolled around in it. Water from someone's body—
or sweat—plus honey. Weird, isn't it?"

"It's got to be a man," Ray-Lynn whispered.

Lydia thought the sheriff would scold her for talking, but he only nodded.

"All I know," Lydia said, her voice shaky again, "is
it's someone who must have used a key to get in—
and I think I have the extras now, the one hanging in
the barn and the one from *Daad*'s office at the store."

"Which means it could be someone who had access to his office," the sheriff said. "Gid Reich, your
come-calling friend?"

"He really isn't anymore."

"And not too happy about that, I'll bet." The sheriff
was silent a moment. "But that extra key hanging in
a typically unlocked Amish barn... Who else might
be sweet on you?"

"Sweet on me? You mean the honey connection?
Isn't this someone who hates me?"

"Maybe. The fact the person rolled around in your
bed, took a shower—all that's kind of sexual innuendo or threat."

Lydia didn't know what *innuendo* meant but she
already saw this as a personal threat. She couldn't
wait for her parents to get back home so she wouldn't
be alone here. And the idea of sexual anything—that
eliminated Connor, didn't it? Leo Lowe—she wouldn't
put anything past him. But she sure hoped the honey,
the shower, the bed didn't make the sheriff think Josh
could be a suspect, too!

Lydia made the three of them coffee and served
thick slices of *Mamm*'s bread with apple butter. She,

too, felt she'd been hit on the head when the sheriff told her how Sandra's skull was crushed in back—just as Victoria Keller's had been.

"If the rung fits her head wound," Lydia said, "her skull hitting the ladder must be what killed her. Then it was an accidental death for Sandra as well as Victoria. Sandra may have stirred up a beehive around here—well, I shouldn't put it that way because of the honey—but I never believed someone would kill her for that."

The sheriff asked, "You got any ideas on who the intruder over at Josh's could have been?"

"Maybe the same one as here, you mean? Leo Lowe would be my first guess. And you said he wasn't home when you went to question him, and that's when someone was in this house."

"Are you going to be all right staying here alone tonight?" Ray-Lynn asked. "You can come home with us and sleep in our guest bedroom, and then I can go to the hospital from there. You need a good night's sleep."

"I really feel I should stay here, Ray-Lynn. But I thank you both so much. I'm hoping my parents will get home soon, and we can all rest easy again. I'll probably sleep downstairs on the sofa again and wedge chairs under all the outside doorknobs, too."

She realized then she had not taken them into the side parlor where she'd found her father's medications, but she'd seen nothing in there to link to an intruder. She'd already blurted out to Josh about *Daad*'s quilting and didn't need anyone else to know. Ray-Lynn would probably want to spread the word far and wide, and then Lydia would be in trouble, as if she wasn't in deep enough already.

And two awful new thoughts hit her. If Sandra had been killed for getting involved in Lydia's search for her birth parents, was Ray-Lynn, who was helping her, safe? And that strange, warped warning in her house and her bed—was she herself in physical danger, too?

Saturday morning as Lydia waited in Dr. Bryan's hospital office, she was proud of herself for getting five hours of sleep, but then, she'd been exhausted. The furniture store would be open today, though she wasn't going back in until Monday, depending on when *Daad* was released. She wanted to be sure she was home with *Mamm* to take care of him, at least a half day.

Her stomach had cramped when the nurse at the cardiac care desk had herded her into the doctor's office instead of letting her go straight to *Daad*'s room. Dr. Bryan wanted to speak with her privately first, the nurse had said. Had *Daad* suffered a setback, and the doctor wanted to break the news to her? Maybe he was going to release *Daad* and only wanted to give her some special instructions, especially since he'd said that *Mamm* might not be a good nurse for *Daad* at times, because she was taking those sleeping pills.

Lydia's exhaustion made her understand better why *Mamm* took those pills, however scary the side effects were. Yet, even without any medication, Lydia now felt as if she was moving and talking but was not herself, like it was all a dream, a nightmare. All she'd wanted was to learn some things about her birth parents and it had led to so many problems.

Dr. Bryan came in and closed the door behind him. He was carrying his little laptop computer again, but he put it on the desk, then leaned over to shake her hand.

"Lydia, we'll keep your father until Monday morning, but your mother has hired a local driver to take her home this evening and come back when he's released. I think he may actually rest better if he's alone tonight and tomorrow."

Lydia nodded. Surely her parents hadn't been arguing when *Daad* was ill. Maybe it was just having *Mamm* there that kept him talking and awake when he should sleep.

The doctor said, "By the way, I talked to your mother about her sleeping pills. I just said you'd scooped up pill containers and didn't realize you had hers, too. I talked to her about the possible side effects. She said she was aware of them but didn't think they were bothering her that way. Though they can be addictive for some people, I think I convinced her to go off them until your father completely recovers."

"Oh, that's good."

"Of course, she's been off them a couple of days already. But here's the thing I really wanted to discuss with you. Your father's blood pressure pills you brought me—they resemble Hytrin. Here," he said, getting up and lifting a huge book from the shelf behind him, "let me show you the picture."

He sat down in the chair beside her and flopped open the big book called *Physicians' Desk Reference.* He pointed at a page with colored pictures of pills. "See the Hytrin capsules here? Bright red, slightly oval shaped?"

"*Ya*—yes. Did I bring the wrong container?"

"The right container, but the wrong pills. It's obviously not your fault. Those pills—" he reached over to his desk and shook the container she'd brought him yesterday "—are not Hytrin." He unscrewed the safety cap and spilled one out onto the page next to the photo in the book.

Daad's pills were red, they looked the same but— Lydia gasped. "Those aren't oval but round. They look like red M&M candy or Red Hots!"

"Sharp girl. M&M'S are exactly what they are."

"But don't those have an *M* on each piece?"

"They do, but the *M*s have been carefully scraped off with a fingernail or sharp object, probably a knife. I experimented—easy to do." He showed her the side that had been scraped. She could barely see where the *M* had been, and the chocolate was barely visible beneath the red color.

"Did you ask my father?"

"He insists he never noticed a problem. I suppose Amish homes are a bit darker with only lantern light. He said he took the pills into his furniture store once or twice. He does wear glasses for close work, and if you don't pay real close attention, you could swallow these with water before the sugar or the chocolate inside melts. I believe your father. So the question is, who would do this? It's not a joke or prank. It's deadly, or could have been, at least. He needs to be on his medicine, not sugar and chocolate."

"Did you ask my mother, too?"

"After I talked to him. She claims she has no idea— he got the pills, took the pills. She's quite upset, especially because she thought I was implying that, when she didn't realize what she was doing—you know, the side effects of her sleeping pills—she'd switched his. But I told her I was not implying anything of the kind."

"No, of course not. They don't get on sometimes, but nothing like that."

"I've had my nurse phone your father's prescribing physician and the pharmacy. They are both puzzled, and I believe them."

"But that's—terrible." Her mind raced. Surely, *Mamm* was telling the truth about not tampering with *Daad*'s pills. But he'd taken them to work. She should look into that, she should—

"Lydia, I'm advising you to let your local law enforcement know about this. I'm going to have to report it here in Wayne County."

"I will. All right," she agreed, but Sheriff Freeman was so busy with the investigation of Sandra's death.

The doctor went on, "I've got him on good BP meds now, but your family must be wary, be careful. You need to ask yourself who had access to these pills after he brought them home and who would want to harm or kill your father."

It was only noon with broad sunlight glaring off the snow, so Lydia asked Ray-Lynn to drop her off at Josh's. Although she had shared so much with Ray-Lynn and the sheriff, she was not yet ready to accuse someone of trying to murder her father. She had to think it through, not jump to conclusions yet. And be careful who she told.

"I think *Daad*'s getting released Monday morning," she told Ray-Lynn, half-afraid she would read her mind that something new was bothering her. "So I'll help *Mamm* get him settled in. I'm pretty sure I can come with Josh for your Wednesday evening manger scene at the church."

"That'll be great. We can use any help you all can give with those animals since you said Hank can't stay for the whole thing. Now, you just be careful walking home from Josh's and going into that house alone, daytime or not—maybe ask Josh to go over with you and wait till you've looked around inside."

"At least I've got all the extra keys now, because I'm sure *Mamm* has hers in her pocketbook. Oh, and *Mamm* should be home tonight anyway, so *Daad* can get more rest. And me, too, if *Mamm* and I don't take to arguing."

"Lydia, I'm glad you won't be alone, but people can easily have extra keys made, you know. Right up at the hardware in town. Ding-dang, that might be an idea."

"What?"

"If Clint Fencer comes in for his usual lunch today, I can ask him on the sly if anyone's made extra keys lately. But then Jack would probably kill me for interfering in his work again," she added with a sigh.

Ray-Lynn shook her head, and Lydia couldn't help but wonder again: Had someone been in their house before recently? Someone who switched *Daad*'s pills? Someone who wanted to kill him? And did that point to Gid, who was ready and able to take over the store, whether Lydia, who had cold-shouldered him, was available or not? Surely, *Mamm*'s side effects from her medicine would not cause her to dump his pills, then change them. *Mamm* liked M&Ms and usually had a sack of them in the pantry, but then there was often a dish of them at the store, and Lydia wasn't sure who replenished that. No, that's right—Gid had given Naomi petty change for that and asked her to get some just last week. Lydia should look at them, see if the red ones were missing. She'd check *Mamm*'s sack of them, too. Oh, how had it all come to this?

Lydia realized she was gripping her hands so tight together that her fingers had gone white. She had to tell Ray-Lynn about *Daad*'s pills, so she could tell the sheriff.

"There's something else, something I hope you will tell the sheriff."

"If it has something serious to do with Sandra's death, how about you tell him yourself? He's been a little touchy lately about my coming up with official things he doesn't know. I don't want to let you down, but... Or why don't you write it down and I'll give it to him? Then I can honestly say I don't know what it's about," she suggested, digging a scratch pad and pen out of the console between the two of them.

"Oh, sure. All right. I understand."

She scribbled down what the doctor had said and gave his name. Folding the paper in fourths, she handed it to Ray-Lynn. She fought to pull herself together as Ray-Lynn turned into the drive by Josh's barn. All she needed was to lose control in front of Ray-Lynn, who would tell the sheriff that much, at least. But Lydia knew all too well she'd get another grilling from Sheriff Freeman, not about Victoria or Sandra's deaths, but about someone trying to hurt her father. Was there any way all three things could be connected?

As Lydia went in the front door of Josh's barn, the alarm-system donkeys began to bray and were soon joined by the familiar gurgles and snorts of the camels.

"Who's there?" came Josh's shout from the loft where Sandra had fallen.

"Me, Josh! What are you doing up there?" she asked as she walked toward the back of the barn.

He appeared above her and quickly came down the ladder. She could see he'd nailed it back tightly to the loft, but he hadn't replaced the lowest rung he'd given the sheriff.

"That crazy cat," he told her. "She took each kitten by the scruff of the neck and carried them back up there, so I'm feeding them—and don't like it. But I can't see moving them again."

He hugged her, and she clung to him. He had shaved again. Her lips grazed his smooth cheek as she said, "Thank heavens, the possible accusations are past, the media people are gone and Christmas is coming."

"How's your father?"

"They're going to release him Monday morning, so I think I'll be able to help you at the Community Church on Wednesday, to really start the Christmas season for the valley."

"Okay, what else is wrong? There's something else."

It amazed her that he knew her that well. She blurted out about the way the kitchen, bathroom and her bed had been tampered with. "Now keep calm," she said, as she felt his muscles tense. "There's more."

"You know who did it?" he demanded. "Gid?"

"I *don't* know. But someone substituted candy for my father's blood pressure pills. He's blessed to be alive since he's been taking sugar and chocolate instead of his medicine. It's like someone wants him hurt or dead. His doctor's going to write it up, and I wrote a note for Ray-Lynn to give Sheriff Freeman."

He pulled her hard to him again. "That points to Gid again, doesn't it?"

"Does it? What if Leo Lowe thinks I'm out to hurt his father, so he tries to hurt mine? What if Connor—"

"Connor?" he interrupted, holding her out stiff-armed and staring into her face.

"Yes, what if Connor wants our land to expand his? I know there's been bad blood between *Mamm* and Connor—his family—but I can't believe he'd do something like that. Only, Connor was the first one to knock on my door after that awful night. He said his mother sent him to see if I was all right, but he seemed so eager to know how *Daad* was, like he might be checking up on his own handiwork."

"How about I sleep here in the barn tonight—I've done that before—and you stay at my house? No one has to know. The only other good option is that I sleep in your kitchen by the back door, but I can't leave the animals alone with all that's going on. How about Ray-Lynn staying with you?"

"She suggested that, but I turned her down. *Mamm* will be home later today."

"Does your mother know about your father's medicine?"

"Yes, the doctor told her, too. It will be the two of us tonight, so you won't have to worry."

But *I* will worry, Lydia thought. Spending the night with just her mother, without *Daad* there as a buffer, might be as unsettling as being in the house with the intruder.

21

Lydia was grateful to have *Mamm* with her that night—and not. Silent snow was falling outside, but Lydia wished it could be more quiet in here. After their meal, she'd explained about the intruder and the things tampered with. She told *Mamm* she wished now that she'd called in the sheriff.

Mamm had exploded. "But who? And in my house? My kitchen and bathroom? And then you paraded the sheriff and Ray-Lynn through here? And now you say you wrote to him about *Daad*'s fake pills! He'd better not think it was me, always looking at the mate, they are, when there's a family problem."

She jumped up from the table and went straight for the cupboard where Lydia had put the honey jar.

"*Mamm,* don't touch that in case Sheriff Freeman has to use it later for evidence."

"Nonsense," she said, snatching the jar down, turning the sink faucet on full blast, thrusting it under the spray and rubbing it vigorously. "No one will want this jar for that. No one in this household has done anything wrong! Now I'll have to clean tonight."

"No, you don't. I haven't touched my bed yet."

"What? Left it that way, messed and dirtied? Every bit of that has to be cleaned, the bathtub, too. I won't say, 'What is this world coming to,' because I know! An intruder in my house. We need to check the windows and relock the doors!"

Lydia got up from the table and went over to where *Mamm* had scrubbed the honey jar, even dumping the rest of the thick contents into the swirl of water.

"*Mamm,* I was thinking, we'd best not spring all this on *Daad* right away. I'm sure his pills being fooled with was enough of a shock."

"To us all. I think that doctor blamed me because of the so-called side effects of my sleeping pills. Like I would put candy in his pill bottle and not know it! *Daad* said he took the pills to work with him a couple of times, but no one in this house would harm his pills! When he first got them, I made him take them in front of me so he wouldn't forget. He's so forgetful sometimes."

She started to cry. Lydia pulled out the closest chair and sat her in it.

"Lydia, I'm sure I'm not doing things I don't know," *Mamm* choked out as Lydia handed her a tissue from the box on the counter.

"Of course you're not, or we'd see signs of it. This is all too much right now, but I do think we need to have the locks on our house changed."

"We'll ask your father."

"He won't be home until Monday and, like I said, do we want to spring all of this on him now? I think we should make the decision to change the locks. I can stop at the hardware store on Monday morning, ask

Clint Fencer to come out to take care of it. And then
we dare not put an extra key in the unlocked barn. I
have that one now and *Daad*'s keys from the store."

"But who would do this? Though I don't like to
speak ill of the dead, it's that Sandra's fault one way
or the other. You know what your father whispered to
me before they took him away to do that test and fix
his heart? He said, 'If I die, I'll tell Sammy you're still
grieving for him.' In Heaven, he meant. So how do we
know he didn't put that candy in his pillbox himself,
like he wanted to die? What would be so bad in his
life that he'd want to die?"

"He just meant he was facing heart surgery, and
that's never a sure thing. Heart attacks aren't like the
common cold."

But all Lydia could think of were the words on the
quilt *Daad* had been working on so hard: *Father Forgive,* or more like, *Forgive Father.* Forgive him for setting himself up for death? Was he that unhappy? Was
that why he, too, had pushed her toward Gid when he
usually wanted only her happiness—so the business
would be well cared for after he died? No, no, that line
of thought was crazy. The Amish abhorred suicide, for
all life was sacred.

Fighting not to dissolve into tears herself, she kept
quiet about those fears. Instead, she sucked in a sob
and put her hand on her mother's shoulder. "We'll get
him home, get him better, *Mamm.*"

When she knelt and hugged her mother hard, she
hugged her back. No, surely it could not be *Mamm*
who wanted to harm *Daad,* even if she might have
been on those sleeping pills and not quite known what
she was doing.

Hoping her voice was steady, Lydia suggested, "How about we clean the house together in the morning?"

"As long as I help you change your bed now. Or do you not want to sleep there anymore? Lydia, if you were only married, had a marital bed with Gid, then you'd always feel safe."

Lydia stiffened and set her mother back in the chair. Little cold fingers of doubt—of terror—crept up her back. *Mamm* doing strange things she did not recall because of her medicine was one thing, but wasn't her desperation to get Gid and her together another motive? Because of *Daad*'s heart attack, Lydia knew she'd have to work closely with Gid now. And *Mamm* seemed almost eager to erase the signs of the intruder.

"*Ya,* let's change my bed together," Lydia said, but she was thinking that, first thing in the morning, she was going to check out the sack of candy in the pantry to see if the red ones were low or missing.

Despite the fact that Sunday was to be a day of rest, Lydia and *Mamm* worked hard, cleaning the house, tending the horses. Lydia was relieved that *Mamm*'s M&Ms stash in the pantry had quite a few red-coated ones, but were there enough? That wasn't such a large medicine bottle, and it had been only about one-third full. Lydia had tried scraping the *M* off several red pieces with a kitchen knife and then her fingernail. Both worked quite well, although a bit of the chocolate showed through, just as it had in the doctor's office. But the change in color wasn't that noticeable. And, as Dr. Bryan had said, it was dim in Amish homes.

Most people would just shake one pill out and down it quickly.

"I'd like to clean up his quilting nest in the side parlor," *Mamm* had said. "But then he would get upset, and he'll need something quiet to do while he heals at home. I still say we need to ask his permission before you try to get all our locks changed. Sad world to have to use locks, let alone have to change them. When I was growing up, we hardly ever locked the house and nothing came of it."

Nothing came of it. The words echoed in Lydia's head. So much had come into her life lately, most of it bad. But not her growing love for Josh. And not her gratitude that *Daad* was coming home tomorrow.

Monday morning early, Ray-Lynn stopped by to tell them that *Daad* would not be released until 3:00 p.m. Lydia had given Ray-Lynn's phone as their contact number. She also gave Lydia a note behind *Mamm*'s back that the sheriff would look into the pill substitution as he investigated Sandra's death.

As soon as Ray-Lynn left for the restaurant, Lydia hitched Flower to ride into town to the hardware store to ask for their locks to be changed.

"You should be heading straight for the furniture store, not running errands in town," *Mamm* had protested.

Ya, Lydia told herself again as she set out, she was ready to have a home of her own, but not with Gid Reich. Maybe one right next door to her family's home would do.

In town she arranged to have Mr. Fencer come out to change the front and back door locks early that afternoon. That way it would be done before *Daad* came home, but while *Mamm* was still there. Lydia wanted to be able to report to her father that she'd recently been at the furniture store so she could assure him things were fine there.

The hired car would pick up *Mamm* at one-thirty, then bring her parents both back by suppertime. Lydia wanted to be there for *Daad*'s homecoming. And, as soon as she thought she could ask him, she wanted to talk to him about the quilt he nearly had finished. Was it to be hers and what did the words on the border really mean?

And, hopefully, with that chat, she could assess whether he could be so depressed or upset that he was suicidal. Surely, he had not substituted his own pills, but she was getting used to surprises. Had Sandra or someone else told him that Lydia was searching for information about her birth parents, and he'd been hurt by that?

As she untied Flower's reins from the hitching post in front of the hardware store, a strange *Englische* man walked up to her. With a broad smile, he flashed a business card at her. "You're Lydia Brand," he stated, not asking a question. "Roy Manning, *Cleveland Plain Dealer.* I hear the county coroner has ruled Sandra Myerson's death accidental just as he did Senator Stark's sister's. Since you were on Joshua Yoder's property at the time of both deaths—found both women dead—do you agree with that ruling? And what is your relationship to those women and Mr. Yoder?"

She was tempted to just keep quiet, climb in her buggy and leave. But wouldn't that look like she had something to hide?

"My relationship with him is that we are next-door neighbors, and I help with his animals. Camels are my favorites, especially the Bactrians like Melly and Gaspar. I think if you research Bactrians and dromedaries, your readers would appreciate knowing the difference, especially at this time of year. Excuse me, please."

She got up into the buggy, backed Flower out and giddyapped her away, despite the fact that Roy Manning ran for his car and, oh, no, followed her. She wasn't sure whether she should drive into the sheriff's to get rid of this pushy, rude man, but what if Sheriff Freeman wasn't there? And the Amish would never ask for a restraining order against someone. She could park at the Dutch Farm Table, but why lead that man to Ray-Lynn, who would hide her, but then be facing Roy Manning herself? If he asked folks in the restaurant about her, they'd be as upset as when Sandra played reporter there.

No, she'd keep to her plans and head for the furniture store, where she could have someone else take her buggy and hide out in *Daad*'s office until the reporter left. He reminded her of a bulldog, nipping at her heels.

She drove directly into the horse shed at work and, leaving Flower hitched for someone else to tend, started at a good clip for the back workshop door. Mr. Manning was waiting for her, walking along fast beside her.

"I won't use your photograph, of course, Ms. Brand. It's just that you and Mr. Yoder are the best eyewitnesses to both deaths. Not eyewitnesses to the deaths, of course, but the bodies being found. And since one woman was Senator Stark's sister and the other someone the senator met with—"

Lydia knew she should keep quiet, but she wanted to protect Bess. "It was her son, Connor, who Sandra Myerson spoke to, not the senator."

"No," he clipped out, almost at the workshop door, "several Stark Farm Christmas workers I interviewed said that when Sandra went to the tree farm to interview the son—Connor, as you said—Ms. Myerson talked to Bess Stark, too, at length, and they both got a bit vocal, gestured a lot, though Senator Stark won't answer my questions, either."

"Excuse me, I'm late for work," Lydia managed to choke out, but she was now more than upset. Hadn't Bess said that she had not met Sandra? So why would she lie about that, since Sandra had met and questioned so many others?

She closed the workshop door in the man's face and asked the men to be sure he did not enter. She rushed to the back offices because, for once, she needed a favor from Gid. He was not in his office but on the sales floor, talking to Naomi.

"A newspaper reporter followed me here, and I don't want to see him!" she blurted out to them. "He may come around to the front door."

"I'll take care of it," Gid said. He went to the door and then stepped outside, only to come back in to tell them the man was driving away. Lydia hoped the reporter would not return when she left or, worse, go to her house. She didn't need another Leo Lowe accosting her or upsetting *Daad* when he got home today. Or running amok in town the way Sandra had, maybe gaining her an enemy who was willing to kill her.

Still breathing hard on the way to *Daad*'s office, Lydia passed the coffee room and, seeing no one was

there, went in. *Ya,* the bowl of festive-looking M&Ms
was there, much depleted from the other day. Plenty
of red ones in the mix, but that meant nothing. Whoever changed her father's pills had probably done it a
while ago.

In *Daad*'s office, she closed the door and sat in his
chair, elbows on the desk, fingers gripped together,
pressed to her forehead. She had to calm down. She
wished she could contact Josh to warn him that at
least one reporter had not left the area, that he'd questioned their relationship, that the nightmare was far
from over.

And should she talk to Bess about what must be a
misunderstanding? She felt bad that Bess had been
pulled into Sandra's death, especially after the loss of
her sister. Lydia closed her eyes, picturing again the
description of Victoria Keller's drawings of flying angels who looked like children. That vision blurred with
an image of the insides of her broken snow globe, then
with the angels on the *Father Forgive Father* quilt.

She jerked alert when a knock resounded on the
door. Gid's voice. "Lydia, are you all right? That man
didn't hurt you, did he?"

"Come in," she told him, grateful he had not just
walked in as if the office were his again. When he
entered, she told him, "No, he was just rude, that's
all. Thanks for making sure he didn't enter the store."

"How's Sol?"

"Coming home this afternoon, so I can't stay long.
But I'd like a complete report of how things are going
here—especially good news—so I can lift his spirits
when he asks."

"All right, good idea," he said, closing the door and

sitting down on a chair opposite the desk. She got up and pulled the drapes open to get more light and so she didn't feel so alone with him. She saw clumps of heavy clouds that might mean more snow, and she sent up a silent prayer the roads would be good for *Daad*'s return.

"Please tell him, too," Gid said as she sat back down, "that things are under control, and that you and I will work well together until he can return. When and if he's seeing visitors, I'd like to visit him—see you, too, outside the store, of course. But if you or your mother need anything done around the house or barn, just let me know."

"That's kind of you," she said, wondering if he'd already helped himself to things in the house and barn. But now it was time to focus on business. "So, what are the sales numbers since he's been gone, and what orders and deliveries are still pending?"

"Glad you don't have a wheelchair for me, Liddy," *Daad* said as he walked into the house with *Mamm* beside him, holding his arm. "They made me ride clear to our hired car in one."

"Standard procedure, the doctor said," *Mamm* put in.

"Well, *ya,*" he muttered. "The doctor said a lot of things."

Lydia kissed his cheek and helped him take his coat off. She meant to propel him clear into his favorite chair in the living room, but he sat down at the table while *Mamm* bustled past with their things. Lydia heard her go upstairs, heard the bathroom door close.

Should she dare to bring up the Christmas quilt al-

ready? No, she'd have to wait a bit, until he was better rested. She had no doubt there would be plenty of
times when her parents were not together.

"Liddy," he said in such a quiet voice that she sat
in the chair across the table to hear him better. "You
found the pills, the fake pills, in my quilting room,
right?"

"*Ya,* after searching everywhere else."

"So you saw the quilt—your Christmas gift."

"I was hoping it was to be mine. It's so beautiful,
Daad. I just love everything about it. It reminds me
of Josh's animals, the manger, of course. I love the
angels that remind me of the snow globe you gave me
so long ago from—" she lowered her voice even more
"—from my other mother."

His eyes teared up. Oh, no, she didn't want to get
him emotional the moment he got home. Would asking
about the words so carefully sewn on the quilt's border
upset him even more when he should just be resting?

But *Mamm* bustled back downstairs and took over
the early supper of soup and sandwiches Lydia had
begun.

"Well," *Mamm* said, "we are both happy to have
our Sol home. We'll find out who changed those pills.
Someone will tip their hand." Without looking at them,
she picked up a pot holder and tipped the big pan of
steaming noodle soup into the three waiting bowls.

22

By Wednesday, Lydia felt things were looking up. *Daad* seemed to be adjusting well to his new medicine. Since both she and Gid had assured him things were going well at the store, he seemed content right now to stay home, resting and working on his quilt. He hadn't noticed the door locks had been changed, and they hadn't told him about the intruder yet. Today was mild, clear weather for the tableau at Ray-Lynn's church. And, as busy as she'd been with her parents and at the store, she would finally see Josh tonight.

Best of all, she had managed to have another reassuring talk with *Daad* when *Mamm* was upstairs. Her parents were going to drive by the manger scene later tonight. "We always support out daughter!" was the way *Mamm* had put it.

"I was wondering about the words on the border of the quilt," Lydia had told *Daad,* coming back into the kitchen where he was lingering over apple pie, coffee and the Amish newspaper *The Budget.* "'Father, forgive' is a Bible quote, but one I usually think of more at Easter time."

He put the paper down, looked up at her and said, "But we all have to be reminded to forgive—even those we love."

"True. Everyone makes mistakes," she'd said, trying to help him when he started to look a bit upset.

"Another good Bible quote, 'For all have sinned and fall short of the glory of God,'" he added, his voice catching. "I know the quilt border can be read as 'Forgive Father' as well as 'Father Forgive.' I've done my share of things to be forgiven for, if you want to read it that way." He cleared his throat, then coughed and reached for his coffee.

"Me, too, of course," she'd said, still wanting to bolster him. She wished she hadn't brought the quilt up again. "And a lot of times problems come from going about the right things the wrong way."

He'd lifted his gaze and met hers. She'd had the oddest feeling he was going to say something else. He bit his lower lip as if to hold words back before he looked down into his cup, seeming to seek some answer there. Lydia almost blurted out that she was sorry she'd involved Sandra in her quest to learn more about her birth parents but that she had been desperate.

"Well, it's a beautiful quilt," she'd said in a rush. "One I will always treasure."

"As you and I will always treasure our time together. Time is precious, Liddy. Time and trust."

Now why, she wondered a short while later, as she walked down their driveway to wait for Josh to pick her up in his buggy, had *Daad* not said, "Time and love?" But "Time and trust"? She trusted him and always had, so why did he say it that way?

She looked down the road, and here came the traveling menagerie: first, Josh's buggy and, behind him, going just as slow, Hank's truck. Hank was pulling an open, penned load of animals in the truck bed, a camel's head showing above the cab as if the beast was driving and had stuck his big, shaggy neck out the roof. Oh, it was Melly.

A car honked and went around the slow-moving vehicles on the two-lane road. Lydia was pretty sure her usually well-behaved Melly actually spit at the car as it roared past.

Josh pulled over onto the berm for her while Hank put on the brakes to wait.

"Slow going!" Josh called to her. "I brought Melly instead of Gaspar since you were going to be there."

"I like things slow lately," she said, climbing up beside him. She saw in the backseat he had the crèche filled with straw for the baby Jesus.

They made a strange parade to the Community Church, but at least it was on this side of town. Lydia's heart lifted even more. *Daad* was healing, *Mamm* was off her sleeping pills and had been a bit calmer lately— and she was with Josh in his buggy, as if she really was the woman in his life. The reporter from Cleveland had not been back, Gid was keeping his distance at the store. And she was going to get to speak with Nathan Hostetler tonight, one of her birth mother's cousins. Considering the tragedy of two deaths lately, and the fact Josh had briefly come under suspicion for Sandra's, but was now in the clear—oh, *ya,* things were definitely looking up.

A crowd awaited them at the church where the three-sided manger had already been erected. The risers for the church choir were set up to one side. Several large lights on poles dispelled the twilight shadows. It would soon be dark, but those beams would illuminate the tableau. Dangling from a wire, a bright six-pointed star outlined by blue bulbs hung above the manger. Straw was strewn on the ground, and Josh took the crèche out of the backseat to put it in its place.

Striding here and there, Ray-Lynn looked nervous. Unlike the other folks, costumed in plain or fancy robes waiting to become characters in the tableau, she was in slacks and a long coat—camel hair, no less.

"Glad you're here!" she called out as she ran over to the truck. She was carrying a clipboard with papers fluttering from it, but at least the wind was fairly mild. "A few folks who got the time wrong have been by already. Hank, Josh, we've checked the angel platforms more than once, but when you get the animals unloaded, can you take a look at that, too? We don't need our angels taking a header into the roof of the manger during 'Silent Night.'"

Lydia went to watch Melly amble down the ramp Hank had attached to the truck bed. When the animal saw Lydia, she smacked her lips—her form of an air kiss.

"I love you, too, big girl!" Lydia told her, and took hold of her bridle while Hank and Josh unloaded the ox, donkey and four sheep, then put them in a makeshift pen away from the road.

As Lydia led Melly in that direction, a flash went off in her face. For a moment, she couldn't see. Melly balked, snorted and let out a low screech. She jerked her bridle from Lydia's hand and took off.

Afraid Melly would head for the road and be hit, Lydia watched the camel charge toward a dark figure in the parking lot instead. Bright red-and-blue spots pulsed in both her eyes from the flash, making it difficult to see clearly.

"Melly!" she shouted. "Melly, stop! Stay!"

Josh and Hank came running, but Lydia chased the camel and got to her first, just as another bright light flashed. Photographs! Who was crazy enough to take flash pictures in Melly's face—or photograph an Amish up close?

As she grabbed Melly's bridle to turn the big beast around, Lydia's eyes cleared enough that she could make out the reporter Roy Manning with a camera.

"I should have let her run you down!" Lydia shouted.

"Get away from here!" It was Josh, followed by Ray-Lynn.

"Get off our property right now, sir, or believe me, I'll tell the sheriff. He'll be here any minute."

"I just took a couple of pictures!" the man shouted, but he edged away from them. "Ms. Brand here gave me a lecture on camels, so I thought I'd get a picture of her with one. But I'll trade it for an interview."

"Leave right now!" Josh ordered. "You do know that camels attack on cue, don't you?"

"Sic that thing on me, and I'll sue!" he yelled, but he headed for a car parked in the church lot, revved the engine as if it were angry, too, and drove away.

Josh looked furious as they led Melly, still sputtering, back toward the holding pen. "I think he got me in the background of the photo, too," he muttered to Lydia.

"That's probably what he wanted—us together—not the camel," she told him, keeping her voice down. "At

least that picture shows what I told him about our relationship—only that I work with your animals. Glad he
didn't get us in the buggy together. But what a bad start
for Ray-Lynn's big night. Oh, Sheriff Freeman's here."

"And Ray-Lynn's filling him in. That reporter
could be trouble. I think he's the type to keep hanging around."

Things definitely improved after that as the animals
were moved onto the set and the cast of characters took
their places. The choir began to sing. The sheriff kept
cars going past on the road, unless they wanted to pull
into the parking lot for a longer view. Lydia jumped
each time someone took a flash picture from a car, but
at least the photos were from a distance and only of
the manger scene. She estimated that about one-third
of the visitors were in buggies.

Lydia especially loved the angels, pretty, blonde
teenage girls with wire wings who stood on a platform
hidden behind the manger under the star of Bethlehem.
They held trumpets and pretended to play. The Virgin
Mary cradled a doll, and the church choir sang all the
hymns Lydia loved, even the one with the haunting
tune, "When blossoms flowered 'mid the snow, upon
a winter night..." And Melly, even though they had
strapped the ornate seat on her, seemed to be behaving for the three bearded wise men who more than
once knelt before the manger with their treasures for
the holy child.

Lydia kept watching the buggies that went by, looking for her parents and others she knew. Gid drove by
and pulled in the lot for a few minutes. She talked to
him briefly, hoping he would not hang around, and
he didn't. He told her he had somewhere else to go

and left with a wave. Bess drove slowly past with her grandsons and daughter-in-law in the car but no Connor. Lydia wondered if he was still out spraying sick trees. Wouldn't it get all over town, and beyond, if he was actually defrauding his Christmas customers?

Others from her church passed by in a line of buggies. She saw Bishop and Mattie Esh, and following them, Hannah and Seth Lantz with their two young children. The third buggy in that group carried Ella, a lavender grower, her husband, Alex Caldwell, and their young daughter. They were members of Lydia's church, but a family with a worldly last name because Alex had been reared in the world and was one of the few outsiders to turn Amish. The last family she recognized were wood carver Ben Kline and his new wife, Abigail Baughman, who raised mushrooms, of all things.

But, from the moment she'd arrived, Lydia had wondered which one of the background workers was her distant relative, Nathan Hostetler. By eight o'clock, with only an hour left to go, the donkey and sheep were starting to eat the straw on the floor of the manger and Melly had pulled a turban off one of the wise men. Ray-Lynn, looking frazzled but happy, came up to Lydia and whispered, "Nate Hostetler has some time to talk to you now. He's taking a break on the porch steps behind the tableau. Good luck," she added with a pat on Lydia's back before she darted off again.

Lydia whispered to Josh where she was going and hurried back toward the church.

Josh sure hoped that newspaper reporter didn't show up again, because he was afraid he'd lose his temper and hit him. The guy had dared to come to the barn this afternoon, announced by the raucous greeting of the donkeys. He'd had the gall to walk right in and flash his name card, as if that made everything on the up-and-up.

"I'm busy, Mr. Manning," Josh had told him, once he'd read his card which announced he was a field reporter for the Cleveland newspaper. "And I'd appreciate it if you would get out of my barn and off the property."

"I know the Amish are good businesspeople," he'd said, ignoring that request. "How about I do a story this spring on your petting zoo to bring in a lot of extra people, and you, in turn, answer a couple of my questions now? Like which loft did your friend Sandra Myerson fall from?" He craned his neck to look around. "Oh, I'll bet that one there with the ladder."

"The Amish are law-abiding, nonviolent people, Mr. Manning, but I'm asking you to leave. There will be no answers to questions, no interview. Talk to the sheriff if you must, but—"

"I have. He didn't exactly say so, but you surely must have been a suspect in your former girlfriend's death, at least before the accidental death ruling."

Josh fought to keep his temper locked down. It had gotten the best of him more than once recently, and the results were always bad. Besides, this guy had what they call the power of the pen. All he needed was to throw him out bodily or shove him...

Instead, he forced himself to just turn away—turn the other cheek—and walk over to get Melly out of the pen. He was tempted to spit at the guy, just like a camel.

"Just a few questions about your relationship with Ms. Myerson, then," the idiot dared to ask, following but at a distance, so he had to shout. "I've interviewed the Columbus friends you have in common, but the fact she came here several times, was asking around, some say about your current girlfriend—seems Ms. Myerson still cared about you and wanted you back..."

That, Josh thought, was too close for comfort. Was this guy fishing for a way to imply that either he or Lydia had wanted Sandra out of the way? The last thing he needed was Manning hitting on the possibility he had shoved Sandra off that loft.

Josh flexed his fists and fought to keep from throwing the man out. Then he realized he should get Melly and maybe let her do the dirty work.

He swung the gate to the pen open wide and called Melly out, Gaspar then Balty. With an open sack of feed in his hand, he walked straight for Roy Manning, the three camels shuffling in quick step behind him. He even threw a bit of camel feed at the man's feet, so the animals crowded closer and swung their big heads toward him.

Ya, thank the Lord. Cursing, the man raced for the door he'd come in. But as he started his car, Josh wondered if the intruder who had been lurking around his barn could be someone like that reporter.

Josh had hoped he wouldn't see Manning again, but he'd figured he might—and then here he'd turned up tonight at the tableau...with a camera.

Josh shook his head to clear the memory and walked along the fence to look at the manger scene from the side. His animals were pretty much behaving. Hank had been picked up to go to his son's birthday party, though he'd left the truck for another *Englische* guy to drive the animals back home.

And, Josh saw with a glance back at the lighted church steps behind the manger, Lydia was finally getting to talk to a Hostetler relative who might have known her birth mother.

"Did Ray-Lynn tell you that my birth mother was Lena Hostetler?" Lydia asked Nathan Hostetler.

"She only said you were related, and then were adopted by the Brands," he told her. He was soft-spoken. Tall and lean with a sun-weathered face, he wore a trimmed beard, not an Amish one, and seemed quite nervous. He was dressed all in black, as were the other church members who were background workers.

"I believe you are a distant cousin of my mother, Lena," Lydia said. "I was hoping you or someone you are related to could tell me what you recall about her. She and my father, David Brand, were killed in a buggy accident when I was very young, so I don't remember either of them. Any details or memories would mean a lot to me. I wonder if I resemble her or David at all."

He shifted on the step beside her. Frowning, he averted his eyes. "Not so much," he said. "Well, hair color. I remember them, of course, family reunion, weddings, including theirs, Christmastime. But there are many Hostetlers, some still Amish, who are disappointed my family left the church to become Mennonites."

"I understand that. Is there anyone else you could mention that I could talk to, someone who knew Lena better? And do you know if she collected those little plastic snow globes?"

"Are you sure you got your facts straight?" he asked, sitting up straighter and turning toward her for the first time. "I mean, it was a while ago, and their tragic accident and all..."

"But—"

"The thing is, I think you got the adoption thing confused. It's been years, but I remember my mother— she passed nearly ten years ago—saying you were adopted all right, but by David and Lena."

"No, I was adopted by the Brands, Solomon and Susan."

He shook his head and shrugged. "Sure, well, I know Lena and David would have been good parents had they lived. Growing up, Lena took care of her younger siblings, loved kids. That's why I remember my mother saying she'd been sick somehow—Lena— and couldn't have kids, but then got one."

Lydia wanted to burst into tears, to tell him he was wrong. But what really scared her was that this man's comments more or less matched what old, blind Mr. Raber had told her. She recalled he had said of Lena Brand that she did not look pregnant, that *They had no child—and then they did.* Could two people who had known her parents—although not well—be so confused?

She was going to ask him for more, for anything to prove to herself he was wrong. It had been years ago. His mother could have been ill when she told him about Lena and David's child. But could it be—no, no way—that the Hostetlers had adopted her and, when they were killed, she was adopted a second time? No, she just knew Lena and David were her birth parents!

"Mr. Hostetler, is there someone else who might know even more about the Brands, so that—"

It was all she got out before Ray-Lynn appeared, out of breath. At first Lydia feared Melly had acted up again, but Ray-Lynn blurted, "Your parents are here—drove in the parking lot for a closer view. Your Dad stayed in the buggy, but your mother... I mean, she was talking to Josh, but I told her I'd find you so they didn't have to look for y—"

But *Mamm* was hurrying their way. She must have followed Ray-Lynn.

"Oh, and who is this?" *Mamm* asked, looking at Mr. Hostetler.

Ray-Lynn answered as he and Lydia stood. "This is Nathan, our church custodian. They're both just taking a little break."

"Oh, so I see. I'm sure you both worked hard to put this lovely Christmas scene together," *Mamm* said with a smile, but Lydia could tell she was upset. Maybe because her daughter was sitting alone with a strange man, one not Amish. Hopefully, she didn't know he was a Hostetler.

"I thank you again for all the hard work you and the church men did to set things up here," Lydia told him, and tried to move *Mamm* away. But she wasn't budging.

"Nice to meet you, Mrs. Brand," he said with a nod of his head. "I'm Nathan Hostetler, and my wife sure loves your family's furniture."

"Nice to meet you," *Mamm* said, finally turning to leave with Lydia at her side.

"Hostetler, but not an Amish one," *Mamm* said, her voice as chilly as the air. "So I find my daughter talking to a stranger in private."

"If you call the brightly lighted church steps private," Lydia said as they made their way toward the manger scene. "I assure you, *Mamm,*" she said, trying to keep her voice light, "I'm not going to run off with a Mennonite or a married man."

"I know," she said, obviously not wanting to pursue the topic when Lydia figured she would. "Just you be sure you don't run off with an Amish man who left the faith to live in the world, who wants to marry a girl with enough money to keep his petting zoo going."

Lydia's nostrils flared and she gritted her teeth as they headed toward the buggy where *Daad* was waiting. Sadly, it sounded as if her undeclared truce with *Mamm* was over, and was it only because she was panicked that Lydia was chatting with a Hostetler? Why did *Mamm—Daad,* too—have to be so secretive about her past? Did they fear she might reject them or were they just overly protective since they'd lost Sammy?

"A nice manger scene!" *Daad* called to her from the buggy. "The biblical animals add a lot, but I really like the angels."

"They're my favorites, too," Lydia said, and smiled at him. She wondered if, like her, he was thinking of her snow globe and the angelic figures on the quilt that would soon be hers.

And she vowed that this wonderful man, in every way a father to her, would know, even when she told him she was seeking news about her birth parents, that he, Solomon Brand, would always be the father of her heart.

23

Although her parents wanted her to go home with them in their buggy, Lydia stayed to help Josh take the animals to his barn and get them bedded down.

"Bedded down?" *Mamm* said. "Then how do you plan to get home?"

"*Mamm,* Josh lives barely a quarter mile from us," she said, trying to keep her annoyance in check. "His buggy will still be hitched, and he can easily run me home."

"Your mother just means," *Daad* put in, "don't you be walking the road or through the woodlot alone that late."

"I won't. Josh wouldn't let me."

"I'll wait up, *ya,* I will," *Mamm* said as she took the reins from *Daad.* She must have decided it would be too much for him to drive home. And they were gone.

Josh came over. "Did Mr. Hostetler tell you anything useful?"

Lydia shook her head. "He thought I was adopted by the Hostetlers as well as by the Brands. The thing is, that's what Mr. Raber from Amity said, too, but I thought he was just senile. I'm going to have to find another Hostetler who knows what really happened. What if it's true? About two adoptions?"

"That can't be. It was a long time ago and followed a tragedy. They're confused. Are you sure you can't just ask your father?"

"I'm afraid to so much as tell him or *Mamm* I'm looking into my past. It's a miracle they haven't figured it out so far. They're so different from each other but both fragile. Come on, let's get these animals home."

Holding the envelope with Josh's payment from the church on her lap, sitting beside him in his buggy, Lydia treasured every minute of their slow journey. She could tell he was nervous, probably since Hank wasn't driving the truck behind them. It was a friend of Hank's who didn't work much with animals. But all went well, and the Beiler boys came out to help them unload.

"Everything all right?" Josh asked them. "No problems?"

"Just that the east side old milking door blew open a little bit ago," Micah said. "I mean, the wind wasn't much tonight, but we heard it bang, so we went down there. That old lock was broken."

"*Ya,* we had to nail it closed with a couple of boards," Andy added. "And somehow the sheep you keep down there in the old cow milking area got loose in the barn—broke the latch on their pen, I guess. Musta been an accident, but we finally caught them all. Just got the last one back in the pen."

Lydia saw Josh stiffen. His facial muscles tightened to a grimace.

"We don't need more accidents," he muttered, "not

even something minor. That's the wing I'm going to have remodeled soon, so it sounds like I'll need a new door, too. Lydia," he said in a louder voice, "you take Melly in. Andy and Micah, get the donkey penned up and fed, then you can head home. I'll take the sheep and check things out down by the old cow stanchions. Oh, and your week's salary's in an envelope on my desk."

"*Danki,* Josh," they said, almost in chorus.

Lydia led Melly to the camel pen where they were greeted with welcoming snorts and gurgles. She made sure the water and feed pans were full, but the boys had done a good job. She walked with the two of them to the front barn door and watched them leave in Andy's small courting buggy. Realizing she was still holding Josh's payment envelope from the church, she headed back yet again to his office area. She wondered how the mother cat and her kittens were doing in the loft and glanced up at it. And screamed.

It was hard to see from here, but—but… She tried to shout for Josh, but no sound came out.

"Lydia! What is it?" Running feet. Josh's voice, still distant. "What—"

He skidded to a halt next to her. She pointed upward. He squinted into the lantern-lit dimness of the barn and gasped. Painted in crimson on the side of the loft, one on each side of the ladder, were two crudely drawn angels. They both had their haloes pierced by devil's horns, and the larger angel held a pitchfork as if guarding the very gates of Hell.

And under that angel, in heavy, freshly dripping paint—or blood—the ladder leaned against the huge word *KILLER!*

* * *

"Oh, no. Look," Ray-Lynn said to Jack after they parked side by side in their garage that night. "Lydia left her purse in my car for safekeeping and evidently forgot it. She was so harried at the end, she won't even remember where she put it."

"Do Amish women put as much stuff in those as non-Amish?" he asked, looking at the plain black bag Ray-Lynn was holding out.

"Are women *women?* Ding-dang, I'm tired, but I've got to get it to her tonight."

"Get back in, and I'll drive. I swear, honey, you just ought to adopt one of these Amish girls you're always sticking your neck out for. Okay, I know," he said, snatching her car keys from her. "With Lydia, that adoption joke came out way bad."

"Let's get the boys back in here," Josh said. "Can you catch them?"

"They're gone. Should I take your buggy and go after them? But you know they didn't do this."

"No, I don't want you out on the road alone at night. I know they didn't do this or even see it, or they'd have said so. The broken door and the sheep made a diversion to get them away while someone came in the back. I hate to start locking barn doors. And that mess better not be blood, but it seems like it's turning black, maybe clotting. I didn't count the sheep. If someone's killed one of them…but it's obviously a reference to Sandra's death."

They clung together, still staring aghast at the message and pictures.

Finally, Lydia whispered, "But why the word *killer?*

Is it accusing you or is that the signature of Sandra's killer? Or is it meant to keep me from trusting you? Who could hate you that much?"

"I don't think *killer* is a signature. It's—" his voice wavered "—it's pointed at me."

"Gid left the manger scene a while ago. Said he had something to do."

"It could be someone Sandra knew. Or if it's to drive a wedge between us, even your parents."

She pulled away from him. "My parents? You think they would do this—or ruin our snow angels? Can you see my *daad* climbing up here right now or my mother, either?"

"I just meant for motive. They must still want you to stay away from me. Let's try another way of looking at it. Someone wants to scare me into moving away, to leave here."

"Connor might want our property, so maybe he'd like to own yours, too."

"What about Leo Lowe? The sheriff hasn't found him yet, has he? Why is he on the run or in hiding if he didn't hurt Sandra? Lowe was watching you from out back, so he could be the one who's been hanging around here. This could be a threat to be sure you don't try to go to the media or re-open the case against his father."

"How about that off-the-wall reporter Roy Manning?" Josh asked. "He ticked me off here today, and I'm sure I returned the favor. We probably both angered him at the church."

"You didn't tell me he bothered you earlier today."

"I didn't want to worry you... And now this. But I can't believe Manning ruined the snow angels. It's more like him to just come busting in instead of lurking."

"Josh, there's something that's really been eating at me. What if someone doesn't want me to keep asking questions about my real parents? What if Lena and David Brand were involved in something dangerous— or there's some secret I'm not supposed to know."

"I'm praying none of this is aimed at you. Or at least that it just has to do with us becoming a couple."

"But even Bishop Esh and his wife act like there's something they can't tell," she said, her voice shaking.

"You know his sense of honor and duty. Probably someone—most likely your father and mother—asked him once to promise not to talk about it, so you would really feel like their child, to protect you."

"*Ya,* that would be like them at least."

"And I can't blame them for that." He hugged her and kissed her cheek, then walked slowly toward the loft, climbed a couple of rungs and reached up to touch the bottom of one angel's robe. "It's sticky," he called down to her. "Not blood, I think, or it would smell more coppery. I'm not sure I want to get the sheriff in on this."

"That right?" came a voice behind them as a flashlight beam swept across the horrid drawings and word as if pinning Josh there. "Come on over here, Ray-Lynn. Looks and sounds like it's a good thing we came."

It was, Josh thought, almost the same nightmare after Sandra's death. The sheriff had separated him and Lydia. Ray-Lynn waited with Lydia by the front door, while he and the sheriff went into his barn office. And he could tell from the questioning the sheriff might actually think he'd done that paint job himself.

"Calm down, Josh. Once again, I find myself having to interview young Amish guys to back up your story, that's all. But I believe you that the Beiler kids said the sheep got out and they had to go down to the long wing of the barn. For sure that might have given someone time to come in the back way and do this in a big rush. It's not exactly a Rembrandt."

"I'm just making sure you don't think I did that. The boys or Hank would have seen it while we loaded the animals. And why would I make a mess of the snow angels I told you about? Since it was in the papers where Sandra died, the placement of that painted outrage could have been put there by anyone."

"Just sit tight now. I didn't say you did that, but I've got to run through all the possibilities. You got any paint on the premises?"

"Sure, but not red. No Amish man or woman is going to paint anything bright red. It's the verboten color of martyrs' blood—our ancestors' blood in Europe before we came here—the reason we fled to America."

Jack Freeman flipped his notebook shut and shoved it in the inside pocket of his leather jacket. "So you don't mind if I look around?"

"Of course not—again," Josh said.

"Look, Josh. I'm trying real hard to figure out who's behind that crude graffiti because it will probably lead me to Sandra's killer. Yeah, coroner's ruling or not, I feel in my gut that murder is still a possibility, though, no, I don't think *killer* is supposed to be a signature, either. And since you were close to Sandra once, you sure want that looked into, too."

"*Ya,* of course I do."

"Besides, the motive for what seems to be an attack on you could actually be an attack on Lydia, too. Let's look at this another way. What if someone is desperate to keep her from turning up info about her birth parents? Maybe Sandra opened a can of worms asking around about that. So someone panics and gets crazy enough to kill her—or at least argues with her and gives her a shove—hoping to pin it on you."

"Maybe," Josh admitted. "Lydia came up with the same possibility. Sandra was asking way too many questions. But that could mean Lydia's in some danger now, and she's got to be protected."

"If that theory is correct, you got that right. So he or she—the killer—enters Lydia's house, moves things around, messes up her bed to imply a threat and scares the living daylights out of her. Lydia's here a lot, you two are starting to be seen as a couple, 'least that's what Ray-Lynn says. So the intruder tries to either scare Lydia away from you or scare both of you to shut you up, make you leave—together or alone—I don't know. So don't just figure I'm out to nail you. And I'll be talking to her formal betrothed, Gideon Reich, soon."

"They weren't formally betrothed. Gid wanted it. Some assumed it because it looked so—so perfect."

"Got that."

"I hate to do it, Sheriff, but taking a cue from Lydia, I'm going to put locks on all the barn doors and hope someone doesn't come in a loft window high up."

"She changed her locks?"

"*Ya.* See, I had a key hanging in the stables where I sometimes keep the buggy, too. Tradition, once we all went to keys and locks in Amish country, is to keep a spare in the barn or shed. Relatives or friends come calling and you're not home, they know where it is. That's sure got to change. But I had that back door to the barn locked, so you'd better ask the Beiler boys if they unlocked it. I doubt it since it's locked now."

"It's the first thing I checked after I sat you down here. And you should have checked it earlier."

"I was too shocked to think of that at first," Josh said, standing even though he hadn't been dismissed. "Look, Sheriff, Lydia needs to get home or her parents will worry. Her mother hears about this, and it will be the straw that broke the camel's back." He glanced at Melly and Gaspar, who seemed ever so interested in eavesdropping on all this from their pen across the way. "And then they won't let Lydia near me so I can help protect her."

"Maybe her keeping clear of you will be best, in case you're the target. Meanwhile, I'll have to get that artwork documented and photographed, but I don't intend to tell the newspapers, especially that *Plain Dealer* reporter Manning. It's something I'll keep quiet to help nail the mad painter when I get this figured out. By the way, Roy Manning came in my office, asked all kinds of questions." The sheriff got to his feet and patted Josh's shoulder. "But the fact I overheard you say—not admissible in court now—that you didn't want me to see this picture and message means, if you painted it yourself, you might have only wanted Lydia to see it, not to drive her away but maybe to be more scared and trust you more."

Josh exploded, "I didn't deface my own barn for Lydia or anyone else! I said, the Beiler boys—Hank, too—would have seen it. Sheriff, the paint is barely dry. For sure, someone did it when the boys were lured away just before we got here. I just don't need this to get all over town, and at Christmastime when the animals are going out here and there like at your church tonight!"

"My thinking exactly. Just wanted to get your take on the far-out possibility that you did it. Now, I know Amish privacy and all that, and the fact, deep down, your people don't trust law enforcement, but that's not helping us here. Just work with me, not against me, from here on out, Josh. You hear me?"

"Loud and clear," he said, but he saw how this man operated. Get cozy, friendly, supportive, then toss in another foursquare hit to the head, hoping to spring some sort of confession loose.

"Ray-Lynn and I will take Lydia home and tell her mother we stopped by and volunteered. Say, one more thing. Why wasn't your right-hand man, Hank, with you at church tonight instead of that other guy?"

"A family birthday. Hank's oldest boy. You don't think he—"

"Just covering all the bases. I would have liked to document those snow angels you two were talking about, too. Now don't you wash that paint job off or repaint your wall till I send my desk gal, Peggy, out to get a good photo of it from all angles tomorrow morning."

"Fine, but then I want to get rid of it."

"Now, Josh," the sheriff said, in his best small-town voice that Josh knew he put on sometimes, "getting rid of something or someone is not gonna help things at all. You want to say goodbye to Lydia, you make it quick now." He walked away to stare up at the horrible paintwork again.

For one second, Josh couldn't decide whether to keep what he knew from the sheriff or not, but he figured he'd better tell him that much. "Sheriff, I do have something else to show you."

One hand on his holster, he turned back toward Josh. "Like what?"

"As you probably overhead when you were eavesdropping," he said, trying to control the bite in his voice, "those snow angels out back had a pitchfork drawn between them, too. Carrots on the head for horns and a pitchfork where we held hands. But— and Lydia doesn't know this—a real pitchfork was stuck in each of the chests."

"And you've got the pitchforks?"

"*Ya,* here in the barn with my tools. I pulled them out and brushed over the snow so Lydia wouldn't get more upset than she already was. It was the same day someone evidently followed her to Amity where she met with an elderly man who used to know her father. She found out that Sandra had been there to interview him first. While Lydia was in his house, someone unhitched her horse and put a camel saddle on it, a heavy saddle that had been stolen from the back of my barn that morning. It's one we used in the pageant tonight. Lydia brought it back from Amity."

"And the reason no one told me any of this before? No, never mind. Don't trust the local law or the feds."

"I'm telling you now—everything. She didn't want her parents to know she was pursuing information about her birth parents. And, *ya,* you're right. Like I said, we Amish don't on the whole trust law enforcement officers. They're the ones who dragged our forefathers off to prison, torture and death."

"Well, get this straight, Josh," he said, walking closer and putting an index finger on his chest. "This is America, times are different, and law officers like me are here to protect and defend, to help. Unless someone Amish has committed a crime and deserves imprisonment and even death, I'm on your side. Got that?"

Josh nodded and stood his ground, meeting the sheriff's piercing gaze. Now, why had the man mentioned imprisonment and death, as if he was still thinking Josh had murdered Sandra?

"Let me show you the pitchforks," Josh said. "I've got extras. Over here with my other tools. My prints will be on them, but maybe you can find a trace of someone else. Or you can use DNA or whatever that new stuff is."

"You volunteering to get printed, despite the fact it's against Amish ways? How about a simple swab of your inner cheek in case DNA ever helps us solve Sandra's death or this defacing of your property?"

"*Ya,* if that's what you need. I'll have to tell Bishop Esh, though, hopefully not get shunned for all that. But I want to stop this, Sheriff, find out who's trying to hurt Lydia and me and why. But most of all, I want to get whoever killed Sandra. The thing is, I suppose most people around here own a pitchfork, so this may not be much help. And can you take them both out the back door and put them in your trunk so Lydia doesn't see them and get more upset if I have to explain?"

"But the thing is, who, except local farmers—and I

don't have a one of them on my list of suspects—would own two pitchforks?" he repeated, shaking his head.

"I'd say the hardware store in town, but these two look well used. You know," Josh said, drawing out his words, "I'm not sure if this will still be true, but one of them had dead pine needles stuck with sap on a couple of the prongs."

"That right?" the sheriff said, pursing his lips. "Well, let's have a look."

He squeezed Josh's shoulder as they walked toward his stash of tools in the corner of the barn. Their working together was a start, Josh thought, because the other option was worse. He had to keep calm. Still, when he passed the bloodred angels and the word *KILLER* again, he felt like ripping the obscenity down bare-handed, board by board.

24

Lydia heard distant screeches and hoots outside. It was barely light the morning after the horror in the barn. So far, she had not told her anxious parents about that, even when Ray-Lynn and the sheriff brought her home. *Mamm,* who waited up, seemed relieved to see her in any vehicle that wasn't Josh's buggy.

Now Lydia pressed her face to the cold window-pane above the kitchen sink to see who was making that noise. Down on the road, she could see a car hit its brakes and swerve. Was there ice on the road? But who was shouting and squealing? Despite the cold morning—new snow had fallen last night—she opened the window over the kitchen sink and stuck her head out a few inches. The horse and buggy that came along after the car went on its way with no problem.

But then another car braked and swerved, and this time she saw why. Two boys were hiding behind the first row of Christmas trees edging the road and throwing snowballs at passing cars. A third car hit its brakes, then sped on. Hoots and hollers filled the air.

Ya, it was Connor's twins. Now, what were their

names again? Bradley and Blaine, something like that, so worldly. Although they were obviously unsupervised this morning and doing something that could cause great danger—their grandmother would be appalled—they suddenly made her remember Sammy. He had died when he was five and these boys were seven, but Sammy had loved to throw snowballs. He'd made a snow fort once with *Daad* and always begged her to play fox and geese in the snow.

Lydia's parents were both still in bed, but she had to stop Connor's kids before they caused a wreck. Besides, a few years ago, Amish boys throwing tomatoes at cars had been shot at by an angry motorist. She closed the window with a bang.

Jamming her feet into boots, she yanked on her coat and tied her bonnet as she went out and down the driveway. You might know the boys had chosen the corner of the Stark land that abutted the Brand driveway. She took such huge strides she was almost out of breath when she got within their earshot.

"Boys! Stop that! You're going to cause a wreck!" she shouted. "Your father will be upset and your grandmother, too!"

As they turned toward her, snowballs in hand, she marveled again at how much they looked alike. Blaine? Bradley? She had no idea who was who. For one minute, she thought they would throw snowballs at her or run, but they probably figured she'd just tell on them. Reminding her so much of their father, they stood their ground defiantly.

"We're just having fun. It's only snow," the boy in the blue coat said. She saw they were dressed for school and had made a mess of their jeans and jackets, as if they'd been pelting each other first.

The boy in the orange jacket said, "We don't care if you tell our dad."

"Why don't you care? You know what you're doing is wrong. You could hurt someone. Won't he punish you?"

"If he does, at least he'll have to talk to us. He's gone a lot and Mom's mad at him, too."

"I see. Well, he's mayor now and he's trying to buy more land for trees, you know, so all that keeps him busy."

"Too busy. Mom argues with him and Gran did, too—real loud. We can't fight with him, so if he hears about this, he'll have to talk to us."

Lydia was astounded. Evidently desperate to get their father's attention, the young boys had laid this plan, one they knew could get them in trouble. And here she wanted to talk to her own father about things, but couldn't because she didn't want to hurt him or cause him to strain his heart.

"So, you gonna tell him?" the boy in the blue coat challenged.

"I think we need to march right up the hill to your house, and you can tell him what you did and why. It may be that one of those cars you hit just went up your driveway to tell your parents, anyway. It doesn't look good for the mayor's sons to be throwing things at cars, does it?" she asked as the three of them started to trudge up the hill toward the house.

"Boy, if someone drives in to tell him, he might get mad at them, too," the twin in blue said. "But it's that bad story in the newspaper about him that really got him mad."

Lydia's head jerked around. She'd seen the local weekly paper, so what were they talking about? It did have a short article about her father's heart attack and that he was home again. It was only then she realized her parents might find her missing and be panicked.

"Listen, you two," she said. "I have to go back and get my buggy and head for work. But on the way, I'm going to stop in to check with your parents that you told them the truth about all this. So I expect you to get back to your house right now. Besides, aren't you supposed to catch your school bus?"

"Not for a while. They think we went to our room to study."

"Oh, that's a good one. You just go on up to the house now, and I'll be there soon. But what about a bad story in the newspaper?"

"There you are!" a voice boomed. Connor came half walking, half running down the hill, kicking snow ahead of him. For once, he seemed dressed for the cold weather. "What are you two doing out here? You're supposed to tell your mother when you're going outside. Lydia?"

"I saw them doing something they shouldn't have and came out to talk to them," she said, edging away. Connor looked furious, unless it was the chill wind and his exertion that made him so red in the face.

The boy in the orange coat said, "We were throwing snowballs at cars, but not buggies, 'cause we didn't want to hurt any horses."

"Get back to the house, right now!" Connor yelled at his sons. "After what happened to your great-aunt

Victoria, we don't need anyone just disappearing out of the house into the snow. I had to follow your tracks. Get going now!"

The twins looked at each other as if to say, "Mission accomplished," but Lydia could tell they were shaky, too. Thinking Connor would follow them, she started away.

"And you're guilty as hell, too, aren't you, though not for throwing snowballs at cars?" Connor demanded, and came after her. He grabbed her arm and swung her back to face him. "Caught just like kids with snow on your hands!"

"What are you talking about? Let me go!" she shouted back. She was suddenly very afraid of him. Connor could well be the intruder in her house and Josh's barn.

He gave her arm another shake. "That story in the *Cleveland Plain Dealer* could ruin this tree farm and hurt my mother," he said as she pulled free of his grip and almost went off balance. "You didn't think of that, did you—hurt your friend Bess?"

"I said, what are you talking about? The boys mentioned a newspaper article, but—"

"That reporter Manning wouldn't even have been around here if it wasn't for you and your boyfriend getting mixed up in Sandra Myerson's death."

"Roy Manning's been bothering me, but why should he be after you?"

"Oh, yeah, play the little Amish innocent! Manning's the second person you've sicced on me. You're his source, you have to be. You figured out I was spraying diseased trees to sell them fast this season, didn't you? Gave him that story to get him off your and Yoder's backs. I believe you that you don't get the Cleveland paper on your doorstep every morning, but you gave him the info!"

"No! I suspected what you were doing, but we didn't even talk about you, except he mentioned you'd talked to Sandra."

"Nothing like a little diversion, right? Get him after me, so he'll let up on you and Yoder as suspects. That woman was running wild, anyway. Did you make a deal with Manning? Forget Sandra's death, but here— Senator Stark's son is committing fraud on Christmas shoppers. It's true the trees were sprayed with green paint and you're the only one—"

"Connor, I didn't say one word to him about you or your trees. I should have talked to you about it, just like I did to your kids when they did something wrong, but I didn't. But I repeat, I gave Roy Manning no information on you or your trees. And don't you ever even hint that Josh or I had anything to do with Sandra's death. Now I have to go to work."

"I don't believe you!" he shouted as she started down the hill toward her house at a good clip. "You've always tried to horn in here!"

She blinked tears onto her cheeks, then brushed them away with a gloved hand. More than once over the years, Connor had shouted at her as she ran from his land. But who indeed had given that story to Roy Manning and the paper? Or, had he been lurking in the Christmas trees while he watched her house, seen the trees and figured it out himself?

Peggy Fencer, the hardware store manager's wife, who worked in the sheriff's office, took photos of the

bloodred mess painted inside Josh's barn. The minute she left, he got up on the ladder with a can of gray
paint and covered it completely, as if that could end
his problems. A cover-up never worked and he knew
it, but he had to get rid of the offensive message. Being
this close, seeing the quick, angry strokes of crimson
hurt and infuriated him. The person who had done
this was someone desperate, in a rage—just like he
felt right now.

Josh realized he could have left the horrible graffiti for Hank to see, but why? It was bad enough that
Lydia had seen it, suffered for it. He yearned to make
peace with her parents and to propose to her. But her
mother especially detested him. Josh was pretty sure
Gid Reich was just playing nice guy so she'd marry
him, with the pressure from her parents and all. Josh
wanted her in his bed for good, and, here, someone
else was dumping honey on her sheets. But so far she'd
stuck with him, as his *daad* used to say, through thick
and thin.

But, really, what was best for Lydia? Whoever she
married, the furniture store would be in her future
and running that was way out of his realm. Still, if
she insisted on knowing who her real parents were,
Sol Brand could be deeply offended and disinherit
her. Lydia had been hesitant to hurt her parents before.
Now she was terrified she'd trigger another heart attack if she asked Sol about her birth parents, and her
mother would probably blow sky-high.

He was almost tempted to take that burden on himself, to ask the Brands about Lydia's birth parents and
why they would not tell her the truth. What were they
hiding or afraid of?

And then a new thought hit him with stunning force. His father had once told him that his mother, Bethany—called Bessie by her parents, because she couldn't say her name when she was little—had been a close friend of Sol's before they went their separate ways and Bessie married his *daad*. What if Lydia's mother hated Josh because he was the child of an early rival for Sol's affections? Could it be she feared Lydia and he would wed and that would remind her that she could have lost Sol to another woman years ago?

Though Lydia was already late for work, she pulled Flower up the long driveway toward the Stark house. Despite the fact she feared running into Connor again, she'd told his twins that she would stop in to be sure they'd told the truth. Telling the truth…she vowed to face *Daad* down about that today. He was healing, was stronger. Even if he said he'd have to clear telling her about her birth parents with Bishop Esh first, today had to be the day. Because if someone was trying to stop or hurt her, she didn't want to end up like Sandra. She had to know what she was facing in her search and be sure no one had the chance to shove her off a loft or anything else.

To her great relief, even though she hated to hurt Bess's feelings, it was Bess who came to the back door when Lydia knocked.

"I was waiting for someone else, but come in," she insisted. "I heard what the boys did. Thanks for stopping them before they hurt someone or got hurt themselves. They are *really* in trouble with their father, and rightfully so. We don't need headlines about those two causing a wreck on the road on top of the attack on Connor for spraying trees."

"Bess, I can make this quick. I promised the boys I'd stop, that's all, and I like to keep my promises."

"Don't we all? Come in here, I said. It's cold. Connor drove Blair and Brad to school, but I need to talk to you for a few minutes."

Oh, that's right, Lydia thought: his name is Blair, not Blaine. She went in, expecting at least the boys' mother, Heather, to be there, but the big kitchen—two ovens and two refrigerators!—was empty. "I need to get to the furniture store," Lydia told her, realizing she was repeating herself, "but I told the boys I was going to stop here to be sure they confessed."

"They did, apparently happily so, and sadly, just to have Connor's attention," she explained, grabbing a carafe of coffee and two cups as she led Lydia down a hall and into an office where she clicked on a light. The outer wall of drapes was still drawn against the cold in the large room. "He's been so busy and burdened. I do wish you two could get along. Now, I'll get you on your way soon," she rushed on, "but I just need to ask you something. Sit, sit. Just a quick warm-up of coffee and a quicker question."

Lydia expected it would be something else about her grandsons' dangerous prank. A prominent picture of them was on her cluttered walnut desk. This must be Bess's away-from-the-senate office. Family photos and business ones covered the three walls that didn't have windows, cluttered bookcases and filing cabinets. She saw a photo of Bess with the governor. Oh! Bess with a former president!

"I had to have that one taken," she said when she

saw Lydia gawking at it. "Respect the office, if not the man, right? I mean like you and Connor getting along like oil and water all these years," she added, handing her a cup of coffee.

"He blamed me for the bad newspaper article."

"That's my question, and, unlike him, I will believe you. You say you didn't tell that *Plain Dealer* reporter, but did you tell anyone else who might have told him? Josh or Ray-Lynn Freeman, for example?"

"No, Bess, I did not. I thought Connor might be doing something wrong when I saw him spraying paint on the trees and using a couple of pitchforks to shake needles loose, but I told no one."

"Okay, so that's out of the way between us. I believe you. The thing is, it not only hurts Connor locally but me statewide, maybe nationally," she said with a sigh as she sat in the chair beside her and sipped her coffee. "Actually, I'm waiting for someone to help me lay out a campaign for governor."

"Can I ask you something, too?"

Bess looked a bit worried at that, but she said, "Sure. Ask away. Politicians are good at answering questions, you know."

"You said once that Sandra Myerson talked to Connor but not to you when she came to your tree farm."

"Did I?"

"That's what I understood. But someone told me you talked to her, too, and got kind of angry with her. I know that's secondhand information, but why did—"

"Yes, my girl, I did talk to her. Because of my high profile, I just didn't want to be mentioned among the dozens she ticked off around here. I told her to quit nosing around, especially with the Amish, that's all. So, who came up with that information for you?"

"Someone who interviewed several workers, I guess."

"Lydia, if that someone was Roy Manning, I will still believe you that you're not the one who told him about Connor spraying trees, even though Connor says you caught him at it and had the motive that he's not been nice to you for years. Or if you tell me it was Sandra who told Manning—she seemed to know too much about most things—I'll believe that, too. You were taken in by her. Maybe Josh, too. I don't mean you weren't taken in by Josh but that he was taken in by her."

They stared unspeaking into each other's eyes a moment. Bess believed her, yet was still on Connor's side. Well, of course, she would defend her son. Lydia heard in her words a silent challenge not to ask more questions, but one thing comforted her. Whatever people thought of politicians these days, Bess obviously believed in and cherished the most important things— love and trust.

"You'd best get going," Bess said. "I didn't mean to keep you, but I want you to know, Connor's opinions aside, you are always welcome here—at least when I'm around."

Lydia drank a bit of the coffee she'd almost forgotten about and stood. "Does that mean I'm welcome when you're in the governor's mansion and the White House someday, too?" she asked with a little smile.

Bess, who had seemed so tense, smiled back and gave her that one-armed hug around her shoulders as they walked out of the office and down the hall. Lydia

blinked at the brightness of the kitchen with its drap-
eries pulled way open. The entire house seemed lit
by the sun glinting off the snow outside, so why was
Bess's office kept so dim with the curtains pulled?
She'd said she was waiting for someone to help her
plan a campaign, and the driveway passed right outside her office windows so she could watch for a car.

They said goodbye, and Lydia climbed into her
buggy just as a big black car pulled past her and a
man got out. Oh, one of the two who had been talking about Bess running for a higher office at Victoria's funeral luncheon.

Lydia turned Flower around by the attached garage
and started past the house again. Bess had already
taken her visitor inside. Lydia caught a movement in
the house as Bess evidently pulled her office drapes
open. Her face was turned away, so she must be talking
already. But it was hard to really see her because there
were shelves, lots of them, in front of the windows.
Lydia gasped and twisted her neck to look back as
Flower pulled the buggy forward. Now that the drapes
were no longer drawn, sun poured into the gleaming
windows of the office. And there, not only on the win-
dowsills, but on the shelves, were rows and rows of
different-size, shining snow globes.

25

At the store, Lydia hated to seem uninterested or unfriendly, but she was afraid she was going to cry or completely break down. So she just nodded, waved and blazed her way right through the busy back workshop at the store, then made straight for *Daad*'s office, where she planned to lock herself in until she got control again.

It must be pure coincidence, of course, but Bess Stark collected snow globes, ones she might have tried to keep Lydia from noticing. And *Daad* had said years ago when he gave her the snow globe from her birth mother that... Oh, no. Bess as her birth mother—that could never be.

The door to *Daad*'s office stood open. Not Gid in here again, she prayed. She didn't want to face him now when she needed to be alone.

It wasn't Gid. Marta Kurtz, who usually helped her husband clean the store showroom and offices at night, was dusting. Her mop leaned against the open door as if to let folks know she was busy inside. Marta was a very hard and fast worker. Only her brain worked a little slow.

"Oh! Lydia. I thought you weren't in yet. So I'd get this done, all nice and neat for you. Our buggy horse was took sick last night. We couldn't get here to clean, had to deworm him. When I came in, Mr. Reich was working in here, too. He was surprised I was here early, but it couldn't be helped with the horse all sick."

"I understand," Lydia told her, trying to keep from bursting into tears in front of the girl. Gid had been in *Daad*'s office again. Was it on the up-and-up? "So what was Mr. Reich doing in here when you surprised him? He works so hard."

"Oh, going through that bottom desk drawer," she said, pointing. "Left it partly open in his hurry but I closed it. I keep things neat and tidy."

"You sure do. We appreciate your work here and we'll be sure you get your special Christmas envelope. So did Mr. Reich look like he found what he wanted? Did he take something with him?"

"First, he tells me to get out, then said I could stay. He took a little skinny file with him. Still, I'll bet he was looking for a big one. I think he keeps your *daad*'s files real nice."

Dust rag in hand, Marta kept edging toward the door and her mop. "I can just get caught up tonight," she said.

"That will be fine. *Danki,* Marta."

The girl went out and closed the door. Lydia went over to lock it. Though she'd promised herself a good cry, she went directly to the drawer Gid must have been rifling through, sat in *Daad*'s chair, opened the file and pulled out folder after folder and fingered through them.

It sounded like Marta must have seen Gid going through files at other times. With *Daad* out of the way for now, was he searching for something special? And if he'd been through other drawers—*I think he keeps your* daad'*s files real nice,* Marta had said—was he just trying to secretly learn how her father organized his information and ran the business, or was there something else?

"A waste of time, a dead end," she said aloud as she pulled out the last folder in the drawer, this one under *W* and marked Workers. She went through it and found nothing unusual. But as she sighed and started to refile it she saw a folder had either slipped flat to the bottom of the drawer or been placed that way under all the rest. It was plain beige manila like the others and unmarked. Maybe it was even empty.

But no, it contained several pieces of paper in *Daad*'s tight handwriting.

She gasped and skimmed the first page, then the second. No wonder Gid was desperately searching through these files. Her father's notes were dated quite recently, from late October on. It looked as if he'd been keeping a list of large projects—church pews for a new Baptist Church nearby; a large dining room set for a hotel in Columbus; an entire array of shelves and cabinets for a store specializing in men's clothes. And for each of those accounts, her father had recorded an amount of money—several hundred dollars each time that *Daad* had noted as missing. And in each case, G.R.—Gid Reich?—had arranged and overseen the deal. It had to be. No one else had those initials here.

Lydia sucked in a breath through flared nostrils. Bess's snow globes—well, ridiculous to think they were tied to her own pitiful, broken one. But now this. Could the trusted Gid, heir to the throne, as Ray-Lynn had once put it, have been siphoning off money? Embezzling from large accounts where the missing funds wouldn't be noticed like in small orders? And if Gid suspected *Daad* was on to him, would that be motive enough not only to search his files but to mess up his blood pressure pills? *Daad* had evidently brought them with him to the store once or twice. And if her father thought Gid was guilty, maybe that's why he'd let up on pushing her toward the man as much.

She shuffled quickly through the few other papers *Daad* had evidently meant to hide. Sammy's obituary from *The Budget.* Maybe he kept that here rather than at home, where *Mamm* could find it and get upset. A copy of the very article for David and Lena Brand that she and Sandra had found from the *Wooster Daily Record!* So wasn't that proof they were her real parents? And a last sheet, handwritten, but not in *Daad*'s tight script.

This note was in large writing with fancy loops on some letters. It was addressed to *Sweetheart Sol,* but it wasn't in *Mamm*'s handwriting. Surely, her father had not been untrue to his marriage, however unhappy her parents obviously were.

Sweetheart Sol,
Let's meet out past the pond again after dark! Ah, the forbidden seems so sweet. The entire

earth comes alive when we're together. You help
to heal me, and I don't feel so alone anymore.
Forbidden love but wonderful love!
Your Bessie

Lydia gaped at the worn paper, the faded words.
Bessie? Bess Keller Stark? Sure, there were other Bes-
sies around here, even a couple of Amish girls she
could think of. And if Victoria Keller was known as
Vicky by her family, couldn't Elizabeth, or Bess, have
been called Bessie? Or if *Daad* and this woman had
an affair, maybe it was his pet name for her. This note
sure must have meant a lot to him since he'd dared to
keep it a long time, for the paper was old and worn—
it looked as if it had been often handled. Did it mean
he'd been untrue to *Mamm* or was it before they were
wed? And when was it written?

Lydia's heart was pounding so hard she could hear
it echo in her ears. Surely, Amish Solomon Brand and
Englische Bessie Stark had not been sweethearts, even
though they'd grown up as neighbors. Well, Amish/
Englische happened, of course, the forbidden part
noted here by "Bessie." What this could mean staggered her.

Despite his recent heart attack, Lydia had to make
Daad tell her the truth tonight. If he refused, she'd
insist she was going to ask Bess if she'd ever heard
anything about the tragic buggy-car accident that took
David and Lena Brand's life. If Bess was at all involved, he would tell her the truth instead of letting
Lydia face down Bess. *Daad* had always been funny—
touchy—about Bess Keller Stark.

* * *

It was late afternoon when Lydia got home—she'd promised she would not drive anywhere after dark—and she was relieved that *Mamm* had gone to bed early. Better yet, *Daad* was in his quilting room so there was no way *Mamm* could wander downstairs and overhear them. Best, *Daad* had said, "Give me a couple of minutes, then come in to talk. And keep your eyes closed because your Christmas quilt is almost done."

He had somehow sensed she needed to talk—or else he did, she thought as she hurried upstairs, used the bathroom and washed up. Gid had been too busy with the Christmas rush to corner her today, which was just as well. She wasn't sure how good she was at keeping secrets, pretending things were going well when they were in such a mess. Besides, it would have been hard not to try to get him to admit irregularities in the big accounts, and then she'd ruin what must be *Daad*'s undercover investigation. Maybe that's why he had said nothing to her about it before.

Although Lydia had been tempted to bring the page with *Daad*'s embezzlement findings home with her, she had put it carefully back. As for the note from Bessie, perhaps she'd never find the courage to tell *Daad* she knew he'd kept it all these years—unless he still refused to talk about her birth parents. And, of course, to bring it up with *Daad,* she'd have to admit she'd seen his information on Gid's possible embezzling. But she had brought the love note with her.

She tiptoed to her parents' room and put her ear to the door. *Mamm* used to take long afternoon naps when she was using those pills. But with worrying about *Daad*—and, *ya,* about her daughter, she'd looked especially tired lately. Then, too, maybe her insomnia had set in again to tire her out.

Lydia went downstairs and, finding the side parlor door ajar, knocked once and went in. *Daad* had rolled the quilt almost closed on its frame, but she saw one of the four hems was not sewn yet.

"I don't want you to work too hard," she said, "even on that."

"It's not work that will do me in someday, Liddy. Here, sit down," he said, indicating the chair he'd been using, then pulling around the other one from the far side of the quilt for himself.

"Of course, you want to know how things went at the store today."

"If things are all right, save that until later. I need to tell you about your mother."

She gasped. Had he read her mind? Guessed her torment somehow? But no—no. He must mean *Mamm*.

"Is she all right?"

"I learned from the fact I've been counting her sleeping pills that she's back on them again. Liddy, I've kept this from you, but she sleepwalks at night and sometimes during the day, just like Dr. Bryan warned us about."

"Have you stayed up at night to make sure she doesn't hurt herself, like on the stairs?"

"*Ya,* but not since I've been back from the hospital, because I thought she was off the pills. Before that, I stayed up at night, even tied her wrist to mine so I knew when she got up. Sometimes she just went to the bathroom, but other times..." He shrugged. "And she recalls nothing of what she does at night, but she's sure-footed. I'm not afraid she'll fall. She takes the stairs, moves around the house, even cleaning things sometimes. Twice she made bread. I just slept nearby, so exhausted. But even asleep, she seemed to know what she was doing."

"So we have to get her off the pills again. You can't be worrying about her, following her. You need sleep to recover. We'll get her help, get her off those for good."

"It's just I'm at my wit's end with her again. I don't mean to use you instead of Bishop Esh, kind of like a marriage counselor. But the doctor will have a fit if he sees I'm stressed out."

Lydia felt doubly deflated. *Mamm* was a problem, her parents' marriage was as good as dead, and now did she ever dare to bring up what she'd seen at Bess's today and found hidden in his desk drawer? But wasn't the Lord giving her these clues so that she could confront him? Or was this new problem with *Mamm* to show her she should hold her peace again, or maybe even ask Bess if she knew *Daad* well years ago, instead of upsetting him even more? She could mention to Bess that her real mother had collected snow globes, so did she know any Amish girl around here who did that?

But then she could lose Bess's friendship and support. Strange how much it meant to her. Over the years, Lydia's heart had swelled with joy, even excitement, when Bess was near. And would a woman who had set her sights so high and was planning a campaign to reach the stars ever admit she had an illegitimate Amish daughter?

"Liddy? Are you all right?" *Daad*'s voice sliced through her agonizing.

"Just upset about *Mamm*."

He took her hands in his. She was shaken to see tears in his eyes.

"*Daad,* I'll help you watch her at night. Can't we put a bell on your bedroom door? Maybe the bathroom doorknob, too? If she's in a sleep-awake state when she gets up, she wouldn't notice the bell, would she? In the morning, we'll insist she must get off the pills and go back to her doctor for another kind of medicine tomorrow. I can go with her."

"And one more important thing. I want you to know I'm not promoting Gid as a husband for you anymore. It just seemed so perfect, so right at first. There are others who can run the store after I'm gone. Just wanted you to know," he repeated.

Touched, she nodded. *Daad*'s hands were shaking. *Dear Lord,* she prayed, *don't let him have another heart attack. And help me to help him and Mamm, but to somehow get the answers I need without hurting them.* After all, she thought with a twinge of anger, she'd asked *Daad* before about her birth parents and he'd put her off and turned her down, just like Bishop Esh had. Even if she did ask *Daad* again, he still might refuse to tell her. Maybe asking Bess, as pushy and scary as that seemed, was the best way now.

Just before dinner, *Mamm* appeared, seeming in a calm and kindly mood. So was *Daad* reading this all wrong?

That night, Lydia rigged bells on the outside knobs of the bedroom and bathroom doors, then left her own door open so she could hear better. She also hid *Mamm*'s pills under her own pillow. But if *Mamm* didn't open the doors quick, like she always did, maybe the bells wouldn't sound at all. No matter what happened, tomorrow she would use the phone in the shanty way down the road and make *Mamm* a doctor's appointment. Things had to get better.

Then, as soon as possible, she'd ask Bess her big question. But Bess had so easily talked her way out of her lie about not speaking to Sandra. So would Bess even tell the truth, especially if it meant admitting to any kind of deceit or scandal? She was obviously really clever at bending questions her way. As kind as Bess had been, she'd protect herself from anything or maybe anyone who stood in the way of her ambitions, Lydia thought. Did she really know Bess Stark at all?

Lydia jerked awake. Had she heard a bell? She'd been in and out of light sleep, keeping her ear tuned to any sounds. She looked at the beside clock. Almost 4:00 a.m.

She got up and peered out in the grayish hall. The bathroom door was closed. Had *Mamm* or *Daad* gone in there? She'd wait just inside her bedroom door to see who came out.

She kept silent when *Daad* padded barefooted toward their bedroom. Strangely, she had the urge to stop him, to demand to know if Bess Stark could possibly be her birth mother. But would the next assumption be that *Daad* was her real father? The instinctive love she'd felt for them both over the years pointed to that, didn't it? Yet, how wrong of them to keep that from her, how cruel. It would be terrible for *Mamm* to know that—or did she? What if she'd been forced to take in her husband's love child? Maybe she had no idea. Or if she did, was that the cause of the problem between her parents? And Bess...she must not want her past to get in the way of her rise to power. Just give your flesh-and-blood only daughter a half hug now and then and go on your merry way. And Connor—did he know? Did he hate her for that, too?

Back in bed, Lydia tossed and turned. She loved Josh, wanted Josh. Was that how it was for Sol and Bessie?

Love...love...

Lydia sat bolt upright. Someone was in her room, a woman in white. For one half-waking, wild moment, she thought it could be Sandra's ghost, but she didn't believe in that.

No, it was *Mamm*.

Gooseflesh iced Lydia's skin as *Mamm* said in a whisper, "I have to find Sammy. I have to keep him safe."

When Lydia tried to speak at first, she had no voice. She cleared her throat. "*Mamm,* Sammy's not here, and you have to go back to bed."

Though her face was in darkness, *Mamm* turned and looked at her. She wore not only her long-sleeved, floor-length, white flannel nightgown but a white prayer *kapp,* which made her look as if a halo hovered over her head. Her feet were bare. Her long hair was down, not even plaited in a big braid but wild around her face and shoulders.

Lydia got out of bed, went to her. If she was looking for Sammy, so long drowned in the pond, was she lost in a dream or nightmare? She turned her head toward Lydia but did not respond to what she'd said. Now she ordered, "Don't try to stop me. I have to find him fast."

To Lydia's amazement, *Mamm* shoved her back onto her bed with such strength that she bounced. *Mamm* rushed from the room, and Lydia heard her bare feet on the stairs.

Lydia scrambled up again. Should she wake her father? No, she didn't want to alarm him. She could handle this herself, get *Mamm* to bed in the guest room or the sofa and sit with her until she went to sleep.

Barefooted, in her nightgown, Lydia followed her downstairs. How could *Mamm* be so quick when she usually moved much slower?

Downstairs, Lydia's panic increased. Where had she gone?

She heard the back door open, then close.

Dear Lord, was her mother going outside in that state? And surely not to the pond!

Lydia rushed through the kitchen to the back door. She saw *Mamm* had pulled on a coat and was walking out through the white blankness of the snow, heading in the direction of the pond. The ice must be frozen pretty thick, but who knew if she could break through it? More than once Josh's father's cows had gone through in the winter when the Brands used to own the pond.

Lydia jammed her feet in boots, not fastening them. The first coat on the rack was *Daad*'s. She yanked it on and ran outside. And here she had promised herself, *Daad* and Josh she'd not be out alone after dark. What if Leo Lowe or the intruder or—

She should have shouted for *Daad,* but she didn't want him out here in this cold. Not taking time to fasten her boots—she realized too late they were *Daad*'s and too large for her feet—she clomped along at a shuffling run through the snow. Starlight and moon-light helped a bit, but how could she be so far behind? And, *ya,* it sure did look like *Mamm* was heading for the pond.

"Mamm!" she shouted, cupping her hands around her mouth as she ran. Her voice seemed so small under the vast, dark sky. She fell once, scrambled to her feet again. "Stop, *Mamm!* Wait for me, and I'll help you find Sammy. It's Lydia! Wait up!"

As she crossed behind the woodlot, Lydia could see a light was on in Josh's barn. Was he still sleeping there to keep the animals secure? Could one of them be sick? And would he hear her if she called for him?

"Mamm! Mamm, stop!" she cried, trying to ignore the frigid air that bit deep into her lungs. Her nose was going numb. Her head hurt, and her eyes watered, blurring her vision. Some of the snow she was wading through kicked up her bare legs.

Out of breath—did those pills give someone strength as well as mess up their mind?—Lydia passed the back line of Josh's land and past the gate Victoria Keller had gone through and perhaps hit her head on. What if *Mamm* slipped on the ice and hurt herself? Lydia recalled there had been three pairs of boots in the back hall, so was *Mamm* barefoot? And was this confusion just caused by the pills, or had she finally been broken by her guilt and grief over Sammy's death?

Lydia peered ahead and saw that *Mamm* had taken something, maybe a rock or tree limb, and was pounding on the ice a few feet from the shore. The pond was deep, almost no shallow edges. At least she'd get to *Mamm* now.

Shrill cries of "Sammy, Sammy, I'm breaking the ice so you can get out!" shredded the night air. "Come back up! I'm here, I'm here!"

To Lydia's horror, she recalled those last few words were the exact ones *Mamm* had said over and over the day Sammy died, when she wouldn't leave the pond, not even when the volunteer rescue squad came, not until *Daad* lifted her in his arms and carried her home. And those were the same words she had whispered at Sammy's funeral when the elders shoveled soil into the grave, and it thudded upon the lid of the small coffin.

Lydia had almost reached her when *Mamm* stood and lunged out on the ice she'd broken through. Except for that black hole, the coating of snow made it hard to see where the ground ended and the pond began. *Mamm* went into the water, thrashing, screaming. Maybe it had shocked her from her trance.

On the edge of the pond, Lydia got down on her stomach and started to reach for her, but the broken ice cracked farther, opening a bigger, jagged hole. Lydia's right arm and leg went in before she could claw her way back to the bank. Frigid water instantly soaked her coat and nightgown. Her boot was gone. Her hand and foot went numb.

As she clambered to safety, she saw *Mamm* had used a rock to break the ice. She had to get something long to hold out to her, pull her to solid ground. Maybe a tree branch.

"Sammy! Sammy," *Mamm* was screaming, but she kept going under.

"Josh! Josh, help me! Help meeeee!" Lydia shouted toward the barn, praying the dim light within meant he was there. But even if he heard her, maybe he couldn't get here in time, just like when Sammy drowned.

Lydia lay belly down with her hips in the snow and her upper torso stretched across the jagged ice and choppy, frigid water. Again and again she reached in vain for *Mamm,* who kept flailing, gasping, going under.

26

Lydia heard a deep voice cutting through *Mamm*'s shrieks and her own desperate cries for help. A man's voice. Was he calling for Lydia or Liddy? Even if it was *Daad,* with him so ill, she needed help.

"Lydia? Lydia, you out here?"

Josh, distant, but his voice sounded so good.

If she stood so he could see her, would *Mamm* slip under the ice? "Here," she screamed. "*Mamm*'s in the pond. Help meeee!"

But there was no reply. It seemed endless days dragged by. She kept grasping for *Mamm,* feeling the ice beneath her breaking. Had she imagined his voice, his love?

Then he was there, panting, throwing himself flat beside her. "Get back. Lydia, get away, too much weight!" He grabbed a handful of her coat and slid her off the ice.

Scrambling to her knees, leaning forward, she gripped her cold hands together and blinked back tears. In one hand, Josh held a horse's rein that he'd made into a big noose. Sweating but shaking, Lydia watched him try to lasso *Mamm* with the rein, once, twice, again.

The leather loop snagged *Mamm* under one armpit, around the side of her neck and her flailing wrist. He yanked it tighter, but *Mamm* seemed to fight, not help. She no longer cried Sammy's name but she seemed insane to struggle so.

"I may choke her," Josh cried, "but I've got to get her out." He stood, moved a few steps back and pulled, dragging the thrashing woman closer.

Lydia reached for *Mamm*'s arm, helped to pull. Finally, she stopped struggling. Together, they dragged her out sopping wet on her belly. Lydia carefully rolled her over, face up, while Josh loosened the strap, then pulled it from her.

Daad suddenly appeared, wrapped in a quilt, wearing untied shoes on his feet, shuffling through the snow. He fell to his knees beside *Mamm,* wrapped her in the quilt and pulled her to him, lifting her head and shoulders against his thighs.

"Thank God for you, Josh," *Daad* said, tears streaming down his face. "But—she's out—not breathing."

Mamm's mouth gaped open. Josh lifted her eyelid; her eyes were rolled back. Lydia sucked in a sob. Josh put his ear to *Mamm*'s lips and shook his head. He pulled her gently away from *Daad,* flat on the ground. Lydia watched in fear as he gave *Mamm* three of his own breaths, mouth-to-mouth. Then, stiff-armed with his hands linked flat on her chest, *Daad* hovering close, Josh began to press, then release his weight on the unmoving woman. Lydia couldn't recall the name for that procedure but she knew the world's ways were sometimes a blessing.

"Lydia—I—may—have—you run to Starks' for a phone—the rescue squad," Josh said in rhythm to his movements. "But late at night—volunteers—it may take a while—for them—to come."

Josh began counting. *Daad,* trying to help, echoed his numbers. Suddenly *Mamm* choked, sucked in a breath and opened her eyes. She gasped, spit up water while Lydia and Josh helped her to sit up and *Daad* chaffed her hands.

"I want to—die—too," she whispered, her voice rasping. "I killed Sammy. Did I kill someone else? I told her—stay away from my Lydia."

She coughed more and sucked in ragged breaths. *Daad* said, "Don't talk now, Susan. Shhh!"

But she went on, gasping her words. "Why, you should have heard—the things—she asked—me!"

Even in the dark, Lydia's and Josh's wide gazes slammed together. Did she mean Sandra?

Josh looked quickly away, but Lydia's thoughts terrified her. What if *Mamm* had taken one of those pills during the day? In her strange waking-sleeping state, could she have confronted Sandra in the barn—the loft? *Mamm* had been there to give Josh bread just two days before that. Maybe she'd seen Sandra drive into his place and had come over just to talk, to warn her to keep away, to keep quiet about Lydia's adoption. And then...? No. No, impossible.

Daad cradled *Mamm* against him, bending over her as if he could warm her. Josh put his hand on *Daad*'s shoulder, gripped it. "The barn's the closest place, and I've got heated blowers we can train right on you," he told them. "The heat's turned down in the house, and the three of you can't all get in my single bed, anyway.

I'll carry her there and get blankets from the house for everyone. Lydia, help your father. We're all going to freeze. We can't stay here. Everyone up. Now."

He lifted *Mamm,* and they obeyed, a straggling band trudging through the snow. It was only then Lydia realized she had one bare foot, and it had gone numb. Limping, weaving, they went through the gate and Lydia closed it behind them. Slowly they made their way across the animal enclosure toward the open camel gate in the barn. How beautiful it looked to her, that dimly lighted doorway: safety and salvation. *Mamm* ill but alive.

Daad had been near death's door, too. Were they being punished for not telling her about her birth parents?

Lydia's mother was conscious, clinging to her husband. Josh helped Lydia wrap them in camel blankets. He moved one of the two lanterns closer to them, as if that would provide warmth, and handed Lydia the other, and then he trained both warm blowers on the three of them.

"I'll be back fast with dry clothes and house blankets. Lydia, rub and wrap your foot. And there's some hot coffee left in my thermos."

Josh reopened the back barn door they'd just closed and ran for the house. He knew he had to keep moving. He hadn't been in the water, but he'd gotten wet from the splashing and carrying Mrs. Brand. Besides, he'd run out with the horse rein but no coat. How had Mrs. Brand gotten in that pond? Had she been trying to kill herself and then decided that she wanted to live? Lydia's father had needed a heart surgeon, but her mother needed a psychiatrist. At least Lydia had been there to call for help.

He fumbled to unlock the back door. His hands were freezing, shaking, and it was so chilly in here. Maybe he'd turned the heat down too far when he went out with the animals. Had to hurry...Lydia could have broken through the ice, too, drowned the same way her little brother had, the way her mother surely would have if he hadn't heard their screams and shouts. He could have had two more dead women on his property. He had felt so blessed when Lydia came into his life this second time, but now he almost feared there was a curse on her family.

He tore inside his house and pounded up the stairs. If only he had time to heat water, but he had to get all of them in dry clothes. Maybe he should have brought them here, but they'd barely made it as far as the barn.

In his bedroom, he stripped the quilt and both blankets off his bed, then grabbed his clean clothes, even for the women. Flannel shirts, pairs of pants, socks, slippers and shoes. A change of clothes for himself. He jammed it all into a bundle, using the biggest blanket to cover it.

When they were dry, he should take them home in his buggy, but he hated to leave the animals alone, even for that long, with all that had been going on. If KILLER wanted to hurt him even more, would he attack the animals to accomplish his sick mission?

On his rush back downstairs and through the kitchen, he grabbed a box of crackers and a sack of cookies.

His arms so full he could hardly see where he was

going, he engaged the lock from the inside, then stumbled out into the cold.

He went at a lurching run toward the barn. How many times had he wished Lydia and her family would drop by for a visit and now this. He remembered Mrs. Brand's first words when she regained consciousness. He knew what she meant when she said she'd killed Sammy since the boy had somehow gotten past her and headed to the pond. But what about her dazed question, *Did I kill someone else, too?* She'd seemed to refer to Sandra with all her questions. Had Sandra confronted Lydia's mother? Here? *Ach,* people said a lot of things when they were in shock.

It might be a good idea to shout for Lydia to open the camel door. But as dark as it was out here, barely starlit with no moon, he could see something was written—painted—on the entrance he'd run through more than once tonight. The same crude, quick writing. This time, the paint was dry. Since he'd left the door open when he'd run back and forth, the words could have been there awhile: U KILLED S.

When Josh came back in, Lydia thought he looked like he'd seen a ghost. No doubt, the shock of all this was setting in for him, too. She'd rubbed her foot and wrapped it in a towel, then done the same for both of *Mamm*'s feet. Her toes had looked blue. She had gotten some hot coffee down her mother and made *Daad* take a few sips. Josh, at least, didn't look as if he needed coffee. He looked wide-awake and his face was red, but not the kind of red from the cold. Was he scared or angry?

"Here," he said, dropping his bundle on his plank

desk. He told Lydia, "We'll all have to wear my clothes and cover up with these blankets until I can buggy you home. Unless you think your mother needs a doctor right now."

"She needs a doctor, all right, but not now," Lydia whispered. "A doctor tomorrow, for sure. Best we just all get warm."

Josh carried *Mamm* into his office, and behind stacked bales of hay, she and *Daad* got on dry clothes and wrapped themselves in blankets. Lydia went to change on the other side of the camel pen behind the kneeling, sleeping animals, who woke and tried to nuzzle her and nip her hair as if to say, *Join us. We have room here in the hay.*

Josh had gone around the corner where the old milking wing started. Unfortunately, all the hubbub annoyed the donkeys, who began protesting in their usual brays and haws.

Once Lydia got her pants cuffs and shirtsleeves rolled up, holding up the too-big trousers, she hurried back to her parents. "*Daad,* are you two doing all right?" she asked. "Can Josh or I get you something else from his house? He brought crackers and cookies."

"We're all right, Liddy," *Daad*'s wan voice floated to her. "All covered up, warmth coming back."

As she moved away from her parents, Josh came striding toward her in his dry clothes. He still looked upset. "Sorry we got the animals stirred up, so—"

He stopped in midthought as his eyes traveled over her, dressed in his clothing. She knew her hair was a mess, and she had cinched in his too-loose trousers with some twine and was still shivering from what had happened as much as from the cold. She wore so many socks on her tingling foot that she hobbled when she walked. She was shaken to her core, and she saw now Josh was trembling, too.

They moved farther away from her parents into a barely lit corner of the barn. Josh pulled her into a warm embrace, pressed tight, her soft curves to his hard angles. Her arms around his waist clamped her to him; his arms around her back felt like steel— trembling steel.

"You should lie down, too," she murmured, her lips against his warm throat. "You'd better not buggy us home right now. You strained your muscles. You're shaking."

His only answer was to kiss her hard, his demanding mouth moving over hers. His skin felt warmer than hers. His beard stubble raspy, his tongue commanding. He broke the kiss as quickly as it began and whispered in her ear.

"Lydia, the KILLER painter has been at it again. I didn't see it on the outside of the camel door until I came in with the clothes. It's dry, may have been there for a while—well, at least since after I came in here to check on a sick sheep a few hours ago. When I ran in and out to get to you, I was in such a rush, and then the door was open when we came back in."

His deep voice, his emotion and urgency vibrated through her as he held her close. Strange that even with all the terror they'd been through tonight, she felt warmed by his body, by her desire and love for him.

But she leaned slightly back to see his face. "Is the message the same as before?"

"It just says U KILLED S. The word *you* is not

spelled out, like someone was used to sending messages on Twitter or something. Or, was just in a hurry."

"Twitter? A worldly phone? Could KILLER have come into the barn when you were out, too? Should we look around again? I've been trying to give *Mamm* and *Daad* privacy, but could he be behind a stack of hay bales, too...or up in the loft?"

"I'm going to get a pitchfork for protection, take a lantern and find out," he said, setting her back. "This has to stop now, but you wait here."

"You'll have to tell the sheriff you're still being harassed," she said, clinging to his hand as he started away. "Maybe he can do a stick up."

He almost smiled. "A stakeout? Like stay outside in the cold all night, walking back and forth between your place and mine? And I'll bet your father didn't lock the door when he went out. Considering what happened to your place—your bed—you'd better ask him. I swear, I'm going to do a stakeout myself. But *ya,* I'll have to get the sheriff out here again, as much as his continued questions gall me."

Josh got the extra lantern and a very old-looking pitchfork and started to make a circuit of the barn. Lydia tiptoed near her parents and whispered, "*Daad,* did you lock our house door?"

He sat up beyond the bales, rose and tiptoed away from her sleeping mother. "I didn't, but don't worry, Liddy. No one will disturb a place, especially this time of night. Not in Amish country."

She remembered that she and *Mamm* had not told him about the break-in at their home. Nor did he know about the first message scrawled under the loft. Or that the person who might be Sandra's killer—Victoria's, too, for all they knew—was in the area tonight, throwing red paint around instead of honey this time. So should she blame him too much for not telling her important things? People had their secrets and their reasons, maybe not to hurt but to protect those they loved.

But no way did she want to go home alone now to secure those doors with their new locks. For all she knew their keys might have been taken by now. Without another word, she hugged her father good-night and went back by the camel pen to wait for Josh. The barn had gone silent again but for the creak of its old wooden bones in the wind. She couldn't even hear Josh until he suddenly appeared.

"Nothing I can find, even in the lofts," he whispered as he came back with the pitchfork and lantern.

"You were right," she said. "*Daad* didn't lock the house when he went out in such a rush. So far, we haven't told him about our intruder. But after all he's been through tonight, maybe he's ready to hear some things he'd rather not—just like I am."

"Your burning question?"

"*Ya,* I'll try again. Josh, it has to be something… well, something bad to make them keep the truth about my birth parents from me. Each time I get ready to demand he tell me, I think the Lord is giving me signs to wait longer, but all this can't wait. *Ya,* I need to ask him or Bess about the truth."

"Bess? Oh, you mean she's lived around here long enough that she might remember something about your birth parents? And being *Englische* instead of Amish, she's more likely to tell you than your parents or Bishop Esh would."

Lydia agonized whether to confide in him about

the huge collection of snow globes, about the letter she'd found to Sweetheart Sol from his Bessie. But she'd seen too many secrets, and she trusted Josh. In a quiet voice, she blurted out everything except *Daad*'s suspicions about Gid's embezzlement.

"Bessie?" Josh said when she told him what the letter said. "I don't know if Congresswoman Stark was ever called that, but that was my mother's nickname among family and friends instead of Bethany. So there's a coincidence for you. My father always called her Bessie. Lydia," he said, taking a deep breath before plunging on, "they were close friends years ago."

He'd spoken so matter-of-factly. A coincidence, he'd said, though Lydia's stomach did a cartwheel. Another Bessie! And one in *Daad*'s early life. As much as Lydia had feared the wild possibility that her real mother was Bess Stark, it would be even more of a disaster if it was Bessie Yoder, now deceased, because then Josh would be her half brother.

Lydia was grateful when Josh buggied them home at dawn. They had whispered for hours, then had finally fallen asleep, leaning together on hay bales near the front door. Before exhaustion claimed them, he'd tried to keep Lydia from thinking a massive collection of snow globes was enough to prove maternity, but he'd even more strongly assured her that his mother and Sol had been no more than friends. Yet so many things had shocked her now that it seemed no nightmare was impossible.

To her relief, nothing was painted on their house or barn, and inside the house things seemed to be as they had left them in their haste to chase *Mamm* outside.

Daad got *Mamm* to bed and sat with her while Lydia fixed them tea, then made a quick tour of the house to be sure all was well. Nothing strange in the pantry or refrigerator, she noted, except both ice cube trays in the freezer section were empty. The way *Mamm* had been today, she'd probably forgotten to refill them, though who would want cold drinks today?

Lydia filled the trays and put them back in the refrigerator. As soon as she got out of Josh's clothes, she was going out to the phone shanty way down the road because she wasn't ready to let the Starks know *Mamm* had run outside just as Victoria had. She had to call their family doctor for a recommendation for someone to treat *Mamm*'s problems.

But when she went up to change and opened the underwear drawer of the cherry chest in her room, she found that her panties and stockings had been moved around. But then she saw that wasn't the worst. Her undergarments were all wet, soaked with cold water—melted ice cubes?—and a note crudely printed in red ink read U R NEXT.

27

Though she was exhausted, Lydia walked into the sheriff's office at 9:00 a.m. that morning. She had the threatening note in a plastic zipper bag and intended to tell him about the new sign on Josh's back barn door. She'd gotten *Mamm* a late-afternoon appointment to see her doctor today, but Lydia vowed she was also going to drop in at the store and stop to see Bess Stark.

And tonight, no matter what happened, she was going to talk to her father about her past. Whatever threats she and Josh faced, they needed a new beginning, and she was determined to have that. If, she thought with a shudder as she looked at the bloodred ink through the plastic sack, her father had not loved Josh's mother at one time. And if she—Lydia—was not NEXT.

"Come on in, Lydia," the sheriff said after his receptionist went back to his office to tell him she was here. "I can see by your face something else happened. Everyone all right?"

"Not really," she told him, trying to stem the urge to cry. She'd never had time for that cry yesterday. But she only sniffed once as she sat in the chair Sheriff Freeman indicated. She blurted out about her mother's near drowning last night and the new message on Josh's door. She blushed when she told him about melted ice cubes in her underwear drawer, then handed him the note.

"Ice cubes in the drawer, hmm? Makes me think your intruder was watching the near tragedy in the icy pond. He's either saying to you, 'I've been watching you' or, once again, like this note, 'You're next—in the pond.' Or worse, since we have two dead women."

"I've been so exhausted I didn't think of that—that he'd been watching my mother nearly drown." She shuddered, but she had to pull herself together. "Oh, I almost forgot," she added as she watched the sheriff frown over the note. "Josh says you can take pictures of the latest paint job and he wishes you could do a stake-out. I wish you could keep an eye on our house, too."

"I just may have to do that, at least at Josh's, since he's alone there and you've got your folks back. I used to have 4-H animals when I was a kid, showed them at the state fair, slept with them all night in the sheep barn, no less. Yeah, I just might have to help Josh tend his herd for the night, even though I'd have to make a showing at a party for local businessmen the Starks are giving at our restaurant."

"Oh. Tonight? What time is that?" she asked, hoping she could get to Bess before then.

"Eight. Bess didn't want to make Ray-Lynn close the place early on her regular customers. You've done good to bring me this information and this note, Lydia. I'm working on all angles, including someone switching your father's pills. Anything else I can help you with?"

She sighed and thought how nice it would be to have him inform Gid, Bess, Connor, even *Daad,* that he would interrogate them if they didn't tell her the truth.

"Gid Reich," the sheriff would say as he took him into custody, "have you been embezzling from the store? And have you been trying to scare Lydia away from Josh with those messages on the barn and in her house? Maybe you've been backing off from her in public because in secret you've been stalking and frightening her, hoping she'd run to you. Or, worse, are you trying to get rid of her father so you can take over the store as well as her life?

"And, Mr. Mayor," the sheriff would say to Connor when he arrested him for painting Christmas trees and Josh's barn, "I'm hauling you in for questioning, too. I hear you've been mean to Lydia, your neighbor, for years.

"And, Congresswoman Stark," he would say, holding up both hands when Bess rushed in to rescue Connor so his arrest wouldn't hurt her career, "did you once keep secret company with Sol Brand? Did you have his baby and give her away?

"And, Sol, I know you're recovering from a heart attack, but I need to ask this, anyway. You've been a loving adoptive father to Lydia, but are you her real father, too? She needs to know. And, Sol, is your marriage bad because your wife lost your son or because she can't love Lydia—or you because you were unfaithful?"

"Lydia, you listening?" the sheriff asked, leaning closer and tapping her arm. She jerked her head. Had she nodded off? "You're exhausted. You almost fell asleep sitting here. Can't you go on home, get some rest?"

"I'll sleep tonight, Sheriff. Things to do, but I thank you and Ray-Lynn for all your help. As my father used to say when I saw he was exhausted and I begged him to get some sleep, 'Someday, Liddy, I'll sleep forever.'"

They both stood. "Then you have a good, safe day," he said, and patted her shoulder. "And be extra careful."

She had to, Lydia thought as she went out. There was nowhere to go but up...was there?

"So, Lydia," Gid greeted her outside her office at the store, "you may think you can't live with me, but can you live without me? I mean running the store for you and Sol while you have other serious concerns. How's he doing?"

"Better," she told him, not breaking stride or going into her office where he could corner her. She headed toward Naomi at the front desk. Lydia hoped she was having a good day, at least.

"Can I stop in to see him, then?" Gid asked, matching her strides. "You probably can't brief him about things in depth, since you haven't been here much."

She knew it would look suspicious if she kept avoiding this man. If he was the one behind the paint jobs and house intrusions, she couldn't give him a clue she was on to him. Just before they reached the front desk—Naomi was busy with customers, anyway—Lydia stopped, turned to Gid and forced a weak smile.

"I've just been so worried about *Daad*. We are all grateful for the job you do here for us."

"Which I am honored to do. Lydia, you look really tired. Circles under swollen eyelids on your pretty face. You aren't helping your mother sit up with him at night, are you? Is there anything I can do to help there as well as here?"

"No. *Danki*. You've done enough," she managed before she went up to Naomi's desk to chat. Perhaps Gid *had* done enough—even too much.

When Lydia hurried home to go with her parents to *Mamm*'s doctor's appointment, she found a note from *Daad* on the kitchen table.

Liddy—Our driver came early to tell us he'd been called that the dr.'s appt. had been moved up. Do not worry that you wanted to go with us. Mamm's exhausted and sore today and has the chills, is coughing and doesn't remember much about last night. I told her you and Josh saved her. I'm hoping this dr. will recommend mental dr. Get this—your mother says you should visit Josh and thank him again.
Love and blessings,
Daad.

It was a bit of a victory about *Mamm* and Josh, but Lydia, once again, regretted people not telling everything. If *Daad* had known about someone being in the house—twice—he would never have assumed she should stay here alone. And *Mamm* had probably been too out of it to object. So Lydia's own secrets had put her at possible risk of danger. And had *Daad*'s secrets about her parents put his Liddy in real danger somehow? She did not want to be "next" about anything but getting answers and a normal life.

She decided to do the unexpected. She would not stay here alone but would go back to the store after closing time and search Gid's office. If he was the one lurking outside her home, she wouldn't be anywhere around when he showed up after dark.

When Lydia entered the store through the back door with her master key, it seemed an alien place. She had put Flower, still hitched to the buggy, in the shelter of the big horse shed. At least there was a sliver of moon tonight, because no way were there interior or exterior lights in an Amish establishment. But she had planned ahead and brought two flashlights with her.

Yet, even inside, everything familiar seemed so strange. The back door closed behind her with a hollow thud. The cleaning couple weren't here yet, and she planned to be out when they arrived. The silence of the usually busy, noisy workroom stunned her. Her pulse picked up as she swept a flashlight beam on the sawdust-sprinkled floor and headed toward the door to the short hall with the offices.

She was surprised she had to use her key again, but that was best. She hadn't realized this area was locked at night. On second thought, so she wouldn't have to open this door again, she wedged a small block of wood there to keep it ajar.

She wondered what the vast alleys of furniture inside the showroom would look like after dark. However well she knew the layout, would she get lost? But she would not go into that big room tonight.

She went to Gid's office, as he must have gone to

Daad's more than once recently. She hesitated at his office door, but it wasn't really fear she felt, just anticipation. Yet she was going to be risking everything tonight—doing this, stopping to see Bess then talking to *Daad* however late he got home. No more just being curious or afraid. She was getting answers.

She used the master key again and went into Gid's lair, closing the door. A sweep of both beams around the room caught nothing out of place. His desktop looked tidy. But, oh, so many files, just like in *Daad*'s office. She'd never have the time to go through those if he'd hidden something the way her father had. Maybe this was a desperate, too-crazy idea.

She turned off one flashlight, put it down on the desk and, opening his central desk drawer, swept the other beam inside. Everything in its place. After all, Gid was a by-the-rules bookkeeper and controller. Her flashlight illumined only paper clips, pencils, pens. And—oh!—red pens. She'd heard that accountants talked in terms of black-and-red ink. She had no doubt Gid could have written that note she'd found this morning in her drawer.

She jumped when she heard a distant, muted noise. Had something dropped or toppled over? Had the door she'd wedged open closed? It was on a tension bar. But if it had closed itself, it wouldn't be with a bang.

She closed Gid's drawer and tiptoed to the door, putting her ear to it. No other sounds, except the tick-tock of the clock on the shelf behind his desk. But then—someone walking in the hall? She clicked off her flashlight.

Maybe Marta and John Kurtz were here early to clean, and she could tell them she'd just come in for something she needed for *Daad*. But she'd have to get out of Gid's office, or Marta might just blab to him.

She opened the door but still stood inside, barely breathing, listening in the utter blackness. Had someone passed in the hall, or did footsteps echo from the other direction? She heard nothing now. Though Amish to her core, it suddenly seemed the lack of electric lighting was not a blessing, as Bishop Esh had called it in a recent sermon.

From down the hall, someone cast a wan light on the wall, coming this way from the back room. She was about to call out to Marta when someone coughed. A man. Had Marta's husband come without her tonight?

Instinct told her to dart away, and she did, after closing Gid's office door quietly behind her. On her tiptoes, she rushed down the hall toward the coffee room, then into the maze of showroom furniture she'd thought could be downright dangerous in the dark.

She crawled under a desk and huddled there. Shifting shadows etched the outline of an Amish man—she could tell by his hat—as he approached and walked past. She dared not stick her head out to look up. *Ya,* Amish trousers stuffed in plain black boots. Had Gid hired a new night watchman, not trusting the Lord to care for this place at night, or could that be John Kurtz, come to clean? Or Gid himself? Had he stopped by and found Flower and her buggy? But he would have called out to her, wouldn't he?

She wanted to confront the person but she dared not. Especially not since this could be her house intruder. Yet she ached to know who it was, what he was doing here. Without others to help carry things, it would be hard to steal store merchandise, and they never kept money on-site at night. So what business could this person have?

She was going to make a run for it. Then she could see if the doors had been broken into on her way out. If it was a break-in, she'd get the sheriff. If not, she'd go home, get the note from Bessie to Sol in case she needed it then go to confront Bess.

As she crawled out from under the desk and started away, she chanced a look back. The man's lantern cast his shadow on the far wall, and she could hear him opening and closing drawers, maybe over by the dining room highboys or corner cupboards. But looking for what? Something he'd put there rather than in his office?

On tiptoe again, she hurried from the big, dark room. When she could turn on her flashlight again, she tore down the office hallway to the workshop door. It was closed. She had to fumble for her key. Then, as she turned it in the lock, it hit her: she'd left one of her two flashlights in Gid's office on his desk. But she dared not go back for it now. If that was Gid in the showroom, he hadn't gone into his office—yet. Maybe he'd think the cleaning people had left it.

Despite the fact she had to run farther toward the horse shed, she was glad she had not left Flower and her buggy outside to be seen. Because Gid's horse and handsome buggy were tied to the back hitching post.

"Okay," Sheriff Freeman told Josh as he surveyed the barn once again, especially studying the paint on the outside of the camel door, "tell you what. Let's you and me take turns staying awake here tonight.

We can hot bunk—that's what they call it in the navy and marines. Guys take shifts, sleep in the same bunk when the other one's not there. And that cot of yours looks a lot better than some of the bunks I had in my days in the service. I've got to go into town to help Ray-Lynn—and I'm a guest—at a party Bess Stark's giving later tonight. But you'll only be alone about an hour then. How's that for a fast plan?"

"Suits me," Josh said. "I'm just hoping when you're in here without me, the donkeys don't rile the others up, so you can sleep. And when one of us is on watch outside, let's go through the woodlot and take a look around the Brands' house and barn. They're probably back from seeing the doctor in Wooster by now, but you never know if someone's hanging around over there."

"Their place was dark when I went by, but sometimes lanterns don't light up windows well. After what Lydia said happened at the pond last night, no wonder they might have gone to bed already. You got more coffee over there? It's gonna be a long night," he muttered.

"I'll go brew a new pot in the house and be right back," Josh told him, and went out the camel door.

He glanced back at the terrible message U KILLED S. In a way, he had.

Panicked that Gid would hear her buggy and follow, Lydia took a different way home, repeatedly looking back on the road as she urged Flower from a trot to a gallop. Since he didn't follow her, at least she knew he was busy elsewhere. It wouldn't take a minute to grab the Bessie note, the broken snow globe, go to the bathroom then rush back to the buggy and head for the Starks' next door.

But, as soon as she drove up she realized that, unless her parents had gone to bed when they got back, they weren't home from Wooster yet. The house was as dark as it was outside. Maybe they'd been sent to the hospital there. Poor *Daad* must be tired of hospitals right now. Maybe that chill and cough of *Mamm*'s had gone into something worse, like bronchitis or pneumonia. Besides trying to get the truth out of Bess tonight, Lydia figured she could use her phone to call the driver her parents had hired.

She hesitated a moment at the back door. She'd have to get these locks changed yet again since *Daad* had left the house open last night and someone had come in. Someone who had obviously been watching and—

"Hey, Ms. Brand," came a man's voice close behind her.

Lydia gasped and turned.

A squat figure emerged from the shadows next to the house. Leo Lowe! He was wearing a bulky coat with a hoodie. She couldn't see his face but she'd never forget his voice. Had he been in this area the whole time the sheriff had been looking for him? Her knees went weak and she propped herself up against the storm door.

"Oh, Mr. Lowe, you startled me. Please leave me alone," she told him, trying to keep her voice strong and calm. "The sheriff's looking for you so you'd better leave town."

"I know. Listen, I didn't kill Ms. Myerson."

"Then you should not have run. You should go turn yourself in, tell the truth and clear it all up."

"You told the sheriff I scared you—threatened you and bad-mouthed Ms. Myerson," he said, his voice rising. "That's another reason he was looking for me, the wife said." He came closer, just one step down from where she stood with her back against the door.

"But I did not ask for a restraining order or file a complaint. We Amish don't do that."

"Don't have any truck with violence neither, right? Yet you don't think the guy next door knocked Ms. Myerson off for her big mouth? I'll bet the newspapers think he's guilty."

Leo must be the person who'd painted on Josh's barn, accusing Josh to throw suspicion away from himself. He surely didn't mean Connor was the guy next door.

He came up another step. If she could just unlock the door behind her, dash in. But if Leo was her intruder, he had the latest key. And she'd heard criminal acts got worse. Someone who at first just spied might later break in, damage property. She saw again her messed-up bed, her underwear. Then the criminal got bolder and would try an assault, or worse…

She did the only thing she could think of besides run and, in the snow, he could probably catch her, anyway. With her back truly against the wall, she lied.

"Get away from me, or you'll really be in trouble. Sheriff Freeman said he has no case against you and he just wanted an alibi from you, not from your family and friends he visited. Besides, he'll be here soon."

"Yeah—you're right about my family at least. He's been talking to them."

"I said we Amish don't testify, but I will privately

tell the sheriff I don't think you had anything to do with Sandra's death."

Dear God in Heaven, he had a knife! It glinted in the pale moonlight and then went dark against his black clothes.

"You mean that?" he demanded.

"*Ya*—yes, and I'm hardly going to run or hide out like you. I've got my family waiting for me inside." Steady, she told herself. He might know that was another lie. "Besides," she continued, clearing her throat, "my friend, the sheriff's wife, told me—"

"Yeah. Ray-Lynn. I checked out their place a couple of times, and he didn't even know I was there."

He was bold. Desperate. And she kept imagining the thrust of that knife.

"I was saying," she went on, "Ray-Lynn told me that the sheriff would be in his office in town late tonight, so why don't you get it over with—the hiding out, I mean. Clear your name with him, get back to your family, especially your father, who must be very worried about you. I'm sorry he went to prison for hitting an Amish buggy, but I was only an infant, and that's all said and done. And...forgiven."

"Forgiven," he repeated. "Yeah, I hear you Amish are good at that, too, like they forgave the man who killed some Amish schoolgirls over in Pennsylvania."

He was calming down now, wasn't he? But he still didn't budge. A long time seemed to stretch by. And he still had the knife. She felt frozen in place, afraid to flee, afraid to stay here, afraid for her life as Sandra must have been in her last moments.

"You forgive my father for hitting that buggy, killing your folks?" he asked.

She almost told him, *If they were my folks.* But instead, she said, "We all need to be forgiven." Those were *Daad*'s very words to her when they talked about the quilt he'd made for her.

"I'll go see the sheriff," he said, and turned away. He went into a half run down the driveway. Only then did she realize she was hardly breathing and that, even in this cold, she was dripping with sweat.

Eager to get to the Starks to use their phone, she unlocked her back door and dashed inside. The winter night was young, and she had much to do.

28

Lydia almost lost her courage when she saw how beautiful Bess looked—how worldly. No long denim skirt or casual clothes. She wore a turquoise wool dress and a chunky gold necklace and earrings to match. Even her high heels—really high ones—matched her dress. Makeup highlighted her pretty face even more.

Lydia began to tremble. Of course, there was no way in all God's creation this woman could be her mother. They didn't even look alike—well, maybe eye color and the shape of the mouth. But Lydia didn't look like *Daad,* either. Did she have a bug in her bean to pursue this?

"Sorry to bother you when you're going out," Lydia apologized. "I'm hoping I could make two calls from here instead of going way down the road to the phone shanty."

"Of course you can," Bess said, smiling and encircling her shoulders to bring her inside. "As you can see, we're stepping out, but we don't have to leave yet. Since Connor is mayor now, the family is giving a holiday appreciation dinner for the small businessmen in town. We had invited your father, but I believe he planned to send Gid Reich to represent your family, even before he had his heart attack."

Family, family. She knew she shouldn't even ask Bess if the two of them could be family, but that note she had in her sack with the broken globe would always haunt her. *Ach,* Josh was right. That didn't really prove anything.

"Well, you look beautiful, Bess."

"I have to work at it more and more the older I get. I admire you Amish for not worrying one bit about outward appearances—and for having no TV in your homes, let alone the internet. My rivals have been trying to make a big deal out of Connor spraying those trees. Here, let's go into my office, and you can make your calls from there. The others are upstairs getting ready, and my special guest from Washington is meeting us there. Heather's in the bathtub, so Connor's riding herd on the boys."

"Good. I got the idea that's exactly what they needed and wanted."

Bess led her into the room with the snow globes, but the curtains were closed again. She sat Lydia in the same chair she'd been in the other day and handed her a phone—no cord attached. "You have to punch the talk button, then dial your number," Bess told her. "By the way, we're having the party at Ray-Lynn's and the sheriff's restaurant. Ray-Lynn's been a great help."

"That's the way she is. She's helped me and several others I know. Actually, I'm calling my parents' driver to see why they're not back from Wooster yet where my mother had a doctor's appointment. And then the sheriff because he needs to know the son of the man who hit my parents' buggy years ago was outside my house just now. I think I talked him into going to the sheriff."

Though Bess had started to step out into the hall, she came back and sat again, turning toward Lydia. "He didn't hurt you? If he's like his father, he's a loose cannon. Isn't he the one the sheriff put out a bulletin on? You can just stay here when we leave, until you find out when your parents are coming back, because you don't need to be out on these roads after dark."

Lydia thanked her and, when Bess went out, quickly made her calls. Her spirits were buoyed when the sheriff's night dispatcher put her right in touch with him. After she explained things, he said he'd planned to spend the night with Josh, but had been called by his dispatcher that Leo Lowe was indeed at the station. He was on his way there, then hoped to stop by the party at the restaurant before "hustling" back to Josh's barn. "And I'm gonna have to lock Lowe up tonight, Lydia, so don't you worry about him bothering you again."

It made Lydia feel so much safer, stronger, especially when she talked to her parents' driver to be sure they were all right. He was en route back to Homestead without them because her mother had been admitted to the hospital with pneumonia, and *Daad* wouldn't leave her. Lydia made plans for the driver to pick her up the next morning to go into Wooster. If she had to have her big talk with *Daad* in a hospital corridor or lounge, so be it. She had to end this agony of waiting. And who knew, maybe the sheriff might get out of Leo Lowe that he was the intruder, the barn painter, even Sandra's killer. A man with a knife could

easily have been enough to scare someone into stepping backward off a barn loft.

Ray-Lynn and her staff at the Dutch Farm Table
were decorating to the hilt for this Stark family party
tonight. Ropes of pine boughs tied with red velvet rib-
bons circled the main room. Two Christmas trees—
of course, donated by the Starks—studded with shiny
balls and swagged loops of colored glass beads and
lights shed a soft blur of color. The place smelled of a
delicious blend of pine, fresh-baked bread and coffee.

Her Amish girls were now working like mad to
clean up after the last dinner customer left. They were
carrying some of the tables out into the back room to
make a more spacious dining area. Ray-Lynn had the
red-and-green tablecloths and centerpieces ready. The
Starks were paying well to rent the venue and have
Ray-Lynn's kitchen staff prepare the feast of turkey,
two kinds of potatoes, a salad buffet and too many
pumpkin and pecan pies to count.

It relieved her when Jack called to say he had Leo
Lowe in custody—thanks to Lydia—but he was still
planning to "stop by" to greet everyone.

"I sure hope you'll be here," she told him, holding
her cell phone with one hand and gesturing where
the tables went with the other. "Especially since the
Starks are the hosts for this. Besides, Bess's new significant other is going to be here, some mover and
shaker from D.C. Ding-dang, I'll just bet he's advising her on a statewide or national campaign, and he's
been around here a lot more than anyone knows. Jack,
it can't hurt for you to know people like that. Maybe
he can pull someone's chain to get you a deputy with

all that's gone on here lately. You can't help it that your
last one didn't work out."

She watched her waitresses flapping open and ar-
ranging the tablecloths Bess had sent over. Even as
she listened to Jack, she grabbed the fancy name tags
off the counter to place them herself.

"I said I'll be there, honey," he went on, "but it'll
be brief. I'm going to lock this guy up for one night
and depose him tomorrow 'cause I'm spending most
of the night with Josh, keeping an eye on things there."

"But if you have him in custody, and he's the one
who threatened Lydia and had it in for Sandra, Lydia's
and Josh's worries are over."

She started to place the name tags: Bess Stark,
Heather Stark, Mayor Connor Stark...

"He actually has a solid alibi for the day and night
Sandra died, and only ran 'cause he thought no one
would believe him since he'd threatened Sandra and
Lydia," Jack explained. "No, the guy who I think killed
Sandra Myerson, who's been painting up a storm on
Josh's barn trying to blame him, isn't Leo Lowe. I got
a gut feeling her killer's still out there, getting closer
and even more desperate."

Lydia's heartbeat kicked up the moment Bess came
back into the room after she made her phone calls.
"Some hot chocolate for you," she said, putting a bright
green mug on the desk in front of her. "Listen, we'll
be leaving in half an hour, but I can give you a guest
bedroom for the night."

"That's very kind, but I should go home. So you
have a minute to talk now?"

"Of course," she said, but she looked suddenly wary. "Your phone calls—is everything all right?"

"*Ya*—yes, fine with that. Bess, I happened to notice from outside yesterday that you have a beautiful collection of snow globes. You must have been collecting them a long time."

"Quite a while. I consider them seasonal decorations, don't have them out year-round. And they seem to fit better here than in my Columbus office or condo."

"But you must be an expert on them. I have a very special one. It's broken, but I intend to fix it. My father gave it to me years ago and said it had been my mother's—my real mother's—but I was not to ask questions about her. It always bothered me, intrigued me, and lately I tried to have someone—Sandra Myerson—help me find out about her, especially since no one, not even Bishop Esh, seemed to want me to know much about my past."

"No doubt because it was so tragic with that fatal buggy crash."

Bess had glanced at the snow globe Lydia had drawn from her sack, then quickly away. A frown line appeared above her penciled eyebrows, and her red lower lip pouted, then quivered.

"But then several people told me that Lena Brand—supposedly my real mother—never had a child."

"Did your father tell you that?" she demanded, her voice almost strident.

"No. I heard that from both a friend of Lena and David Brand and one of Lena's cousins. But I was just wondering if you had a snow globe similar to this one which has meant so much to me. I was devastated when it got broken and am determined to put it back together."

Lydia got up and walked beside the desk, back to the low bookcases and the curtained window above them. She pulled the cord that drew the curtains open and gazed at the rows of snow globes—and found one almost identical.

"Oh, there, see?" she said, pointing at it before turning back to face Bess. "This one and mine really resemble each other."

Despite her high cheek color, Bess's face had gone pale. She said nothing, then finally murmured, in a whisper, "I can't help you, Lydia."

"Well, maybe just one more thing, then."

"This is not the time for this."

"There's never been a time for this! But I have to know. I have a note here my father saved—he is really my father, isn't he?—that I found hidden in his desk drawer at the store. It's from someone who loved him a long time ago before he married *Mamm,* someone who signed her name Bessie. I haven't told him I found it yet because of his heart attack, but I'll have to now. Besides you and Josh's mother growing up around here, who could this Bessie have been? I won't tell others, really. And your sister knew about it, didn't she, since she drew those pictures of angels carrying a baby away?"

Bess looked frozen. She didn't move, but two tears tracked down her cheeks. Lydia stood aghast at what had spilled from her, especially the last thought about Victoria, since she hadn't fully reasoned that out before.

Finally, Bess moved. She stood and went to the

door, which stood slightly ajar. Lydia thought she would walk out, but she closed it. She turned back, leaned against it. They stood facing each other across the big desk, Lydia with the note outstretched in her hand, Bess staring at it but making no move to look at it closer.

"Yes, God forgive me for hurting you," Bess said, her voice a mere whisper. "Sol and I...after my husband had been dead two years... Yes, my girl, yes."

Bess opened her arms, and Lydia went to her, half joyous, half afraid. Bess pulled her hard into her embrace. They both cried, Lydia shaking but holding on tight to stop the tilting of the room, Bess crying, then kissing her wet cheek, again, again.

"It was a terrible decision to have to make—to give you away, but I was ready to run for public office the first time. I was widowed, a single mother with a young son who was spending the month of July with his aunt Vicky. But Sol and I—that one insane summer..."

Blinking back tears, Bess hesitated. She put Lydia in one chair, pulled two tissues from a brass container on the desk, sat down next to her and handed her one of them. She scooted her chair closer. Their knees almost touched.

Bess leaned forward as she talked. "Connor was thirteen when I got pregnant with you. He and I moved away and lived with my sister Vicky, who wanted you for her own. But Sol said an Amish adoption was best, as he wasn't married yet, hadn't even proposed. Bishop Esh weighed in on it and suggested it be a secret—a sealed deal. Vicky was hurt and angry, and I regret that. But Sol found a distant cousin of his whose wife wanted a child."

"David and Lena Brand."

She nodded and took Lydia's hands in her own. "And then that buggy catastrophe, but at least you weren't with them. I was both glad and sad when Sol insisted on taking you in when he got married. He told your mother—then his wife—whose child you were, of course. But to see you growing up and not as mine..."

Her shoulders shaking, she started to cry again.

"Mom, you ready?" Connor's voice came from the other side of the door. He knocked but didn't come in. "Whose buggy is that out there? We've got to get going."

"I'll be right out. No, you go ahead without me, and I'll be a little late. It's important," she called to him. Bess got up, opened a little door in the tallest bookcase and stared at herself in the small mirror there. "Wow, time for major repair."

"You have just done major repair—helped me. I won't tell anyone, except my father, that I know. Well, Josh, if I marry him someday. I don't want to hurt your career. And Connor—"

Bess turned back, grabbed another tissue and dabbed under her eyes. She blew her nose. "And Connor has a half sister he should love and admire. That was one of the hardest things, besides not being able to be with you enough. Connor maybe sensed how much I loved you, and he took it out on you sometimes. I mean, he knew I'd had a baby, but I told him it died. Too—too many lies. That one he evidently figured out later."

"Victoria—your sister Vicky—had a note in her hand the night she died. It said, 'To the girl Brand baby. Your mother is alive.'"

Bess turned and put both hands on her desk to steady herself. "She was saying things like that a lot, the worse her Alzeimer's became. Truth from a demented woman and lies from a supposedly sane one," she whispered as if to herself. "She never forgave me for not letting her adopt you, but back then—a single woman... That wasn't common like it is now. But that's one reason we brought her here, so she wouldn't tell others the truth. Somehow, over the years, she'd tracked you down or guessed who you were, and Connor caught on, at least got suspicious then, I think, though he didn't exactly say so."

Lydia wanted to comfort Bess. But what if Connor was the one who had shut Sandra up? Maybe he was the intruder who was trying to put the blame on Josh. But no way could she spring that on Bess tonight, too, maybe never.

Bess shook her head, straightened up and went into a desk drawer. She produced a purse and took out more face powder, looking now in the tiny mirror attached to the skinny silver powder case.

"I still think you should stay here tonight," Bess said. "We can talk when I get back, and I won't stay long. We need to make some decisions about how to handle this, who to tell."

"I told you I'm willing to keep your secret. It's just that I had to know or I'd go crazy, and then Sandra Myerson jumped in with both feet and... Bess, now *Mamm* is really ill, and I can't hurt her or *Daad* more.

He's made me a Christmas quilt that says Forgive Father all over it."

Bess teared up again. "And it will hurt her more if we declare our relationship."

"Mom!" Connor called outside the door. "Heather's going ahead with the kids, and I'll wait for you. Let's go. You're supposed to be the greeter."

"More later," Bess said to Lydia with a forced smile. "For the two of us, much more later, my sweet, smart girl. Stay here a bit, then, and when you go out, just be sure the door is locked. And don't be too hard on your father. If you love Josh Yoder—and I think you do—you understand how loneliness and passion can make you be careless. But one more thing."

With her purse on her arm, she came over to Lydia and took her face in her hands. "Don't you ever think Sol or I regretted you for yourself. I mean, as much as we were upset then that people would know we'd made love, and we were upset with ourselves that my pregnancy caused such problems, we have always been proud of our girl. We just didn't get to share you together."

Bess kissed her cheek again and wiped a tear away with her thumb. "Take care, my Lydia and Sol's Liddy. I'll see you as soon as I can, and we'll talk more."

She went out, leaving the door ajar. Lydia could hear Connor starting in on her, "That's Lydia's buggy, isn't it? Here's your coat. You go with Heather and the kids, and I'll be sure she gets home, then be right over."

"Connor, I don't know."

"Well, there's a lot I don't know, but I'll just follow her home in the buggy, all right?"

Lydia wanted to run out and protest, but since he

was clearing it with Bess and he knew the two of them were friends, he wouldn't dare do anything out of line. Would he? She grabbed the old Bessie note and her broken snow globe from the desk, stuffed them in her bag and went directly outside while Bess, Heather and the boys were just heading down the driveway in one of their three cars.

Lydia was relieved she didn't have to say a word to Connor. Thank heavens, he just stormed to his car and got in. Their big garage threw huge blocks of light out so she could see to unwind her reins and get up into the buggy. But she hadn't even turned Flower around to head down the drive when Connor came running at her and seized Flower's bridle.

"By the way, I heard what you told her before she closed her office door," he shouted up at her. "And you know what? I wondered about that all along, what with the weird stuff Aunt Vicky said. I saw my mother once, years ago, just stop the car and watch you play Andy-over in your front yard with your little brother. Sometimes I thought she was stalking you, but never knew why. But it's gonna have to stay a secret because she's going places and not with an Amish daughter in her campaign ads!"

"Let my horse go, Connor! If you want to talk about this later, we'll wait until she can meet with us."

"Meet—that's good. That's what she does, you know. Meetings, events, campaigns. She may have stopped to give a speech to the tree shoppers and workers below. She's hardly ever here except at election time in her district or holiday time like this. Especially since my dad died, where has she been?"

"But your boys are feeling the same thing about

you, so you can change that for them—change yourself."

"Stay away from us and keep quiet! I don't get
enough of her, and now there's you! Oh, don't worry
that I'll give the big secret away, and I'll see to it you
don't, either. I'll follow you home, so get going."

But she was suddenly terrified to get going. Connor
in that big black car was going to follow her home? An
image leaped into her brain: the newspaper picture of
David and Lena Brand's broken buggy and dead horse
on the road. No, she had to get away from Connor.
She pictured him with those two pitchforks he used to
knock snow off the trees, pictured the pitchfork drawn
in the snow and painted on Josh's barn.

But maybe she could get down the driveway to the
Christmas tree workers and just stay there until he
had to go. After he left for town, she would not turn
in her driveway but head straight for Josh. If Bess had
known he'd overheard them, would she have trusted
Connor to see her safely home?

"Giddyap!" she shouted to Flower and snapped the
reins. But they came loose in her hands—cut off by the
traces. She bounced back in her seat, hit her head on
it then slid sideways onto the floor. Now she'd have to
run from Connor, run through the trees to her house.
He was the one! He'd made sure she couldn't flee!

But she jumped down from the buggy just in time
to see someone in black Amish garb, carrying a pitchfork, run into the garage and swing the handle hard
at Connor. She felt dizzy and her right ankle hurt,
but had someone come to her rescue? Connor cried
out and sprawled flat on his face on the concrete
next to his car, which was still running, puffing out

smelly smoke into the cold night air. Then his attacker, Amish hat pulled low, pitchfork in his hand, turned and rushed toward her.

29

Staring toward the lighted garage, Lydia squinted to see who her rescuer was. Josh? But to have struck Connor so hard, even to help her... Dizzy, she was a little dizzy. Was it— No, not *Daad*.

Oh, Gid! Gid rushed up to her. She started to say she'd been wrong about him, but he hauled her up hard by her arm and dragged her nearly off her feet into the garage. Pain shot through her ankle. She must have twisted it when she'd jumped from the buggy.

"You had it all," he ranted, "and threw it away. You had your chances with me, even after you turned into an icicle."

Blood! She saw blood under Connor's head on the concrete floor. But didn't Gid want to impress Connor, work with Connor?

"Why did you have to hurt Connor?" she cried.

"I regret that, but he's been asking around about who put that newspaper man, Roy Manning, on to his doctoring the trees. If he came under fire for fraud, I thought he might ask me to help manage this place. It's amazing what one can learn by lurking around this area. But then I was afraid he'd trace an unsigned note I sent to Manning's office in Cleveland."

"You told Manning! Your entire life is a lie."

He gave her a hard shake. "So," he explained, "here's the story people will figure out—with Roy Manning's articles—about all this. Connor was furious when he found out you sent that note to Manning. Besides, Connor wants your land, so you two got into an argument after his family left. He threatened you, and you hit him with this pitchfork. Somehow he knocked you down with his car engine running and, well, both of you died, such a tragedy. Lydia, except for losing you, this has worked out so well it has to be the true plan for my life—not a lie."

Gid was crazy! If he'd known what she and Connor were really arguing about, he'd have been able to blackmail or ruin Bess and *Daad*. While she tried to yank free from him, he went on and on. About following her to Amity, about taking the camel saddle, about honey in her bed and ice in her drawer and in her heart. But—was he going to hit her with the pitchfork, too? He'd said she would die with Connor.

"Years of planning, months of courting," he muttered. "So perfect for both of us to have the store, and then that female friend of Yoder shoves her nose in, tries to discover your real father and mother. That's all I need, that the store doesn't come with you. But you didn't even take the hint. You didn't stop pushing even when she died, did you? Started playing detective on your own, just like her."

"You're embezzling from the store—big accounts. And you killed Sandra!" she cried as he pulled her farther into the garage.

"And Sol was starting to catch on about the money, wasn't he? I'd guess you're the one who left the flashlight in my office when I went to remark some price tags. As for Sandra…I have a lot of work to do before we talk about that. But I want to thank you for finally giving me the perfect way to stop you. I've been losing sleep for weeks, keeping an eye on you and Yoder late at night, despite the demands at the store, waiting to find a good way to get rid of you or both of you—and your father. I regret Connor has to go, too, but it just happened. It's necessary."

She glanced back at Connor, sprawled, unmoving. Her half brother. Was he dead? If she screamed, even here in the depths of this huge garage, would the sound carry clear down to Christmas tree workers or customers below?

As if Gid had read her mind, he hit a button that noisily closed the garage doors, all three of them inside while Connor's car, still running, spewed out fumes. To her amazement, Gid dragged her to the back of the car. Did he mean to put her in the trunk? Did he plan to actually drive Connor's car somewhere, stage an accident like the one that had happened to Ray-Lynn when she was pushed off a cliff?

But he shoved her to her knees behind the car's fender, forced her head low so she looked and breathed directly into the exhaust pipe. Then from a backpack she hadn't seen he wore, he produced the oxygen mask he sometimes used in the store's back workroom when the smells of shellac and wood stain were strong. He'd always kept it in his buggy in case cars that passed him smelled bad. One-handed, not letting go of the arm he'd twisted up her back, he lifted the straps of the mask behind his head and turned on the flow of air so the mask began to hiss. A cord connected the mask to a small canister in his pack.

And then, though she knew almost nothing about cars, she remembered reading how a local *Englische* family—it had been parents and a young brother and sister—had died from carbon monoxide poisoning because their bedrooms were over the garage and their car was left on. And how a space heater of some sort had taken the lives of an elderly couple because it wasn't vented right.

"No, Gid!" she cried, again trying to yank her arm from his bruising grasp. With her free hand, she clawed backward at him, but his grip didn't loosen one bit. She screamed, "Let me go!"

"Your old theme song, right? Let me go, I want Josh, not you. You think he can keep the store going when your father's gone? I'm an ambitious man, who can do a lot of good with my money. Soon your father won't be the richest Amish person in these parts."

She gasped and started choking, but more of the pieces fell together. Gid must have switched *Daad*'s pills at work...because he knew *Daad* suspected him of embezzling, or maybe Gid wanted control of the store sooner. Gid followed her here tonight, saw her buggy and his chance to blame Connor for her death... or would it be the other way around?

"You— Did you hurt Victoria Keller?"

"That old woman? No. Why would I? I didn't even know about her."

At least he hadn't killed her, too, but he might have wanted to if he'd known how the old woman's—her aunt's—note had set all this in motion. But now...so dizzy from hitting her head, she felt out of it, like Victoria. And this poison smoke. That poor widow she had visited to find out about Victoria, the woman's house was filled with the bitter smell of smoke... And *Daad* always built a fire in the fireplace at Christmas, like the old days, *Mamm* always said. But Lydia loved Bess, too, wanted time with Bess...

"Sorry, Lydia," Gid said, the oxygen mask distorting his voice and making him look like the monster he was. "*Ya,* I confronted Sandra, but it was her fault. I was watching Yoder's barn. In she went, so I thought I'd settle things with her, tell her to lay off, shut up about you maybe being the child of some dead tree trimmer, like she claimed, and not Sol Brand. In the loft, I only pushed her. She stumbled, she killed herself."

Lydia tried to concentrate on his words so she could argue, but her thoughts were so very floaty, so smoky.

"Don't fight me now," he said. "I read this kind of death is like going to sleep. It just sneaks up on you. You know, Bess Stark may want to invest in the store when I volunteer to oversee the tree farm now that her son will be gone. I can handle the store and that, too. You never knew, did you, how clever I can be? I have the perfect alibi because I'm going to that Stark party where Bess and the sheriff will see me tonight..."

Her thoughts were shutting down, her life drifting away. Maybe if she pretended to be limp... unconscious, he would let her go, walk away, away...

His words rolled past her, around her like the fumes. Bess was her mother and had loved her father... She pictured the three of them together in a different life, playing Andy-over where the ball bounced on the roof and went clear up to Heaven. Aunt Victoria was flying like an angel, and there were her nephews, Connor's twins, playing in the snow, and Connor didn't hate her anymore, and *Mamm* forgave *Daad* and gave Lydia a lovely Christmas quilt with the words *Forgive Mother* all around the edge of the heavens with white clouds like smoke.

"And if you think I'm letting Yoder off the hook for seducing you away from me—no way. He and that animal barn are going up in smoke!"

Above all, that infuriated her. The barn, Josh, those animals—her animals. A surge of strength rolled through her, but she knew she had to seem to faint, even to die.

She slumped against the car's fender, deadweight. He lowered her to the ground right where she was.

Thank the Lord, Gid dragged her away from the back of the car, put her over by Connor. She kept her eyes closed, though he left her facedown.

Lydia fought hard to stay awake but to stay limp. "Leave!" she wanted to scream at him. "Get away from me!"

An eternity passed. She had a terrible headache. He dared to pat her on the back, and then she heard him get to his feet. He moved away, but left the car engine on, the exhaust pouring out.

Finally, she slitted one eye open and watched his feet move away, much as she had seen him at the warehouse earlier tonight. He hit some button that lifted one garage door. She longed to run out after him, suck in fresh, cold air, but she stayed put until he closed it again. Then she crawled the short distance toward Connor.

Was he dead? He'd hated her, but he was her brother, and more important, Bess's beloved son. She felt at the side of his neck. Yes, alive. She stumbled to her feet and opened the car door, driver's side. If she turned the key, would the car engine stop? Oh, *ya,* it did, but she had to get Connor out of here and call for help. And, get the volunteer firemen to Josh's barn in case Gid meant he would burn it down right now.

But what if Gid was still outside? He was stronger than her even when she wasn't weak and dizzy, nauseous, too.

She got out of the car and stumbled to the door that went into the house. It was four steps up since the house was built on the hill, so could she carry Connor into the house?

She tried that door but it was locked. She had to open the garage door, get rid of the fumes, scream for help.

But as she shuffled toward the door to find the button Gid had used, it opened, and there she stood, sucking in fresh air, preparing to face Gid again.

Josh wished the sheriff would get back from the party at the restaurant. It felt as though he'd been gone longer than an hour, but then no one could cross Ray-Lynn. Josh hoped Lydia and her parents were getting along tonight, and that her mother would receive some mental counseling. The Amish didn't put their trust in such worldly doings, but he'd been convinced she needed something she wasn't getting among the Plain People. No, Susan Brand needed worldly help.

And that's what Jack Freeman was to him, worldly help. Josh didn't doubt the man's sincerity. He even liked him, despite it all. He and Ray-Lynn had been supportive of many Amish Josh knew, including his Lydia. He could only hope, by Christmas, eleven days away, he could see his way clear to ask Lydia to marry him. Even if they had to buck her parents, even if Gid Reich turned hostile, even if—

Was he crazy, or did he smell smoke?

He got up from his cot, checked the two kerosene lanterns he had inside then made a jogging circuit inside the barn. Nothing, but the smell was strongest in the old wing of the barn where they used to milk the cows. There must be a fire outside, and the smoke was drifting in here, but a fire in all that snow?

He grabbed a pitchfork, went out the camel door. The Beiler boys had boarded up the door in the milking wing where the intruder had broken in. As he ran along the back of the barn, he skimmed the walls for a newly painted threat. Was this yet another ruse to get him outside? Still, smoke meant he couldn't stay put inside but had to check.

Josh turned the corner into the slap of cold wind. He ran toward the spot where his young neighbor Amos had claimed he'd seen someone that panicked the mule he was trying to ride. Josh's thoughts raced as fast as his feet. If there was a fire nearby, his watering hoses were coiled in the barn. And other than an iced-over drinking trough and the pond way out back, there was no usable water or firemen for miles and long minutes away.

As he turned the next corner, he gasped. Light and heat blasted him from a burning pile of hay, shoveled and shoved up against the door. Although the fire hadn't spread far sideways, the door and the eaves above it were already aflame.

Car headlights blinded Lydia. Bess! It was Bess!

"Lydia, what happened? I came back because I shouldn't have left you like that, shouldn't have left you ever. I don't care what they think of me at our party or anywhere else, we need to talk more. And I know Connor's got a temper, so—"

Lydia lunged into her arms, then pulled her into the garage toward Connor. "Gid Reich hit him—left Connor's car on—door down to kill both of us. We have to get him out."

Together they pulled him outside. Bess got on her phone, called 9-1-1. Connor wasn't breathing. And, though Lydia had never done what they called CPR, she gave Connor three quick breaths, then tried to push on his chest the way Josh had saved her mother.

"Tell them to get the volunteer firemen to Josh's barn!" Lydia called to Bess. She was so dizzy she was going to keel over on top of Connor, but she had to keep going. It was hard to keep her arms stiff since she was shaking so hard. "Gid said he planned to burn his barn. I have to run over there."

After Bess called the fire department, she kneeled next to Lydia and took over pressing Connor's chest. Lydia knew she couldn't use her buggy, so she'd have to run to the tree customers below to get some help. She'd ridden horses as a girl, just not Flower. But it would take time to completely unharness her. Despite her twisted ankle, she had to run to Josh, warn him, even if she had to face Gid again.

"Help me put Connor in my car," Bess said. "This

is taking too long. I'm driving him to the hospital, and I'll drop you off. Try to lift his legs."

They got him in Bess's car. Maybe their attempts at CPR or maybe moving him worked, but he began to choke and haul in huge breaths where he lay on the backseat. "What in the—" he hacked out. "Gid Reich, got to stop him."

"Just lie there," Bess said as Lydia got in the front passenger seat. "On our way to the hospital, Lydia and I are going to warn Josh that Gid means to start a fire over there."

"I overheard you talking," Connor choked out. "About Lydia…my half sister…"

"Blame me if you want, but not her," Bess insisted as she turned the car around and started fast down the hill. "She was trying to save you in there."

Without even slowing down when the car neared the Christmas tree workers, Bess continued down the driveway and did a sharp, squealing turn onto the road. She pushed a button that put all four windows down to let the fresh, cold air in. They roared past Lydia's house. She was not so dizzy now, not nauseous. Power poured into her body. She was with her family. She had to warn Josh.

But as they approached the Yoder barn, they saw the old milking wing was red with leaping flames.

"Stay in the car, Connor," Bess ordered as Lydia opened her door and got out.

"You kidding?" Connor said, though his words were still slurred. "He's gonna need help!"

Limping but ignoring the stabs of pain in her ankle, Lydia tore toward the closest gate. It had been padlocked since the intruder had scared Amos Baughman there. She hiked up her skirt and climbed it. To her amazement, Connor shoved himself underneath it. She saw he had a lot of dried blood in his hair and on the back of his jacket. He threw up on the ground, then just crawled on and hauled himself to his feet.

"Connor, go with Bess to the hospital!" Lydia shouted.

"Don't start bossing me around just because you're my sister!"

It looked to Lydia as if Josh had almost all the animals in the back holding area, but no one was fighting the fire. She grabbed a nearby pail and went to crack through the ice on the drinking trough, but saw he'd already done that. She dipped the pail into the icy water and threw it as high as she could, until Connor took it from her and filled the next bucket himself.

Despite her fear for Josh and the animals, her eyes teared up with thanks that Connor was helping. And that Bess—her beautiful coat and dress now a mess—had crawled under the gate, too.

Lydia ran to find Josh and saw him bringing the last of the braying mules outside. It was chaos with the entire menagerie crowded in the fenced animal yard, especially because, snorting, braying and baaing, they shied away from the flames racing along the roof of the milking wing, and crowded around Josh. Lydia counted the camel heads in the flickering light. *Ya,* Josh had them all out, and, no doubt, at the expense of time to fight the fire.

She worked her way toward him. Several sheep, evidently recognizing her, cuddled closer. "Gid Reich did this!" she shouted to him over the noise of animals and crackling flames. "He tried to kill Connor and me and said he was going to burn the barn! Bess is my mother, and *Daad* is my father."

Josh looked doubly shocked as he took that all in, but he pushed a donkey away, and as he grabbed her hard, they heard the distant wail of sirens. They stood with their arms around each other while sheep bumped them, and Melly appeared from the crowd to snort a kiss on the top of Lydia's head.

"It's the sheriff and the fire truck," Josh yelled as they looked down the road at the approaching, pulsating lights. "With these flames, they don't need me to show them where the fire is. And I see the mayor and our state senator—your other family—throwing buckets of water. They'll tell them where to park."

Despite the danger and the din, the two of them stayed among the animals—their animals—that smoky winter's night and held on tight. They would lose the milking wing of a barn, but, Lydia thought, it was the one Bess had given money to rebuild. Despite all that she'd been through, she felt inwardly calm, content and so in love. And that she had finally come home.

30

Mamm had started weekly counseling sessions with a psychiatrist, whom she'd gifted with friendship bread. And Lydia had told her that she knew who her birth mother was. Still, she and Lydia managed to put a feast on the table for Christmas Eve: turkey with cranberry sauce, tomato pudding, candied sweet potatoes, pumpkin pie, *Mamm*'s bread, as well as the traditional side dishes of fudge and peanut brittle. Lydia thought she would burst with the meal and with gratitude and joy.

Because Josh was sitting at the table with them. Because *Mamm* had accepted him as Lydia's come-calling friend at last, mostly, so far, because he had saved her from the pond. Somehow nearly dying there had made *Mamm* accept Sammy's death at last. After all, *Mamm* had slipped past *Daad* to get to the pond just the way Sammy had sneaked past her.

After dessert, *Mamm* said, "At least that Leo Lowe was released since you didn't testify against him, Lydia, but I hope they are feeding Gid Reich on bread and water in jail today. After his trial for murdering your friend Sandra, he'll have years of prison time, even though they still say Victoria Keller's death was an accident. But to think he was taking money from the store, too. I am struggling to forgive him. Forgiving people and myself, that's what I'm working on."

Lydia and *Daad* exchanged glances. After the barn fire, which, thank the Lord, had burned only the wing of the barn that Josh was planning to redo anyway, she and *Daad* had finally had their talk. He'd agonized for years, he'd said, for not telling her the truth about her past, but his promise to the bishop, Bess and *Mamm,* kept him quiet. But, he confided, he'd intended to tell her anyway when he gave her the quilt, however afraid he was that *Mamm* would never forgive him. But now, perhaps that would change, too, especially because she'd accepted the lovely centerpiece on the table.

"Lydia," *Mamm* said, "you be sure to thank Senator Stark for that decoration she sent over with Connor. I'm afraid it's just for pretty, which we don't do, but it smells good, and you tell her I put it on the table."

Lydia glanced from the pine bough, cone and candle arrangement to *Mamm*'s face. Not smiling but kind, almost sweet. And offering an olive branch in exchange for a pine bough to Bess as well as to *Daad.*

"I'll tell her, *Mamm.* Let me help you clear the table and wash up while *Daad* and Josh chat a bit."

"Ya," Daad said. "I want him to see my quilting loom, but first he can help me bring in Liddy's Christmas gift. I know the big day is tomorrow, but I can't wait," he said, and winked at Josh as if he was already in on this.

From *Daad*'s quilting room, the two men carried in a stunning cedar hope chest and put it on the floor next to Lydia.

"Oh, it's lovely!" she cried and fell to her knees to open it. The clean scent wafted out, and there lay the Christmas quilt.

"We'll soon have more than that in there," *Mamm* said, stepping closer to put one arm around Lydia's waist. "You'll need sheets and towels and more quilts in case someone asks to marry you real soon."

Daad had already announced at the table that he would train a new man to take Gid's place so that, although Lydia would inherit the store someday, she would not have to work there anymore in case she found other interests. Right now, *Daad* just beamed, *Mamm* nodded, Josh grinned, but Lydia was so overcome with happiness she cried.

"I'm so glad you stopped in!" Bess greeted Lydia with open arms. Connor's wife, Heather, stepped forward to hug Lydia, too, and Connor shook hands with Josh, though he only nodded at her. In the awkward welcome, Bess said, "Come in, come in, both of you."

They sat in the living area where Aunt Victoria's coffin had lain only a month ago. To think that her aunt had lived next door where she could have visited her, however ill she was, made Lydia sad. So much had happened, she thought.

She sat next to Josh on the white leather sofa while Connor sat on the floor with the twins where they'd evidently been playing a board game called Battleship. Heather hovered near Bess, who sat in the big chair across a coffee table from them.

"I know you said you were eating at home," Bess said, "but can we offer you anything? Hot cider?"

"We're fine," Lydia said. "Too full. Oh, and *Mamm* thanks you for the pretty centerpiece."

Bess didn't take her eyes off Lydia but she tilted her head toward Connor. "Your brother picked the pine boughs and cones himself."

Connor looked up. "Not spray painted, either. I'm paying a fine for that."

"And—not because of that," Bess said, slapping her hands on her knees, "I'm thinking of keeping the important job I have now in the Ohio senate and not reaching higher, not yet. And then I can spend more time here, at home—with my extended family."

"Aw, Gran," Blair put in, "Brad and me thought it would be way cool if you were the president, and we could visit the White House."

"Perhaps I can arrange that, anyway. Enough of Battleship right now," she told them. "Go ahead and ask Mr. Yoder your question."

Both boys stood and came over to Josh. Wiping his hands nervously on his pants pockets, Blair said, "Mr. Yoder, we know you got the Beiler boys to help you, but we'd like to see your animals more and when we're not in school, I mean in the summer—"

"Or," Brad put in, "even after school if we get all our homework done."

"—can we work for you—not even for money but just for fun?" Blair finished for them.

"That would be great," Josh replied. "I could use the help and Lydia would be a good one to teach you about the camels especially."

The boys beamed and glanced at their father as if for more support when he surely had given them his permission for this already.

"I know they'll work hard to help," Connor said, getting to his feet. "But in the holiday season, they're going to have to split their time, or else you get one and the tree farm gets the other because they have to learn this business, too. Shake hands with Mr. Yoder, boys, to seal the deal. And," he added, clearing his throat and coming closer to put a hand on Lydia's shoulder, which she covered with her own hand, "it's fine if they work with their aunt Lydia."

She bit her lower lip, smiled up at Connor and fought tears again. His words were so sweet she might as well have heard the angels sing.

"It came upon a midnight clear," Josh sang to Lydia as he helped her down from his buggy at the front door of the animal barn. It was nearly midnight, almost Christmas Day. They were going to check on the menagerie, he'd said, before he took her home. Hand in hand, they strolled past the pens where most of the animals slept, though their lantern occasionally caught the reflection of a watchful, liquid eye. Even the mules and camels kept quiet.

"Let's look at the sky," Josh said, and, leaving the lantern on his desk, they went out through the camel door together. His voice was a bit shaky, as if he, too, had been swept away by all the emotion they'd shared tonight.

It was cold outside, but the stars were brilliant and the quarter moon seemed to slant a smile down at them. They stood, arms around each other, gazing at the endless heavens above the Home Valley.

"Lydia," he whispered so low the breeze almost blew his words away, "I hope you know how much I love you. We've been through a lot to get to this point, and I would be honored if you would consider being my wife."

He'd never looked so serious, almost scared, she thought as she gazed up at his handsome face, bathed in starlight.

"I would love to share my life with you—and the Yoder zoo."

"I can't imagine my life without you."

"You don't have to."

"I even want you enough to have two mothers-in-law, both of them a challenge."

Upon that winter's night, Lydia laughed, threw her arms around him and kissed him hard.

* * * * *

Author's Note

I love to write about Amish country and its people. I guess that's pretty evident since this is my ninth Amish romantic suspense novel. The earlier ones include a stand-alone, *DOWN TO THE BONE.* Then came the trilogy *DARK ROAD HOME, DARK HARVEST* and *DARK ANGEL.* Most recently I wrote the HOME VALLEY TRILOGY consisting of *FALL FROM PRIDE, RETURN TO GRACE* and *FINDING MERCY.* I also contributed a Home Valley novella for the anthology *DARK CROSSINGS,* entitled *THE COVERED BRIDGE.* And here we are with this seasonal story, *UPON A WINTER'S NIGHT,* also set in the fictional—but very real to me—Home Valley.

In these stories, it has been so fulfilling to follow the lives of young Amish women who find danger but also the loves of their lives. And, in the most recent books, to see Ray-Lynn's trials and triumphs—and how she finally married Sheriff Jack Freeman—has been great fun, too. Who of us wouldn't like to be friends with such interesting heroines and to get Ray-Lynn's glimpse into the fascinating world of the Plain People? I hope these books have given my readers this look into their lives.

Special thanks to my talented and insightful MIRA Book editors, Miranda Indrigo and Nicole Brebner, for traveling with me through these Amish novels.

A quick note about cell phones. Most Old Order Amish are holding the line against these devices despite the fact that cell phones work without the forbidden phone lines coming into their homes. This intrusion by the outside world has been a major problem in the past. Still, most Amish are permitted to use them at their places of employment. Before committing to the church, Amish young people sometimes have these phones, which they must give up later. However, on our most recent trip to Ohio Amish country, my cell phone would not work because there were no towers in the rural, hilly areas. I was also told that I had the "wrong kind of phone," because only one carrier works "around here." When we drove out of that immediate area, the phone worked fine again.

Special thanks goes to Lance White, managing editor at the *Daily Record* newspaper in Wooster, Ohio, who filled me in on how the paper stores its old clip files. The *Daily Record* helps to sponsor the excellent, longtime Buckeye Book Fair every year in Wooster where I've been able to sign many books and meet many readers. Some Amish also attend, and it's been enlightening to talk to them.

Amish furniture, which is beautifully crafted, features prominently in this story. I have visited such stores and purchased a lovely dining room table and chairs set from a place much like the one the Brands own. If you would like to see the vast array of Amish-built pieces, two websites I found useful are www.furnitureheartland.com and www.Amish-

FurnitureGuide.com. Now that farmland is so expensive and the Plain People continue to have large families, more Amish men are turning to various crafts. Some work in the stores, some work at home and buggy their pieces in.

Amish friendship bread is no doubt similar to other such "yeast starter" recipes, but the best online site I found for the Amish recipe is www.armchair.com/recipe/bake002.html. I also have the recipe on my website www.KarenHarperAuthor.com with some other Amish recipes that figure in earlier books. You might have noted that *Mamm* did not share the recipe and yeast starter, as is traditional, but preferred just to give only the bread, perhaps since she felt it was all she had to offer and she didn't want others making her specialty. However, in the spirit of Christmas, and since she is now dealing with her problems, I think she will give people the recipe and the starter as well as the bread, so that they may "pass it on."

As Sandra told *Daad* when she met with him in the story, Christmas always puts us in a kind of time warp. The past becomes the present again as we remember Christmases past and the dear ones who have gone on before us. Like life, the holiday season for many is a mixture of sadness and happiness. But I hope your celebrations and memories will be joyous.

Karen Harper